*She would need an eternity
to forget him...and the passion
that enflames her heart still.*

A Scottish Love

The male of the species always bore more plumage.

As Shona stepped to the side, her gaze never leaving Gordan's face, he reached out one finger and trailed it over her cheek.

His blue eyes were alive with mischief as she stepped out of his reach.

The texture of his skin would be as soft as she recalled, especially that spot right at the corner of his mouth. Or his temple, where she'd feel the beat of his blood beneath her lips.

She wouldn't remember.

She couldn't.

"You're welcome, Shona," he said finally.

Then she was free, walking swiftly toward the room she and Helen had shared, all too conscious of his gaze on her.

By Karen Ranney

A Scottish Love
A Borrowed Scot
A Highland Duchess
Sold to a Laird
A Scotsman in Love
The Devil Wears Tartan
The Scottish Companion
Autumn in Scotland
An Unlikely Governess
Till Next We Meet
So in Love
To Love a Scottish Lord
The Irresistible MacRae
When the Laird Returns
One Man's Love
After the Kiss
My True Love
My Beloved
Upon a Wicked Time
My Wicked Fantasy

KAREN RANNEY

A Scottish Love

An Imprint of HarperCollinsPublishers

AVON BOOKS
An Imprint of HarperCollins*Publishers*
10 East 53rd Street
New York, New York 10022-5299

Copyright © 2011 by Karen Ranney
ISBN 978-0-06-202778-8
www.avonromance.com

First Avon Books mass market printing: December 2011

Avon Trademark Reg. U.S. Pat. Off. and in Other Countries, Marca Registrada, Hecho en U.S.A.
HarperCollins® is a registered trademark of HarperCollins Publishers.

Printed in the U.S.A.

10 9 8 7 6 5 4 3 2 1

To Irene Mercatante.
Some people are friends.
Some are examples.
Some are blessings.
Irene is all three.

A
Scottish Love

Chapter 1

Autumn 1859
Inverness, Scotland

Gordon MacDermond was standing at the door of her parlor. Standing there staring at her, as if she'd invited him into her home. As if she should smile and welcome him.

She'd sooner greet the devil.

For a moment, Shona just sat there and watched him. Sounds faded away, even the air stilled, leaving Gordon standing there alone, illuminated by the sunlight streaming through the open door.

He took a few steps into the room, his eyes never leaving hers.

Her heart beat so fiercely she could feel the tremors in her throat. And why were her palms so damp?

It was only Gordon.

A stranger would look at him and see a tall man with symmetrical features, a straight nose, and a square jaw. A woman might note that his chin looked stubborn, a correct assumption about his character. His mouth turned up on one corner. As a boy, it had given him an amused air. As a man, it made him appear cynical. His brows were gently curved, his blue eyes intent, almost piercing. His hair was cut shorter than was fashionable, but Gordon had never cared for fashion. A man as handsome as he could do anything he wished, including refuse to grow a beard.

The expression in his eyes was decidedly different, however, from the young man she'd known. The youthful enthusiasm, the smile, the eagerness in his gaze had been replaced by caution.

He'd seen too much. But then, hadn't they all?

Seven years ago, they'd been so foolish, so naïve, and unaware of the world. Now, all of them were a little too knowledgeable about what could happen when they ventured far from home.

Her brother said that Gordon had emerged unscathed from the wars in the Crimea and India, and seeing him here was proof that he'd been luckier than Fergus.

She slowly stood, but didn't speak. What could she say?

Get the blazes out of my house, Gordon MacDermond.

For however long it was her house.

"Countess," he said, inclining his head. His attention, however, was drawn to the four stalwart lads at the other end of the room. A frown replaced the look of caution on his face.

Suddenly amused and intensely grateful for it, she sat once again, watching him take in the scene.

The drawing room was shrouded since the only window was heavily curtained. The lumpy horsehair sofa on which she sat was at right angles to the small fireplace. A straight-back chair sat nearby, atop a faded Brussels carpet. Over the mantel was an engraving of the Morton coat of arms, a bit of conceit that her husband had commissioned a year before his death.

How often had she wished for the money that garish bit of nonsense had cost? She couldn't even sell it.

At the far end of the drawing room stood four men, each of them standing silent and respectful.

"Those men are naked," he said.

Her gaze, insultingly slow, took in Gordon's well-polished shoes, up past the trousers of blue serge to the matching coat and vest. When she met his eyes, she smiled again, immeasurably pleased at his frown.

"Not quite naked," she said. "They've merely removed their shirts."

"Why?"

Was it any of his concern? Still she answered him, not because he deserved a response, but because the answer would annoy him.

"They've applied for the position of footman," she said.

"Should you be interviewing them without their shirts?" he asked.

If it disturbed him that she did so, he didn't allow it to show in his voice. Now a small smile curved his lips, but she knew him better than that. He was not amused. His eyes were flat and expressionless.

"Undoubtedly not," she conceded.

Helen came to stand beside her. Helen's cheeks had been scarlet for more than an hour. Her companion was filled with all sorts of maidenly virtues, whereas she hadn't been a maiden for almost a decade now.

"You're measuring their attributes, is that it?"

She smiled again. Very well, she could match him in sangfroid.

"Perhaps I'm ensuring that the candidate doesn't have a wasting disease," she said. "Or merely establishing that he has the strength to assume his duties."

All four of the men were absolutely perfect. The man second to the end was thinner than the rest, but his stomach muscles were better developed. The man closest to her had the most impressive shoulders, and as she watched, flexed them in greeting. The candidate to his right could roll his chest, as if he were purring. The last man had a habit of standing with his legs farther apart, evidently needing the distance to accommodate his, well, *attributes*.

For five years she'd been married to a man forty years her senior. Gazing at four half-naked young men didn't seem that much a crime. She would hire each one if she had the funds. Unfortunately, she didn't even have enough money to hire a parlor maid, the reason Helen had answered the door and escorted Gordon into her home.

She almost turned and asked Helen to see Gordon to the door again. Give him back his hat and his gloves and send him on his way.

We don't need Gordon MacDermond here.

But because she knew why he'd come, she didn't give voice to his banishment.

"You may dress now," she said, sending the four candidates a smile. "Please leave your name with Miss Paterson," she added, nodding toward Helen.

The cheeky one winked at her as he dressed. For a moment, she was tempted to wink back.

Gordon didn't look pleased.

What a pity.

They didn't speak as the men dressed, the strained silence punctuated only as each man gave his name to Helen. One by one, they filed out of the parlor, following Helen to the front door.

When they were gone, she glanced over at Gordon, who returned her look steadily.

Go away, Gordon.

"Congratulations, Sir Gordon, on your baronetcy," Helen said, returning from the door.

"Oh, yes, you won something, didn't you?" she said.

"No," he said, tight-lipped. "It was awarded me."

"Pity they didn't award Fergus," she said, forcing a smile back into place.

"You think receiving a Victoria Cross is nothing, Countess?"

"A baronetcy can be inherited, *Sir* Gordon," she said. "You can do absolutely nothing with a Victoria Cross except brag of it. A baronetcy would have made up for a lot."

He looked at her as if she were a stranger. *Never a stranger, Gordon. Never a friend, either.*

"Fergus is a fine man. Any woman would recognize that."

"Oh, I'm certain you're right," she said, sending him a look sharp enough to sever his ears from his head. "If she can overlook his limp and the fact he's in constant pain."

He didn't respond, ratcheting up her anger even higher. She took a deep breath and composed herself before continuing.

"You were his commanding officer. You should have kept him free from harm."

"It was war, Countess."

"He went to war because of you," she said, with enough equanimity that she impressed herself. "He didn't attend Military College. You did. He wasn't versed in artillery. You were. He didn't know anything about war. I daresay you studied it."

She smiled, tamping down the anger once more. "He went to war because you were going, and as his best friend, you should have protected him."

"Your husband bought Fergus's commission. If you were so against him going, you could have prevented it."

"If you wish to see Fergus, he's in the garden," she

said, waving her hand toward the other woman. "Helen will show you the way."

Helen leaned close.

"Are you all right, Shona?" Helen asked.

No, dear God, she was far from all right. She bled from so many internal wounds she was surprised there wasn't a pool of blood at her feet.

"Yes," she answered calmly, forcing a smile to her face. "I'm fine, Helen, thank you."

She waited until they were out of the room before closing her eyes and leaning her head back against the chair.

Was Gordon's arrival the answer to a prayer? She couldn't leave Fergus here to be tossed out into the street. She had to make arrangements for him. The letter, delivered by messenger yesterday, had stepped up her timetable and also made her situation even more dire.

If she asked him for help, would he agree? Or would he refuse just to punish her?

She was just as beautiful as she'd always been. The last time he'd seen her, she'd been in the first flush of youth, testing her newly discovered feminine power and at the same time, relishing it.

He'd fallen at her feet and nearly begged her to walk on him. He would have done anything for Shona Imrie. He'd extended his heart, his fortune, and his future. Instead, she'd married the Earl of Morton, a man who could give her a title and a large estate. At the time, Gordon hadn't had a title and his home was modest. The only thing he possessed that the Earl of Morton didn't have was youth.

Evidently, that hadn't counted for much.

The years had polished the beauty of the young woman, made her even more alluring. The black of her mourning emphasized her ivory complexion, made her pink mouth look lush and inviting.

Her eyes were a startling gray, the thick black ring around the iris accentuating their smoky color. He'd once told her that she had eyes that beckoned a lover to become lost in them. She'd only laughed and held out her arms.

He'd entwined that long brunette hair around his wrists, pulled her closer for another kiss. Her lips were cloud soft, and he could still taste her on his mouth. Her nose had a slight upturn at the end. A very patrician nose, he'd laughingly announced one rainy afternoon.

"To match the rest of you."

"And what part of me is patrician?" she'd asked.

He'd spread the blanket wide, stared down at her plump breasts, still rosy from their lovemaking. "You've very noble breasts," he said. "Very aristocratic. Look how your nipples harden even now, as if demanding the attentions of my tongue."

Did she remember?

How could she forget?

Helen said something to him, glancing over her shoulder. Instead of admitting that he hadn't been paying attention, had been years and miles away, he smiled, and asked, "Have you been with the countess long?"

"The earl was my second cousin," she said. "After my father died, he took me in and I became the countess's companion."

He couldn't imagine the girl he'd known needing a companion, but then he couldn't envision Shona being married to the Earl of Morton. He'd practiced pushing that image away for years. Improvidently, he wanted to ask her what Shona had become. A shocking woman, one who routinely engaged in the kind of behavior he'd just witnessed? He restrained himself and asked, instead, about Fergus.

"Is he not well?"

She nodded. "He's still quite thin," Helen said. "He's not yet recuperated from his injuries."

The fact that Fergus's left leg hadn't been amputated after Lucknow was a miracle. Guilt spiked through him. He'd not seen Fergus for six months, ever since they'd returned from India.

He followed Helen down a small set of steps and into the garden, feeling the grass sag beneath his feet. Shadows stretched from the tall hedges on either side of the narrow rectangular yard, creating a cool and lush sanctuary. In the middle of the lawn was a bright patch of sunlight. A chair had been placed there, and a man sat with his head tilted back, eyes closed, allowing the sun to bathe his face.

Gordon wasn't a coward. Yet in that moment, he almost turned and walked in the other direction. The man who sat in the chair, bathing in the sun, was too thin to be his boyhood friend, his best friend.

They'd grown up together, sharing secrets and dreams, playing among the crags and boulders of Ben Lymond. As men, they'd suffered the privations of soldiers in battle. They'd depended upon each other and supported each other even as they'd stared death in the face.

"There you are, lazing in the sun, just like a cat," he said, before Helen could speak.

Fergus turned his head, and Gordon almost winced. The narrow face was gaunt; the mischievous grin present during most of their adventures was gone. Instead, his friend's face was sallow and marked with lines of pain and suffering.

"Is this what happens once you get the Victoria Cross? You think you never have to work another day of your life?"

Fergus made as if to stand, but Gordon had already

seen the cane propped on the other side of the chair. He reached Fergus's side and placed his hand on his friend's arm.

"It's not necessary to get up," he said.

"Good God, you're still trying to be my commanding officer," Fergus said, smiling with what looked to be some effort.

He squatted beside the chair. "You've had a bad time of it," he said.

Fergus smiled with more enthusiasm. "You've been listening to Shona."

He shook his head.

Fergus chuckled. "Is she not talking to you, then? Or is she still interviewing her footmen?"

"Do you realize she had them take off their shirts?"

"I'm the one who put the notice in the paper," Fergus said, the grin reminiscent of their boyhood. "She deserves a bit of fun." His grin faded. "She's the one who's had a bad time of it, Gordon."

He tucked that information away to think about later. Right at the moment, he was more concerned with Fergus than his sister.

Liar.

"I came to see how you were doing. I've just gotten back."

"You left the London lassies expiring in grief, then."

"Only a few."

"You've become a damn national treasure."

He felt himself warm. "Hardly that."

"A baronetcy," Fergus said, his smile broader.

"The others?" he asked, changing the subject, and named names, men who had been under his command at Sebastopol and then at Lucknow and for whom he still felt responsible. Men of the Ninety-third Sutherland Highlanders, no better group of men.

"Macpherson died of his wounds. So did Dubonner. Marshall isn't doing well, I hear. But the others are all hale and hearty."

"I should have come back earlier," he said.

"When the War Office summons you, Gordon, even you can't refuse them. Especially when the general adds his persuasion. The months in London couldn't have been enjoyable. Unless," Fergus added, "there really were lassies vying for your attention."

"Only a few," he repeated.

From somewhere, Helen had found a chair, and began to drag it across the lawn. He stood, went to her side, and took it from her, thanking her with a smile.

"He's dead," he said, placing the chair opposite Fergus and sitting.

The two words were remarkably free of emotion. No anger, grief, or even relief tinged them.

"Dead? I thought the old man would live forever," Fergus said, staring off into the distance.

"I'm sure he planned it," he said dryly.

"How did it happen?"

"In his sleep. He would have hated it. He wasn't commanding anyone, and wasn't in the middle of one of his towering rages. He simply didn't wake up."

They exchanged a look, one that both commiserated and remembered. How many times had he come to Gairloch to escape his father? How many times had he and Fergus engaged in boyhood pursuits, neither talking about the man who would punish him when he returned home? Lieutenant General Ian MacDermond made his displeasure known in whatever way was most convenient—shouting, switch, or cane.

"Should I bother to express my condolences?" Fergus asked.

"To the devil, perhaps," he said, smiling. "Can you

imagine the general ordering Beelzebub around? Hell wouldn't stand a chance."

They sat in silence for several moments.

"Is that why you've come home?" Fergus asked after a moment.

"Because the general can't command my life anymore? No, I'd already begun the process to leave before he died. Who knows? Maybe his dying was the final repudiation. I've decided to take over the Works."

Fergus's eyebrows rose.

"You've left the army entirely, then?"

He nodded.

"To do what? Make gunpowder?"

"For now. I've an idea, however, something that I've been working on for a while now."

Helen was suddenly there, a tray in her hands.

"I've brought a wee dram of whiskey for you, Sir Gordon, and tea for you, Fergus."

"Why does he get whiskey?" Fergus complained.

Helen just clucked her tongue, but didn't answer.

He took both the cup and glass from her, thanked her, and the minute she went back inside, handed the glass to Fergus.

Fergus downed the whiskey in one swallow, leaving Gordon to stare at the tea. The brew smelled of flowers— or stinkweed—and was weak enough he could see the bottom of the cup.

"What is this?" he asked, taking a tentative sip.

"Something to build up my blood, I think. I never know what god-awful concoction Shona or Helen has dreamed up now. They're bustling around me all hours of the day and night." He glanced toward the house. "In fact, I'm surprised one of them hasn't come out and rescued me and put me down for my nap. I should probably thank you for that."

He didn't want to talk about Shona now.

"So about the baronetcy—" Fergus began.

"More my father's work than mine," he said, interrupting.

Fergus shot him a look. "Not what I hear. I repeat, you're a damn national treasure."

He shrugged.

"You've gone and gotten modest. Unlike you, Gordon."

He smiled, suddenly glad he'd come. No one else poked at him like Fergus. Perhaps he needed that.

Fergus placed the glass on the arm of the chair. His hand trembled with the effort, an indication of how weak he really was.

"Is there anything you need? Anything I can do?" He patted Fergus's arm, hating the thin frailty of it.

"Come and see me from time to time," Fergus said. "Rescue me from the care of women."

"That I'll do," he said.

"Even if Shona refuses you."

"I won't give up," he said, standing. "You know that much about me."

"You did once," Fergus said.

Those words were a damn bullet to the heart.

He smiled with ease, charming Fergus into a laugh. Her brother hadn't laughed in a good long time. Perhaps she should forgive Gordon for that alone.

Once, she would have forgiven him anything.

The past swooped in like an arrow's point, spearing her heart.

"He's got a bright future, Shona," General MacDermond had said, standing in the Acanthus Parlor at Gairloch. A particularly odious room colored olive green, with carvings of acanthus leaves strewn over the ceiling in a montage that had pleased one of her ancestors.

"You can see, surely, that if he remains here, that future will be blighted."

"He has the Works," she'd said, aware that Gordon had inherited the three armament factories belonging to his maternal grandfather.

His father had glossed over that with a thin smile.

"If he marries you, Shona," he'd said, his voice strangely kind when he'd never been kind to her in the past, "it will be because he pities you. Or because you're Fergus's sister. I doubt you'd want to be such a burden."

They'd been in such desperate straits, however, that she'd known something had to be done, including marrying the first wealthy man who'd offered for her. Someone who hadn't wanted to marry her out of pity.

But marrying Bruce hadn't turned out at all well.

Here she was, seven years later, in an even worse situation. Now, not only did Fergus need her help, but Helen depended upon her, too. This time, marriage wasn't a solution to their problems.

Nor was thinking about the past.

She had a plan, however, and unfortunately, Gordon MacDermond was going to have to play a role in it.

"I promise I'll be back," Gordon said. "Even if it means bodily moving Shona to see you."

Fergus only chuckled, as if the thought of that confrontation was amusing.

Gordon said good-bye, crossing the lawn to the steps. He didn't expect Shona to be standing at the back door, watching him. Nor did he expect her words as he entered the house.

"Did you disturb him?" she asked, waving the piece of paper in her hand toward the garden.

"Disturb him?" he asked.

"Bother him, confound him, annoy him. Ask him questions that make him remember or think. That sort of thing."

He studied her for a moment. Tiny lines radiated outward from the corners of her eyes. The years had made a mark, but a subtle one.

"He's not dead, Shona. Or a bairn. He's a man. He's going to remember things without my prompting him. He's going to feel things despite your wrapping him in a blanket of concern."

She glanced away, the line of her jaw firm, her lips whitened as if she held back words.

If he were another man, he'd have said or done something to comfort her. If it were another time, she might have allowed him to do so. Neither was the case, so he remained silent.

"How did you find him?" she finally asked, still staring out the back window.

"Weak," he said, startling himself by uttering the truth. "Despondent. Why the hell didn't you let me know?"

"Would you have come, Gordon?" she asked, still not looking at him.

"You know I would."

She nodded, the point too easily conceded.

"Will you let me know if he needs anything?"

She looked down at the paper she held in her hand.

"He needs a home," she said, surprising him. "My husband's nephew is taking possession of the house in a short while. Fergus needs a place to live." She folded the paper, still not looking at him. "My new house is being readied," she added. "But, for a few weeks, conditions will be difficult for Fergus."

"He can stay with me if he wishes."

"You're back, then. In Inverness."

"Yes," he said, not giving her the whole truth. To compensate, he offered her a bit more information, something he wouldn't have ordinarily told her. A peace offering? "I've left the War Office."

"No more soldiering?"

He smiled. "No more soldiering."

Now she looked at him, her thin smile not matching the expression in her eyes. He'd had years of studying Shona Imrie. Shona Imrie Donegal.

He disturbed her.

"The Empire may crumble," she said, "without you to fight for it."

She hadn't lost the ability to infuse her words with derision.

"Indeed," he said, still smiling amiably.

She turned, leaving him no choice but to follow. As they headed toward the front door, she glanced over her shoulder at him.

"Why didn't you ever write to Fergus? If you were so concerned for him?"

He was wrong to think she'd conceded the point.

"And have my letters returned?"

She stopped, squared her shoulders, but didn't answer, merely opened the door, standing aside for him to leave. He picked up his hat and gloves from the side table.

"How soon will your husband's nephew be taking possession?"

She skirted that question, asking one of her own. "How soon can Fergus come and live with you?"

Evidently, she was desperate enough to allow some of her anxiety to show.

"Give me two days to make arrangements," he said.

She nodded. "That will be acceptable."

As he left the house, she stood queenlike at the door, her hand on the frame, her smile firmly fixed and false.

* * *

Had she just made the worst mistake of her life?

Shona watched as Gordon strode toward his carriage, never turning and looking back. He wouldn't. Once on a set course, Gordon MacDermond was as immovable as Ben Nevis.

He walked with confidence, as if the world should give way before him. He was Colonel Sir Gordon Mac-Dermond, son of Lieutenant General Ian MacDermond, both father and son national heroes, renowned for their prowess in battle and their courage in the face of desperate odds.

Each man had proved himself to be a modern Highlander.

The air was humid, the breeze from the river pausing to caress her cheek. With the back of her hand, she brushed back a tendril of hair that had come loose, but otherwise didn't move, watching him enter his carriage.

Gordon had brought the past with him, and the past was not her friend.

Identify every part of a problem and handle each part separately. That's how she'd survived Bruce's illness. First, she had to address the issue of money.

Slowly, she closed the door, unfolding the letter again. Good news, of a sort. The worst news, if she chose to be sentimental. But sentimentality was for fools and those who'd no need of wealthy Americans.

Dear God, anyone with a fortune would do.

Once, she'd had armoires filled with dresses and delicate lace undergarments. She'd worn jewels that sparkled in the gaslight. Her home had been a mansion set into a landscape so perfect it looked like a John Constable painting.

Circumstances changed, however, a fact she'd learned only too well in the last two years.

What a shock it had been to learn she was penniless.

She'd known that Bruce's estate was entailed, but she'd stupidly assumed that, upon her husband's death, she'd have some income of her own. Both she and his great-nephew, Ranald Donegal, had been informed that neither was the recipient of any funds.

Bruce had died insolvent.

Her husband had never hinted at his penurious state. Nor had he told her that his great-nephew was an incredibly dislikable man. Ranald was twenty years her senior, but neither his status as a relative by marriage, nor the fact that he himself was married with seven children, had stopped him from groping her at every opportunity. She'd vacated the house she'd shared with Bruce as soon as she could, retreating here to Inverness to live out the duration of her mourning. Two weeks ago, her official mourning was over.

Two weeks ago, she'd also learned that Ranald was coming to Inverness for the express purpose of occupying the house she'd made her home for the last two years.

Her choices were narrowing by the minute.

Did she stay here and attempt some sort of agreement with Ranald? Would he allow Fergus to stay as well? She was neither naïve nor unschooled. Sooner or later, the arrangement would lead to her becoming an unpaid servant or sharing his bed while his wife and her brother slept under the same roof. She doubted Fergus would agree to such a thing even if she allowed it.

Or did she attempt to find other lodgings, with no funds, no likelihood of funds, and no foreseeable funds in the future?

The jewels Bruce had given her had been sold to keep food in the house and coal in the grate for the first year. In the last several months, she'd sold anything, everything, of value.

She took a deep breath before reading the letter once more.

Her solicitor had done what she'd begged him to do a year ago. He'd found a solution for her financial woes, a solution that required selling Gairloch, the castle belonging to the Imrie Clan.

To support the two people who'd come to depend on her, she was going to have to do something quickly.

Helen entered the room and she folded the letter, tucking it into her dress pocket.

"We're going on an adventure, Helen," she said with a smile.

The other woman looked at her, head tilted. "What sort of adventure?" Helen asked cautiously.

"We're going to Gairloch."

When Fergus was settled, she'd go home, and back to the past for the very last time.

Gordon had a hundred questions, all of them revolving around the Countess of Morton. None was likely to be answered anytime soon.

Nonetheless, he couldn't dismiss the thought that there was something he should have seen, known, or asked before being escorted from her home.

The surge of nostalgia he was feeling was idiotic. So, too, his rage at seeing her calmly assess the half-naked men in her parlor.

The girl he'd known had been stubborn, prideful, heedless, and exciting. He'd felt alive in her presence. He'd gone from attempting to avoid his father to challenging the old man because of Shona. She was so brave and daring that he could be no less. He'd laughed with her, held her when she wept, discovered the secrets of Invergaire Glen and their own bodies.

She'd been his first love.

Yet for five years, she'd been the circumspect Countess of Morton. Not one rumor followed her; not one inveterate gossip carried tales from Inverness to London. The girl had either matured or become more adept at hiding herself beneath her new, titled, role.

He'd seen her twice in those years, both times from afar. When he'd gone to war, it was almost a relief. He'd have no reason to see her, to watch her with her husband.

He should have told her what he'd planned, but he'd acquired the habit of reticence, at least around Shona.

He might have loved her once, but he didn't trust her.

Chapter 2

"**I** don't understand," Fergus said. "Why can't I go with you?"

"Because the journey would be too difficult," she said, tucking the blanket around his knees, careful not to touch the area on his thigh where he'd been struck by a fusillade of bullets. "And I want to make sure you're safe."

Fergus narrowed his eyes, a habit of his when he didn't believe what she was saying.

He was older than she by three years, and when she'd begun to care for him after he'd returned from India, he'd responded by saying that she didn't make it easy to be her patient.

"It isn't easy being your younger sister, either, Fergus," she said, which always silenced him for a little while.

At the moment, however, she didn't have time for patient wheedling.

"Fergus, please," she said. "I must go and you're in no condition for travel."

"I don't want to sell."

She'd told him what she'd planned all along. Had he simply pretended that it would never come to pass? Or that no one would have pockets deep enough to buy the castle?

She could always tell him the truth—that there was

no money at all—but if she did, he'd assume the responsibility for their welfare, just when he was incapable of shouldering the burden.

He'd already suffered. He'd already proven how brave he was. He didn't need another worry in his life, especially when he'd not completely healed from his wounds.

"If you don't want to go with Gordon," she said, keeping any hint of panic out of her voice, "I can make other arrangements. He'll be here any minute. Tell me what you want."

He watched her in that careful way of his, eyes the same gray shade as hers noting every movement. He used to tease her, but since he'd come home from the war, he did so less and less.

"I'll go with Gordon," he said, "but I don't want to sell."

The knock on the door was opportune.

Helen opened the door and Gordon strode in, dressed in an outer coat today, one of black wool that accentuated his height. With him was another man, as tall as Gordon, with arms that bulged beneath his clothing.

"Are you ready, then?" he asked Fergus, never sparing a glance at her.

Fergus nodded.

"Are those your things?" Gordon asked, pointing to a pair of trunks in the corner.

Fergus nodded.

Gordon motioned to the man accompanying him, and he effortlessly scooped up the trunks as if they weighed nothing, and disappeared through the door.

"Need some help?" Gordon asked.

Fergus grinned, the first time he'd done so all day.

"Just a boost to my feet," he said. "After that, I can manage."

Gordon reached down and placed his hand under Fergus's arm and helped him rise. He looked as if he were studying every one of Fergus's movements.

As they made their way to the door, she stood there, hands gripped in front of her.

"I'll see you soon," she said, but Fergus didn't turn. He only nodded, no doubt still angry with her.

Gordon was the one to glance in her direction, his expression conveying an understanding of her sudden distress. As if he knew how very much she hated depending on his kindness. Or as if he knew how close she was to crying.

She was not about to weep in front of him.

Keeping silent was difficult, but she managed it, nonetheless, while Fergus was helped into Gordon's carriage. Gordon stood silent beside her on the steps, taller than she'd remembered, broader of shoulder. He smelled of some masculine scent—or was that just him?

She wanted to lean closer. Instead, she wrapped her arms around her waist, waited patiently with a small and placid smile curving her lips.

He pulled out a card from his inside vest pocket and handed it to her. Her hand curled around it, felt the warmth from his body, and stared down at his distinctive writing.

Meet me today. I'm thinking of you. Missed you. Notes they'd shared over the years.

"My address," he said.

"Yes."

He looked as if he wanted to say something further, but censored himself.

"It's chilly today," he said.

How many times had she been taught that one could never go wrong with a comment on the weather?

His glance encompassed her attire from her dress to her shoes, an examination of the same ilk she'd given him only days ago. She hoped she'd been a tenth as annoying.

"I'm not cold," she said.

She didn't want him to show any concern, or act gentlemanly, or—God forbid—make her remember how kind he could be when he wanted.

Just go away. Take Fergus with you and remember he was once your dearest friend.

Soon enough, they were situated, and as Helen bid Fergus an emotional farewell, Shona stepped back, waving from a vantage point far enough away that no one could see the tears in her eyes.

Gordon entered the carriage. The last time he and Fergus had traveled together had been on the return voyage from India, and the other man had been half out of his mind from fever.

Even now, six months later, Fergus was too thin, too pale, but what was more disturbing than simple physical appearance was the fact that the enthusiasm, the excitement that used to dance in Fergus's eyes was missing. In Sebastopol, he'd been the first among them to see the amusement in a situation. Even in India, he'd found something about which to comment in a droll fashion, garnering laughter from his men.

Although he'd been an exemplary soldier, Fergus's mouth had been a detriment to his advancement. How many times had Fergus made a remark about the stupidity of their generals, their orders, or even their mission? How many times had he wished Fergus would just shut up?

Now, he would have preferred the Fergus from Sebastopol or the Siege of Lucknow. Not this quiet, too polite stranger.

"I lied to your sister," he said abruptly. "And to you."

Fergus turned his head, regarding him unsmilingly.

"I've a house in town, but I've my mind set on going home," he said. "It's been too damn long since I've been there and I'm missing it."

He turned to face Fergus, surprised at the other man's smile.

"You've a choice," he continued. "You can either go to the house, where my staff has been advised to welcome you, or you can come with me."

"To Invergaire Glen?"

He nodded.

"I choose home," Fergus said. "It's glad I am to be going there myself," he added, his smile growing in scope, leaving Gordon with the distinct impression that his old friend was amused at a secret jest.

The carriage was hired; Shona hadn't the money to maintain her own carriage and horses. Now she and Helen sat inside the vehicle, a small basket of provisions at their feet. The leather of the seats was cracked, the interior of the carriage musty-smelling, and the upholstery stained in places as if the roof had leaked.

She hoped it was only water damage.

After the driver deposited them at Gairloch, he would return to Inverness, then come back for them in two weeks' time. To pay for his services, she used the money she'd made selling two bonnets and several of her better dresses.

Dear God, soon she'd be down to bartering her unmentionables.

She wondered if Helen was worried about this journey. Helen rarely complained, however, a trait that made her an excellent companion. Yet she also rarely asked any questions, a meekness of character that occasionally grated.

This day reminded Shona, oddly enough, of when she'd arrived in Inverness, but for its contrasts, not its similarities.

Back then, she'd been genuinely mourning Bruce, a very nice man, a kind and thoughtful husband. If no excitement ever entered her marriage, if one day blended into another seamlessly, if she was endlessly bored, it was to be expected. After all, Bruce was much older and had his life arranged to suit him. He was old enough to be her grandfather, she'd heard one old biddy say once, a thought she tried not to have on those rare occasions when Bruce came to her bed.

Back then, she'd been draped in black, swathed in it until she felt as if she couldn't breathe.

Even though she was no longer officially in mourning, she had little money to purchase new clothing. The dress she wore was black, with white collar and cuffs. If they were of a more similar figure, she might have borrowed a dress or two from Helen. But the older woman was shorter and less fulsomely endowed in the bosom. Wearing one of Helen's dresses would have made her look like a plump ptarmigan.

"Are we not going to call on Fergus first?" Helen asked.

She shook her head. "He's barely had time to settle in," she said.

"Two days."

She looked away, wishing Helen wouldn't pursue the subject.

"You don't wish him to know."

"He knows," she said quickly. "He just doesn't want to sell Gairloch."

"Then why not see him before we leave?"

Her gloves needed mending again. She hated darning her gloves, but if she didn't, the seams became worn and split, making her look impoverished. Once, she would have thrown away a pair in such a condition, then made her displeasure known to the shopkeeper.

When had she bought these? More than three years ago, but that's all she could remember.

"Or is it Colonel Sir Gordon you don't wish to see?"

Why had Helen suddenly become so curious?

"I've never known him as Colonel Sir Gordon," she said tartly. "He's only Gordon to me. I've known him since we were children."

"Do you find him very changed?"

Such an innocuous question from someone who normally didn't question anything. Had Helen suddenly become perceptive? If so, that might prove uncomfortable.

She didn't particularly want to think of Gordon. Not as a hero, not as Colonel Sir Gordon, not as the first Baronet of Invergaire, or the heir to the Invergaire Armament Works. Not even as Gordon, who'd been her first love, as well as her first lover.

"Yes," she said, her voice steady. "I found him greatly changed. I hardly knew him."

She laid her head back and closed her eyes, lying with such ease that she should have been ashamed.

The time had come to begin to live her life, whatever shape or form it was to have. Bruce belonged in a time labeled *then*.

Just as Gordon belonged in *long ago*.

Chapter 3

More than three hundred years ago, England withdrew its broken and exhausted troops from Scotland, drained from years of Henry VIII's rough wooing of Scotland.

Mary, Queen of Scots, was fifteen years old, and about to be wed to the Dauphin of France in Paris. The powers in Edinburgh were concerned about the bargain. If she bore a child, the crowns of Scotland and France would be united. If she proved barren, the crown of Scotland would be forfeit to the French.

John Knox began to preach the doctrine that was to reform the church in Scotland.

And in Invergaire Glen, on the shore of Loch Mor, near Moray Firth, the Imrie Clan began building Gairloch.

They carved a foundation at the base of Ben Lymond. Using the topography God gave them, they created a foundation and quarried the yellow-white stone for the building. Three years passed before a roof was erected and the first clan member moved into the fortified structure. In the next twenty years, when they weren't warring to protect the land and their country, they continued to build.

In 1592, the castle was complete, in the era of the Duke of Lennox and his men who were allowed, by decree of the Scottish Parliament, to root out the inhabitants of the Highlands. If slaughter was necessary, so be it.

The Imrie Clan looked to their fortifications, added two more wings and three more towers to Gairloch. The road was redesigned to be winding and circuitous, giving full warning to the inhabitants that a visitor approached.

No one, least of all the Imrie Clan, ever called the massive building they'd constructed a castle. Instead, it had been called Gairloch from the first stone laid on the foundation by its warlike laird.

As the final stone was set into place, a piper played a pìobaireachd in honor of the men who'd died in the construction of Gairloch, and for those who would die in the future for the sake of the clan.

Die they did. As the generations continued, they each gave their blood sacrifice to Scotland, to the Highlands, to the very land on which Gairloch had been raised. The earth itself seemed to demand it, and these hardy Scots resolutely and with great respect surrendered their husbands, sons, and brothers first to clan warfare, then to the endless battles with the English.

A hundred years ago, the last battle had been fought, and with it came a sigh of relief throughout Scotland and Invergaire Glen. The time had come for a respite, for a period to nurse her wounds, breed sons in decimated clans, and plan for the future.

Gairloch had weathered the years well. When people passed, many miles away, they viewed a bit of magic. The deep green of Scottish pines gave way to the sight of the huge building of yellow stone with Ben Lymond at its back.

Even from a distance, Gairloch looked proud, as if it knew its own history.

Tales were told of the ferocious lairds who'd guarded Gairloch for generations. In this place in the Highlands, the members of the Imrie Clan had earned their reputations.

Now, only two were left heirs of Gairloch: Fergus and his sister, Shona.

Helen was gawking.

"It's a good hour until we reach Gairloch," Shona said. "I know it looks closer, but that's because of Gairloch's size."

"You didn't tell me it was so . . . huge," Helen said, her voice filled with awe.

Gairloch had five towers and from a distance looked like a massive round structure. Instead, four wings had been built around the original square keep. The castle was a labyrinth of corridors and hallways, some connecting, but most managing to confound a visitor.

As a child, she'd wondered if Gairloch had been built with confusion in mind. Her father had verified her guess. "In case they were ever invaded, the original Imries had wanted to ensure their clan didn't perish."

"One could get lost," Helen said now.

She smiled. "I did when I was little. Fergus and I learned, quick enough, to remain in the public rooms. Gairloch is cold most of the time. It's best to stay near a fireplace."

Loch Mor glittered in the distance, a mirror for the sun. The hills of Invergaire Glen were purple with heather. Both sights were a greeting, as well as a reminder of how long since she'd been home. Seven years, to be exact, ever since her marriage, but it seemed as if nothing had changed.

"What's that?"

She knew what Helen had seen before she looked. On

the other side of the glen sat another house, not nearly so grand, but proud in its way. Built a hundred years ago, of the same yellow stone as Gairloch, the house looked like a smaller, plainer brother.

"That's where Colonel Sir Gordon MacDermond lives," she said. "His father, the general, named it Rathmhor." She smiled, remembering the barely veiled derision in the village when the plaque had been affixed to the outer gate. "He liked the sound of it."

She looked toward Gordon's home. "It's said that after the Forty-five, the Laird of Gairloch befriended a man, a Lowlander, named MacDermond. He convinced the man to come north and live within the shadow of Gairloch. MacDermond was a piper, and a very accomplished man." A tale she'd offer up to the Americans. "So MacDermond came north, with his family and the remnants of his clan, and settled in Invergaire Glen."

"The story doesn't end well, does it?"

She shook her head. "The piper fell in love with Invergaire Glen and made his home here. But he fell in love with the laird's wife as well."

She and Gordon had wondered once, in the little crofter's hut they'd made their own, if the tale was true. Perhaps the MacDermonds had been lured to Imrie land for just such a time, for Shona Imrie and Gordon MacDermond to fall in love. Back then, it had been easy to believe in fairy tales.

"What happened to them?"

She turned to Helen. "They disappeared," she said.

When Helen didn't comment, she continued. "The laird let it be known that his wife had been unfaithful and refused to allow anyone to speak of her from that day until his death."

"Perhaps he died of a broken heart," Helen said. "Can you die of a broken heart?"

No, it wasn't possible. The heart only ached unbearably for years and years, a comment she wasn't about to make.

"Don't worry about getting lost," she said. "We don't use the east or west wings. Fergus and I closed off most of Gairloch and only lived in a small part of it. In addition, we have a caretaker there who knows Gairloch better than any of us."

Old Ned had offered to act as caretaker for the castle when Fergus went away to war, and had done so in the intervening years.

What was she going to do with Old Ned?

"Will the Americans want to buy such a large place?" Helen asked.

"Evidently, he's a very wealthy man," she said, recalling the letter from her solicitor. "He's made his money in a variety of ventures and now pines for the land of his ancestors."

The words sounded bitter, so she modified her tone. "His grandmother was a Scot and he wants to buy a castle for his little girl."

"Too bad Gairloch doesn't come with a resident ghost," Helen said. "No doubt it would add to the atmosphere."

Gairloch had ghosts, both those of the spectral world and of memory. But she'd let Helen warm up to Gairloch first before learning all its secrets.

"We'll have just enough time to clean Gairloch a little before they arrive," she said, glancing over at Helen. "I'm sorry to ask for your help in this chore. I know it isn't the duty of a companion."

"I like a variety of duties," Helen said with equanimity, tugging down her bodice and straightening her spine. "I've no objection to acting as a housemaid for a Highland castle."

She felt a surge of affection for the other woman, and wished there was some way to thank her for her willingness to help.

Four years ago, Helen had arrived on their doorstep, dry-eyed but announcing to her second cousin that she had no other option.

"I've no other place to go, Bruce," Helen had calmly announced. Her father had died, leaving her without funds, and her money had run out. She was, as she'd said, dependent upon her more affluent relations.

Bruce had turned to Shona with a helpless look.

"I could use a companion," she'd said, stepping forward to greet Helen. From that day to this, she hadn't regretted the decision. She wondered, now, if Helen did.

What a pity she didn't have a relation of two to whom she could appeal. The three of them would be a sight standing on an uncle's doorstep, pleading for shelter and a meal.

She shook her head to dispel that dour image.

From their earlier conversations, she knew Helen had never married. Nor, as she'd once said, had she any desire to care for a man.

"Not to say they're obtuse, Shona," she'd said. "But they do not hear much of what is said to them, and what they do hear, they willfully misconstrue."

She'd wanted to ask, but never had, if a lost love had soured Helen to all men, or if it was a case of never having been courted.

Her face was unlined and her brown hair lustrous and thick, without a betraying strand of gray. But her hair invariably escaped the bun she carefully arranged each morning and frizzed around her face as if attempting to give some softness to her angular features and long nose. Her teeth were regrettably crooked, the front two longer than the others. She seemed painfully conscious of them, so when she smiled it was with closed lips. Although her appearance seemed stern, her brown eyes always seemed to be smiling.

Helen was possessed of a generous nature and a caring heart. How would she have managed without Helen's companionship all these months? When she needed someone to listen, Helen did so without censure. On those rare occasions when Helen offered advice, her counsel was always practical and laced with compassion.

The carriage bounced and rattled down the approach to Gairloch, a reminder that it had been a very long time since the drive had been raked or refreshed with gravel. The sudden lurch of the carriage made her grab for the strap above the window.

Luminous sunlight filtered like rain through dark clouds, as if this brilliant September day fought a battle against the impending storm. For a while, she thought the storm might win, but a swift breeze pushed the clouds to the west as they approached Gairloch.

She found herself breathing deeply of the Highland air, as if she'd been holding her breath for seven years. Although Fergus had visited her several times, she'd never returned to Gairloch after her marriage.

But she was here now, for as long as Gairloch was home.

"Shona," Helen said, nearly pasting her face to the window. "Isn't that Colonel Sir Gordon's carriage ahead?"

"What?"

She peered out the window to find that the carriage in front of them was remarkably similar to Gordon's.

"It can't be," she said. "He's supposed to be in Inverness."

Helen didn't say a word.

"He can't be here," she said in the face of Helen's silence.

Please God, don't let him be here.

She had a feeling God was a Scot, however, and an unforgiving one at that, because she was certain that Gordon MacDermond, Colonel Sir Gordon, was ahead of them now.

The very worst thing that could happen.

They'd taken two days to make a journey that would normally take only one, in deference to Fergus's leg. Stopping the carriage periodically to allow him to exercise helped alleviate some of the stiffness. Otherwise, the pain increased until he was nearly gasping.

"Is there nothing they can do?" Gordon asked as he'd helped Fergus back into the carriage on the first day.

"I'm lucky to have the leg is all they'll tell me. There've been times when I was ready to saw it off myself."

The journey had been a difficult one on Fergus, but not once had he complained. Instead, he remained stoic, a man who seemed several decades older than he'd been a mere six months ago.

Gordon disliked feeling helpless. MacDermonds always succeeded—one of the general's sayings.

Three years had passed since Gordon had last been home. Rathmhor would be there, as it always was. Not as large as Gairloch, or as imposing a presence. History was lacking in the house his ancestor had built a hundred years ago. No ghosts roamed the corridors. Unless, of course, it was the shade of his boyhood self, thin to the point of emaciation and terrified of his father.

He'd been an only child, although his mother had died trying to give the general another son. Perhaps one day, he'd be able to think of his father without the veil of the past obscuring his view. Perhaps, one day, he'd be able to do the same with Shona. He'd be able to see her as a woman he'd once loved. Simply that and nothing more.

He was going home. Home to Invergaire Glen. Home of his childhood, his misery, his greatest failure. Yet, in a strange and incomprehensible way, Invergaire Glen was also a place of endless enchantment.

He'd dreamed of being a hero as he'd played on the slopes of Ben Lymond. He'd tossed stones into Loch Mor with Fergus and learned of his own competitiveness. He'd gone to war from Invergaire Glen, looking around him with the studied ease of a soldier, wondering if he'd ever see Shona or Gairloch again.

Against innumerable odds, he'd survived. He'd emerged unscathed from both the Crimean War and his battles in India. Small scars marked inconsequential wounds, but he could walk without assistance and suffered no pain.

Gairloch greeted them, held sway over the glen, announcing its presence to all who drew near.

As they pulled off the main road to make the approach to Rathmhor, Fergus began to laugh.

Before he could ask the source of his merriment, he saw the approaching carriage himself.

"Do you know them?" he asked. Just as the words left his mouth, he saw Shona's face in the window. "You knew about this, didn't you?" he asked as the carriage began to overtake them.

Fergus didn't answer, only waved at his sister as they passed.

Gordon pounded on the roof, getting the attention of the driver. Once the carriage had stopped, he gave him a new destination: Gairloch.

The front, or Upper Courtyard, was narrow, designed to trap the clan's enemies. The Lower Courtyard was approachable through an iron gate in a back wall, and as they traveled through it, he readied himself for battle.

Shona was standing at the top of the steps when they reached the courtyard.

The breathy sigh of the wind was a precursor to a storm still on the horizon. An apt welcome home. But this wasn't home, regardless of the time he'd spent staring at Gairloch or thinking of the castle and its female inhabitant.

Miss Paterson stood behind Shona, her prim mouth pursed. About whose actions was she more disapproving—his or Shona's?

"What are you doing here?" Shona asked, as he exited the carriage. He was turned to help Fergus, but the other man waved him away, the anticipatory smile on his face more than a little reminiscent of Fergus as a boy.

He turned back, began to mount the steps, but halted halfway to the women. He was not about to attack a formidable opponent without reinforcements.

"What are you doing here?" he countered. "I thought you'd be in Inverness, welcoming your nephew."

"My husband's great-nephew," she said. "I never said I was remaining in the city."

"Nor did you tell me you were coming home."

"Nor did you, Gordon MacDermond."

Miss Paterson whispered something to her, but she waved the comment away. Perhaps her companion was reminding her of his title. As if Shona would give a flying farthing about that.

"I've brought Fergus home."

Her face changed, became a porcelain mask, cool and expressionless.

"You couldn't even do the one thing I asked of you, Gordon?"

"Evidently, I couldn't," he said, annoyed at her. Instead of behaving with a modicum of politeness, she'd launched a verbal salvo at him. "He seems pleased to be at Gairloch," he added, a comment that did nothing to ease the look on her face.

She glanced behind him to his carriage.

"Fergus was not healthy enough for the journey."

Where had she learned that frosty tone? The Countess of Morton was very much present in her speech and demeanor at the moment.

He took another step toward her, annoyed at her, at him, at the situation.

"He fared quite well," he said, lying. "He isn't a bairn, Shona."

Her face stiffened and those lovely eyes cooled. "Where were you for the last six months, while he suffered from his wounds? Partying in London?"

"Yes," he said, smiling at her look of surprise. "I find I'm quite good at it. I'm told I'm very charming, perhaps even influential."

She shook her head, then glanced back at Miss Paterson. Did having an audience mitigate her words?

"I still don't want to sell, Shona," Fergus said from behind him.

"Dearest Fergus," she said. "Why have you come?"

"To stop you," he said, smiling faintly. "It's not a good thing you're doing, Shona."

She bent her head, staring down at the steps. A moment later, she took a deep breath, exhaled it, then glanced up, the look of pity on her face annoying Gordon.

Damn it, she didn't have to treat Fergus as if he were helpless. He'd been wounded, but he'd survived. Granted, the minié ball had nearly taken off his leg, but he'd kept it. He might limp for the rest of his life, but Fergus had such tenacity that it wouldn't hold him back from whatever he wanted to do.

The man had been awarded the Victoria Cross. For that reason alone, he should be treated with some dignity.

Gordon stepped in front of her when she would have reached out to her brother.

"He's not a bairn," he whispered to her. "Let him do it."

She looked as if his words lit her anger. Those gray eyes were the smoke of a fire that burned inside.

The climb up the steps was slow and difficult for Fergus. He was standing on his own, but it was doubtful that he would continue in that position for much longer.

Shona simply turned and entered the doorway, leaving the rest of them standing there.

Gordon wasn't entirely certain he'd won that battle, but the war wasn't played out yet.

Chapter 4

"**H**as he been starving?"

Shona stared at the almost empty shelves of the pantry. What had Old Ned been eating? From the looks of the larder and now the pantry, not very much.

Shame pierced her.

"Perhaps he has friends in the village," Helen said, carefully placing her finger in the ledger to mark her spot. She turned to Shona. "Maybe that's where he is now."

Old Ned hadn't been at the gatehouse when they'd arrived. Nor had calling him resulted in his appearance.

"I hope he hasn't starved to death," she said.

"Isn't he a grown man?"

"He's my clansman," she said, glancing over at Helen. "I should have thought of him earlier. But I didn't."

"He should have been able to fend for himself."

A true statement, but she still felt a sense of responsibility for the man.

The pantry was located off the cavernous kitchen. Three sides of the room were covered with wooden shelves. And only a small portion of one lone shelf held any supplies at all. The larder had been likewise as empty.

"Well, it's obvious we need to acquire some food," Helen said, a note of determination in her voice.

Yes, but with what funds? Foolishly, she hadn't given any thought whatsoever to these days at Gairloch, but it was all too evident that she needed to do something and quickly. The two of them—and now Fergus—could hardly subsist on a bag of oats.

She had the clan brooch, an heirloom set in diamonds and emeralds. She wouldn't sell it, unless she was desperate.

At the moment, she was reaching the outer fringes of desperation.

"I don't suppose we have any tea anywhere," Helen asked.

She shook her head.

Three large tables stood in front of her, their surfaces scarred from decades of sharp knives. She could recall Cook using the one in the middle to knead bread, her large hands turning the flour mixture into a magical rising bubble in the bowl. Above her hung pots and pans capable of producing a meal for a hundred people, now connected by a dozen or so dusty cobwebs. The windows on the far side of the room overlooked the bluff above the loch and had been opened so the breeze could clear out the smell of mold and mildew.

"We should have packed more provisions," she said. But even in Inverness, the larder was nearly bare.

"Would you be able to borrow anything from one of the neighbors?"

"We have no neighbors," she said. "Other than the MacDermonds. And we shan't be borrowing anything from him."

Her stomach felt cold at the thought. She fixed a smile on her face so Helen wouldn't see the degree of her distress and left the kitchen.

Gairloch was pining for care; the signs were there in the festooning of cobwebs in the corners, in the palpable air of neglect. Each room held its own version of a musty smell. The floors were dull, the surface gritty and needing sweeping.

The castle had been designed for protection and not for the comfort of its inhabitants. In the main keep there were no windows, only arrow slits that had been bricked up when the rest of Gairloch was added. The kitchen was toward the back of the castle, in the most remote area, attached to the rest of the building by a long, narrow hallway. For that reason, cooking smells never tainted the dining room. But the distance from the kitchen also guaranteed that their meals were often cold as well.

Almost in the center of the original keep was the staircase, winding up to the second floor. In later years, a banister had been added, but the steps had been built for a right-handed swordsman to defend his home, and they still canted down, making them difficult to climb. The servants' stairs, located in the rear of the castle, were much easier, a suggestion she would make to Fergus.

She did not treat him like a bairn, and who was Gordon to suggest that?

Seven years ago, a mountain of debts faced them. Bruce had offered for her at the best possible time. Had Fergus ever hated her for that? Had he ever resented her for disregarding his pride in her rush to save them from their hopeless situation?

She'd never asked.

What had he expected her to do? Starve to death with him in Gairloch? Defer to him simply because he was male?

At least, with Bruce as her husband, she'd had the money to purchase Fergus's commission. He'd never mentioned that, either. Had he, at least, thanked Bruce?

To her right was the Clan Hall. The ceiling soared

upward, the arches resembling a cathedral. Sound echoed strangely here. If the laird, sitting on his throne-like chair in the corner of the room, so much as whispered, the sound would carry throughout the cavernous room.

In the next quarter hour, she and Helen discovered that most of the linens were usable. All the mattresses were lumpy and needed to be plumped back into place.

Their work, however, couldn't take her mind from the two questions plaguing her: where was Old Ned and what were they going to eat?

As they made their way up the sloping stairs, Gairloch was too still, almost as if the castle were grieving for its crowds, for the merriment once inside its walls, for the sheer tumult and noise of its clan.

If tears would help, she'd indulge in a bit of weeping, but when had tears ever been of use? They wouldn't change the situation, and they certainly wouldn't magically provide any tea or biscuits. Or money. If tears would have helped, she'd be a wealthy woman by now.

She waited for Helen on the second floor landing, then turned and headed for the third floor. Here, the staircase was newer and easier to navigate.

"It's a very large place," Helen said.

"Some of the rooms are very small, and hardly count as rooms."

"Unless you have to clean them," Helen said.

"There is that," Shona agreed with a rueful smile.

How would they manage? The Americans would want to see everything, especially since they were thinking of buying the place.

Gairloch seemed to sigh around her, as if hearing her thoughts.

She hesitated at the end of the corridor. "I haven't any idea which room Old Ned might have taken as his."

Glancing at Helen, she smiled. "Pick a direction, and we'll begin looking there."

Helen pointed to the right, and they headed toward the south wing. Each of them began on opposite sides, knocking on doors before pulling them open.

"How many servants did you have?" Helen asked from the other side of the corridor.

"Four dozen when I was growing up," she said.

The days of plenty, when no one spoke of penury. Days of wealth, when the clan brooch had been designed as a bauble for the laird's lady, and people would come for miles around to celebrate any number of events at Gairloch.

She shook her thoughts free of the past.

At the end of the corridor, they looked at each other.

"The family quarters are in the north wing," she said. "Perhaps he's there."

"You do think he's dead?" Helen asked hesitantly.

"I hope not," she said. Not only would she hate that he'd died caring for Gairloch, but his death would weigh heavily on her conscience. She should have sent him word before now. She should have inquired as to his health and well-being.

Why hadn't she?

Because she'd been too consumed with her own survival.

Besides, what would she have done if Old Ned had said he needed funds? What excuse could she give him if he'd told her that Gairloch was in need of repairs? Something always needed to be fixed, shorn up, remortared. The castle was so large that they could begin on one side, and by the time they were finished, that first side would need repairs again.

"What's that?" Helen whirled and stared around her.

"What is what?"

"That noise. It sounded like someone was crying."

Now was perhaps not the best time to discuss the ghosts of Gairloch, so she only shook her head. "No doubt another window is open somewhere and it's the wind."

Helen glanced at her. "It doesn't sound like the wind."

"We have a great deal of wind at Gairloch. It's always blowing hard," she said. "Because we're on a bluff overlooking the loch."

Helen didn't look as if she believed one word.

They found Old Ned fast asleep in the middle of the laird's bed, in the Laird's Chamber, in the very suite of rooms her parents had occupied and which she'd planned to ready for the Americans.

Not only was he fast asleep on the counterpane, fully dressed—a fact she secretly blessed—but he was soused. A half-empty whiskey bottle lay at his side, attesting to the source of his condition. The odor of whiskey and onions, a particularly odd combination, wafted through the room. He was snoring, loudly, evidently having missed their arrival and subsequent inventories.

His brown trousers were stained, his boots caked with dry mud. The white shirt he wore had been new a dozen or so years ago, but she had no idea when it had last been washed.

"Is he a drunkard?" Helen whispered.

She shook her head. "Not that I ever knew," she said. "I've never seen him look so disreputable."

At least his boots hung over the counterpane. A blessing, since it had been made in France and was still a lovely blue. Gairloch blue, her mother had called it.

She grabbed the top of one muddy boot and shook his foot.

"Ned," she said, in a voice just this side of a shout.

One hand rose in the air as if to greet her, then descended to the mattress while he snorted in his sleep.

Like it or not, he was her charge. She grabbed his pants leg, shook it, and shouted his name.

"Ned! Wake up!"

Ned rose up like Lazarus, eyes open wide. A second later, his mouth opened as well and he began screeching like a banshee.

In the Family Parlor, Gordon turned to Fergus. "What's that?"

The other man simply shook his head, both of them looking upward.

Gordon put down his glass—their arrival at Gairloch had called for some reminiscences among good Imrie whiskey—and stood.

Fergus waved his hand toward the second floor. "Go and find out what's amiss, Gordon. Try not to strangle my sister."

He didn't promise anything as he followed the sound. Abruptly, it stopped, but he headed toward the family quarters. He'd been here to visit Fergus once when he was ill. He'd never been inside Shona's room, but he knew exactly where it was. The second floor, third window from the left, facing Rathmhor.

"Shona?"

Miss Paterson peered out from around a heavily carved door at the end of the corridor.

"Colonel Sir Gordon! Whatever are you doing here?"

"The screaming, Miss Paterson. What's wrong?"

"I'm afraid it's the caretaker, sir."

Helen stood aside, an almost welcoming gesture. He entered the room to see Ned sitting on the edge of the bed on the dais, Shona standing beside him, patting him on the shoulder.

"It's sorry I am, Miss Shona," he was saying. "I

thought you were the *bean tuiream* myself, I did." He raised rheumy eyes to stare at her. "I sleep when I can during the day so as to be on guard for the ghosts at night. I don't live here, truly. Not in the Laird's Chamber. I'd never do that."

"It's all right, Ned."

He shook his head mournfully. "It's to keep the ghosts guessing," he said. "If they don't know where I'm sleeping, it confuses them."

Shona turned to look at Gordon. "I thought you left," she said, in the coldest voice he'd ever heard. He was surprised icicles didn't form in the air between them. She stepped down from the dais, but didn't approach him.

"We need to get Fergus settled," he said, pushing his annoyance at Shona to the background for the moment.

"Nothing is ready at the moment," Shona said.

"What needs to be done?"

"The mattresses aired, the sheets aired, the rooms swept, and the cobwebs and dust swept from the rooms."

"All that?"

"Yes," she said, her face set in stern lines. She might look the same after a lifetime of disappointments, her face devoid of humor, no sparkle of amusement in her eyes. He missed, suddenly, the girl she'd been, his companion in exploration and sin.

"Then I'll take him home to Rathmhor," he said.

Her hands were fisted in her skirt. The girl he'd known would not have been so restrained. She would have spoken the words trembling on her lips, and expressed the irritation he saw in her eyes.

"Ned, pick a room on the third floor and make that one yours."

The man straightened enough to look up at her. He'd not shaved in a few days, and it looked as if he'd not changed his clothing for longer than that.

Slowly, he nodded.

Was Shona fool enough to believe Ned would obey her?

Without comment, she walked over to the bed and picked up the bottle of whiskey. The look she gave him promised a discussion about his drinking at another time.

"We'll go and ready my brother's room," she said, glancing at Helen. "You needn't worry about Fergus." A nod to Helen and the two women were at the doorway.

"What can I do?" he asked.

"Leave," she said. "Go home. We'll muddle along quite well without you."

"Shona," Helen said, looking at him, then at her employer.

Shona shook her head as if to silence the woman.

"Thank you for bringing Fergus home," she said, but the look she gave him wasn't filled with gratitude. She was angry, but holding back her words. When had she learned to master her temper?

Perhaps he didn't know her as well as he'd thought. But he wanted to, a realization that kept him silent. This woman with her flashing eyes and soft smile was a contradiction, an anomaly, and he wasn't comfortable being ignorant around Shona Imrie.

"Fergus doesn't want to sell Gairloch," he said, well aware that his friend could speak for himself. But he wanted to goad her, test the limits of her temper. "Why do you?"

She calmly folded her hands in front of her, turned in the doorway, and surveyed him. "Once, you might have had a right to question me, Colonel Sir Gordon. That time has passed."

"Has it?"

There, another spark of emotion, something lighting her eyes just for a second, like a summer storm.

"Have you any provisions, Colonel Sir Gordon?
Something we might be able to borrow?" Helen said,
taking a step toward him.

He glanced at Helen in surprise, then back at Shona.
Her temper was loosed from its cage, evidently, from the
look she gave her companion.

"It's just that we haven't planned well," Helen said,
taking a precautionary step away. "What with Fergus's
arrival now." Her words trailed off as she glanced at
Shona.

"Of course," he said, "I'll have a wagon sent over."

"That's not necessary."

She smiled at him, a gracious and irritating countess-
like expression as if he were her subordinate. A beggar
at her door who'd offered to share his meager rations
with her.

Like hell.

"Don't be an idiot, Shona," he said. "Would you
starve for the sake of your pride?"

He strode to the door. Shona moved aside quickly, but
he stopped in front of her.

"Why?"

"Why what?" She glanced up at him, then away, not
meeting his eyes.

"Why are you so set on selling Gairloch?"

His memories were suddenly more uncomfortable
than he'd thought they could be, with her betrayal still
sour on his tongue after all these years.

"I don't owe you any explanations."

"When have you ever explained yourself, Shona?"

She looked up at him.

"Once, I thought your arrogance charming. The
sign of a girl who knew her mind. Do you not think of
anyone but yourself? The great Countess of Morton."

Her lips thinned, but she didn't speak.

"Fergus doesn't want to sell," he said softly. "Why are you so set on it?"

"It's none of your concern," she said.

Her eyes were a clear gray, the color of rolling clouds before a Highland storm. The smile was gone and a tinge of pink colored her cheeks.

She looked like the girl he'd known, tumultuous, willing to argue a point simply to win. He'd entered into her game eager enough, pitting his reason and his logic against her more emotional arguments. They'd debated and shouted, disputed, and countered each other over a myriad of subjects, none of them important, and all of them memorable.

"It's none of my concern? Very well," he said softly, conscious of Helen and Old Ned.

With a smile, he stepped through the doorway and left her before he could say something he'd regret.

Or she could further wound him with her words.

Chapter 5

Rathmhor was only a fraction the size of Gairloch and lacking the splendor of the home of Clan Imrie. The house was stolid and square, a labyrinth of corridors and hallways he'd managed to learn as a toddler. He was never so cold as when he was in Gairloch or so happy. Here, at home, he was warm but almost always miserable.

He'd not been home since the general died, and that, in itself, was cause to hesitate at the gate. His father had been intent upon guarding what was his, and even in this peaceful glen, he'd erected a stone fence and iron gate to announce to all that this was Rathmhor. On one pillar was the house's name. On the other was the Latin word: Prodeo. *Go forth*, the motto of the MacDermonds. How like them to take a Latin term instead of a Gaelic one, as if to show these stubborn Highlanders that they were somehow better. Go forth they had, into battle, into war, into any type of contest they could find in the civilized world. They'd proven themselves, father then son, and now, he alone was returning.

He'd written his housekeeper and informed her that he was coming home. Mrs. MacKenzie would marshal up the household troops, ready them for inspection and welcome. An unofficial recognition that he was the head of the household now and not the oft absent general.

His earliest memories of Rathmhor had been filled with terror. As an only child, he'd been doomed to carry all the general's hopes on his skinny little shoulders. A lifetime of work had gradually transformed him into the man the general had wanted for a son.

The general had gone to battle, and so had he. The general had won acclaim, and so had he. The general was a national hero, and so was he. The general had been a lonely man, but Gordon was damned if he was going to continue in his father's footsteps.

The elder MacDermond had never been awarded a baronetcy. The old man's pride had struggled with irritation when the son had outstripped the father. He'd known that, and maybe it was for that single fact alone he'd taken delight in being addressed as Colonel Sir Gordon in his father's company.

Go forth, Gordon, into the lion's den. But, of course, the great lion of the MacDermonds was dead.

His father had arranged the macadam coating on the road from the gate to the front of the house, which meant that the approach was smooth, the carriage wheels almost soundless.

Mrs. MacKenzie stood by the steps, the household staff arranged in a semicircle in front of the house.

He exited the carriage, his smile firmly affixed. When he reviewed the troops, he was somber and intent. Here, at home, his demeanor could relax a little, especially since the general wasn't around to critique his performance.

Would the household staff feel the same sense of relief he did?

Mrs. MacKenzie was short and plump, with a habit of smiling in the middle of any provocation. Even with her crown of white hair piled high on her head, she didn't come to his shoulder. He'd often wished she'd been around when he was a boy. She might have been a refuge for him, a place to go when he was frightened and trying, desperately, not to show it. He bent down, and surprised her by kissing her on the cheek, a gesture he'd never before performed.

A hint, perhaps, of the changes to come.

"Colonel Sir Gordon," she said, softly, placing her hand against the spot he'd kissed. She bobbed a curtsy. "Welcome home."

He stood back and stared up at the stone edifice. After being away, he was always struck by how much Rathmhor looked like an English fortress. A stolid, square building set into the Glen of Invergaire, jealously guarding its terrain as if fearing an advance of Imries.

"Your staff, sir," Mrs. MacKenzie said, sweeping a hand toward the two dozen or so people standing patiently.

He stood at attention, realized what he was doing, and forced himself to relax.

"You had a lookout from the tower," he said, smiling.

She bobbed her head, her face flushing a little. "It's only fitting that we be waiting for you, sir."

The tower was the only part of Rathmhor that didn't fit its English appearance. A single conical shape set back from the front like a jester's hat atop the structure. Or a jealous cousin of the spires and towers of Gairloch.

As a boy, he'd retreated there often enough, to send a signal first to Fergus and then to Shona. When had irritation over her constant presence altered to become interest? When he'd first confided in her and she'd hugged him? Or when he'd first placed his cheek against the softness of her hair and felt a tug of some previously unknown emotion?

He'd first felt lust when thinking of Shona. Would he always couple the two in his mind?

"Everyone looks well," he said now, pushing thoughts of the Countess of Morton from his mind.

He fell back on his ability to recall names and events with ease.

Cook was a woman of middle years who'd been with them ten years or more, and favored the French way of cooking, something his father had appreciated. His own taste was less continental and more Scots. Granted, he wouldn't do well with a diet of haggis, but kedgeree would satisfy him fine, as would any type of salmon.

Two of the younger maids he remembered from his visit before he left for Russia. Three other girls, however, were new.

"Hello Maisie," he said, stopping in front of one of the upstairs maids. "Are you and Robbie still seeing each other?"

She bobbed an awkward curtsy, and flushed. "We're married now, sir."

He smiled and moved on, greeting the stable master and three of his helpers. How many people were required to care for one man?

When he was done, he made his way back to Mrs. MacKenzie.

"Have we enough food to spare, Mrs. MacKenzie?" he asked.

She looked surprised at the question, but answered quickly. "Yes, sir, a few haunches of beef and venison. Some mutton as well, if you've a taste for that."

"Send half of that to Gairloch," he said.

"Gairloch, sir?" Her expression changed from affable to annoyed in the blink of an eye.

"Do you object, Mrs. MacKenzie?"

"That Ned is a wastrel, sir. Never does a bit of work around the place. Mumbles about ghosts the whole time instead of working. A drunk, he is, and you know I don't hold with that."

She allowed whiskey into Rathmhor for one reason only: the house wasn't hers.

"The laird and his sister have returned," he said, hoping she wouldn't question him further.

She did even worse. Her eyes widened, her face paled, and she began to weep, the tears falling down her cheeks silently.

"Oh, sir, is it true?"

He reached out and patted her on the shoulder. "Why don't you dismiss them?" he said, aware of the audience of interested staff.

"Of course, sir," she said. "And I'll be about sending over some food for the Imries. Imagine, sir, after all these years, they're home. Imagine."

"I didn't realize you were so fond of the Imries, Mrs. MacKenzie," he said as she turned and clapped her hands together. Evidently, that was a signal for the staff to disband, which they did quickly enough.

She turned to face him again. "Invergaire Glen isn't the same without the Imrie Clan in residence."

"You sound as if you're from the village," he said, surprised.

She nodded. "I am, sir. My family's from here, but I didn't return home until my Alfred died. In the army he was, sir. One of your men."

Startled, he began to run through a roster of men in his mind.

"Oh, not yours, sir. He was in the Ninety-third." She glanced up at him and continued, "He never made it to the Crimea, but he did see service in Halifax."

She slowly began to walk toward the house, and he accompanied her, feeling a curious reluctance to enter Rathmhor.

"I didn't know, Mrs. MacKenzie," he said.

Of course his father would have hired a soldier's widow.

"And why should you, Colonel Sir Gordon?" she asked, reaching up and patting his arm in a decidedly maternal way. "You've barely been at Rathmhor since I was hired. Soldiering, you were, you and your company. It's proud I am to be serving you, sir, and if my Alfred was alive, he'd feel the same."

"I'm no longer with the Ninety-third, Mrs. MacKenzie. Or a colonel."

Surprised, she stopped and faced him. "Have you given up your commission, then, sir?"

He nodded. The War Office could no longer force him to command men who willingly went to their deaths for the honor of the Empire. War was for young, optimistic men. He was still young, but he wasn't as optimistic as the War Office would wish of him. Instead, he'd become a realist.

You're a damn coward! Words from his father. Maybe the old man had died simply to spite him. Or maybe he'd died from rage.

The funeral had been sparsely attended. Only in his adulthood had he fully accepted what his child self had somehow known: no one liked General MacDermond. He may have been respected for his almost foolhardy courage and his skill at devising cunning battle strategies, but when the battle was over, people avoided him.

Unfortunately, Gordon hadn't been able to do the same.

He and Mrs. MacKenzie hesitated at the double doors. Something should be carved on the lintel. *Beware, all who enter, thou shalt be judged lacking.*

God forgive him, but he was glad the old man was finally dead.

* * *

"You're angry with me."

Shona didn't answer.

Helen sighed heavily, which garnered her a quick glance.

"You shouldn't have said anything," Shona said.

"Why not? Should we starve, instead?"

She halted in the corridor, took a deep breath, released it, then forced herself to turn and face Helen.

"You surprised me. When I first knew you, I thought you such a timid soul, afraid of offending anyone. I suspect, however, that you aren't like that at all."

Helen blinked several times, but didn't defend herself.

"You're very fierce when you need to be."

"I don't like being hungry," Helen said. "Or too prideful for my own good." The latter sentence was whispered, but Shona still heard.

"Perhaps I was," she said after a moment. "Thank you. There wasn't anything else to do, was there?"

"Unless you wish to drink yourself into a stupor like Old Ned," Helen said. "I take it there's plenty of whiskey about?"

"We're in Scotland," she said, smiling. "Of course there's whiskey about."

"It's what one neighbor would do for another," Helen added. "After all, we're in the wilds of the Highlands, alone but for Rathmhor."

"We're not all that isolated. The village is just over the hill. It's become quite prosperous in the last few years, Fergus says."

If they'd had any money at all, she would have shopped there. Unfortunately, they were down to the money she had in her reticule, a ridiculously small amount given that she lived in the largest house in this part of Scotland.

With any luck—a commodity that had been scarce of late—Gairloch would save them.

"Well, I for one hope Colonel Sir Gordon will hurry."

"We've brown bread and jam," Shona said. "In the basket."

"No tea, however," Helen announced dejectedly.

"I'm sure there are a few bottles of wine in the cellar. We could invent a new kind of repast. Sandwiches and wine."

"What if we get tipsy?"

A condition devoutly to be sought. A few sips of wine might take away the edge of this day, dull the absolute misery she felt. No, then she would be as bad as Old Ned, who chose drunkenness to escape the ghosts of Gairloch. She had her own ghosts, but one of them was alive, well, and not far away.

The past was striking with too much force, and everything hurt. She was no longer a child, and she couldn't withdraw to her room to hug her pillow and weep. Yet the grief she felt now was so unexpected that she felt off kilter, uncertain and strangely alone, even though Helen was standing next to her.

They entered Fergus's room, the musty smell halting her in the doorway. Was the whole of Gairloch in disrepair?

Resolutely, she strode to the window, opening the heavy curtains and throwing up the sash. The wind around Gairloch was always fierce, as if nature were a warrior and pitted its strength against the castle.

"We need a day or two to air out all the rooms," she said. "But this will just have to do. He shouldn't have come."

"Fergus is as stubborn as you," Helen said, garnering her another look. "Well, he is, and it's no good you looking at me as if I've turned yellow, Shona Donegal. It's the truth and you know it."

"I do," she admitted. "I just didn't know that you knew it."

"You're very personable people," Helen added. "A pretty smile can hide a great many flaws, but it doesn't mask the fact that the two of you very much want to get your own way."

Shona stood at the window, gazing out toward the loch. "When I was younger," she said, "I thought that if I wished for something long enough, or hard enough, I'd get it. It never quite worked out that way."

"You married an earl," Helen said.

She nodded. "True."

"My second cousin was quite wealthy. Until he died."

"True again."

"Was that not what you wanted?"

Now was not the time to continue this conversation. Not when tears were too close to the surface.

"You could always marry again."

An idea that had already occurred to her. Marriage had always been a woman's salvation. Nor had being married to Bruce been a terrible experience. Her heart hadn't been involved, but she'd felt compassion for him and a certain type of fondness. He'd been kind to Fergus and generous as well.

Perhaps another older husband, preferably wealthy, was the answer.

If she could bear it.

Love was not, after all, necessary.

But even marriage was not a certainty of financial security. Look where she was now, as poor as she'd been after her parents died. If she married again, she'd arrange for some provision to be made beforehand, in case of her husband's death.

She was really tired of being poor.

"Right now what I want is for Fergus to be comfortable," she said, smiling determinedly at Helen.

She removed one corner of the counterpane, and Helen moved to help her. Together, they stripped the bed, flipped the mattress, and while Helen went to fetch some of the less musty sheets, she went to the maids' closet and found some rags and a broom.

A little work, that's what she needed. Some physical labor to banish thoughts and feelings as well.

In the next half hour, they put Fergus's room to rights, including filling and testing the oil lamps, refreshing the potpourri in the jar on the dresser, and placing a bouquet of late blooming heather near the bed, the purple blossoms attesting not only to September, but the fact that they were home.

She was grateful that the days were still temperate. The evenings would be chilly, as well as the mornings, but the cold wouldn't start to seep into their bones for a few weeks. By that time, the Americans would have settled in, relishing their Scottish heritage.

They wouldn't, however, be prepared for winter in the Highlands.

But they were wealthy and could well afford the coal to heat the rooms they wished to use. As for the Clan Hall and the Family Parlor, both were so cavernous that it made no difference that each had two tall fireplaces.

Her nose nearly froze on her face if she stepped more than ten feet away from a roaring fire.

"I won't miss the winter here," she said, shutting the window.

Helen didn't say anything, but her look was dubious.

"I would think it would be lovely, what with the snow and ice. Does the loch never freeze?"

She shook her head. "It's too deep, I think."

"I've always liked winter," Helen said. "Until I was alone. Then it seems like a cruel season, don't you think?"

She didn't know quite how to answer that comment. Luckily, Helen didn't seem to expect one.

"I wish I'd married when I was younger. Now it's too late, of course."

Another comment for which she didn't have a response. What could she possibly say? That marriage had been a blessing? That it had given her comfort? It hadn't. It had simply been there, a partnership she and Bruce had shared. She'd attempted to be the wife he wanted, and he'd succeeded in being kind and generous to her.

But for the whole of it? Would she do it again?

Better to be miserable alone than to share that emotion with another person.

They retreated to the Laird's Chamber once more. Old Ned had taken himself off somewhere, but Fergus had taken his place on the bed.

Her heart lurched when she saw him so pale. Fear was immediately replaced by anger. Why couldn't Gordon have done what he'd said he'd do? Why hadn't he remained in Inverness? Why had he brought Fergus here?

Stepping to the side of the bed, she placed her hand on Fergus's clammy forehead.

"Don't hover, Shona," he said without opening his eyes.

"I'm not hovering."

He opened his eyes. "I'm just resting," he said.

"You've hurt yourself."

"I've hurt myself," he admitted. His wry smile touched a corner of her heart, reminding her of their childhood together. "I was trying to demonstrate that I'm not quite an invalid, but those stairs are damnable."

Alarmed, she swept her gaze down to his leg.

"Your wound is worse?"

"No," he said, sitting up. "It just hurts like the devil himself is jumping up and down on it."

She glanced over at Helen who was looking as worried as she felt.

"Helen thinks we're stubborn. You've just proven her point, Fergus," she said. However irritated she was at him, she couldn't harden her heart when he looked at her that way—the corner of his lip tilted in a grin, the look in his eyes unrepentant.

"What are you doing here?" she asked, helping him to sit on the edge of the bed.

"Especially when you expressly forbade me to come?"

"I didn't." Well, she had. "Not in so many words," she said. "I wanted to deal with the Americans myself."

"I don't want to deal with them at all."

She glanced at Helen, as if to concede that her companion was indeed right. They were two stubborn people, perhaps the most stubborn people in all of Scotland.

She had the feeling she would need every bit of her resolve before the sale of Gairloch was finalized, and before she left the past behind.

Chapter 6

Shona awoke at dawn, lighting the oil lamp in the room she and Helen had claimed as theirs. She couldn't bear to sleep in the spacious chamber she'd had as a girl. The view from the window was of Rathmhor, and a secret part of her was afraid that she'd stand there, fingers pressed against the glass, yearning to be seven years younger and desperately in love.

Love died.

A flower withered if not watered. A plant shriveled if not given care. Even the hardy heather could be destroyed.

If not nourished, love perished.

They'd claimed one of the guest bedrooms, a chamber overlooking the winding approach to Gairloch. The last person to occupy this room had been a guest at her parents' funeral ten years earlier.

The sunlight through the window was sullen, as if grudging the start of day.

Shona felt the same.

The room smelled dusty, overlaid with a tinge of mildew. Were the windows in this wing secure? Or had Old Ned simply left them open to the rain? The smell was an admonishment, as tangible as the layer of dust over every surface.

She and Fergus had not been good stewards of their heritage.

Gairloch was the symbol of her clan's honor, filled with so many memories that they could drown her if she let them. Every room held a reminiscence: her father's booming voice, her mother's smile, the sound of Fergus's running feet.

Now she prayed for the courage to say good-bye.

She had no other recourse but to sell the castle. Instead of dwelling on the bad, she should think of the good. Once she sold Gairloch, she'd never have to see Gordon's home. She'd never again have to think of the crofter's hut tucked neatly in the woods, or the path to the loch and the brae where they'd had their picnics so many years ago.

If she sold Gairloch, they'd have enough money to go away to some warmer place, where Fergus could sit in the sun and brown, where the chilled wind didn't hint of winter even in the middle of summer.

Fergus, however, was not cooperating.

For now, she would dust the fixtures, clean the floors, polish the fireplace andirons, sweep the corridors, and brush away the cobwebs. Perhaps she'd even sing in the shadows to banish the ghosts in the unused wings.

Her stomach rumbled, as if to remind her that dinner last night had consisted of only brown bread, jam, some beef tea, and the last of a jarred stew. By unspoken agreement, she and Helen had forced the stew and the beef tea on Fergus, ensuring that he ate, rather than drank, his dinner.

Old Ned had procured a bottle of wine from the cellar and Fergus had appropriated it, making headway to the bottom before their dinner was finished. Since they had no laudanum or anything else he might use for pain, she remained silent.

"Is this all there is?" Fergus had said at the beginning of the meal.

"We're saving the oats for breakfast," she'd said, with more good humor than she felt.

They'd exchanged a look.

"I simply didn't plan well enough," she said, unwilling to let him know the full degree of their poverty. "I should have arranged for provisions in Invergaire Village."

"I hope you will, tomorrow," he said, pouring himself another tumbler of wine.

She bit back in the remark she might have made. What could she say? *There isn't any money, brother. There hasn't been for the longest time. The sale of Gairloch is the only thing to save us.*

He'd never questioned her inheritance from Bruce or the expenses of her Inverness home. He probably wouldn't query her on the money to be spent in readying Gairloch for visitors. That question would be easily answered. She had none. Somehow, she would have to entertain the Americans with creativity and sleight of hand.

Prayers wouldn't hurt, either.

In his defense, Fergus had other things to concern him, such as surviving his injuries.

Her stomach made its presence known again. The idea of breakfast was holding a great deal of interest, even if it was only boiled oats.

Helen, whose face had been buried in a very lumpy pillow, turned her head and blinked several times. Her hair was a nimbus of frizz; her face bore several wrinkles from the sheets. The disarray was disturbing, since Helen was normally so neat in appearance.

"Will he send some food today, do you think?"

Their thoughts were such twins of each other that she smiled.

"If he doesn't, we'll simply have to return to Inverness and sell my clan brooch."

"Would you truly sell the brooch, Shona? It's all you have left of your mother."

Why had she told Helen that in a moment of weakness?

"Memories can't be sold," she said.

"There are a great many weapons in the Clan Hall," Helen said.

She only nodded.

As laird, Fergus wouldn't hear of any of the artifacts being sold. Every one of the swords saved from countless battles, shined and polished with edges kept honed, was sacrosanct, along with the shields, dented and bloody in spots, either indicating a victory or the death of a clan member. Some of the pipes hanging in the Family Parlor hadn't been played since the first years of Gairloch. The reeds were clogged with dust and the bags hung in tatters, but they might fetch a few pennies.

Not if Fergus had anything to say about it.

They might starve to death, but Gairloch would remain inviolate.

Helen threw back the covers from her side of the bed. There hadn't been time to ready two chambers last night, so countess and companion had shared a lumpy mattress in a stale room. Helen stared at the floor as if trying to come to grips with the reality of dawn. With her hair arranged in one fat braid, she looked a great deal younger than once she was dressed all proper and prim.

"We'll make what we can for breakfast," she said, smiling at the other woman. "When that's done, we'll begin cleaning."

Helen nodded. "It will take my mind from my hunger."

She hesitated at the screen and turned back to Helen. "Thank you," she said.

"Whatever for?"

"For not grumbling about the task. I know you were not hired to be a charwoman."

Helen shrugged. "One must do what one must do," she said. A smile trembled on her lips. "You're a countess, and yet I'll wager that you work as hard as anyone today."

"There's no other choice," she said. "Old Ned seems useless. Fergus will insist on helping but shouldn't tax himself."

Helen slid from the bed. "Then we'll have to be enough," she said.

Once dressed and fed—such as it was—they began in the Clan Hall.

The room was cavernous, taking up the whole of the middle of Gairloch. Its mirror was the Family Parlor, reached through a tall arched doorway in the middle of the far wall. Here, however, was where the members of the clan had congregated to adjudicate disputes, pay their yearly rents, or meet before battle.

The room had not been furnished for comfort but for gatherings. In the corner, on a small pedestal barely a foot high, sat the laird's chair. Constructed of wood that had once been painted but was worn and dark now, it had two broad arms, and a tall back inscribed with the clan's badge: five upward pointing spears gathered by a ribbon on which were written the Gaelic motto: *Be afraid of nothing.*

She stared at it for a moment, wondering if any of the lairds of the past faced what she did now—a penury so encompassing that she worried about food.

Two round tables with accompanying chairs sat on either end of the room. Other than a series of benches arrayed against each wall, there was no other seating. Comfortable chairs, settees, and lamps were reserved for the Family Parlor.

The echoes of war seemed to linger in this room, and it had always been odd to her that no one had ever sighted any of the ghosts of Gairloch in the Clan Hall.

"I think it would be best," she said, looking over the room, "to begin from the top down. We'll lower the chandelier, clean it first, then dust, and lastly sweep and wash the floors."

"A masterful plan of attack, my general," Fergus said from the doorway.

She turned, surveying him from head to toe. His clothing was wrinkled, but that was to be expected. His hair was brushed, however, and he'd taken the time to shave. Neither Fergus nor Gordon wore beards, so at odds with fashion that she wondered if it was a small rebellion of theirs.

His eyes, however, were clear, and if he leaned a bit too heavily on his cane, she wouldn't mention it.

"Did you use the back stairs this time?" she asked, arranging the buckets, brushes, and rags as if they held more interest than her brother's health.

"I nearly slid down them," he said.

She quickly glanced up to see the smile he and Helen exchanged.

"I care about you," she said, annoyed. "Or I wouldn't ask."

"You care too much, Shona," he said, entering the room. "One would think you were my mother. Not my younger sister. My much younger sister."

His look was steady and this time she glanced away first.

"We left toast for you," Helen said.

"Found it, ate it, and looked about for more food.

Shouldn't we solve that problem before we begin to clean?"

"I'll solve the food situation," she said, handing Helen a bucket and some rags.

Inside the bucket was a jar of ashes to be used to brush into the carpet in the Family Parlor. If they could finish the almost monumental task of cleaning the Clan Hall, they'd move on to that room.

"We could live here," Fergus said. "We've the forest for wood and there's plenty of game. You could set the kitchen garden to rights. Who cares if there's only the three of us, plus Old Ned, rattling around?"

He could barely walk. Now he was talking of hunting and chopping wood?

She pushed down her impatience, remaining silent as if she was entertaining his idea. He didn't know that she'd spent many, many sleepless hours trying to figure a way out of their dilemma. The lamentable fact was that the three of them were woefully unequipped to fend for themselves, even at Gairloch.

"Have you come to help?" she asked.

When he nodded, she smiled, having figured out a task that would leave him his pride and not exhaust him.

She went to the doorway, pointing to where a rope was wound around a pair of iron spikes set into the wall.

"If you'd lower the chandelier, please," she said, "Helen and I will clean it."

She walked away, determinedly not looking to see if he needed assistance. The chandelier was heavy, and even with the rope on a pulley, it would be a chore. But the effort would require his arms, not his wounded leg, and use enough strength that Fergus wouldn't feel she coddled him too much.

What a delicate thing was a man's pride.

She grabbed her bucket and walked to the other side of the room. Fergus swore, then swiftly apologized. Neither Helen nor she looked in his direction. He would just have to manage. If he asked for her help, she'd be at his side the next second. However, the creak of the pulley indicated that he was managing quite well.

"Damn heavy, Shona," he said, before apologizing for his language again.

She looked up at the lowering chandelier.

For months, worry had filled every moment, but for a few short minutes, it was pushed aside by regret. And, perhaps, grief as she stared at the cobwebs that swept from the corners to tenuously perch on the chandeliers, and then draped from shield to claymore to dirk. A message that the past was dead, given a dust shroud, and decorated by industrious spiders.

Helen's stomach growled, the sound embarrassingly loud in the silence. When she excused herself to go and fill the buckets, Shona turned to her brother.

"I'll have food here by this afternoon," she said.

The villagers of Invergaire would be more than happy to assist them, since all their ancestors had been clan members. But she wasn't about to go door to door, explaining their plight. The shame of even having that thought was painful.

We're poor. We're beyond poor. We're destitute, and we've nothing but Gairloch.

Hardly words she'd utter aloud.

The minister, however, had been a friend of her parents. In addition to officiating at her parents' funeral, he'd married her in the church at Invergaire. This afternoon, she would travel the short distance to Invergaire and beg, because begging was what it would be.

Helen should never have asked Gordon for help. He'd aid Fergus, perhaps, but she couldn't even be sure of that. Not once in the six months since they'd returned from India had he written.

And have my letters returned?

She wouldn't have done that. A still, small voice whispered that she might have. She had no reason when it came to Gordon.

The black dress she was wearing was one of her oldest, so she wasn't concerned about its welfare. She used one of the longer rags to bind her hair. After Helen returned from filling up the two buckets, she did the same.

The chandelier, an elaborate ring of interlocking circles, held sconces for two dozen thick pillared candles. In the last century, glass shields had been placed around the candles so that the hapless visitors standing under the chandelier wouldn't be showered with hot wax.

She'd thought to bring a knife from the kitchen and it was the first tool she used, scraping off dried puddles at the base of the candles.

"Are there any more candles in the pantry?" she asked, turning toward Fergus, who was tying off the rope now that the chandelier had been lowered.

"Is that my new task?" he asked.

"That, and making sure the stove is lit," she said, smiling.

He only nodded and left the room, leaving her and Helen to their chore.

By the time he returned, they'd finished scraping and polishing. The iron would never be attractive, being a dull gray cast, but the glass shields sparkled.

"We've only got three candles," Fergus said.

With the remaining five, they would provide some illumination. Perhaps the Americans would see the dimness of the Clan Hall as atmospheric. A true Scottish castle, complete with shadows and hints of other times.

Raising the chandelier took more time and effort, but once again, she refused to assist Fergus. Nor did he call for help. Instead, she and Helen made quick work of dusting the rest of the furniture, and what weapons they could reach.

Please, God, let the Americans purchase Gairloch.

The last task remaining in the Clan Hall was to sweep and mop the floor. Helen swept while she went into the kitchen. The well was located in the corner of the kitchen, topped by a surround of bricks a foot high. She knelt, filled the buckets, and heated some water in one of the large pots hanging over the table. After the buckets were filled with hot water, she carried them one by one into the Clan Hall.

The stone floor was sufficiently hard—and dirty—that she had little to think about other than her chore. Helen worked beside her, with Fergus periodically replacing their dirty water with clean.

When she reached the wall, she moved to the side to help Helen.

"Now that's a sight. The Countess of Morton scrubbing."

She stopped, frozen to the spot, on her hands and knees with a scrub brush in her hand.

Of course, it was Gordon. Colonel Sir Gordon. What a ridiculous title. Of course, he'd arrived now, when perspiration was rolling off her forehead and her dress was uncomfortably damp under her arms.

Of course, she was filthy.

She didn't look up and she didn't comment. Let him say what he would, a response wouldn't get the floor clean. He said something to Fergus that she couldn't hear, but when both men laughed, she gritted her teeth.

Miserable man.

She glanced at Helen. If she looked as bad as Helen, she was in a deplorable state indeed. Since she didn't hear anything further, she risked a glance behind her. Both men had disappeared from the doorway.

"Do you think he's brought food?" Helen whispered, looking as hopeful as Shona suddenly felt.

"If he has, then he can say anything he wishes about me," she said, rising to her feet.

She glanced down at her dress. In addition to water spots, it looked as if she'd scrubbed the floor with the skirt. Her fingernails were brown, her face warm and no doubt flushed. She probably had streaks of dirt on her face as well, and she knew her hair was a mess because some tendrils had escaped the rag she'd used.

Stiffening her back, she looked around the room.

"We've done as much as we can do here," she said, as Helen finished up her section of the floor and stood.

"Perhaps we'll have a small tea?" Helen asked.

Shona's stomach rumbled at the thought.

She nodded, leading the way to the Lower Courtyard, praying that Gordon had indeed brought provisions.

Provisions?

He'd brought the whole of northeast Scotland with him.

The wagon he, Fergus, and Old Ned were offloading looked to be filled with enough baskets, jars, and canisters to feed them all for a month. In addition, there were two sides of beef.

Did he think they were starving?

Her initial relief was tempered by a dawning awareness that he'd known, exactly, what sort of difficulty they were facing. Embarrassment began a march from her toes, warming her skin as it traveled upward to blossom in her cheeks.

She should have refused his largesse and sped him from the courtyard with a word or two to let him know that she wasn't to be pitied.

There were others to consider, however. Fergus, who'd not yet fully recovered from his wounds. Helen, who'd been rescued from poverty and hopelessness only to be thrust back into it again as her companion. She'd not been able to pay Helen for months now, and the other woman's only comment was that she was happy to have a roof over her head and sustenance.

Sustenance she hadn't even been able to provide.

When he mounted the steps, a side of beef slung over one shoulder, she moved aside. Any comment she wanted to make, was desperate to make, was silenced by his generosity.

She would have to thank him, and not only did that thought rankle, but it was something she'd have to practice.

Would her lips even form the words in his presence?

Seven years earlier, she'd been dependent upon his charity. She hadn't liked it then any more than she did at this moment.

She closed her eyes and prayed for patience and restraint, neither easily accomplished since Helen moved to stand beside her, relaying the inventory in an awe-filled whisper.

"It looks like a canister of chocolate, Shona. Chocolate! Do you know how long it's been since we had chocolate?"

"At least two years," she said, opening her eyes. It did, indeed, look like a canister of chocolate sitting atop a barrel of something that Old Ned was pulling down from the wagon bed.

Evidently, Old Ned had slept the night before and abjured the use of the bottle to scare off the ghosts. Was he more reassured since the three of them had arrived? Or had Fergus simply taken his whiskey away?

Life was so much easier in Inverness. It wasn't better; it was just easier.

She left the courtyard in favor of the Family Parlor, Helen ghosting her.

"We need to work in here," she said, hoping that Helen wouldn't ask about food for the moment.

Evidently, the other woman heard the resolve in her voice—it wasn't the hint of unshed tears—because Helen didn't say a word, merely stepped over the wet spots on the floor, grabbed her bucket, and followed.

The Family Parlor was a little more comfortable, although it couldn't be said to be a welcoming room. Two settees, recent additions commissioned by her mother, sat in front of one of the massive fireplaces. A few small chairs were scattered here and there, each with a table nearby. The oil lamps hadn't been tended to in at least seven years, and she wondered if they had any spare wicks.

A carpet, another of her mother's acquisitions, covered most of the dark floorboards with an intricately loomed pattern of wild laurel, a plant associated with the Imrie Clan, on a crimson background.

This room held more memories, but even those she resolutely pushed away. She could not be catapulted into the past for fear that Gordon would be there.

"Shall we begin with the chandeliers?" Helen asked.

She glanced up at the ceiling. Four brass chandeliers, each hanging beneath a discolored plaster rose, illuminated a section of the room. The brass was dull, but they didn't have time to polish it completely. Nor was there time to clean the ceiling of its soot.

Neither the Clan Hall nor the Family Parlor boasted windows, since they had been built first, in a time when the clan required defense more than aesthetics. Now she was grateful not to have to contend with dusty curtains such as those in the bedrooms.

Even thinking about everything to do was disheartening.

Her stomach rumbled again. Helen glanced at her, but said nothing.

She tossed the rag she was holding into an empty bucket and sighed.

"Shall we go eat?" she said, trying and failing to keep the enthusiasm from her voice.

Helen nodded.

The three men were still unloading the wagon.

She really must thank him. She'd remember her manners, a little rusty where Colonel Sir Gordon was concerned, and be sweetly appreciative.

He'd be so surprised, he'd no doubt be struck dumb.

Old Ned entered the kitchen, staggering under the weight of a barrel.

"We've got two pails of butter, Shona," he said. "And that's all that's left."

What on earth would they do with two pails of butter?

As she stared at the magically filled pantry shelves, another hideous thought occurred to her. Who was going to cook?

The maid in Inverness had lent a hand, but their menu had been relatively easy. They'd had no haunches of beef to roast, or a crate filled with live chickens.

Yes, living in Inverness had most assuredly been easier.

"I don't suppose you have any cooking ability," she asked, glancing at Helen.

Please, God, let her be uniquely talented in the kitchen. Let her have endless enthusiasm for baking or roasting, or whatever was required with the bounty that lay before them here and in the larder.

Instead, Helen only shook her head.

"We need Mag," Fergus said, entering the room with one pail of butter. He surrendered it to Gordon, who continued on to the larder and a cooler temperature.

She glanced at her brother, smiling at the memories his words invoked.

"Mag was our cook," she told Helen. "But she also had all sorts of stories about Gairloch." A quick glance at Fergus assured her that he wouldn't mention the ghosts quite yet.

Let a few days pass first, before the family histories were completely revealed.

"And she was a fine cook," Gordon said, reentering the room. "I remember her Scottish tablets."

Her smile became a little less genuine and a little more fixed.

How many times had she taken a plateful to Gordon, when they were due to meet one afternoon? How many times had they fed them to each other, the chocolate or orange sweetness a perfect accompaniment to their loving?

"I can make stew," she said, turning to stare at the pantry shelves again. "And scones. I make delicious scones." She'd taken him scones on numerous occasions as well.

Her stomach had stopped rumbling and in its place was a pain so fierce she thought she might be sick.

Go away. Go away. Go away.

"But for now, you'll have what Mrs. MacKenzie sent over," Gordon said, holding a large ceramic container aloft. "A rice and fish dish that's her specialty."

She stared at him. Was there no end to his kindness? Damn him.

Helen reached for the container, smiling. Shona didn't hear the rest of the conversation because she simply escaped the kitchen. Instead of taking the servants' stairs, she went around to the front, concentrating on each one of the curving steps, the better to focus on something else—anything else—than Colonel Sir Gordon MacDermond.

A man she'd loved once. A man she'd adored with

her body, her mind, her heart, and her very soul. A man who'd been her companion in spirit and laughter, who'd held her when she wept. A man with whom she'd felt neither shame nor restraint.

A man who'd died in her memory not once but a thousand times. He could not be resurrected now. She would not allow it.

"Are you all right, Shona?"

Helen was at the base of the steps, her face anxious.

"I'm fine, thank you," she said carefully. *I want to be alone for a while. No, that was too rude, wasn't it?* "I need to wash up a little," she said. Never mind that she hadn't a fresh pitcher of water. In Inverness, they'd had a boiler to produce hot water. At Gairloch, everything was done just as it had been done a hundred years ago.

"Oh, what a good idea," Helen said, putting ruin to the thought of being blessedly alone. "Shall I bring up some hot water?"

She smiled. Would Helen see how much her lips trembled from there? She hoped not. If her companion knew how tenuous her composure, she'd have to spend the next hour explaining that she was truly all right. It was just the press of memory.

"Thank you, that would be nice."

Helen disappeared, and she completed her ascent. Instead of entering the room they'd shared last night, she walked down the hall, to the third door. For a moment, she simply leaned against it, the wood cool against her forehead. She shut her eyes, and pretended that it was ten years ago, before her parents' death, before things changed at Gairloch. She was seventeen, and laughter was her constant companion.

She entered the room and immediately crossed to the window. Most of Gairloch's glass was so thick and wavy that it was impossible to see through. In the bedrooms, however, the glass had been replaced fifty years ago and the view was clear and without distortion. There, directly below her, was the edge of the lawn at Gairloch, an area created only after the clan ceased going off and returning from war. A formal garden had been planned for years now, and the beds just recently marked out. Beyond the lawn was the forest, stretching northward toward the loch.

To her right was a clearing, this one carefully delineated and marked by a rigid boundary of brick and stone. Rathmhor.

Its silly little tower stood as it had ten years ago. If she was still seventeen, she'd be looking for a signal, a flash of mirror, a wave of cloth. She'd smile, then laugh, then leave Gairloch to be with Gordon.

Summer or winter, spring or autumn, she'd found a way to be with him. It was Mag who'd told her of the way to prevent a child. Mag, who'd showed her where the plants grew and how to brew the mixture. When the old woman died, she felt as if she'd lost her mother again.

She pressed her fingers against the glass, blocking out the sight of Rathmhor.

She bent her head, listening to the wind. During autumn, the wind was like a blustery giant blowing chilled air around Gairloch. But in winter, the giant lost his breath, subsiding beneath the flinty cold.

Now, she felt the cold so intently she couldn't tell if it was from inside or out.

"Aren't you carrying your aversion to me a little far?" Gordon asked from behind her.

She closed her eyes, wondering if she had the strength for this confrontation. Folding her arms in front of her, she resolutely turned to face him.

"No," she said, "I don't think so."

"Your meal will get cold, and from what Helen said, you didn't eat well yesterday."

What business of it was his? Next, he'd appoint himself her guardian, pretend to care.

Only a few feet separated them, but it might as well be the distance between Gairloch and Rathmhor.

"I'll eat when I'm ready," she said, well aware that she sounded like a petulant child.

"When I'm gone."

She inclined her head, turning away from him to stare out the window again.

He would not see her cry. No one would see her cry.

"Thank you," she said, unwilling to turn to see if he was still regarding her with that impassive gaze. "Thank you for your generosity." There, she'd gotten the words out.

A moment passed silently until she was certain he'd left.

She turned to find him standing there, back braced against the doorframe, arms crossed, a look on his face she couldn't decipher.

Her chin came up, her shoulders straightened and they regarded each other in silence.

"Shona? I've brought the water."

Helen. Dear, virtuous Helen, saving her.

"I must leave," she said, walking toward the door.

He didn't move.

Why was she always at disadvantage around him? In Inverness, she hadn't expected him. Nor had she yesterday. Today, it was almost amusing that he saw her at her worst. Now, she faced him attired in a filthy dress, her face grimy, her hair still covered in a rag.

Yet he was, despite his earlier effort, untouched, unsoiled, and perfect. His white shirt had been recently ironed. His black trousers were pressed as well. His boots had been polished by some adoring servant. He'd recently shaved, and he smelled of sandalwood while she carried the scent of turpentine, linseed oil, and dirt.

The male of the species always bore more plumage.

As she stepped to the side, her gaze never leaving his face, he reached out one finger and trailed it over her cheek.

His blue eyes were alive with mischief as she stepped out of his reach.

The texture of his skin would be as soft as she recalled, especially that spot right at the corner of his mouth. Or his temple, where she'd feel the beat of his blood beneath her lips.

She wouldn't remember.

She couldn't.

"You're welcome, Shona," he said finally.

Then she was free, walking swiftly toward the room she and Helen had shared, all too conscious of his gaze on her.

Chapter 7

He was damned if he was going to live the rest of his life as a cripple. Even though it was all too obvious he didn't have much choice in the matter.

Fergus looked down at the cane in his left hand, loathing it. Hating, too, the fact that he needed the damn thing to walk or he was apt to end arse up, flat on the floor.

He made it to the Clan Hall, collapsing on one of the benches, happy that Shona, Gordon, and Helen had momentarily disappeared. He wanted a few moments alone, without solicitous comments, without Shona looking at him as if he were a bairn in nappies.

Closing his eyes, he leaned back against the wall, allowing the silence of Gairloch to enfold him. Here, he was an Imrie, a man preceded by a hundred other such men, made more by the heritage he shared. At Gairloch, he could almost feel the whispers of advice, encouragement, and support, and it wasn't wishful thinking or the presence of the ghosts. Here, he felt as if he was a better man, simply because he was the Laird of Gairloch.

How could Shona think of selling his birthright? She'd never answered when he questioned her, only said it would be better for both of them to be away from Gairloch. Better for whom? Not for him. As for her, it was time she and Gordon made their peace with each other.

His eyes flew open when thunder sounded at the door.

When no one appeared, he stood with some difficulty and left the Clan Hall, moving down the corridor to the front door, an entrance rarely used since most people were aware that the Upper Courtyard had been designed to trap Clan Imrie's enemies.

The wooden door was as old as Gairloch, the foot-thick timbers fastened with iron. A sturdy log, supported on brackets across the door, ensured that no one could enter without a battering ram.

The latch was cumbersome, and once that was dispensed with, he removed the log. As he worked, the thundering knock sounded again. He knew better than to call out that he was working as quickly as he could. The wood was so thick no one would hear him.

Finally, he opened the door, the log falling and ringing against the stone floor.

Two people stood on the other side. A man tall and broad enough to be considered a giant, dressed in dark green livery and with a head as bald as a newborn babe's. He, evidently, had been the one impatiently pounding on the door and, from his expression, he wasn't happy about it.

The other person was his opposite in all ways.

If the giant was the beast, the woman was beauty.

She was exquisite, and Fergus was not given to exaggeration. Her black hair was as dark as a Highland midnight. Her eyes were a piercing blue like the water at the edge of Loch Mor. She had a little heart-shaped face, a straight short nose, and a chin that ended in a sharp point. Later, he would think that her pink mouth was a little too large for perfection, but now it was arranged in a smile so blinding, revealing even, white teeth, that he could be excused for being momentarily dazzled.

"I know, for a fact," she said, in an unexpectedly jarring accent, "that you aren't the Countess of Morton."

"No," he said. "I'm not. I'm her brother." He introduced himself in a singular and previously never used manner. "I'm the Laird of Gairloch."

Her swooping black eyebrows rose in a perfect arch. She raised her left hand and waved it in the direction of the giant. "This is Helmut," she said. "My father's bodyguard."

"And you are?" he asked, bemusedly thinking that she withheld her own identity as if it were a treasure to be sought.

In truth, he knew before she spoke, knew as he spotted the grand traveling carriage beyond the gate. The coachman had evidently thought he'd be wedged in the archway.

A feeling like doom settled over him then, as deep as the fog that hung over the loch in midsummer.

"I'm Miriam Loftus," she said, twinkling up at him. "Thomas Loftus is my father."

"The Americans," he said. A recognition, more than an announcement.

"You're early," Shona said from behind him.

He glanced back at his sister, sighing inwardly. Shona hadn't had time to clean up, and next to the American woman, she looked the worse for wear. Of course, Miriam Loftus hadn't been scrubbing all morning.

"I didn't expect you for five days."

"You're the Countess of Morton?" the American asked, her tone rising at the end of the question as if unable to believe that the unkempt woman at his left was actually titled.

He almost winced, awaiting Shona's rebuff. But his sister surprised him by stepping back, out of the doorway.

"Give them directions to the Lower Courtyard," she said, and was gone.

"Bloody hell! Why in the name of God are they here now?"

"Shona!"

She looked up to find Helen on the stairs, her mouth agape in shock. Behind her was Gordon, his face carefully expressionless.

"Put me in chains," she said, throwing up her hands. "Pillory me. Pour boiling oil on my head and rend my clothing. I restrained myself. You should have heard what I was thinking."

She stalked to the rear of Gairloch, wishing that God was, indeed, a Scot. Let Him deal with this situation because she most certainly couldn't.

Yes, she could. She must.

Fergus had gone to war; she could greet the Americans.

Why had they arrived five days early? Why had they arrived before she had time to put herself in order?

She'd disliked the American woman on sight, and wasn't that a terrible thing to admit? Would she have liked her under any conditions? After all, if everything went right, they were going to buy her heritage from her.

Miriam Loftus could have at least seemed out of sorts or fatigued by travel. No, she'd been radiant, evidently captivating Fergus enough that he'd stood there agog.

She didn't enter the Lower Courtyard right away. Instead, she went into the stillroom, whisked off the rag binding her hair, gathered it up, and tried to make it appear less nestlike in the snood at the base of her neck. She washed her face and hands and, after glancing down at her dress, realized that nothing could salvage it.

At least the floor in the Clan Hall was clean.

She straightened her shoulders, took a deep breath, and walked to the door to greet the Americans.

"I do apologize, Colonel Sir Gordon," Helen said. "Shona's been under a great deal of strain lately."

He smiled down into Helen Paterson's earnest face. "Gordon is fine, Miss Paterson," he said.

"Oh, I couldn't."

Helen Paterson was a stickler for propriety, then. He tucked the information away for later. Did she find being a companion to Shona an onerous duty?

"You needn't explain Shona to me," he said. "She's always had a fiery temperament." And he was oddly pleased to have been witness to it. The proper—almost brittle—countess was only a façade.

"You've known each other since you were children," she said. Another glance back at him, this one filled with curiosity.

"Did she tell you that?"

"Shall we go and welcome them officially?" Fergus asked from the bottom of the stairs.

He surveyed his friend. Fergus's face was flushed, but he didn't look otherwise exhausted.

"Are you up to it?" he asked, knowing the minute he said the words that Fergus wouldn't appreciate them.

To his surprise, the other man only nodded.

The corridors of Gairloch were wide enough to accommodate the three of them walking abreast, Helen between them, as silent as Fergus.

He'd stroked a finger down the side of Shona's face and she'd flinched.

Her gray eyes had been ice cool, direct and revealing nothing of her thoughts. The Countess of Morton in all her frosty demeanor. At least, until the scene at the door. What would it take to make her disappear again? Now, that was a foolish thought. Even more disturbing was the surge of anticipation he felt.

Someone tapped on her shoulder and, without turning, Shona knew who it was.

Gordon had bedeviled her all during her childhood, until she was seventeen. She could still remember the exact moment he'd begun to see her differently—not as Fergus's bothersome younger sister, but as a young woman. She'd been experimenting with her maid, trying to decide on just the right way to wear her hair. Finally, they'd threaded ribbons through her curls, the same shade of ribbon that matched the decorative hem and sleeves of her dress.

The dress hadn't been special; the occasion had been a simple day at Gairloch, but when she'd come down the steps, he'd been there, waiting for Fergus. He'd turned and looked up at her, and in the silence, she'd somehow known it would be different between them from that moment onward.

Now she took a few steps to the right, away from him, unwilling to remember any more scenes between them.

The coach that entered the courtyard a minute later was magnificent, certainly the equal of any she'd seen at a royal residence. Since it was wider than the narrow roads of the Highlands, she doubted if the owner had considered his destination when purchasing it. At least it looked well sprung and more than capable of carrying six or more people.

The coachman, dressed in the same livery as the giant beside him, was an older man, seemingly expert at handling the team of six matched chestnut horses. The leather hardware was adorned with silver that gleamed in the early afternoon sunlight. Shona wouldn't have been surprised to see gold trim on the doors.

Two wagons entered the courtyard after the coach, the first loaded with a mountain of trunks. The second wagon held barrels and crates and boxes piled on top of each other.

"The stables are going to be crowded," Fergus was saying.

Her brother was right. She counted fourteen horses so far, and more if the Americans had outriders or another wagon following. With any luck, there was some feed in those barrels.

Sitting in Inverness, she'd thought the wealthy American would come, she would impart the history of Gairloch, he would be charmed and make an offer on the castle. She'd thought her biggest obstacle might be Fergus's recalcitrance.

Not once had she considered that he might have such an entourage accompanying him. Or thought about the logistics of having to house all of them.

Or feeding all of them.

The food Gordon had brought and unloaded only a little while ago now seemed paltry in view of the fact she had Thomas Loftus and his daughter, their three drivers, and who knew how many other people to feed. Not to mention the giant. How much did he eat?

She couldn't very well advance on Mr. Loftus, demand to know if he wanted to buy the castle, then finalize the sale tonight. Some charm was necessary, even though she felt charmless. Some tact and diplomacy was called for, just at a time she was certain she had none.

A tap on her shoulder again. She turned, annoyed, but instead of Gordon, Helen stood there. A call to good manners. Helen was more than her companion. Recently, she'd acted as her conscience, too.

An inclination of Helen's head was enough of a reminder that Shona nodded, curved her lips into a welcoming smile, moved down the steps, grateful that the wagon from Rathmhor had been moved to the side of the courtyard.

Gairloch looked its best in the brightness, its pale yellow stone appearing almost white in the afternoon sun, the gravel of the courtyard sparkling. Behind her, arranged on the steps, were Fergus, Gordon, and Helen.

The men were quite properly attired, and handsome specimens, even if she grudgingly allowed that label for Gordon. She and Helen, however, were disreputable sights.

The carriage slowed to a stop in front of the steps.

She folded her hands in front of her, her posture and poise mimicking her mother's when she'd greeted important guests. Of course, her mother had been attired in the finest French fashions, her hair arranged by a personal maid devoted to her mistress, and even the air around her perfumed by scents Shona could never afford.

Very well, she'd have to do the best she could.

The giant reminded her of the Russian soldiers Fergus had described to her when he could be persuaded to talk about his wartime experiences. Tall, broad-shouldered, his bearing erect, everything seemed overly large about him, from his hands to his feet. His head was perfectly bald, and his beard groomed to a point.

Why did Mr. Loftus feel the need for a bodyguard?

The giant jumped down from his perch, opened the door, and bowed low, as if before royalty. A delicate foot appeared. A moment later, the giant extended his hand, rolled down the carriage steps, and offered his arm for the American heiress.

"Well, at least they look wealthy enough to afford Gairloch," Fergus said from behind her.

Miriam Loftus emerged from the carriage slowly, like a butterfly from a chrysalis. Like wings being unfurled, her smile spread across her face; her eyes, blue and clear, seemed to summon their gazes.

She was attired in an emerald green coat over a long skirt, both the tight-fitting coat and the matching hat improbably edged in fur. If she thought Scotland was cold in September, she wouldn't like January very much.

Tiptoeing across the gravel, as if it were dangerous waters she crossed, Miriam Loftus gave the impression of being almost too delicate, too feminine to manage the distance.

Shona's shoes were not so delicately made. When she wasn't conscious of it, she stomped across the floor.

Perhaps Gairloch deserved a princess and not an irritated countess in residence.

Miriam's glance encompassed them in a measured way, as if the American woman was gauging the reaction of her audience to her arrival. Helen was obviously beneath her notice because her glance barely hesitated there. Fergus received a sweet and tender smile. Gordon, however, was the recipient of a coy sideways look.

Shona could feel her own expression freeze.

The giant did not accompany her across the gravel. Instead, he turned toward the carriage again, this time to assist a man in dismounting. A rather corpulent individual, bearded and mustached, and dressed in a suit of midnight blue, emerged from the vehicle. His black hair was dusted with gray at the temples. His face was round, almost porcine in appearance, with a small flattened nose and eyes as blue as his daughter's, only a more piercing shade. His smile, however, possessed a surprising warmth. The amiable expression firmed up his face and gave a hint of how handsome he'd been as a younger man.

She felt the shock of his gaze immediately, as if he were measuring her not as the potential seller of Gairloch but as an adversary. The daughter had evidently learned that trick from her father.

She didn't have to like the Americans. All she had to do was welcome them to Gairloch.

Yet another person exited the carriage, a woman this time. The giant turned away as if uninterested in her descent, giving Shona a clue that she was a servant. Added to that impression was the fact that the woman was wearing a uniform, of sorts. A large blue apron covered the whole of her bodice and skirt.

Her hair was blond, but pulled back into a bun covered by blue net. Her eyes, a soft brown, were flat and expressionless. Neither her attire nor her expression could diminish her beauty.

Shona heard an indrawn breath and turned to look behind her. Fergus's face had drained to white. He was staring at the woman who'd emerged from the carriage. In the next moment, she caught sight of him, and the two of them might as well have been alone in the courtyard.

Slowly, he descended one step, the effort obviously costing him. When Gordon grabbed his arm to help, Fergus shook it off.

Time was acting very strange, as if the minutes slowed to view this tableau with more detail. She wasn't conscious of the American and his daughter, only of Fergus, and that look of pain on his face. She'd seen that look only a few times, when the discomfort reached a level he could no longer hide it.

The woman and Fergus were the center of attention, but if either of them cared, they didn't show it. He halted, some ten feet away, taking in her appearance slowly. She returned his look for a very long moment, then very deliberately looked away before reaching inside the carriage.

Without a word, Fergus turned and retraced his steps, this time taking advantage of Gordon's assistance.

Chapter 8

Before Shona could ask what had just happened, Fergus and Gordon disappeared into Gairloch.

Thomas Loftus advanced on Shona as if she were a wall he intended to breach. Before she could welcome him to Gairloch, apologize for her brother's behavior, or say a dozen or so other acceptable remarks that might have eased the tension of the moment, he stuck out his hand.

Bemused, she put her hand in his, and found it being enveloped by large, fleshy fingers.

"You're very young to be a widow," he said, his look taking in the whole of her appearance. He finally released her hand, and she grabbed her skirt with it.

She couldn't think of a rejoinder, so she remained mute, her smile firmly fixed in place.

"I've caught you at an importune time," he said.

Yes, he had, but she only demurred, remembering her mother's lessons. "We're happy to welcome you to Gairloch at any time," she said.

"That was your brother?" he asked, staring up at the door. "The Laird of Gairloch?"

Her embarrassment over Fergus's actions was suddenly tinged by a surge of protectiveness. She found herself curiously unwilling to apologize for him.

"He stared at you as if you were a ghost, Elizabeth,"

he said, turning to the young woman who'd mesmerized Fergus. "Do you know him?"

"We might have met in the Crimea, Mr. Loftus," she said softly, her accent that of London.

"Elizabeth is a nurse," Miriam said, taking her father's arm. "Father's regular nurse didn't make the voyage well," she added, flipping her hand in the air as if to dismiss the woman's illness and the woman herself.

"I'm sorry you're ill," Shona heard herself say in a direct disregard of proper manners. She knew better than to comment on the state of someone's health, especially a stranger's health. Especially the health of a man who was offering her the first sign of hope in a very long time.

"It's of no account, Countess," he said, his tone indicating that the topic was not one for discussion.

She bit the inside of her lip, reminding herself that she didn't have to like the Americans, only be cordial to them.

"As you can see," she said, drawing on her mother's example, "this is the main courtyard for the castle. The builders of Gairloch devised a way to fool their enemies with the Upper Courtyard."

"We'll get a tour later, if you don't mind, Countess," Mr. Loftus said, interrupting. "We're tired and would like to be shown to our rooms."

Their rooms. Dear God, their rooms.

She turned and sent a panicked glance to Helen, one that was intercepted by Gordon returning from assisting Fergus up the stairs.

"We're in the process of readying your rooms, Mr. Loftus," he said, coming down the steps. "In the meantime, can I interest you in some fine Scottish whiskey?"

When Gordon smiled, the corners of his eyes crinkled up, the effect utterly charming. His delaying tactic might give her enough time to slip up the stairs and ready the Laird's Chamber for Mr. Loftus, and another room for his daughter. And another one for the giant? What about the nurse? Surely, she should be close to her patient?

"Who are you?" Miriam asked, smiling sweetly up at Gordon.

Helen spoke up from behind her.

"This is Colonel Sir Gordon MacDermond, Baronet of Invergaire," Helen said, for all the world like a chirpy little sparrow given the ability to speak.

The Americans appeared to be impressed. Gordon was, perhaps, a striking figure, a handsome man in the prime of his life. He gripped the American's hand, and they shook as if they were adversaries testing each other's mettle.

"If you'll give us a few moments," she said, wishing for hours, instead, "we'll have everything prepared for you."

"In the meantime," Gordon said, extending his arm for Miriam, "shall we go into the Clan Hall?"

Fergus had disappeared, and Gordon stepped into the breach. From his quick glance, he seemed to know that Shona was balancing on a fulcrum of irritation and gratitude.

She murmured something, futile words to explain her additional rudeness. The Americans didn't seem to notice, even though the giant never let her out of his sight. She didn't have time to worry about him now, or the nurse, or Fergus, or the extent of the gratitude she would owe Colonel Sir Gordon after this.

She raced Helen up the back stairs, stripped the bed in the Laird's Chamber, wishing that the smell of whiskey didn't permeate it still. Had Old Ned spilled it on the mattress? With any luck, Mr. Loftus would think it an affectation of Scottish castles, that they all smelled of spirits.

"Where is Old Ned?" she asked, as Helen returned from the linen press, her arms filled with sheets.

"I haven't seen him. Maybe he's in the kitchen, eating."

"Kitchen." She straightened. "Someone needs to cook," she said, panic gripping her. "I didn't know there'd be so many people. He never indicated he'd have this many people with him." She began to count them off on her fingers. "His daughter, his bodyguard." She stared at Helen. "Why does he need a bodyguard? Never mind," she added, shaking her head. "The nurse." She took one of the sheets from Helen. "I need to talk to Fergus about that. That's four people. Counting the drivers, that's three more. That's seven. Plus us. That's ten. Plus Ned. Eleven people! And I can make tea and toast. And scones. Oh, and stew, but anyone can make stew, can't they?"

She was beginning to babble.

Other than a little too much hero worship of Colonel Sir Gordon, Helen was an excellent companion and wouldn't divulge her lack of control. Even if she gave in to hysterics, which Shona was only too afraid she would in the next few moments, Helen wouldn't tell anyone.

"I'm quite good at cream soups," Helen said.

"Yes, but do you know what to do with a side of beef? Or venison?"

The two women looked at each other.

"Not to mention preparing rooms for all of them."

"I'm exhausted already," Helen said, "and we've barely finished with this room. Where are you putting Miriam?"

Only one room would do for the wealthy industrialist's daughter: her own. Thankfully, it didn't need more than a cursory airing out, a quick dust, and a change of sheets.

An hour later, they'd managed to prepare four rooms, all of them in the family wing. She moved Fergus's belongings to the guest wing while she and Helen selected adjoining rooms, moving their own trunks by sliding them down the hall runner.

When they were done, they surveyed the bedrooms for the Americans one last time. Everything had been done in a slipshod, hurried manner that embarrassed her, but at least they had a chamber for each of Loftus's entourage. The drivers would have to bunk in the stable, unless the American preferred all his staff to be housed in Gairloch proper. If that was the case, she needed more time to prepare more rooms.

"Vases of heather," she said.

Helen nodded and no doubt put it on a list in her mind. A cook, Shona added silently. Good humor when dealing with Fergus. She needed to be valiant in the coming days, and not so prickly. She could not be upset by the Americans' manner, or Fergus's actions.

And Gordon?

Gordon was a separate matter entirely. Gordon was a pebble in her shoe, a wisp of hair brushing against her face, a shutter that slapped against the wall. He was a constant, unremitting irritant.

They retreated to the Clan Hall, but not before they each took a little time to change and freshen themselves. Helen had a lovely blue wool to wear, while the majority of Shona's wardrobe was composed of half mourning, dresses with white collars and cuffs.

She was flushed, her hair was a disaster, but she was clean, an improvement over an hour earlier. When they entered the Clan Hall, the Americans—and Gordon—

were nowhere to be found. Instead, they were ensconced in the more comfortable Family Parlor. Gordon was standing by the fireplace, the very picture of a Scottish baronet posing in his castle. All he needed was a pair of hounds at his feet, a few dirks and shields mounted behind him, and to be attired in a kilt, and the picture would be perfect.

He had the legs for a kilt.

The last time she'd seen him in a kilt was when she'd said farewell to Fergus at the ship that would take him off to war. Both men had been dressed in the traditional Ninety-third Highlanders: the red coat and kilt with sporran and bandolier. Gordon's jacket had held only two medals. How many more had he acquired since then?

She hadn't spoken to him then, nor told him how handsome he looked. Bruce had been with her, and her husband deserved a wife who clung to her vows, even mentally.

Dreams were something else.

Gordon was acting the part of host even though Gairloch didn't belong to him, in the face of Fergus's absence. She would owe him for that, too.

"Your rooms are ready," she said as she and Helen swept into the room. "Would you like something to eat first? Or to begin our tour of Gairloch?"

"Later," Mr. Loftus said, standing. He was flanked by his giant and his nurse. Which did he fear more, disease or an enemy? "We'll get settled first, Countess, then eat, and tomorrow we'll look over the place."

She folded her hands in front of her and nodded, emulating her mother once more. Had her mother ever felt this churning of emotions and thoughts? In all her memories, she'd seemed almost divinely guided by tact and composure.

"Will the laird be joining us?" Miriam asked, rising from a chair with a studied grace.

Shona nodded again, wondering at her own composure when lying. She didn't even know where Fergus was at the moment, let alone if he'd consent to join them.

"Sir Gordon says he won the Victoria Cross. How utterly wonderful."

Was the woman daft? The price for that honor had been steep indeed. Fergus would probably always be in pain, always walk with a limp, and always have difficulty raising his left hand above his shoulder.

She knew, suddenly, how her mother had done it. She'd simply numbed herself to her surroundings, pretending as if the absolute inanity spoken by her guests was so much noise, like the screech of eagles, or the sough of the wind.

All Shona had to do was ignore the American woman.

Miriam made a point of stretching with a little shiver at the end of it, as if she were a kitten who'd just felt a chill. The gesture called attention to her petite body, snug in her coat, and especially to her plenteous bosom.

Did Americans stuff their corsets?

"Have you a maid, Miss Loftus?" she asked. "Will she be arriving later?"

"Good heavens, no," Miriam said with a little laugh. "We Americans are used to doing for ourselves."

The expression on the nurse's face lasted only a second before it was smoothed away.

"I can certainly dress myself, and Elizabeth helps with my hair." Miriam studied her for a moment. "I can lend her to you, if you think she might be able to help."

Surprise at the insult kept her mute, even after Miriam went to her father's side, grabbing his arm as if needing his protection. "Will you be escorting us to our rooms,

Gordy?" she asked, her mouth curved in a perfectly acceptable social smile.

Gordy? Gordy?

Perhaps that was better than Colonel Sir Gordon, but not by much.

Gordon only smiled back at her, while Helen, bless her, stepped forward. "I will do so, if you don't mind, Miss Loftus." She turned to the American industrialist. "I'm afraid the stairs are rather steep, Mr. Loftus. Will that be a problem?"

His look was as direct as Helen's words. "Not as long as I've my man here," he said, motioning to the giant. "I find myself in any rough patches, Helmut will get me out."

Helen nodded, then turned and glanced at Shona. She raised an eyebrow, evidently a signal of some kind. Shona didn't have any idea what she wanted until Helen approached her and whispered one word.

"Cook," she said, then inclined her head toward Gordon.

This day was a day of firsts, wasn't it? She'd scrubbed a floor on her hands and knees, fluffed mattresses, in addition to performing all the duties of an upstairs maid. She'd welcomed a group of people into her home—people she wasn't certain she could come to like.

Now she was to go to Gordon MacDermond, and beggar herself?

Her stomach rumbled, reminding her that she hadn't eaten since breakfast and afternoon was rapidly advancing. If Fergus was about, she would have appealed to him to solicit Gordon's help, but her brother had disappeared.

She smiled as the Americans left the room, feeling as if her face might split in two as she did so. Hypocrites were the worst kind of people and she was acting the part at the moment. She not only disliked herself for doing so; she despised the circumstances that made it necessary.

Perhaps she should place the blame on her grandsire, who'd spent a great deal of money at the gaming tables. Or on her mother, who saw nothing wrong in flitting off to Paris to buy gowns that were rarely seen, except for her parents' infrequent visits to Edinburgh. Or on both parents equally, when they had the unfortunate luck of being in the wrong place at the wrong time, both succumbing within days of each other to a virulent influenza. Only hours after they'd been interred in the chapel at Gairloch, the creditors had come calling.

Very well, she'd do what she must, just to keep up appearances for a little while longer.

Her hands trembled; it was fatigue. Her stomach was suddenly nauseous; she hadn't eaten since breakfast. A piercing pain sat in the middle of her forehead; she hadn't slept well the night before.

She made her way across the room, wishing Gordon didn't appear quite so large and imposing in his stance. He folded his arms and watched her, remaining silent. He must know she wanted something, because a glint appeared in his eye, a mote of humor.

Halting several feet away, she took a deep breath, her gaze never leaving his.

"We need a cook," she said. Perhaps she should have phrased the request a little less baldly. "Gordon, we need a cook." That wasn't much better, was it? "Colonel Sir Gordon," she said, moderating her voice so that not one scintilla of sarcasm appeared in it, "we need a cook."

"Do you, Countess?"

Did he maintain that even tone while commanding his men? Did he keep that same expression on his face so his troops couldn't figure out exactly what he was thinking? Once, she'd known. Once, she'd been able to discern each one of his emotions.

But, then, they'd been lovers.

Seven years ago, when the world was a kinder place, they'd loved each other. A time when she'd been ignorant of the pitfalls that lay ahead, before war or penury. Years before she realized the sheer determination she'd need to get through each day.

Dear God, had she ever been that innocent, that naïve?

"Is there anyone at Rathmhor who would like to apply for the position?"

By the time quarterly wages were due, Gairloch would have been sold, and she could afford to pay a cook. If, for some reason, the American changed his mind, it wouldn't matter about wages. They'd starve to death because she wouldn't be able afford to buy food.

She clasped her hands together tightly in front of her, firmed her lips into the semblance of a smile, pushed the pain of her headache away, and looked up at him.

Had he grown taller over the years? He'd certainly become a more commanding presence. She'd read of the horrors of the war in India. What had he seen? Surely. enough horrible deeds that there wasn't a trace of the young lover she'd known in his face. Only the shadow of the Gordon MacDermond she'd known and adored.

But, then, she wasn't the girl she'd been, either.

His silence didn't bode well. He didn't speak, but his eyes were restive, playing over her features, studying her hair, her face, her dress.

She knew she didn't look the part of countess, and felt even less so. She hadn't become used to her title, especially since she and Bruce were not often in society. Her servants addressed her as Your Ladyship and even that had taken some acclimation. She and Helen had agreed that they would not have formality between them. Only today, with the Americans, had she reverted to being the Countess of Morton.

If a title helped sell Gairloch, then so be it.

She whirled to leave the room, his words slowing, but not stopping, her.

"I'll send over a likely candidate tomorrow."

She hesitated at the door, turning to look back at him. "I'd prefer this afternoon," she said, wondering why he smiled.

The Americans must be fed dinner, and Thomas Loftus didn't look as if he'd be satisfied with a bit of cream soup and toast. And that giant of his, what would he eat? A side of beef at each sitting?

"This afternoon it is," Gordon said.

His blue eyes twinkled at her.

Don't do that. Do not attempt to charm me. I can't be charmed by you. I mustn't be.

She nodded, intending to leave before she could put breath behind the words.

His question stopped her.

"Why are you so intent on selling Gairloch?"

At that moment, she wished she had more experience in society. More than the occasional dinner or rare ball that Bruce agreed to attend. Her husband was older, and in the last few years, hadn't been a well man. With a bit more sangfroid, achieved through countless societal obligations, she might have been able to answer that question with a haughtiness that would discourage further interest.

Instead, all she could do was stare at him.

"I would have thought that coming home would be a blessing, of sorts," he said. "Unless you don't consider Gairloch home anymore."

"Why are *you* here?"

"Because it's home," he said, a smile still in evidence.

"It never has been before," she said. "You were always off soldiering."

"I've come home."

"For how long?"

"For good." Finally, the smile was gone, but in its place a regard that was proving to be a bit too intense. "I'm opening the Works," he said.

Now *that* was a surprise.

"Why?"

"If I tell you, will you tell me why you're set to sell Gairloch? I've some interest in the people who'll become my only neighbors, you know."

"I would think Miriam would be just the sort for you," she said.

She'd never before been petty for the sake of it, but his resurgent smile irritated her. "Perhaps you can convince her that the crofter's cottage is the perfect trysting place."

His smile vanished.

"Or perhaps she'll marry an old earl, to better herself. I hear some women do that."

She didn't have a rejoinder for that.

"Perhaps you're right," he said easily. "Perhaps Miriam is just the sort for me."

This time, she did leave, and not one word or question he asked could have made her stay.

To blazes with a cook. She'd find something for the Americans to eat even if she had to prepare it herself.

Chapter 9

A hundred years ago, a man came to Gairloch, a man made friend by the laird. A man with experience in war, Brian MacDermond nevertheless possessed a gentle manner. None suffered from his temper. Not one person felt his rage. That was given for his enemy in battle, and for the person gone from friend to foe.

His birthplace was far away, in the border lands, the disputed lands that faced and defied England. In his early years, he'd spent too many nights reiving against the English, punishing them for the fact of their presence, if nothing else.

Brian MacDermond and Magnus Imrie had fought together in the last rebellion, had healed together, each congratulating the other on the fierceness of his wounds and the scars they would make. Each man had eaten roasted hare over an open fire, talked of shelter with longing in his voice when the pitiless rains fell. When failure found them both accepting and unsurprised, they planned for what future the English would allow them. One coaxed the other to put aside his petty border wars for another life, one dedicated to raising sons amid the peace of Clan Imrie.

And, so, to the Highlands Brian MacDermond went, accompanied by his earthly possessions, a wagon filled with what he'd inherited or won in reiving. With him *were seventeen people, members of his clan who, if they doubted the wisdom of this northward migration, kept it secret.*

By urging the Lowlander north, Magnus accomplished two tasks—brought into Invergaire Glen a man of great strength and bravery, a man who would play the pipes no matter that they were now banned. He also, by his actions, put into motion a love so strong that the echoes of it would be felt a hundred years in the future.

"Where have you been?" Shona whispered, catching sight of Fergus before he entered the dining room.

He stopped and stared at her. He looked tired, which had the effect of mitigating her irritation more than his careless shrug.

She'd spent the last three hours fulfilling the Americans' wishes. Hot water? *Yes, of course, it would only be a moment.* More Scottish whiskey? *That would be no problem at all, Mr. Loftus.*

Gordon hadn't just sent an applicant for the position of cook, but the undercook from Rathmhor, in addition to a young girl who was serving as maid and general helper.

Shona really wished she had the option of sending them back to Rathmhor with a curt instruction to tell their employer to kiss his own well-formed arse, but she didn't. Besides, the younger girl—Jennie—was obviously excited to be there, smiling throughout her introduction.

"We're to tell you that it's a bit of vacation for us," the younger girl said, bobbing a curtsy. "It's Gairloch, after all, Your Ladyship."

In other words, she didn't have to pay them.

"Where were you?" she asked Fergus now.

"I needed some time alone," he said, and from the look on his face that was all he was going to say.

"Are you going to have dinner with us, then?" she asked.

He nodded again, staring at the entrance to the dining room with reluctance. She couldn't blame him. She didn't want to spend the next hour in the company of Miriam Loftus and her father, either.

Or was it seeing the nurse he dreaded?

"What is she to you, Fergus?"

He waved her question away, and she huffed out a breath, annoyed beyond measure.

What a bother men were.

He turned and entered the dining room, and she followed a moment later, saying a little prayer that the meal wouldn't be as dreadful as she feared.

The dining room had been carved from the Clan Hall, partitioned off a few decades ago to allow for dining in a more sophisticated manner than trenchers and rough-hewn tables. This table was mahogany and had been imported from Edinburgh two dozen years ago. The chairs were carved in the same pattern and upholstered in a deep red fabric. Fergus had heard it called something else, once, but he couldn't remember the name.

He was damn lucky to remember who he was at the moment.

Elizabeth was there, attending to Thomas Loftus as if he were a wounded soldier and not a hale and hearty-looking wealthy American. He was seated at the head of the table in his chair, an odd thronelike chair that had been passed down from laird to laird.

In the American's case, the word should be lard.

None of them noticed him until he was almost at

the table, and then Miriam smiled at him, a lovely and gracious mistress-of-the-manor smile that Shona should have worn. Instead, his sister was a few steps behind him and he could almost hear the grinding of her teeth.

Loftus merely nodded at him, intent upon his tumbler of whiskey. Perhaps he should have invited Old Ned to the dinner as well. The two men could have discussed the relative merits of different casks in the cellar.

At least Gairloch had plenty of wine and whiskey on hand.

Miriam turned to him, extending a delicate hand, an encouragement for him to sit beside her. He'd gladly take that particular chair, since it would be as far from Elizabeth as possible. She still had not looked in his direction.

Shona sat to the left of Mr. Loftus, while Helmut sat to his right. He couldn't help but wonder if the body-guard also chewed the man's food for him first.

Was the American so loathsome a creature that he was in danger of being killed? Or did he simply put too great a price on his own existence?

The soldier who did that endangered others, a fact he knew only too well.

Elizabeth was thinner than he remembered. The look in her eyes was more cautious. Only the smile was the same.

Was she as solicitous with Thomas Loftus as she'd been with the men of the Ninety-third? Did she fluff his pillow, leaning over to brush back his hair? Did she come so close that her patient smiled, thinking himself in heaven and this glorious woman an angel?

Every day, for weeks, he'd gone to check on his men. Miss Nightingale's contingent of nurses had helped to save countless wounded. Elizabeth, working in the ward where most of his men had been taken, gave them the first ray of hope and beauty in a very long time.

Did she remember those days? How could she forget them? He remembered every moment of battle, every second of every war. He'd been desperate to survive. And afterward, those little bits of respite he'd been given were even more precious.

Did she recall how he'd told her, when the Ninety-third was being sent home to Aldershot, that he loved her? Would she wait for him? Or had she forgotten that, too?

Evidently, she had, or she wouldn't be ignoring him so pointedly now.

He directed his attention to Miriam Loftus. The American woman was quite lovely and very much impressed by his title of Laird of Gairloch, if he wasn't mistaken. Twice, she'd asked him to describe the duties of his rank. Did she think him a duke? Or an earl, like Shona's husband?

He didn't know what Bruce had done during his life. When he was younger, of course, he'd attended Parliament. He'd proposed a number of good works in his time. When Shona had married him, however, the man had been older, a little worn, and tired. A man who was damn lucky to get Shona Imrie, even if he was an earl.

For all the love he had for his sister, he wasn't blind to her faults. Too impetuous, rash, and emotional for her own good. Lately, however, she seemed to have developed a wide practical streak. If she hadn't, he wouldn't be talking now to an American woman with an atrocious accent, and a way of treating others as if they were beneath her notice.

Unless they had a title.

As for being the Laird of Gairloch, his main duty was ceremonial. Once, the Imrie lairds had been responsible for the welfare of the clan. If any of his ancestors had been faced with the bleak circumstances he now found himself in, they'd probably have resorted to stealing cattle again.

The idea of being a reiver struck him as a damn sight more agreeable than selling Gairloch.

Someone with skill had produced this wonderful dinner, a feast he had every intention of enjoying despite the company or the fact that Elizabeth, the woman he'd once loved, was pretending she didn't know him, hadn't kissed him, hadn't looked at him with love in her eyes.

"New cook, Shona?" he asked, between listening to Miriam's endless tale of the voyage to London, the carriage trip to Gairloch, and being aware of the awkward silence at the other end of the table.

She nodded, her firm look warning him to be more politic around the Americans. Who cared? He didn't. He wasn't for selling his birthright anyway. With a little economy, they would manage. His sister, however, was notoriously stubborn. Once Shona was set on something, God Himself couldn't dislodge the thought.

She hadn't entertained much as Bruce's wife, but Shona knew a disaster when she saw one. Mr. Loftus refused to be engaged in conversation, and when she'd attempted to say something to the giant, the American had interrupted her.

"Helmut doesn't speak very much English, Countess. He's German."

She didn't speak a word of German.

Miriam had changed for dinner. No doubt most of those trunks the giant had hauled up the stairs were hers. Just how long did they plan on staying? Was Mr. Loftus going to make an offer, then remain at Gairloch? Or was he going to return to New York? Or, an even more hideous thought, was he going to spend a few weeks here in order to "experience" Scotland?

She'd much rather concentrate on Miriam's dress, a peacock blue silk adorned with bangles. The garment bared her shoulders and too much of her bosom, especially for a dinner in a remote Scottish castle.

Miriam was directing all her attention to Fergus, who was looking pained from time to time. Not that anyone would know. He was the epitome of decorum, answering questions, passing a platter, and pouring the wine.

Thank God the Americans didn't object to the dinner being served a la Russe, which eliminated the necessity of footmen or maids.

What was Mr. Loftus's ailment that he required a constant nurse? She and the woman had exchanged a look, curiosity meeting curiosity. Here was someone with whom she might have been able to converse, if the nurse hadn't been sitting on the other side of Mr. Loftus. Helen, however, was engaging the woman in conversation when Elizabeth wasn't directing her attention to her patient.

Mr. Loftus was concentrating, rather fiercely, on his dinner, and when he wasn't eating, he was drinking. Helmut had poured him three glasses of whiskey so far, and the meal was only half done.

But everything tasted wonderful. Was it because she was so hungry or was the woman in the kitchen just such a wondrous cook? She suspected both were true.

"When did you lose your husband, Countess?" Mr. Loftus abruptly asked.

She kept her voice low, but it vibrated with emotion. "A little over two years ago, sir."

"Sudden, was it?"

Of all the subjects in the world, the last one she wanted to discuss was Bruce, but she forced a smile to her face and answered him. Perhaps a bit of truth would dissuade him from continuing the subject any further.

"My husband had been ill for some time," she said, staring down at her plate.

"You're not a bad-looking woman," he said, a comment that had her gaze jerking up to meet his. He was regarding her over the top of his glass.

St. Gertrude and all the saints. Was he *interested* in her?

Fergus began to cough, but she didn't dare look over at him. Her brother was trying not to laugh. And Helen? Helen was looking as shocked as she felt.

"Thank you," she said.

"Have you no plans to marry again?"

She shook her head, desperately focusing on her glass of wine. If she drank all of it right down, would she become tipsy immediately? She didn't dislike the feeling, and it might fog the evening substantially so that she could deal with Mr. Loftus.

"Are you married, Mr. Loftus?" Helen asked, smiling brightly as if she didn't know the question was almost vulgar and, at any other gathering, unpardonably rude.

However, the Americans seemed very direct people and this dinner had been different from the beginning.

Mr. Loftus merely glanced at Helen. "I've been a widower for many years, ma'am."

"Please call me Helen," she said. Another gaffe, one that the American didn't seem to note.

Was all propriety to be set aside for the duration of their visit? If so, she might as well stand, throw her napkin down on her chair, and stomp off, intent on her room. Except, of course, that she was desperate to sell Gairloch, which meant she had to remain in place, like the queen on a chessboard.

Thank God for Helen.

At the moment, she was smiling toothily at Mr. Loftus, such a blinding gesture of goodwill that the man put his glass of whiskey down and stared at her in return. The look wasn't entirely complimentary, more in the lines of someone who'd spotted an oddity in his environment.

"My mother was an absolutely beautiful woman," Miriam announced, looking directly at Helen.

Even the most charitable person couldn't label Helen beautiful, but she was kind, and that virtue meant more than looks.

"What was her name?" Shona asked. Another insipid question, one more designed to deflect Miriam's wrath than any curiosity on her part.

Miriam turned to her and gave her a look of such incredulity that she might as well have been one of the stable cats given the power of speech.

Without answering, Miriam turned back to her father. "Must we speak of dead people?" she asked.

Shona had the most incredible wish to slap the young woman silly.

Fergus took the opportunity to interject a comment, no doubt because he'd seen the look in her eyes.

"Do you find Scotland interesting, Miss Loftus?"

"It's a very odd place," Miriam said. "Quite empty. And you all speak strangely."

Fergus smiled, but the expression was a little thin.

"Were you a nurse in the Crimea?" Shona asked, turning toward Elizabeth.

"I understand you have no boiler at Gairloch," the nurse replied. "What is the most convenient method to obtain hot water here?"

"Merely use the bellpull," she said, fervently hoping mice hadn't eaten through the wires. "Someone will bring you what you need."

The nurse nodded. "As for the Crimea," she said, abruptly standing, "I was with Miss Nightingale's nurses." For the first time, she looked directly at Fergus. "I don't remember you," she added before turning to her employer. "I'll go and ready your room for the night, sir."

With that, Elizabeth left.

The entire dinner party had taken on the aspects of a nightmare. Perhaps she was truly asleep, having fallen, exhausted, onto a newly freshened mattress. She closed her eyes, counted to ten, then opened them again to find that nothing had changed.

Fergus was smiling at Miriam, the expression curiously unsettling. She knew the effort her brother was making, just as she'd known the nurse had been lying.

Elizabeth Jamison escaped upstairs, running as if a monster were chasing her. Of all the places in the world to come but to his home. To have to sit across the table from him and wonder about the signs of pain at the corners of his mouth, to see the blankness of his eyes when he looked at her.

She'd been counseled, too many times, that men form an attachment for a nurse in the field. A nurse takes the place of mother, sister, lover, friend, she'd been told. Much care should be given not to reciprocate affection in any way, so as not to form a bond based on illness and recovery.

He'd been the talk of the ward, the officer in charge, the one who'd kept everyone's spirits up, even in the worst of times. When another brave soldier had died, he was the one to speak to his men. He was the one who'd refused to allow them to sink into despair, joking with some, listening to others. He'd been there every day he could, their leader, brother, and comrade in arms.

Who wouldn't love him?

She wasn't the only nurse to have fallen under his spell and now, here he was, and here she was, at his home.

She opened the door to Mr. Loftus's room and closed it behind her, leaning her head against the wood. She needed to be calm, to show nothing of what she felt.

Otherwise, she was very much afraid she might begin to cry.

Chapter 10

Gordon headed toward the Invergaire Works. Instead of the carriage this morning, he'd chosen one of the horses he'd purchased in Inverness and sent on to Rathmhor. The mare was young, restless, and the perfect mount, untrained enough to keep his attention and possessing a gait that made the journey enjoyable.

The clouds skimmed over the sky as if blown by God in a fit of temper. The heather shivered in a cascade of purple against green. The grasses stood proudly, almost in regimental order, saluting the wind as it passed.

Both Gairloch and Rathmhor were nestled in a glen framed by Ben Lymond on the northern side, and Loch Mor on the southern. To the east was Invergaire Village, where clan members too numerous to live in Gairloch proper went to live in times of peace. To the west, the Invergaire Works formed the fourth side of the square.

Invergaire Village had been a cooperative venture. When the time came for a member of the Imrie Clan to turn away from his warlike ways, he was given a small parcel of land by the laird. He could use it to his own benefit by farming it or raising cattle.

A hundred years ago, several of the old ones banded together, each surrendering a portion of his land to create a common area for all of them. Thus was Invergaire Village formed, on the north edge of Loch Mor. The villagers, none of whom was bound by allegiance to the Imries after the Forty-five, nevertheless treated the laird and his family with fondness and respect.

Around the same time, his ancestor Brian MacDermond had uprooted his clan and come to the Highlands. He'd disappeared a few years later, never to be seen again. A feud had begun when his family demanded that the Imries explain Brian's absence. The discord had lasted for years, until memories faded. Somehow, the fate of Brian MacDermond hadn't seemed cause enough to continue the feud with the powerful Imrie Clan.

For decades, the Imries and MacDermonds had been friends, the echoes of that long ago dispute being revived only on ceremonial days. The Laird's Day, for one, when the Laird of Gairloch paid tribute to the elders of Invergaire Village and to the MacDermonds. A way of accepting blame for Brian's disappearance while never admitting to causing it.

What would Fergus offer this year? Would his tribute have to be larger because he'd missed the ceremony for a number of years? He'd been off fighting for the Empire, giving his talents to the army.

One of a countless number of men ready to die for his country.

As a colonel of the Ninety-third, Gordon's movements and behavior had been controlled by his orders and his superiors. As a Scot, the MacDermond of Rathmhor, his life was constrained by tradition and expectations.

His father had expected a great many things from him, and for the most part, Gordon had delivered. He'd followed his father's way for the majority of his life, his path veering from the general's only in the last months.

Sometimes, he wondered if the old man had died when he had to spite him, a last act of repudiation. Two nights before the general's death, he'd informed his father of his plans, as well as the fact that he'd surrendered his commission. The resultant attack of temper had been enough to stop anyone's heart. His father had made his displeasure known as loudly as possible, then proceeded to renounce his son.

Part of the general's annoyance might have been the fact that Gordon was the legal owner of the Works, the companies he'd inherited from his maternal grandfather when he was still a boy. Or the fact that there wasn't a damn thing he could do to stop Gordon.

As a child he'd feared the general. As a man, he'd loathed him.

White clouds boiled on the horizon, prefaced by an advancing army of white streaks. A perfect September day in the Highlands, the breeze carrying a hint of chill.

The Invergaire Works, some seventy-five years old now, had once provided employment to the inhabitants of Invergaire Village, those who didn't have a yen for sheep, farming, or kelp drying and harvesting.

They'd produced gunpowder in the building for decades. But the Works had shut down while he was in India. Too many problems, not enough employees, and poor management had rendered it a liability.

However, the Glasgow factories were still producing black powder, shipping it worldwide. Some of the bullets that had grazed him in the two wars he'd fought might well have come from his own factory.

A bit of irony that he'd shared only with Fergus.

He was damn tired of war. But countless graveyards were filled with men who hated war. If a man wanted to survive, he killed. If he wanted to win, he destroyed. The only thing good about war was its end. The best commanders understood that.

If he could accomplish what he wanted, the Works

would be greatly changed in purpose and expanded in people.

The red brick building was three stories tall, with two enormous smokestacks sticking out of the roof. The windows were black with dust and powder, the weeds nearly overgrowing the walk and the steps up to the door.

On the second floor, tall windows allowed natural light to stream into the work floor, since oil or gas lamps would have been too dangerous to use around the gunpowder.

He opened the iron door and stood just inside, the smell curiously that of spices and herbs, not charcoal, sulphur, or potash.

Once, two dozen people had labored here, earning a good living, if a hazardous one. But only one explosion had ever occurred here, and that was a result of an error in mixing the powder's formula. Thankfully, no one had died, and those who'd been hurt had only minor injuries. But the entire west wall had had to be rebuilt, as well as a portion of the roof.

The manager's office was located at the east end of the building and equipped with a large window so that he might oversee the work on the floor. Since the position had been vacant for nearly a year, he expected the office to be empty as well.

Instead, Rani Kumar waved his hand at him without looking up. "Providence has delivered you here just when I need supplies."

He smiled.

Today, Rani was dressed in the European fashion—trousers, shirt, vest, and a jacket hanging on a nearby hook. Although he'd eschewed his more comfortable tunic and pants for European attire, in other ways, Rani hadn't changed in the months since Gordon had seen him. He was still short and slight, his black hair straight and hanging chin-length. Still given to an unconscious autocracy.

"Do you have eyes on top of your head?" he asked.

"I saw you through the window," Rani said, finally looking up from his notes. His gaze was a direct and unflinching brown-eyed stare. He finally smiled, moving from his perch on the stool to clasp Gordon on both arms. "It's good to see you, my friend."

"And you, Rani. Was the voyage tolerable?"

Rani moved his head from side to side, a gesture to mean that it was neither horrible nor pleasant but somewhere in between. As a Hindi, Rani had perfected an enduring silence about most things, which meant he was inscrutable to most of the British East India Company with whom he'd worked for years.

A native of Hyderabad, one of the states that hadn't joined the Sepoy Rebellion, Rani had been instrumental in providing supplies to the company Gordon had commanded in India. He'd long suspected that Rani had been a prince in Hyderabad, or at least closely aligned with one. His education was the equal of—or surpassed—his own, and his mannerisms sometimes indicated a man annoyed by underlings.

Or perhaps that was just Rani's reaction to the daily prejudice he endured.

"He's *foreign,* sir." How often had he heard one of his own sergeants say that?

As a Scot, he'd experienced the prejudice himself. Perhaps that, more than anything else, had made him come to Rani's defense initially. Doing so had led to a friendship, conversation, and a mutual interest in what might become a joint discovery.

"How long have you been here?" he asked now.

The other man moved back to his stool, waving his hand in the air again. "Two months only."

"You should have sent word."

"It is of no account, Gordon. I have been very comfortable."

He looked around the office. "You haven't been sleeping here, I hope?"

Rani shook his head, smiling. "I have a very nice room in a house run by a very understanding lady of Scotland."

Which meant that his landlady had not shown him any overt prejudice. They'd had numerous discussions on each nation's intolerance. The East Indians he'd met hadn't been enamored of his country, either.

"I'm a Scot, Rani. In Scotland a man is valued for who he is. The more independent, the better."

The other man had only smiled when he said that. Another discussion they'd had numerous times.

He drew up a stool, and sat opposite his friend.

"You were supposed to be my guest."

"One's employer should not be one's host," Rani said, still smiling.

"I would say we're partners," he said.

Their relationship was one of symbiosis. He needed Rani to develop the formula. Rani needed a place to make the blasting powder as well as financial backing. Both of them, together, could achieve each man's separate dream.

Rani's ambition was to do something for his family, his town. And his goal? Not more wealth as much as autonomy. He'd been a loyal servant of the Crown, a respectful officer, a dutiful son. Had he ever been himself?

"I have good news," Rani said, reaching over and picking up a piece of paper. "I have finished my calculations," he said, handing the document to Gordon. "I believe that we have the perfect blasting powder."

He stared down at the paper, realizing that he

couldn't understand Rani's notations. He wasn't a scientist; he was a soldier. He'd watched minié balls explode, watched as smoke obscured the battlefield, had calculated how to make a rifle's aim more true, but all these things had been possible because he'd been exposed to the Works since he was a boy. Black powder was as familiar to him as the sound of battle. Anything more required the expertise of others.

"What do you need from me?"

Rani pulled a list from his vest pocket and handed it to him. "A few supplies."

"You'll have them as soon as I can arrange it," he said.

Rani nodded. "As soon as I have the last ingredient, we can begin testing."

The minute they did so, the whole of Invergaire Glen would know what he planned.

His father had called him an anarchist. The general had meant it in symbolic terms only. Even though he mentally questioned his superiors, he'd never disobeyed an order. Even though he thought the upper echelon of the British Army was occupied by the bored sons of peers who'd nothing better to do than play soldier, he'd grudgingly succumbed to their plans for him.

Now, however, it amused him to think of how much an anarchist he was actually becoming. In a matter of weeks, he'd be able to produce an explosion that would shake the world.

"What do you mean, he wants biscuits?" Shona stared at the cook uncomprehendingly. "Who eats biscuits at this time of day?"

"He wants something like a scone, but not sweet. And round."

The undercook from Rathmhor, who'd proven to be

so talented in the kitchen, frowned down at the two bowls of rising dough.

The bread making had been halted to accede to Mr. Loftus's request. Unfortunately, neither of them really knew what he wanted.

"He wants them big and fluffy so he can soak them in gravy."

"Give him scones," she said. "Can you cut them into rounds?"

The girl nodded. "Should I put raisins in them?"

The idea of raisins and gravy didn't sound palatable to her, so Shona shook her head.

"Make them savory instead of sweet," she suggested. "That ought to suit him."

She was not given to hysterics, but it was barely one o'clock in the afternoon, and she was already feeling panicky. Despite her attempts to interest Mr. Loftus in conversation about Gairloch, he'd been more concerned with the state of his stomach.

His portion of breakfast had astounded her. At the rate he was eating, they'd have only enough food to last for another week. But, then, he'd brought some provisions. Not as much as they would need, but it was something. Gordon had contributed feed for the horses. At least they wouldn't starve.

Perhaps Mr. Loftus had a particular malady, one involving hunger.

She'd seen the nurse twice today, once at breakfast, and another time when she'd come to fetch some hot water for Mr. Loftus's shave. Evidently, the giant—Helmut— performed the valetlike chores for the American.

What a very strange group they were. But, then, she couldn't have imagined that anyone wishing to purchase Gairloch would be anything but extraordinary. After all, the price was prohibitive, and the idea of buying a castle in order to experience one's Scottish roots was a bit odd as well.

Not once had Mr. Loftus said anything about his Scottish ancestors. Nor had Miriam paid the slightest attention to any of Shona's determined conversation this morning. Surely, if she was going to pretend to be a Scot, even one a few generations removed from the mother country, she should begin to appreciate the history of Gairloch.

No, Miriam's attention had been for Fergus. Unfortunately, her brother had seemed more than willing to bask in her smile.

It was enough to give Shona a rash.

Where was Miriam now? Hunting down Fergus in order to spend more time with him? Or was Fergus giving the American woman a tour of Gairloch?

That would never do.

She knew quite well that he didn't want to sell the castle. What he didn't know was how close she was to resorting to the almshouse. The idea of being dependent on the charity of others made her stomach clench. As did the notion of living in a little parish cottage off Shoe Street, given food, fuel, and a ration of pity. Not to mention having to endure endless preaching.

The idea of it kept her awake at night, while humiliation fed her dreams.

How was she going to pay the Inverness shopkeepers what she owed them? She'd managed to convince most of her creditors to grant her a few months, in view of the possible sale of Gairloch. But if it didn't go through, she didn't know what she'd do. If the magistrate, in an act of grace, didn't send her to gaol, she still owed the money, plus a fine.

In light of that undeniable future, sentimentality really wasn't very important.

"Where is Mr. Loftus now?" she asked.

"He's in the library," Helen said, entering the room with a tray in her hands.

"Where's Jennie?" she asked, speaking of the girl who was acting as maid for a time.

"Cleaning the dining room. What is Miriam doing? Fussing over her hair. Evidently, the weather in Scotland is damaging to milady's locks."

She'd never heard Helen be sarcastic, but exposure to the Loftus family would drive a saint to swear.

"Have you just served tea?" she asked, glancing at the contents of the tray. An empty plate, a cup and saucer, and a small china teapot, from her mother's company china.

"Just a small portion left over from breakfast. Mr. Loftus is longing for scones, the kind his grandmother made for him."

Maybe Helen could decipher exactly what the man wanted.

"I've spent a good long time listening to Mr. Loftus complain about a great many subjects," Helen said. She began removing the empty dishes from the silver tray. "Did you know that, in addition to being a financier, he runs railroads?"

Shona shook her head.

"He does. He also owns two shipyards and is looking at property along the Clyde."

"That would give him something to do in Scotland."

"He was very fond of his grandmother," Helen said. "Quite a lovely woman, I understand, with a voice like a sparrow."

Shona frowned. "Sparrows don't sing."

"Mr. Loftus thinks they can. I didn't correct him."

"You're a wonder, Helen. Truly."

Helen smiled. "I'm very used to listening to my father.

He had a tendency to go and on about things as well. It's amazing, really, how often people just want to be heard. Mr. Loftus seemed gratified that I was paying attention. Evidently, Miriam doesn't."

She bit her lip rather than comment on the American girl.

"Any complaints about Gairloch?"

"Oh, he's quite filled with complaints about Gairloch," Helen said airily, not understanding that the words were like a spear to Shona's heart. "But along with the complaints, he has numerous plans."

"Plans?"

"He intends to install a boiler immediately. As well as new device they have in New York City. An elevator," Helen said, sounding the word out slowly. "A platform to hoist people from one floor to another. He said it would make it easier for him."

Shona looked at the cook, then sat on one of the benches in front of the table, uncaring that flour dusted her dress. "Then he's serious about purchasing Gairloch?"

Helen looked at her oddly. "Of course. Why ever would he come all this way?"

To bedevil her; to cause her hopes to rise. She only shook her head in answer.

"He hasn't seen the whole of Gairloch yet."

"I imagine he will after his nap."

"He's napping now?"

What about his bloody scones?

"Elizabeth insisted upon it," Helen said, wiping the tray. "She's quite a lovely girl."

Evidently, Helen had managed to learn more in a few minutes than she had in a day.

"I don't suppose you know where Fergus is?"

Helen shook her head.

"Then we'll plan on giving Mr. Loftus the grand tour this afternoon."

Until then, she was going in search of her brother. Before she could leave the room, however, Helen stopped her.

"Mr. Loftus did ask me the strangest question," Helen said, placing the tray in its spot in the pantry. She returned and faced Shona. "He wanted to know if we had any ghosts."

"What did you tell him?"

Helen looked a little shamefaced. "I know it was wrong, but all I told him was that every Scottish castle had its share of ghosts. He evidently wanted one."

She studied her companion for a moment. Perhaps she'd delayed too long. Before any more time passed, it was time to tell Helen the truth.

Chapter 11

"**G**airloch does have ghosts," Shona said. "Not just one, but two."

Helen looked startled.

Shona sighed and stood. "Come with me," she said, leaving the kitchen.

Several moments later, she stood in the Clan Hall with Helen beside her. Today, the room reeked of linseed oil and turpentine, and the yellow soap she'd used to scrub the floor.

"We have two ghosts," she said. "One called the *bean tuiream*, or weeping woman, and the other who's a piper." She smiled. "All my life, I hoped to see one of the ghosts, because the Imrie who did was said to have great good fortune."

"Did you?" Helen asked, wide-eyed.

She shook her head. Despite nights of sneaking down to the Clan Hall, shutting her eyes tight and wishing—and praying—for a peek at one of them, she never had. Truthfully, she wanted to see the piper more than the *bean tuiream*, because she didn't want to be saddened by a ghost.

She'd imagined what the piper would look like if he ever appeared, the amorphous shape of the figure as he gradually formed, attired in an emerald-hued kilt and white shirt, holding the pipes on his shoulder, his gaze on the far horizon.

Helen looked at her, no doubt remembering the sound she'd heard a few days ago. The weeping woman was heard by most people, but she didn't get a chance to reassure her companion.

"What utter blatherskite," Miriam said from behind her. "That is the right word, isn't it? You Scots have such colorful terms."

"It's not nonsense," Shona said, turning and facing the American woman.

"You must tell Father. He'll be so amused."

Miriam, dressed in a striped blue and white dress—not the one she was wearing at breakfast—approached with a swaying gait that made her skirt swing much farther than decorum decreed.

"You cannot believe such things, surely?"

"Scotland is a much older country than America, Miss Loftus," she said, feeling for her composure and finally finding it. "After another thousand years, people in your country might feel the same."

"I doubt it," Miriam said. "I've never heard anything more ridiculous. Ghosts?"

Helen's glance was filled with caution. As if warning her that she wasn't in a position to be dismissive of Miriam. Nor could she say exactly what she wanted to say, which wasn't the least polite.

Perhaps she'd been spoiled in her life, always being able to say, within the limitations of good behavior, exactly what she wished whenever she wished. At the moment, however, she had no power at all. Not even that of a verbal rebuff.

Instead, she tucked away her irritation for another time and forced a smile to her face. She didn't need to look in the mirror to know the expression was forced and false.

"Will your ghosts be pleased at having Americans living here?"

She was very much afraid that the Gairloch ghosts would not be pleased with the ensuing departure of the last of the Imrie Clan. But if Miriam had such derision for the ghosts, what would she say to that comment?

Even she and Fergus treated the ghosts with some respect. Not that the ghosts demanded it. Tradition did, handed down for a hundred years, ever since the piper's haunting lament had first been heard in the corridors of Gairloch.

The pibroch wasn't a warning to the Imries. She'd often wished it had been. Perhaps they might have been able to prevent their parents from going to Edinburgh. Or somehow prevented the death of a baby sister even years earlier. Her grandsire had said that the ghost played when he would, when the time suited him and not otherwise. For that reason, when she heard the far-off, faint sounds of the pipes, she stopped, recalled the day, and wondered at the reason for such a sad sound.

None of this would she share with the Americans, however. They might be buying Gairloch, but they'd no claim to her memories.

Perhaps it was necessary to be a Scot to understand. Blood had seeped into the soil of the Highlands. Freedom had been a cause so necessary to her ancestors that they'd willingly fought for it, died for it, and enshrined it in their songs and stories. Proud men rebelled against a yoke of any kind, whether it came from another clan, an invader from the north, or the English.

Surely an American would understand that, but she

couldn't be certain, and for that reason, Shona held her tongue.

"I'm sorry you don't believe," she said. "Perhaps our ghosts will make an appearance for you."

"That would be vastly amusing," Miriam said. "I should like to tell my friends about a Scottish ghost. Will he be wearing a kilt? Or be as handsome as your friend Gordon?"

"Colonel Sir Gordon," she corrected.

Helen glanced at her, but Miriam only smiled.

In the middle of the Clan Hall, surrounded by weapons wielded by her ancestors over three hundred years, Shona had the distinct impression that the American woman had just drawn first blood.

"The willing horse is always worked to death."

"What's that, Shona?" Helen asked.

"Nothing," she said, embarrassed to have been caught grumbling. "Just something my father always said."

He'd also said: *He that talks to himself speaks to a fool*, but she didn't bother repeating that comment.

After Mr. Loftus awoke from his nap, he'd finally agreed to a tour of Gairloch. Not before, however, he'd requested a bit of "something" to eat between lunch and dinner. Oh, and some more hot water. Oh, and a jot of whiskey. Oh, and some extra blankets since he was cold. Jennie, Helen, and Shona had been ferrying trays up and down the stairs ever since.

He couldn't install an elevator too soon to suit her.

The giant, ever present at the American's side, hadn't offered to help. Evidently, his duties involved carrying the older man's bags or shaving Mr. Loftus. Otherwise, he stood around looking fierce, a role he fulfilled very well.

Fergus had finally appeared for the tour, leaning a

bit too heavily on his cane. However, he was soon looking amused at her annoyance. Let him be amused. Let him be outright joyful. Anything but stand in the way of this sale.

Marching into the small sitting room attached to the Laird's Chamber, she faced Mr. Loftus sitting on the settee, his daughter beside him. Before she could open her mouth to speak, however, he said; "I've been waiting for your tour, Countess. Is there something you wish to hide?"

Her mouth opened, then closed, then opened again.

"Doesn't she know that you've already looked over the castle, Father?"

She looked at Miriam, then at Mr. Loftus, and finally at the giant who stood beside the fireplace straight and tall as if he were a pine transplanted to the Laird's Chamber.

"What do you mean?"

A flush appeared on the American's cheekbones. How much of that was due to whiskey and how much to embarrassment? Did Mr. Loftus even feel embarrassment?

"I never buy something without inspecting it first, Countess."

"You've inspected Gairloch?" Her muscles tensed as her smile froze in place.

"I sent someone to do it for me a month ago," he said. "I'm a businessman, Countess, not a sentimental fool. Shall we begin?"

Wordlessly, she turned and led the way to the corridor.

A month ago? Whom had he sent? How long had he been here? Why hadn't Old Ned reported the presence of a stranger? For that matter, had Old Ned even noticed someone climbing over Gairloch, investigating the walls, or looking over the roof?

She turned and faced Mr. Loftus. "Where would you like to begin?" she asked.

"The oldest part of the castle."

"You've already seen it," she said. "That's the Clan Hall and the Family Parlor."

He nodded as if he knew. "Then we'll begin there."

He'd sat there the night before, and had drunk whiskey there with Gordon upon arriving, but if he wanted to see the room again, she'd show him. She'd give him the speech she'd practiced in the last few days.

If she could think past his surprising revelation.

"Did your inspector find anything wrong with Gairloch?" she asked.

He shook his head. "A little water seepage in the south wing and there's a patch of roof that needs mending. Other than that, it seems in good enough repair."

Relief surged through her tempered by annoyance.

He'd sent an inspector here, had he? Had he discovered everything? If he hadn't, then perhaps the Americans weren't destined to know all Gairloch's secrets.

Chapter 12

They slowly descended the curving steps, Fergus's lips compressed until they were little more than a white line. Elizabeth glanced at him from time to time, until Shona wanted to warn her that he was more stubborn than ill. The pain in his leg would remain with him all his life, she'd been told. A reminder that he should have agreed to the amputation in India.

She couldn't say that she agreed with the physician's assessment. After all, it was Fergus's leg. But sometimes, as now, she wondered if the price he paid to keep it was too dear.

Mr. Loftus was grumbling during the descent, his bodyguard at his right while he clung to the banister with his left hand.

Not one person in the whole party had a joyful air about them, or even an eagerness to be about the tour of Gairloch. Even Helen, who had become the peacemaker for the group, was unsmiling as they entered the corridor. Before they could enter the Clan Hall, an echoing boom sounded at the rear door.

Like a trail of ducklings, Helmut, Mr. Loftus, Miriam, Elizabeth, Helen, and Fergus followed her to the door.

Gordon stood there, his hair askew from the afternoon breeze, his blue eyes hinting at humor. Dressed in a black suit, the white shirt beneath his jacket was the only spot of brightness in his somber attire.

For a second, just a second, she felt her heart lurch. If it had been seven years ago, she would have looked around, first, then stood on tiptoe to kiss him quickly before anyone could see. He would have smiled as he had so often, and placed his palm against her cheek.

Now, she steadied her heart, forced a smile to her face and said, "What are you doing here?"

His mouth twitched as if she amused him.

"Forgive me if my arrival is inopportune," he said, glancing behind her.

She remembered her manners, but only barely.

"Of course it isn't," she said. "It's just that I'm about to give our guests a tour of Gairloch."

He suddenly smiled, the expression sending a tremor of memory through her. How often had he smiled just like that, an expression of such delight that it had lightened her heart? This time, however, he wasn't smiling at her, but at someone else.

"Ah, Sir Colonel Gordon," Miriam said, coming to stand beside Shona.

"Colonel Sir Gordon," she corrected.

"Gordon," he said, moving to enter Gairloch even though she stood in the middle of the doorway.

She finally moved aside so he could enter.

Miriam smiled, the same expression the barn cat wore when smelling cream and wanting a taste. A sidle here, a quick purr, a head butt against a calf, and the cat would be rewarded its sweet disposition with a fingertip of cream. But the cat's amiability would last until it wanted away, and it'd fly out of sheltering arms in a fit of fur and claws.

How long would Miriam's amiability last?

Her feelings for Miriam Loftus had blossomed into an active dislike. Every coy comment, every sidelong look Miriam gave Gordon—accompanied by a flutter of lashes—irritated her.

She would have thought Gordon immune to such nonsense, but he evidently wasn't. Instead, his head was bent as he listened to Miriam's soft-voiced conversation, pitched so low that no one else could hear. One would think the other woman did it purposely, as if to give others the impression that their conversation was intimate and secret.

"You didn't say why you're here," she said, interrupting their conversation.

"I came to speak to Fergus," he said, glancing at her, then at her brother. "But it can wait."

She took a deep, relaxing breath, wished away her incipient headache, and turned, making her way back to the Clan Hall. She didn't care if Gordon and his new ladylove followed or if they were engaged in a torrid embrace in the stillroom.

Surely Mr. Loftus cared about his daughter's reputation?

She caught Elizabeth's glance, wondering at the look of commiseration. If the nurse could tell she was annoyed, then she was not hiding her emotions well enough.

"You'll note the shields affixed to the wall there and there," she said, pointing above their heads as they entered the Clan Hall. "The first known appearance of the Clan Imrie in war was when we fought for King Robert the Bruce against the English at the Battle of Bannockburn in 1314 and at the Battle of Halidon Hill in 1333."

As a girl, she'd counted all the various remnants and souvenirs of war mounted on the walls, asking her father if it was true they'd fought more than a hundred times in the last three hundred years. He'd only laughed and said that it was probably twice that, what with the feud with the MacDermonds lasting nearly seventy years.

"The clan fought against the English in the Battle of Sheriffmuir in 1715, and again in 1745, when we were arrayed against the Hanoverians at the Battle of Prestonpans, Falkirk, and Culloden." Their chief had been exiled in France, where he'd died, the first and last time, an Imrie laird had perished on foreign soil.

Fergus had come too close to seconding that feat.

"Our grandfather," she said, "was a member of the Grenadier Guards in 1815, fighting at the Battle of Waterloo."

Fergus had kept up the warlike tradition when he'd gone off to the Crimea and then India.

Somehow, Miriam managed to have Gordon on one side of her and Fergus on the other, and was now giving both of them a fatuous smile.

Shona bit back her annoyance, and continued. "The early part of Gairloch was actually a square keep," she said. "The walls are six feet thick and a gallery wrapped around the outside of the keep allowed a view of the loch and the road to the west. A hundred years after Gairloch was originally built, a high house, and the north wing, along with the staircase, were added."

Mr. Loftus looked incredibly bored. So did Miriam, who was paying more attention to Fergus and Gordon than to the history of Gairloch.

"In 1787, the largest extension was created. The south wing was added, along with the third floor. There are thirty-five rooms for servants, twenty-seven guest bedrooms, twenty rooms for family, as well as three suites. We've five parlors, a music room, a contingent of rooms for preparing and storing food as well as a number of outbuildings."

"One hundred fifteen rooms in all, less the outbuildings," Mr. Loftus said.

"We count those as rooms," she said.

"Why? They aren't part of Gairloch."

"Nevertheless," she said, "they're counted."

She realized that everything she was parroting now had already been sent to Mr. Loftus. He knew Gairloch history, and, if he'd sent someone to survey the castle, he probably knew more about the structure than she did.

"Gairloch is one of the oldest inhabited houses in Scotland," she said.

"I thought Dunrobin was," Mr. Loftus said, surprising her.

"You know a great deal about Scottish houses, Mr. Loftus," she said.

"The more I know, the better deal I make, Countess."

"Dunrobin is the only structure larger than Gairloch," she said. "It has one hundred eighty-nine rooms."

"Were your ancestors trying to best them?"

"Or they were trying to best Gairloch," she said with a smile.

Miriam barely glanced up. Helmut, the giant, was surprisingly looking rapt, as was Elizabeth. Fergus wasn't paying any attention to anyone, including Miriam. He was acting so aloof that she knew he was angry with her.

She had to do this—there was no other choice.

"Sir Charles Barry, the architect of the House of Commons, was retained to remodel Gairloch in 1845," she said. "There are numerous plans still in the library of his recommendations. He would have added ornamentation to the five towers and—"

Mr. Loftus interrupted. "But you ran out of money."

"Yes, we ran out of money," she said, deciding that she would match the American's bluntness. Frankly, it was a relief to finally admit the truth. Why else did he think she was intent on selling Gairloch? Because she wanted the adventure of a life in London? Because she wanted to travel the world?

"The castle is very old," Gordon said, addressing his remarks to a rapturous Miriam. "You'll find that the Gairloch has a bit of history everywhere," he added. "There, for example." He pointed to a gash on the wooden floor just beyond the fireplace.

"That's where Fergus coshed himself. We were playing soldier."

"You were English, I believe," Fergus said, smiling. "I was Robert the Bruce."

Was he going to point out other places at Gairloch? Memories seemed to swell in the air, mocking her. Over there was an alcove formed by a window seat. One day, Gordon had drawn one of the drapes and kissed her when Fergus had been in the room. In that doorway, she'd stood and watched him walk toward her the year he'd returned from school, his eyes somber, his face even then bearing the look of maturity. He'd been sent away to the Royal Military Academy in Woolwich, and she'd missed him with an ache she still felt.

He'd been special and hers.

Miriam's laughter dissolved the past, brought her back to the present with a jolt.

He wasn't hers and she wasn't his, and it wasn't the past. The time was now, her situation was perilous, and if she wanted to do anything about it, she had to stop being foolish and concentrate on the task at hand.

Miriam glanced at her. "Did you tell the countess about the new name for the castle, Father?"

"New name?" she asked.

Fergus came to stand at her side. She reached out and placed her hand on his arm, hoping he wouldn't speak. She knew exactly what he'd say. Gairloch was an old and venerated name throughout the Highlands. Calling it something else would be a sacrilege.

"Lochside," Mr. Loftus said.

She only smiled, clamped her hand on Fergus's wrist, and gave him a look. He returned it, eyes bright with anger.

"A pity," Gordon said. "I would have kept the name Gairloch. It's very distinctive, whereas I know at least three other homes with the name of Lochside."

Mr. Loftus only nodded, neither agreeing nor disagreeing.

She was torn between being thankful to Gordon for his efforts and being annoyed he was there at all. She settled for something in the middle, a simmering kind of resentment kept in check by her determined smile.

Elizabeth seemed to be feeling the same emotion. Her smile was tight, her expression bland. Were nurses trained to reveal nothing of their true thoughts? They must be, or else Elizabeth had a natural affinity for burying herself behind a very pleasant, if innocuous, smile.

"Are you planning on living here year round?" Gordon asked.

"Are you?" Miriam asked.

What an annoying woman.

Gordon, thankfully, didn't answer the question, only smiled. Miriam smiled back. How very amiable everyone was suddenly.

Her stomach was churning and it wasn't hunger. Nothing had gone right, from the Americans' arrival days early to Fergus's silent and disapproving presence, to this moment.

"And you?" Miriam asked, turning to Fergus. "Are you planning on remaining in Invergaire as well?"

She sent a cautionary look to her brother, but Fergus was ignoring her. Instead, he was looking toward the nurse. "I don't know, Miss Loftus. Once, I could have told you my plans. Things have changed since then."

Without another word, he left them, walking with stiff and halting steps to the doorway. He never turned, or glanced back, and so didn't see Elizabeth watching him leave.

"Can we continue?" Mr. Loftus asked, annoyed.

Shona turned to find Gordon watching her, his look unreadable.

He'd always had that gift of silence, his eyes steady, as if he absorbed everything to study it later. Part of his demeanor was, no doubt, a result of being the general's only child. One did not speak unless the general commanded it. Part of it was due to Gordon's own nature. He seemed to analyze a situation carefully, pull it apart, and put it back together.

Why did you come? Are you here to witness my humiliation? My hawking of Gairloch to the highest bidder?

Shona Imrie Donegal, the Countess of Morton, brought low. Would that please him?

She watched as Gordon offered his arm to Miriam once again, and the two of them preceded everyone out the door, as if Gordon were leading the expedition and not her.

Gordon was torn between following Fergus—after all, his errand today had been for that purpose—or remaining where he was and watching Shona. As the drama unfolded, he found himself fascinated by her behavior. Even as a girl, she'd had a touch of arrogance about her. The Imrie pride, he'd called it. But now, she was almost brittle with it, her chin at an angle that dared the world to see anything but the Countess of Morton. A variety of expressions crossed her face: annoyance, sadness, and then a tightly controlled expression he'd come to expect from her.

But her hands were trembling.

She was not as composed as she wanted the others to think. Why? Did the idea of selling Gairloch not appeal to her as he'd thought? Or did she simply dislike his presence?

With his free hand, he reached out and gave Shona's arm a brief, supportive squeeze. He heard her draw in a sharp breath. For a moment, she looked as if she might turn to him, but then she pulled away.

He smiled at the sight of the pulse thudding rapidly at the base of her throat.

In that instant, he decided he wasn't leaving, even if it meant he had to be attentive to Miss Loftus. Clinging women annoyed him, and Miss Loftus clung like a barnacle. She hadn't released his arm once since they'd left the Clan Hall, an action Shona noted more than once.

Good, another reason to stay right where he was.

"Do you ever wear a kilt, Gordon?" Miriam was asking.

Shona frowned, caught Elizabeth's glance, and smoothed her face of any expression. A moment later, the frown was back.

"My uniform is a kilt and a jacket, Miss Loftus," he said. "So, yes, I've worn it quite often."

"Please call me Miriam," she said, looking up at him with a rapturous smile.

Shona had been wrong to liken Miriam to a cat. She was a pigeon, instead. A very pretty little gray and white pigeon with a very plump chest, beady little eyes, and an inquisitive look, its little head twisting back and forth on its sturdy little neck. Pigeons pranced, they didn't quite walk. Miriam didn't quite walk, either. Since she was so close to Gordon, she didn't have that opportunity to sway quite as much, thereby causing her skirts to rise above her ankles. But she did lean a great deal. Now, she was pressed against him, her breasts against his arm.

He was glancing down at her as if every single word out of her mouth was something to be cherished and remembered.

She caught Elizabeth's smile, and felt a flush race through her body.

She was Shona Imrie Donegal, Countess of Morton. She did not have to endure such behavior.

Yes, she did.

Suddenly, she was so sad that she couldn't bear it. She wanted to find a refuge, some place at Gairloch that didn't hold the remnants of memory. She wanted to slip out of her skin, somehow, and be someone other than who she was. The weight of the past was nearly bringing her to her knees.

But she had no choice but to lead Mr. Loftus and the others through a tour of the kitchen, larder, and pantry, the stillroom, the armory, the conservatory, and the pharmacopeia. He'd already discovered the study, so that was spared an inspection. But she did open the library with the key she'd placed in her pocket that morning. Gairloch's library was the last of its treasures.

The first volume had been added when the castle was barely twenty years old. A studious son of the laird had wanted to study for the priesthood. When that had not been possible, he'd educated himself, intent on spreading knowledge throughout the clan. He'd procured a Bible richly adorned by monastic scribes and it sat in pride of place on a brass stand on a small table.

This room alone was worth the price she was asking for Gairloch.

The library now boasted over a thousand volumes. She knew the exact number—one thousand, one hundred sixty-three—because it had been her task to catalogue each and every one of the books. From the time she was thirteen until the summer before her parents died, she was expected to use any of her free time to complete the task. Fergus had been given the duty of inventorying all the stored armament, not only those items displayed in the Clan Hall, but the attic filled with weapons collected by the Imries over the centuries.

Some of the books were priceless and had been old when they'd been acquired by members of the clan. They'd been lovingly placed here because they represented knowledge, not because of any thoughts of their intrinsic worth. At the same time, no one had given any concern as to their protection. Because Gairloch sat on a bluff, there was little danger of flooding, but still, she worried about damage.

Mr. Barry's plans had incorporated expanding the library upward so that it would take up two floors, instead of simply being housed on the first floor. Since there'd been no money to expand the room, four rows of bookcases were separated from each other by a passageway three feet wide between them, creating a shadowed labyrinth.

"Then, he had the audacity to insist that we sleep in the smallest rooms imaginable. Father almost purchased the inn right there and then."

Evidently, Miriam was expounding on her journey again. Shona thought she'd heard every excruciating detail, every item that had amused, annoyed, or stood between Miriam and her comfort. Thankfully, she was not included in this conversation.

Poor Gordon, having to listen to all that whining. She stifled her smile.

Mr. Loftus didn't look impressed about the library. He wrinkled his nose at the smell, and she wanted to tell him that was the scent of knowledge, at least that's what her father had always told her. No doubt it was a combination of leather and old paper, as well as bookworms.

"Gairloch is a huge, drafty old place, isn't it?" Miriam asked.

Shona could feel herself tensing. Helen glanced at her, a message in her eyes. Helen, more than anyone else, knew the state of her finances.

She nodded, forced a smile to her face, but before she could speak, Gordon said, "It is quite large. But it has a wonderful history."

Miriam looked up at him adoringly, as if she were a baby bird and he had just brought her a nice juicy worm.

"You should tell the story of Gairloch," Miriam said. "I love the way you speak."

The woman had the most annoying accent, one that flattened her voice, and made it almost nasally. Most of the time, she barely spoke above a breath. She shouldn't be likened to a pigeon at all, or a baby bird, but an emaciated bird on the brink of dying, so frail it could barely flap her little wings.

Gordon, however, seemed to be fascinated with the sound of her voice, and with Miriam herself, because his attention had barely faltered during this whole, horrible tour.

"Your grandmother lived around here, didn't she, Father?" Miriam asked, turning her attention momentarily to her father.

He nodded. "She was an Imrie," he announced, fixing a stern look on Shona.

Oh dear God in heaven.

Miriam looked at her. "Are we cousins of a sort, Countess?"

"There are a great many people named Imrie in Scotland," she said, as calmly as possible.

Please, do not let them be family.

"She taught me that a Highlander believed in family first, then clan, then everyone else."

He was going to teach her about Highland traditions? Her smile thinned and she kept silent with some difficulty.

"I've heard that there is never a sight more stirring than a man in a kilt," Miriam said in her little bird voice.

Shona prayed for patience, and perhaps a little Gairloch whiskey while she was at it.

"I should very much like to see you in a kilt, Gordon."

Her face must have become flushed, because Mr. Loftus looked at her strangely, as did the giant. Helen elected to study the wainscoting while Elizabeth was examining the carpet.

Were they all pretending not to hear?

Very well, she'd do the same.

Let him dress in his kilt and show his fine legs to Miriam Loftus. Let him strut about like a rooster. She didn't even care if Miriam slid her hands all the way up those lovely thighs to cup one perfectly rounded buttock. Let the woman salivate with lust. Let her eyes glaze over with desire. Let them couple on the dining table, the courtyard, on the banks of the loch, anywhere they wished.

It was none of her concern.

He might have been a fixture of her past, and an important figure in it, but she'd grown beyond him. She was no longer the girl she'd been.

"Are you up to the third floor, sir?" she asked Mr. Loftus. "We can access the attics from there."

"We don't have to see the whole of the place today," he said. "We're planning on being here a few weeks, Countess."

A few weeks? A few weeks? Panic rendered her speechless. How was she to feed them all for a few weeks?

"We'll save the third floor for another day. Maybe tomorrow," he said. "And the attics. And the dungeon. I should like to see that."

"We don't have a dungeon," she said, forgetting to smile. "Just an area where the whiskey is kept."

He nodded. "For now, I'd like to rest awhile."

"Of course," she said as Elizabeth went to his side.

"Shall I come with you, Father?" Miriam said, momentarily diverted from salivating at Gordon.

He smiled fondly at her. "On no account. I'll just rest before dinner." He glanced at Shona. "A small repast to tide me over might not be amiss."

Again?

"Some tea?" Helen suggested, once again coming to her rescue.

"A bit of whiskey, instead, I think," Mr. Loftus said. "With some venison from dinner last night."

Mr. Loftus left the room, escorted by Elizabeth and the giant. Helen followed soon after, heading toward the kitchen, leaving her alone with Miriam and Gordon.

At the moment, she didn't like either one of them very much. When Miriam smiled up at Gordon and cooed something at him, she felt some internal control shatter.

"He looks quite lovely in his kilt," she said, smiling at Miriam. "You could tell all your friends about a Highlander who posed for you." She turned her smile on Gordon, increased the brightness of it, and said, "Maybe he'll bend over and show you his arse. And a very fine arse it is."

With that, she turned and left the room to the sound of Miriam's gasp.

This time, her smile was real.

* * *

Gordon found her in one of the southern parlors on the second floor. Shona was standing, facing a section of tartan that had been draped over a patched bit of wall. The hole had been caused by one of the previous laird's fists, he'd been told, and the wall never painted, no doubt to forever enshrine the laird's temper.

The Imrie pride went back several generations.

"Did you accomplish what you wanted?" he asked, leaning against the doorframe.

"By being rude?" she asked, not turning to look at him. "No," she said.

"I would suggest that it was a little beyond rudeness. Do you really think I have a very fine arse?"

She clasped her hands together, bent her head to stare at them. "Consider your lecture delivered. I'll go and apologize."

They were in the same room, but she might as well have been in London. She was back to form, the arrogant Imrie.

He moved from the doorway, walking toward her. What did he want? To see if her hands still trembled? To smell her perfume?

"Do you know Elizabeth?" she asked, surprising him.

"No."

He stopped behind her, close enough that he could reach out and touch her. Right there on the nape of her neck where she was sensitive. How many times had he placed a necklace of kisses on her skin? How many times had she shivered in delight?

"Did you please your husband in bed?"

Her shoulders tensed.

"Not even in Sebastopol?" she asked as if she hadn't heard his question. Ah, but he was made of stronger stuff than that. He knew how to flank the enemy, use his artillery to confuse them.

He took one step closer, leaned down until he was only inches from her neck, and softly blew on her skin.

She flinched.

"I knew some of the nurses in the Sebastopol and India," he said calmly, "but I never met her." He wouldn't tell her that Fergus had confided in him. If Fergus had wanted her to know, he would have told her.

Slowly, carefully, as if it were something she'd thought of doing before he began teasing her, she took a step forward. Too many more steps and she'd have her nose to the wall.

"Why does Fergus act the idiot around her?" she said, turning.

Her hands were clasped tightly in front of her.

He smiled. "You'll have to ask Fergus."

"He won't answer." She took a deep breath, exhaled it. "He's changed since the war, Gordon." She turned to face him.

"Men do."

"Then why are you so eager to go away to war?"

"To protect what's ours," he added. "Perhaps to prove ourselves."

"Why, when you come back damaged and broken?"

"I didn't make the war, Shona. In the end, the generals do."

She shook her head. "No, but you were eager for it."

"And you sleep safely in your bed because men like me stand ready to defend those who would harm you."

"You couldn't wait to go, I understand."

"Why should I stay?"

He didn't move his gaze from her face, not even when she paled. This, too, he'd learned as a soldier. To always face the enemy, to never allow his own fears or inadequacies to surface.

"There wasn't much here," he said. The woman he'd loved had married someone else, an act of betrayal he'd come to accept. But never understand.

"Did you love him?" he asked, feeling his temper rise. He forced himself to calm. "You never said."

"Why are you here?"

Her attention drifted away from him, to a spot on the floor.

"To talk to Fergus, but he's taken himself off again."

"It's Elizabeth," she said. "He won't remain in the same room with her for long."

"Women have that power over men. They either make our lives better or miserable. Did you make your husband's life miserable, Shona?"

She took a step to the side, as if to avoid him. He found himself mirroring her move, the sudden flash of panic in her eyes interesting him.

"Are you afraid of me?"

"I want you gone," she said, pointing up her chin.

He took another step toward her.

"*Why* are you afraid of me?"

Her eyes widened.

"Do you think I'd punish you for what you did? How could I do that? What punishment would be fitting, Shona?"

"It was a very long time ago," she said, taking a step away until her back hit the wall.

"An infinity," he agreed. "And yet, I can remember every single word Fergus said. 'She's to marry the Earl of Morton.'"

She didn't respond, but he didn't expect a response. He smiled. "I wondered, for a time, if you were with child. Would it be mine? Or his? Then, when there was no announcement of the blessed event, I wondered if you'd simply lusted after the earl. Did you play me false there, too, Shona? Did you keep his bed warm, at the same time you met me?" He took another step toward her. "Or was it just his money?"

He reached out and touched the very tip of her nose, but she jerked her face away.

"I had money, Shona. Oh, we wouldn't have lived in a castle like Gairloch, but our home would have been large enough. I'd inherited the Works then, and could have provided for a wife well enough. Why not my money?"

Her eyes flashed. "It was seven years ago, Gordon. Seven years."

"An infinity," he said again. "Would you go back?" he asked, a question that evidently surprised her from her startled expression. "Would you go back seven years ago, Shona? Would you do things differently?"

She looked down at her clasped hands. Her voice, when she finally answered, was faint. "Please go away, Gordon. Leave me alone."

Oh, if he only could. If he could banish her from his mind, he would have, seven years ago.

Could a man lust after a woman he didn't trust? Evidently, he could.

"Did you please him in bed?"

She closed her eyes.

"Didn't he ever want to know why you weren't a virgin?"

She sighed, opened her eyes, and regarded him somberly. "If he was curious, he never once mentioned it."

He turned, walked toward the doorway, something else he'd learned from war. When to stay and fight to the last man, and when to retreat.

"Yes," she said to his back.

He glanced over his shoulder at her.

"Yes, I pleased him in bed," she said, her gaze direct. Her smile, light and fleeting, was more a goad than a genuine expression. "You were a good teacher."

He silently contemplated her a moment longer before turning and leaving the room.

Damn her.

Chapter 13

Fergus stood at the window of the west tower, a place of refuge for him. From here he could see the whole of Imrie land, imagine the clan going forth on raids or to war, coming home in wagons, or buried in far-off places, only their shields returned to represent a life lost.

From here, he could see the forest around Gairloch spread out like a flattened hand over the glen, fingers of green stretching toward Loch Mor. The trees were already hinting at winter, turning gold and rust. Here and there, clumps of gorse sheltered quail, offered flowers for the deer to nibble on during their scamper up the hills. From the other side of Gairloch, the view was of the rugged yellowish gray and black base of Ben Lymond.

Nature had blessed the day with color. The sky was a blistering blue, with not a cloud to mar the perfection of it. The loch glinted silver in the afternoon sun. There, on the horizon, the sky darkened. Not an approaching storm but night come to soothe this part of the world.

In both Russia and India, this view had been a lodestone for him. After he'd been wounded, it had been a place to imagine when pain stripped every other thought from his mind. He'd lain aboard the ship bearing him home with his eyes closed, a determined smile on his lips, wishing himself here.

Shona didn't understand that. She didn't understand

that all he had left was Gairloch. Take that away, and who was he? No longer the laird of the Imrie Clan. No longer the steward of this land. He had no money to support anyone, even himself. He had a Victoria Cross for "most conspicuous bravery and extreme devotion to duty in the presence of the enemy" and an annual pension of ten pounds. Hardly enough to maintain Gairloch. Nor was it enough to support a family.

He knew nothing about farming, but it was just as well. The land might appear lush and green, but it was an inch of soil atop rock. He might do as other lairds were doing, raise sheep. How did he get the money to buy sheep?

"I thought you'd be here."

He glanced over his shoulder at Gordon.

"I should have remembered you knew about this place."

"Your hidey-hole, then? Have you gone to ground like a fox?"

"What better time? Gairloch is filled with Americans and Shona walks around just waiting to snarl at someone."

Slowly, he turned and faced his friend.

Gordon didn't respond, but then he rarely did when Shona's name was mentioned.

With Gordon, he'd climbed Ben Lymond or reenacted famous battles in which the Imries had played a significant part. He'd imagined himself a laird of old, holding a wooden sword aloft and shouting the clan motto, "Be afraid of nothing," in Gaelic. Gordon had no choice but to play a minor role as transplanted border reiver or one of the English.

That had all changed when Gordon returned from school. Then, he and Shona were rarely apart. A blind man could have seen what they'd felt for each other.

"Is Elizabeth the nurse you told me about?" Gordon asked now.

He saw the look in Gordon's eyes, that implacable "I'll wait forever" expression. As a commanding officer, it had been intimidating. As a friend, it was just annoying.

"Yes," he said.

Gordon didn't answer, merely waited.

He turned and stared out at the view again. Would he ever tire of looking at Loch Mor?

"What happened between you?"

"What do you think happened?"

"I've just met with your sister. I'm not in the mood for another taste of Imrie pride."

Fergus smiled. "Is that what it is? I thought it was a taste of Imrie reticence."

Gordon's laughter exploded in small tower. He couldn't help but smile despite his mood.

"When the hell have the Imries ever been reticent?" Gordon finally said.

He shrugged.

"What happened?" Gordon asked, relentless in his curiosity.

"I fell in love. She didn't."

He discovered that he loved her smile, the sound of her voice, even her laughter.

"She kept telling me that she'd been directed never to socialize with patients. I told her I wasn't her patient, and we weren't socializing, merely sitting in the garden. She said she couldn't accept flowers from me when I picked a few and presented them to her."

His gaze shifted to the cupola above them. The ceiling had been carved into patterns of the night sky: stars and a quarter moon.

Gordon didn't speak. When the hell had he learned

that endless patience? The rest of the story was even more pitiable, and Fergus spoke it quickly before he lost his nerve.

"All of my letters were returned," he said. "Then, I'd heard that a ship had gone down and several nurses had been aboard. I thought she was one of them."

"You never discovered differently?" Gordon asked, his voice holding the same measure of incredulity he'd felt.

"Not until she walked into Gairloch yesterday," he said.

"Have you talked to her?" Gordon asked.

He shook his head.

"What the hell are you going to do about it?"

He hadn't the slightest idea.

Thankfully, Gordon didn't press him for an answer.

"I came here today for a different reason entirely," Gordon said. "I need a manager for the Works, and I thought of you."

"Good God, why?"

"You've got to do something, you know."

"Do I?" he asked, turning his attention back to the view beyond the window. "What do I know about managing an ammunition factory?"

"About as much as you did manning an artillery emplacement," Gordon said. "Or being a hero."

That coaxed a laugh free. "I didn't mean to be a hero, Gordon. The lads were just in trouble, that's all."

"You single-handedly saved twelve men, as I recall."

He folded his arms, leaned against the window. "I remember being scared out of my wits. All I was thinking was how damn loud the cannon were, and wishing I could run a little faster."

"I need someone I can trust at the Works, Fergus. Why not you?"

Fergus turned and smiled at him. "Haven't you noticed?" He held up his cane. "I'm lame."

"You're not a damn horse. You walk with a limp. At least you're alive."

Fergus felt his anger flare then fizzle, as if he didn't have the energy to keep it burning.

"Is that why you're not going to confront your nurse?" Gordon asked. "Because you see yourself as a cripple?"

"Yes," he said, turning away. "And it's no good trying to reason me out of it, Gordon. You can't talk my wound away."

Without another word, Gordon turned and left the tower.

A good thing, really. The problem with old friends was that they saw too clearly and too much.

No doubt Gordon had returned to Miriam's side to apologize for her poor behavior.

"You'll have to excuse the Countess of Morton. She's being an ass today." Would that be a good enough explanation? Better than the truth, surely. "The Countess of Morton is being flayed alive by the past. She's in pain at the moment and wants to cause the same pain in everyone else."

Gordon had hurt her and he could hurt her again. Could she wound him as easily? If so, she'd never know it. Perhaps he was more courageous than she, but then he'd gone to war.

So had she—against herself.

Shona grabbed her shawl and left the parlor, intent on finding Miriam to apologize. She'd been unpardonably rude, or perhaps just a few steps beyond that. She would make amends, not because it was the right thing to do. Not because her mother had taught her to always be a kind and gracious hostess. No, she would go and grovel to Miriam Loftus because she needed Mr. Loftus to purchase Gairloch.

Gordon would be pleased, but she wasn't concerned about pleasing Colonel Sir Gordon MacDermond at the moment. The sale of Gairloch and moving from Invergaire Glen would be easier if Gordon continued to view her with barely veiled contempt.

How could she bear it if he began to court Miriam?

She pushed that thought away.

No one was in the Clan Hall. She really should go check on everyone, see what needed to be done, what tasks were next. She should do another inventory of the pantry and larder. Perhaps worry some more. About the only thing she could afford to do lately was worry.

What would she do if she saw Gordon and Miriam together again?

She would smile and pretend that it didn't affect her in the least. She would simply clamp a lid down on that part of her that was determined to remember another time, even though it was the very same place.

"He's a very attractive man," Miriam said, startling her.

The room was empty, but she looked toward the door to the Family Parlor. Because of the height of the ceilings, sound traveled well between the two rooms.

She looked toward the corridor, then back at the doorway. She really should leave. Now, before she heard anything else.

"He's almost worth being in this godforsaken country, Elizabeth."

"I thought you were engaged, Miss Loftus," Elizabeth said.

"Do you know why we're in Scotland, Elizabeth?"

"I believe your father's grandparents were from Scotland."

"We're in Scotland, Elizabeth, because I've agreed to

marry Robert Simmons, a protégé of my father's. In exchange, I am to have Gairloch as a wedding present. I'd much rather have a few dresses and an emerald or two. What on earth will I do with a moldering old castle? In the meantime, why shouldn't I find something of interest in this awful country?"

"Yes, Miss Loftus. Shall I tell your father you'll be along?"

"Poor thing, is he feeling unwell?"

"He is resting, but requested your presence," Elizabeth said.

"I'm the only one in this entire moldering place who's attractive and personable," Miriam said.

"Yes, Miss Loftus," Elizabeth said.

Did she imagine it, or was there an edge to the nurse's voice?

"The countess could be very pretty, but she doesn't seem to care, does she? All those very boring dresses. Black and white, as if she's afraid of the tiniest bit of color."

"She's just come out of mourning, I understand."

"That's another thing, she's exceedingly gloomy to be around. All she talks about is Scotland and Gairloch. I quite want to yawn around her."

"I believe she just wishes to tell you about Gairloch, Miss Loftus."

"And ghosts?" Miriam laughed. "How can she expect us to believe in ghosts? Does the woman have any sense at all?"

"It is Scotland, after all, Miss Loftus."

The voices were growing stronger.

Shona went to the fireplace and pushed the brick just below the end of the mantel on the right side. A section of wall opened soundlessly. She slipped inside and pulled down the iron torch holder to close the door.

Three hundred years ago, several defenses had been

built into the castle. One was the Upper Courtyard, one was a well in the larder, and another a series of secret passages connecting the Laird's Chamber with important rooms throughout the castle such as the library and the Clan Hall. The labyrinth of passages connected at one point toward the west, then began to slope downward in a steady descent, the angle of the passage mirroring the ground above it.

She'd used the passage dozens of times, as familiar with its contours as she was her own bedchamber. At the end of the tunnel Gordon would sometimes be waiting, reaching out one hand for her. Her hand in his, they'd laugh together, then race to their meeting place.

She'd never been afraid of the dark, never considered that there might be things in the darkness that could harm her. A good thing, since there was only a small slit of light around the opening of the passage door.

The sound of scrabbling paws reminded her that she'd not been a good chatelaine of the castle. In her mother's day, vermin were effectively eradicated, a process that involved a dozen maids, a fair share of poison, and constant efforts at cleanliness.

She hadn't given orders for boiling water to be used to scrub the kitchen floor. Nor had she placed small tubs of water beneath the bedposts. The smell of dust was another reminder of what she hadn't yet accomplished. Every room needed to be swept, the tapestries on several of the walls carefully shaken, the paintings with their ornate gilt frames treated with a bit more care. And here, in the passages, normally kept as clean as possible, she'd done nothing at all.

The Americans had the money to hire enough staff to care for each and every item at Gairloch, each precious reminder of her heritage. Was it possible to be grateful to her saviors at the same time she loathed them?

A breath of air swept across her cheek. A reminder that the passage connected with other secret corridors in the castle.

She stood on tiptoe, peering through the opening into the Clan Hall. Miriam stood in the doorway, laughing. Amusement no doubt at Shona's expense. What was she ridiculing now? Her hair? Her manner of speech? Her nose?

No, she really didn't like the woman.

She could tolerate remarks about herself, but it seemed pointless to ridicule a place and rude to denigrate an entire country.

Miriam Loftus was simply young and spoiled. The girl was in a foreign country, among strangers.

Had she acted the same once? Had she believed that anything she did or said would be forgiven?

"Can you imagine anything so backward," Miriam was saying. "Ghosts? Poor thing if she really believes in such things."

What did Miriam believe in? Only money? Or perhaps adulation?

"I can't begin to tell you what she said to me. I would have thought a countess would have more breeding." Miriam laughed, a tinkling little laugh that went straight to Shona's spine. "But I do admit that the thought of Gordy naked is a tantalizing one."

Oh, that was just too much.

Throwing her shawl over her head, Shona reached up with her right hand and pulled down on the bottom of the torch holder. When the wall slid open, she raced out of the opening, arms outstretched, hands curved into claws, yelling Gaelic at the top of her voice.

Miriam took one look at her and screamed.

For that perfect second in time, it was worth being foolish and childish and silly.

Miriam, however, clutched her bodice with both hands, and sank to her knees, her mouth still open. For a moment, Shona could only stare at her as tiny little shrieks emerged from Miriam's open mouth.

Elizabeth knelt at her side, patting her back gently.

At least the floor was clean.

Shona pulled the shawl off her head and stood staring down at the woman in amazement. Now Miriam was rocking back and forth, hugging herself, tears streaming down her face.

"Oh bother," she said. "There's no reason for hysterics."

She doubted anyone could hear her over Miriam's loud sobbing. Certainly not Elizabeth, who was murmuring something soothing. Not Helen, who'd come racing in from somewhere. Or Gordon, who stood in the doorway with the oddest expression on his face.

Heat traveled up her spine as ice pooled at the base of it.

"What were you screaming at her?" Elizabeth asked. She was now fanning Miriam's face, which had paled to an alarming shade, something resembling plaster.

"Is there something wrong with her?"

Elizabeth met her gaze. "She's excitable."

Too excitable—a comment she was not about to make, especially since everyone was looking at her as if she'd done something horrible. Very well, it wasn't very mature, granted, but it hardly merited this act of Miriam's.

"It was a scone recipe," Gordon said from the doorway.

Elizabeth blinked at him. "I beg your pardon?"

"Shona was yelling a recipe for scones," Gordon said dryly, his gaze flicking over her as he entered the room.

"It was the first thing I could think of," she said in her own defense. "It's not as if I speak Gaelic every day."

Fergus arrived to make her humiliation complete. He said something to Gordon, and Gordon relayed the events of the last few minutes. Gordon looked as if he was holding back his amusement.

Fergus, however, wasn't.

Embarrassment had her taking a few backward steps out of the room. Fergus's gaze would have pinned her there, but she had no intention of remaining in the Clan Hall. Miriam was being coaxed to one of the benches, and now Gordon—Gordon!—was comforting her.

He might have been rude to her earlier, but he was exceedingly solicitous of dear Miriam now. Would she like something to drink? A restorative? Would she like him to fetch her smelling salts? Would she like his escort to her chamber?

"She doesn't believe in the ghosts of Gairloch," she said, hearing her own voice and wincing at both the whiny tone and the idiotic explanation.

What had come over her?

Helen was coming to her side, her eyes filled with confusion. What could she say to her companion? That she'd suddenly become twelve again? That hearing Miriam disparage Gairloch was like inflicting a wound? Worse, she'd admitted that *Gordy* fascinated her.

She really had no idea the woman was so easily frightened.

"It was just a jest," she said, looking at the circle of stony faces.

No one said a word.

When she slipped from the room, not one person was paying any attention to her. Instead, they clustered around Miriam, Gordon the closest of all.

Chapter 14

Gordon laughed all the way home.

His conscience chastised him for making fun of an incident that had caused Miss Loftus a great deal of distress. But the look on Shona's face when she'd been caught reminded him of too many other episodes in their shared past.

She'd been fifteen the last time he'd seen that wide-eyed acknowledgment of her own stupidity.

The younger Shona had had a habit of tossing her head, as if in defiance of his words, her parents' dictates, or society at large. She'd learned, over the years, to deliver a look of such penetrating disdain that the object of it immediately understood Miss Imrie's thoughts. Nor had she measured her words to determine which ones were appropriate for the circumstances.

He'd thought the younger Shona gone, but she'd been hiding. Today, he'd seen her again. In addition, she hadn't lost that ability to skewer him with words.

Yes, I pleased him in bed. You were a good teacher.

Words that irritated like a burr in his boot.

A carriage was in his drive. He wasn't expecting company, unless Rani had changed his mind about staying at Rathmhor. As he dismounted, one of the stable boys came up to attend to his horse.

"You've a visitor," Mrs. MacKenzie said at the front

door, her round face flushed. "A very important man from the looks of it," she said, following him into the house. "Very important entirely, Sir Gordon. I've put him in the front sitting room."

"He'll have to wait until I'm settled," he said, looking down the hall as if he could see the visitor through the walls. "Did he state his business?"

She shook her head.

"Give you his card?"

Again, she shook her head.

"Why, then, do you think he's important, Mrs. MacKenzie?"

He stripped off his hat, gloves, and coat, leaving them on the chair in the front hall.

"He's a military man, Sir Gordon, with more medals than the general."

An important man, indeed, and an emissary from the army was the last person he wanted to see.

He considered telling Mrs. MacKenzie that he'd been unavoidably detained—for a year or two. But if he refused to see the man, they'd just send someone else.

"Have you offered our guest refreshments, Mrs. MacKenzie?" A testament to his distraction that he didn't realize the question was offensive to a woman of his housekeeper's dedication until she replied.

"A bit of tea and some pastries," she said, her voice curt.

He nodded, knowing he'd have to make amends for implying she'd been negligent.

The front sitting room was exactly twenty-three paces from the front door. He made the journey counting each of his steps, concentrating on the slats of the well-polished floor beneath his boots.

He stood on the threshold, meeting the other man's gaze. The man seated in the overstuffed chair and finishing up the last of Mrs. MacKenzie's pastries was possessed of a bearing the equal to his father's. If it could be said that General MacDermond had a mentor—or even an idol, if he were to ascribe such an emotion to his father—it would be General Horace Abbott. Tall, lanky, with graying hair, an angular face, and a gravelly voice accustomed to giving orders, Abbott was of sufficient rank that Gordon hesitated at the doorway.

The War Office must be worried.

Mrs. MacKenzie had been right. General Abbott was in full military regalia, complete with an impressive array of medals.

If you eat your porridge, darling, I'll give you a pastie.

His long-dead mother's voice made him wonder, suddenly, if medals were the army's equivalent of a pastie. The more medals a man had, the more obedient he'd proven himself to be?

At least they hadn't sent one of his father's subordinates to plead their case. No, this man had the ear of Prince George, the Duke of Cambridge, who'd become the commander-in-chief of the army a few years earlier. As such, General Abbott was often courted, endlessly praised, and continuously feared.

"I'm not interested in going back into the army," he said, before the other man could speak. "So if you've come for that reason, I'm sorry you've traveled all this way. If you've come to extend your condolences, consider them extended."

"I haven't come for either reason," General Abbott said.

He didn't think so. "Why are you here?"

"For a very important matter, Gordon. Otherwise, I wouldn't have disturbed your retreat."

The fact that the man called him Gordon, conveying

a camaraderie the two had never shared, didn't bother him as much as the fact that Abbott was smiling. Nothing good could come from General Abbott's smile.

"I've resigned," he said flatly, closing the door with more force than it required. He didn't sit, but began a slow pace in front of the chair, from the fireplace to the window, now darkening with night.

Abbott didn't say a word, either to urge him to sit or calm or listen, another clue that this wasn't a normal visit. General Abbott was an autocrat. His men were terrified of him because he demanded it. No doubt the general reasoned that terror and deference were brothers.

After several moments of silence, the only sound the thump of Gordon's boots on the polished floorboards, he spoke again.

"It's not a retreat, General. It's my home."

"I beg your pardon, Gordon. I only availed myself of the term your father used."

"My father considered Rathmhor a place to come between wars," he said. "I don't."

Abbott nodded.

"Why are you here?" he asked, tired of being patient. He wasn't Abbott's subordinate anymore. He didn't have to worry about being sent off to some god-awful duty because he'd annoyed the great general.

"To ask a question, and convey a request."

Had Abbott always been cryptic? They'd never actually spoken at length before, since being a colonel didn't put him in the upper echelon of the British Army. But he'd been forced to listen to Abbott's speeches, addressing his line officers, and he'd heard of him often enough from his father.

"Ask your question, General. And your request."

"I understand you're working on a secret formula for an explosive."

It wasn't surprise that halted him, but the amusement that came from being right. Slowly, he resumed his pacing, his gaze never leaving the other man.

"My father," he said, after two passes across the floor. "My father told you."

Abbott nodded. "Was he incorrect?"

"He was wrong to tell you," Gordon said. "He violated a trust in doing so. But, no, he wasn't incorrect."

Abbott drew himself up, a commanding position despite still being seated. "What use do you have for such an explosive?"

"Is that why you're here, General? To ensure I use the formula for the good of the British Army?"

"Let's say that I am. How would you feel about that?"

"Wary," he said.

"The army treated you well."

"The army treated me competently," Gordon said. "I wouldn't take that to mean well."

The general eyed him with some caution, as if just learning the hound he'd raised from a pup had suddenly turned rabid.

"Your father said you were rebellious."

"Did he?" A mark of his maturity, then, that he no longer cared what either general thought of him.

Abbott was silent, seemingly unconcerned that darkness was almost upon them, that the roads leading here were circuitous and dangerous to travel at night, or that there wasn't an inn for some distance.

He was going to be forced by good manners, if not decency, to offer the man a room in his home.

"It's blasting powder, General, for that purpose. Not to be used in warfare."

"You were very good at war, Gordon."

He turned and stared out at the night, wishing the man to perdition. "I was a soldier. I fought where I was told to fight. I won where I fought." He glanced over his shoulder at the general. "Because I didn't want to die."

"For that, you were awarded a baronetcy."

He felt another surge of amusement. "And for developing a way to make rifles shoot straighter."

General Abbott inclined his head in wordless acceptance of that clarification.

"A teaspoon of initiative, General, in an effort to save a pail of blood."

"You're a very bitter young man."

He smiled. "On the contrary, sir, I'm not bitter at all. I'm simply done. I don't want to be a soldier. I don't want to fight any more wars." *And I no longer want to be my father's son.*

"And the Commonwealth? Is it safe?"

Into those few words, Abbott managed to infuse memories of all the prejudice he'd faced as a Scot in the British Army. Although the last battle between them had been fought a hundred years ago, there was still suspicion on both sides. The British regulars made remarks like "soldiers in skirts" when the Ninety-third appeared. A part of him, the Scottish part, looked on the British as a conquering force to be endured. Never once had he truly felt a part of the army, but he was soul and heart part of the Ninety-third Highlanders.

Abbott would never understand that, and no doubt saw his nationality as a threat.

He forced a smile to his face, and nodded. "The Commonwealth is safe from me, General."

"We're interested in seeing what it can do."

That was a surprise. The Duke of Cambridge was not known to be a forward-thinking man. Instead, he was considered to be conservative to a fault.

Did Abbott speak for him? Or only for himself? A question he decided not to ask.

"I'll consider a demonstration," he said.

"I devoutly hope you will."

Was that a threat? If it was, it was a politic one, couched in polite terms and accompanied by a razor-thin smile.

"You'll stay the night, of course," he said, grudgingly offering his hospitality.

"I must decline," Abbott said, the smile changing character to one more genuine. "I've friends not far away. They're expecting me."

Another surprise.

Gordon moved to the door, opened it, and stood aside.

"We're interested in seeing what it can do," Abbott repeated.

"I'll keep that in mind, General."

"You're not going to cooperate, Colonel?"

"I've left the army, General. I prefer not to use my rank anymore."

The other man looked as if he was about to say something further, then evidently changed his mind, merely nodding as he passed Gordon.

He had the distinct impression, as he saw General Abbott to his carriage, that the War Office wasn't done with their efforts at persuasion. A thought that, surprisingly, only amused him.

His father was attempting to pull the strings, even from the grave. Why else would he have told Abbott about the blasting powder?

Nothing would change his mind or his course. Not General Abbott or his father. Not even Shona Imrie Donegal, who might prove to be more of a threat to his peace of mind than any emissary from the War Office.

Chapter 15

Brian MacDermond came north to Gairloch with seventeen people, among them his wife and child, a boy of only three. Fenella, his wife, was a calm and approachable woman with a serene smile regardless of the situation surrounding her. He'd always appreciated her demeanor, and her lack of complaints.

"I have little to complain about," she'd once said. "You're a good provider. You're kind to our child and to me. In addition, you provide for my parents, and never seem to mind that my father is sickly."

The marriage had been arranged, a joining of lands and hands. He'd no complaints himself. Fenella was sweet, of good disposition, and pleasant to all who met her.

When he went away to war, she missed him, she said. When he returned, saddened and sickened, she tried to tend to him. Something had changed, however. He wanted more. He wanted someone to talk with him about momentous things, such as freedom and a man's soul. He needed to share these thoughts he had, things he'd never before considered before facing his own mortality at Culloden Field.

Instead, they shared silence, once companionable, now only devoid of speech. When his mind was trou-

bled, he took to the pipes, setting aside his work on his house for a time. When the sound eased him, he began to build again. The structure would be sturdy and large enough to hold Fenella's parents and other members of his clan, but nothing the size of the giant castle that shadowed the glen.

Sometimes, at night, he'd stand in the glen and watch as the lights in the upper floors winked at him like stars. Sometimes, he'd play his pipes, but by that time, it was not so much in solace as it was in sadness.

The wife of the Laird of Gairloch was a woman with soft brown eyes and black hair. She'd spoken his name aloud when meeting him for the first time, and he'd thought there was magic in her voice. Her name was Anne, a simple name for a complex woman, one who looked at him with questions in her eyes.

By unspoken agreement, they didn't see each other often, and never alone. They spoke, when circumstances forced them to meet, of his wife and her husband, of their fealty and assets. They never discussed either's flaws, or the fact that each felt loneliness more often than any other emotion.

If her eyes strayed to him when he played the pipes, it was in appreciation of his skill, of the fact that he could cause the very air to weep. If he watched her surreptitiously, it was because she was the Laird of Gairloch's wife, and a woman greatly to be admired.

Shona didn't want to go down to dinner, all too aware what her reception would be. Instead, she busied herself with sewing on two buttons, examining the cuffs of a dress to see if they could be turned so as not to show their frayed edges, and cleaning her one and only pair of well-fitting shoes. When those tasks were finished, she relaced her corset since she'd broken a lace tightening it that morning. She kept herself busy so as not to think of the debacle in the Clan Hall and what an idiot she'd made of herself.

Whatever Miriam wanted to say about her, she would simply have to bear it. If the woman flirted with Gordon, she'd smile. If Miriam linked her arm in his and pretended to be helpless and incapable of walking more than a step or two without assistance, Shona would simply ignore it.

The sudden knock on the door surprised her. So, too, did Helen's admonitory look when she opened the door.

"You can't hide in here," Helen said.

"Why not?"

"Because it will only make it worse when you do have to face everyone."

Helen pushed open the door and entered the room. "Whatever could you have been thinking, Shona?"

"I wasn't."

Thankfully, Helen didn't agree, leaving her some dignity.

Her companion sat on the edge of the bed, waving her hand toward the wardrobe. "Are you going to change? Or wear what you have on now?"

"This will have to do," Shona said.

Helen nodded, stood, and reached out to help her button one of her cuffs. She could manage the left one fine, but the right always gave her trouble.

"I wasn't thinking," she said again, staring down at Helen's nimble fingers. She'd just been feeling. All sorts of emotions had jumbled up inside her, resulting in a lapse of judgment. When she said as much to Helen, the other woman just shook her head, lips pursed.

Helen could sometimes be a very tough taskmaster.

"I have every intention of apologizing," she said.

"It should be tonight," Helen said. "I think Miriam will just be more upset if you don't."

Everyone seemed to be very protective of Miriam, even Helen. If Shona had half the hovering nannies Miriam seemed to collect, she wouldn't be in the predicament she found herself. *Shona? Oh, we've provided well for her. She'll never have to worry another day of her life.* Reassurances she might have received from her parents or her husband.

Instead, she was fending for herself while Miriam was congratulated for drawing breath.

Well, that attitude certainly wasn't going to ease the situation, was it? She'd have to get beyond her feelings about the woman. Perhaps if she got to know Miriam, they'd be able to find something in common.

Gordon.

No, that wasn't a thought she wanted to have, either.

She frowned at Helen. "I shall apologize. Or grovel. Or whatever is necessary," she said. "I shall be nearly angelic."

Helen looked doubtful.

She bit her bottom lip, released it, then blew out a breath. "Shall we go in to dinner?" she asked. Her lips didn't want to curve into a smile, but she forced them just the same.

"Is that your angelic look?"

She frowned at Helen again. "I'm practicing."

"Practice harder," Helen said, urging her to the door.

They were silent down the stairs, and once on the threshold of the dining room, she forced her expression into one of contrition, and entered the room.

Elizabeth Jamison hadn't been this miserable for a goodly number of years. Ever since she'd returned from the Crimea, as a matter of fact.

Fergus was smiling at Miriam, his expression so solicitous that her stomach soured whenever she looked in his direction.

Her plate was filled with food, but she wasn't hungry for any of it.

The china was quite lovely, a pattern of purple flowers interspersed with green leaves. The dinner china was different from the morning china which had been different from the china used on the trays sent to Mr. Loftus's room.

That fact illuminated just how much difference there was between their roles in life. Fergus Imrie had not only won the Victoria Cross, but he was the laird of this sprawling, massive castle, the first sight of which had rendered her awestruck.

How could he think to sell such a magnificent place?

"Good evening."

The Countess of Morton entered the room with a bright smile on her face, her eyes darting from person to person. She drew out her chair, took a deep breath, and looked directly at Miriam.

For several heartbeats, they did nothing but stare at each other.

"Forgive me, Miriam," the countess said. "I have no excuse for doing something so foolish. Blame it on an excess of atmosphere, if you will." Her gaze shifted to Mr. Loftus. "I do hope you'll be able to excuse my poor judgment, sir. I would never have caused your daughter any harm."

She stretched out her hand across the table, too wide for her to touch Miriam, even if Miriam would consider joining hands.

"Tell me about the secret passages," Mr. Loftus said.

The countess drew back her hand, placed it on her

lap, and studied the plate before her. A moment passed, then another, before she finally spoke.

"They were designed to keep the laird and his family safe," she said. "The location of the entrances and exits is a family secret, but if you purchase Gairloch, of course, the information will be provided you."

Fergus cleared his throat as if to admonish his sister. The countess, however, wasn't looking at him. Instead, she and Mr. Loftus were regarding each other in a way that made Elizabeth think they were acknowledging each other as adversaries.

She would have thought, prior to arriving at Gairloch, that Mr. Loftus would win every battle he joined. He was very set on getting his own way.

Even though she'd been hired to monitor his health, he didn't pay any attention to her recommendations. He wasn't to drink spirits, but he'd shooed her away the other night when she'd murmured something about his consumption of whiskey. When she'd cautioned him about not eating too many sausages, he'd just waggled his fingers at her, too intent on chewing.

The Countess of Morton, however, was his equal in stubbornness. That was evident from her very posture: shoulders level, chin squared, gaze direct. She might have been forced into apologizing for behavior that had been curiously out of character, but she wasn't pleased about it.

Fergus might well be as stubborn as his sister. From time to time, he would glance at her, and she'd avert her gaze. Earlier, in the Clan Hall, when Shona had pretended to be a ghost, she'd looked at him and found herself mesmerized.

She wouldn't make that mistake again.

"A party," Fergus said in the silence.

Elizabeth glanced at him, then away before their eyes could meet.

"A party?" Miriam said, her eyes sparkling.

The last month had given her enough insight to know that Miriam loved parties, or entertainment of any sort, preferably events that involved other people paying court to her.

"A party," Fergus repeated. He smiled at Miriam. "To celebrate your arrival at Gairloch. A way of both welcoming you and making amends." His look shifted to his sister.

The countess looked panicked, but the expression disappeared too quickly for Elizabeth to be entirely certain she'd read it correctly.

"A party," Mr. Loftus said, sitting back in his chair and regarding Fergus with more favor that he had previously.

"We'll invite the villagers, of course. And the neighboring houses."

"Will Gordon be there?" Miriam asked.

The countess sent an irritated look in Miriam's direction, then immediately smoothed her face of any expression at all.

"Of course," Fergus said easily. "We'll make it the social event of Invergaire," he added. "Everyone will be there."

No, she hadn't mistaken the panic in the Countess of Morton's eyes. It was back, just before she dropped her gaze to her plate.

Everyone else was busy eating. The countess, however, looked as if she were counting the individual blossoms of heather painted on the plate.

What did one call a countess? Your Ladyship? My lady? Not Your Highness; that was reserved for the queen. Instead of addressing the other woman in any way, Elizabeth remained silent, wishing she could assist her in some fashion.

The Countess of Morton looked so miserable she marveled that the others at the table didn't see it.

"Where were you injured?" Elizabeth asked, turning to Fergus. "It wasn't at Sebastopol." There, a way to aid the countess, even if it meant deflecting Fergus's attention to her. Even worse, it meant addressing the Laird of Gairloch deliberately.

"Ah, you do remember me," he said, his smile devoid of humor or even kindness.

"It has finally come to me where we met," she said, having practiced for this very moment, and those very words. She looked around the table. "The laird was quite caring of his men." Turning back to him, she said, "You kept everyone's spirits up. I remember that the most."

"Do you?" he asked, his expression not unlike the frozen mask his sister wore.

She sipped at her wine, wondered why she couldn't taste anything at the moment. Perhaps it was because her lips were numb.

"I had a great many patients, but I do remember you."

"I wasn't your patient."

"Elizabeth came highly recommended," Mr. Loftus said, his booming voice having the effect of a thunderclap. "Because of her work with Miss Nightingale. I wouldn't have anyone but the best."

She turned her smile to him, grateful that his character was such that he couldn't be excluded from a conversation for long. His daughter had inherited that trait.

"If you'll excuse me," the countess said, standing.

"But you haven't eaten anything," Mr. Loftus said.

"I find I'm not hungry at the moment." She hesitated. "Will you want to complete your tour of Gairloch in the morning?"

"No," he said, glancing at Miriam. "My daughter will take my place."

She nodded, looking distracted.

"Could you see if the maids could dust my room?" Miriam said, catching the countess before she left. "And take down those awful curtains? I've never seen anything so ugly. Is there any other furniture to choose from? The pieces are awfully old-fashioned, aren't they?"

The countess blinked at her, then evidently recalling that she had entered the room for the express purpose of apologizing to Miriam, chose not to comment at all. She only nodded, turned, and left the room.

"Perhaps, if your duties allow you, we could discuss what you remember of Sebastopol," Fergus said, completely missing the fact that his sister was distraught.

She'd thought he'd be hurt, that he wouldn't seek her out again. She hadn't planned for him to be staring at her in such a fashion.

Oh dear, now what did she do?

Chapter 16

Her thoughts kept Shona awake for too long. Now, in addition to their approaching penury, she was going to be humiliated beyond measure because of Fergus's idea of hosting a party. The social event of Invergaire Glen?

Dear God, how was she supposed to afford that?

Gairloch seemed as restless, the constant tapping making her wonder if one of the inner shutters had pulled free of its restraint. Tomorrow, she'd have to investigate.

At dawn, she finally left her bed. The bedclothes were rumpled as if she'd fought a war with sleep. She'd won an hour or two, but only that. A dream tugged at the edge of her consciousness. Scraps of recollection: laughter, running along the banks of Loch Mor, watching from her bedroom window, and waiting for a signal from Gordon, waving good-bye as the carriage carrying Gordon and Fergus went off to school, feeling an open wound where her heart should have been.

Of course it would all come back to her. She was at Gairloch, what else did she expect?

She donned one of her mended dresses. After staring at her pale face for a few minutes, she unbraided her hair, brushed it, then pinned it into a snood at the base of her neck.

She was feeling out of sorts and annoyed, neither mood suitable for companionship. Avoiding the dining room and kitchen, she entered the main corridor, hoping not to see anyone. Better to simply disappear for a while than say something she couldn't retract.

She retreated to the library, walking to the end of the rectangular room. An oil lamp, sitting on a small circular table, might have been placed there for the convenience of those looking through the hundreds of books. The lamp had always served another purpose for Shona. She lit it, then went to the farthest bookcase. Reaching up between two old volumes, she pulled the small iron ring protruding from the wall. The entire bookcase swung outward silently.

This was her childhood escape, so familiar that when she stepped inside the passage, she could feel the years peel away. Here, she wasn't the Countess of Morton. She was Shona Imrie, a young woman of impetuousness, sometimes rash and reckless, always in love. She pulled the ring on the inside of the door and watched as the bookcase slid back into position. Holding the lantern high in one hand, she began to trace the path she knew so well.

Using the passages meant no one could see her disappear. No one could counsel her to remain at Gairloch and be a good hostess. For the moment, she wanted done with all of them: the corpulent Mr. Loftus and his daughter, the princess, Fergus with his eternal glower, and Elizabeth who seemed to inspire it. She didn't want to see the giant regarding her with his impassive stare or even Helen, who had taken up the role of keeper of Shona's conscience and good manners.

Will Gordon be there?

Miriam's question from the night before still burned in her ears. Shouldn't the girl be more concerned with her own intended husband? She shouldn't even be flirting. Nor should Gordon be encouraging her.

She passed the entrance leading to the larder. At the passages' intersection, she turned right. Going left would lead to the stables. The lamp cast a yellowish glow, highlighting the landmarks she remembered. Seven years ago, the passage had not seemed so long, but then, she'd been meeting Gordon. She'd picked up her skirts with one hand, holding on to the lamp with another, and nearly raced down to the loch.

The smell of damp earth reminded her of all the times she'd made this trip. Her hand brushed the stone walls, cold and rough against her fingertips. The passage gradually widened, the air smelling of Loch Mor. The tunnel opened up on an outcropping above the loch, the door hidden behind a cairn of stones.

Three hundred years ago, this tunnel was devised as a last means of escape if Gairloch was ever overrun by enemies. How many times had she used it to meet Gordon?

Now, she simply wanted to stand on the bluff overlooking Loch Mor, see the waves whipped by the wind. Perhaps bid farewell to her girlhood and to Gairloch.

Closer to the loch entrance, the dirt floor became level, making the walking easier. Placing the lamp on the ground, she reached up and removed the thick wooden bar laid across the iron door, leaning it against the side of the tunnel. With one hand, she picked up the lamp. With the other, she grabbed the latch of the door, surprised when it opened so easily.

She'd asked her father, when first shown the hidden passages and tunnel, if their ancestors had created the arrangement of rocks hiding the door.

"A firm undertaking, to be sure," he'd said. "But I've not the knowing of it."

Still, for three hundred years, each succeeding

member of the laird's family had guarded the knowledge of the passages and escape tunnel, secrets to be divulged only to an Imrie of Gairloch.

And now the Americans would know.

If she hadn't pretended to be a ghost of Gairloch, Mr. Loftus would never have known of the hidden passages. Resolutely, she pushed both thoughts away.

Loch Mor was large, shaped, she'd been told, like a teardrop. At the broader end, rocks formed a wide beach. On the narrow end, on the bluff where Gairloch sat, was a stone face. Tall elms perched on the edge, their branches hanging above the water, almost as if they longed for a watery escape.

Her ancestors had planned well. Even if the loch flooded, unknown within written history of Gairloch, the tunnel was high enough above the water that it wouldn't be affected.

She extinguished the lamp, set it down on a rock, and found the beginning of a well-worn path with ease. On this side of the loch, the forest was dense. The air was cool beneath the boughs. Purple geraniums poked their heads out from the fallen leaves, surprising her with their appearance. But the temperature was still mild for September; the withering winds would arrive soon enough.

Accompanying her was the sound of insects sweetly talking and the sight of a lone blackbird strutting on stiff little legs across the path. He hesitated, giving her a gimlet eye before continuing on his morning stroll.

She couldn't help but smile.

Sunlight filtered through the trees, dancing on her shoulders as she walked farther. A patch of wild garlic announced her destination as the forest gradually thinned, giving way to a clearing. In the middle of it, crowned like a rough jewel on the mound of dirt, was a crofter's hut.

The cottage had not been treated kindly by the seasons. The thatched roof, now rotted and gray, bulged outward. The wooden shutters hung askew on the lone window. The door looked solid, however. If she opened it, would she find a rickety cot, an unstable table, and two flimsy chairs? The remnants of a crofter's life and, for a short time, a blessed and enchanted place.

Memories swamped her. He'd been ticklish. She'd never imagined he'd be ticklish, and as she reached for his foot again, he let out a masculine yowl of protest.

He held her as she remembered how her father always kissed her forehead before bed, and her mother swept her up into a perfumed embrace. When the grief of their loss engulfed her and she couldn't even speak for her weeping, Gordon's arms were around her.

They sat, cross-legged, on the sagging cot staring into each other's eyes. The one who looked away first lost. Only one Scottish tablet remained on the plate, and it was forfeit to the winner.

Those days had been filled with laughter, tears, and even more laughter.

He'd been her best friend, her lover, and her love.

"Hiding out, Countess?" Gordon's voice held a note of amusement.

She jerked, but didn't turn.

"Have you come to tell me how odious I was?" she asked, still facing the cottage. "You needn't bother. I've already apologized for my conduct."

"Then you're visiting the past."

She clenched her hands into fists, released them, and turned, facing him.

God was a Scot and He was testing her, surely.

Colonel Sir Gordon MacDermond, first Baronet of Invergaire, was the most beautiful thing she'd ever seen.

He was dressed in the uniform of the Ninety-third Highlanders. His kilt was emerald green and dark blue tartan. Red and white plaid socks reached halfway to his knees and were tied with red ribbons hanging nearly to his ankles. The red wool doublet was adorned with gold epaulets, cuffs, and buttons. The sporran hanging in front of his kilt was made of animal skin, adorned with triangles of contrasting fur. Instead of the bear-skin hat—Fergus swore the thing was hideously difficult to maintain and store—he wore a Glengarry cap, a long wool cap with dark blue ribbons trailing down the back.

A brace of medals attested to his foolhardiness, his grin to his charm.

He was so perfectly built that she couldn't help but remember the shape of his shoulders under her hands, the curves of his arm, the feel of his hips. Everything about him was fixed in her memory. Would the image of him always remain there?

"You've seen me in my uniform," he said, the brogue of Scotland thick in his voice.

She nodded, incapable of speech.

He was, like it or not, the epitome of men who'd claimed this land a thousand years earlier. Men like the first lairds of Gairloch, and his ancestors as well. A Highlander in form, bearing, and stubbornness.

His smile broadened, and for a moment, just a moment of wistful thinking, it was seven years ago, and he was home from his first assignment, proud and eager to tell her all about it.

"Do you approve?" he asked, wrapping the reins of his horse around a nearby branch, approaching her with steady determination.

"What are you doing here?" she asked, feeling unprepared to verbally battle with him. The girl from her memories would never have done so. She'd have launched herself into his arms and would be kissing him senseless by now.

Miriam would think him a gorgeous specimen. There, a thought to keep the past from intruding.

She frowned at him, but he kept walking toward her.

"Are you going to Gairloch, then, to show Miriam your pretty legs?"

An arm's length away, he stopped and closed his eyes.

"Are you sniffing me?" she asked.

His eyes opened.

"Stop doing that."

His lips quirked.

"I mean it," she said.

"It's your scent. I like it."

He always had. Once she'd told him, when he'd asked, that it was something her mother ordered from France. Bruce had purchased it for her as well. When it was gone, she wouldn't be able to replace it. The cost was too dear.

"Go on and show Miriam how pretty you are," she said, forcing her lips to curve in a smile.

How odd that they should be talking of another woman here. A place where they'd confessed how they felt about each other.

Together, they'd learned the art of love. He'd been a natural student, with inventive ideas, some of which she'd never suggested to Bruce. She and Gordon had learned to kiss here, from tender pecks to open mouth explorations of tongue and lips. She'd let him touch her breasts as they'd sat on the cot. She could still remember the shock of awareness she felt when his hand first touched her body, each finger tender and exploring.

More than once, she'd been certain she was with child, but thanks to Mag's instructions she'd been safe. More than once, she'd told herself that being with Gordon was foolish, but loving him had been so natural, so normal, so much a part of her life, she couldn't cease.

He stepped forward now, touching her cheek with just the tip of his finger, sliding down to measure the angle of her jaw and hesitating at her chin, a soft and delicate touch she felt to her toes. He leaned closer until his breath bathed the skin he'd just touched. So softly that she might have imagined it, he pressed his lips against her temple. A ghostly kiss, an echo of those they'd once shared.

"Are you jealous, Shona?"

She stepped back, intent on putting distance between them.

"Of course not," she said, unwilling to admit it. "She's to be married, however. You should know that."

His smile didn't alter, but something in his eyes did, a look that shifted to cool. He was Gordon but he wasn't. The boy he'd been was there, but in a lesser degree than the man he'd become. This man was more dispassionate, less apt to allow emotion to show. Here was the commander of men, capable of looking out over a battlefield, seeing death and destruction, and remaining calm in the face of it.

"Are you hiding out here?" he asked, moving away from her, toward the cottage.

"No, why should I be?" She flattened her palms against her skirts. This morning she'd dispensed with her hoops for two petticoats, but now she wished she'd worn them. Female armor.

"Has everyone forgiven you?" he asked, glancing over his shoulder at her. "Welcomed you back into the bosom of the family?"

"They aren't my family," she said. "Well, Fergus is, of course, and perhaps Helen, but not the Americans."

His lips quirked again.

"You didn't answer the question. Are you hiding here until people forget?"

He'd always been direct. They'd talked about everything, every subject except two: his father and his future. He'd known, even as a child, that his future had been mapped out for him. First, military school, and then, the army.

Only once had they discussed it.

"What would you have me do, Shona?" he'd asked. "Immigrate to America? Turn my back on my country?"

"Do you really want to go?"

He hadn't answered her, and she'd realized, later, what a foolish question that had been. He was, like the men of her family, ordained by destiny to fulfill a certain role. He was General MacDermond's son, and expected to follow in his father's footsteps.

"I feel about ten years old around her," she said now, her sharp tone at odds with the rueful nature of her comment.

"Miriam?"

"She doesn't say anything good about Gairloch," she said, hearing the words and wishing they didn't sound like whining. She wouldn't tell him what Miriam had said about her.

His smile was wide, revealing white, even teeth. The expression stopped her heart. Dear God, he was so handsome.

"So you thought to demonstrate a few of Gairloch's finer qualities."

"You believe in the ghosts," she said.

He shook his head. "I believe that you believe," he countered. "That's been enough for me."

Without waiting for a response, he turned and walked away, opening the door and entering the cottage.

She followed him to the door but wasn't foolish enough to go inside. If it was just as it had been, she'd feel a surge of memory. If it wasn't, she'd regret the change.

Memories could wound. She knew that well enough.

Had he been miserable when she'd left? Had he longed for her as she'd longed for him? Even in her marriage bed, she'd shut her eyes and tried to recall Gordon. Bruce had been a kind and loving man, but he wasn't young. Nor did he have Gordon's physical perfection.

But the worst part of their marriage, and it would have surprised Bruce had she ever the courage to mention it, was that her husband wasn't curious enough. He never wanted to know if what he did pleased her. He merely assumed he had. He never once asked her where she wanted to be kissed, or if she was ready for his loving. In the end, it didn't matter, because he rarely visited her bed. In the last three years of their five-year marriage, Bruce had been too ill to contemplate performing as a husband.

The fact that she'd been without a man's touch for five years was the only reason she was remembering what had happened in the cottage now.

"Why did they give you a baronetcy?" she asked.

He turned, his look of surprise making her smile.

"Did no one ever ask you before?"

He shook his head. "It's a boring reason," he said. "Not nearly as heroic as showing valor and courage."

When had he learned that kind of self-deprecating humor?

She didn't speak, curious as to his answer. Just when she thought he wouldn't continue, he spoke again.

"I tinkered with artillery," he said. "I thought it important to increase firing accuracy. Why shoot a musket unless you're certain of hitting the target? I experimented with various barrel sizes and loading techniques, and passed on what I'd learned to my company."

She remained silent, suspecting there was more to the story than he was telling. But, then, perhaps he'd acquired modesty over the years as well. No, the boy he'd been would have been just as reticent in bragging about his exploits. In that, he hadn't changed.

Once, he'd broken his arm, then stubbornly remounted the horse that had thrown him before allowing it to be set. Fergus had told her the story, not Gordon.

"And the army learned what you'd done, of course," she said.

His smile altered character, became wry. "Of course."

And his father? Had he been surprised, as well? That question she wouldn't ask.

"So, you were awarded a baronetcy for your ability to kill."

His smile dissipated faster than the words did.

When had she learned to be so cruel?

"Perhaps," he said.

She wanted to call the words back, undo the last moments, ease the look on his face. He wore an expression of nothingness, as if he were only an effigy of himself.

Shame flushed her skin, made her wish, in that second, to be anyone other than who she was.

"Gordon," she said, stretching out her hand to him.

He turned back and looked at her, his eyes flat and unreadable.

"Forgive me," she said. "I shouldn't have said that."

"If it's what you thought, then you should have," he said, his voice carefully neutral.

Suddenly, she hated all the pretense she'd built up all these years, all the hardened thoughts laid over the hurt and pain.

This man was a stranger, but he'd once been the boy she'd adored. No, he hadn't been a boy when she loved him, but a man on the cusp of becoming who he was now. She'd shared her secrets and her body with him, longed for him, and adored him.

Before she could say anything else, however, he walked away, leaving her no choice but to drop her hand.

Chapter 17

Turning, he walked into the cottage. Seven years ago, they'd congratulated themselves on making this place theirs. Shona had brought flowers from time to time, placing them in an earthen jar, arranging them on the table as if they'd taken up living there.

He'd loved her on that cot, the first time feeling so inept he thought he'd done it all wrong. Her sighs and smile had eased his mind then.

Shona had felt like his mate, his mirror half, her responses the equal of his. He'd never thought she would go away, ever leave him.

He turned to her now. Her face was still stricken.

He wanted to tell her that it didn't matter; that she didn't have the power to wound him. The words, however, wouldn't pass the gate of truth in his mind. She did have the power to hurt him; she always had.

She looked around the interior of the cottage. "We were such fools," she said.

"We were improvident," he agreed. "And definitely unwise."

He wouldn't have traded those memories for his baronetcy or his wealth, but he was damned if he was going to be dragged around by his cock. Whatever fascination she had for him should remain in the past, as dead as her husband.

But, and this admission troubled him more than a little, there was something about her that made him want to watch her when she wasn't aware. She had a habit of tapping her fingers against her skirt, just before she said something she considered important. Otherwise, her features were still, arranged in a pleasant fashion, but attempting to reveal nothing of her emotions. Except for one eyebrow, her right, that arched in a way she probably didn't realize.

He found himself watching for that subtle movement, an indication of her disdain or annoyance.

Her eyebrow arched a great deal in his presence.

Her wardrobe had not improved significantly with her marriage. Today, she was attired in the same dress, black and white, as if to emphasize her mourning. Or was she attempting, in her fashion, to remind him that she'd married and left him?

As if he could ever forget.

Seven years ago, he'd wished she'd been with child. He'd have married her then, before she left him. Or perhaps he himself should have married in the intervening years.

Should he tell her that she'd ruined him for other women? Hardly exactly true, but at this particular moment, it felt genuine.

He turned, staring at the ruined shutter. Suddenly, he pushed it back with both hands as if he couldn't stand the confines of the cottage anymore. The slap of the wood against the wall sounded as loud as a rifle shot.

The sunny morning had given way to encroaching clouds, the weather as unstable as his mood.

"Are you really going to Gairloch to show off your pretty legs?" she asked.

"Do you think they are? As admirable as my arse?"

She ignored the questions, her frown impressive and intimidating to anyone else.

He walked to where she stood in the doorway of the cottage, reached out and drew her closer. He inhaled slowly, the perfume of her summoning memories.

"You'll look like a prune-faced old maid if you keep that expression, Shona," he said, tracing the outline of her lips.

"I can't be an old maid," she said, stepping back. "I've been married."

"Yes, I know," he said. How could he forget?

She looked like she would have spoken, then silenced herself. He watched her do that twice before she looked away.

"You're always watching me," she said finally. "As if you expect me to fall on my face. Or stumble. Or make an idiot of myself." She threw her hands up in the air. "God knows I've been doing that often enough, lately. No doubt I've given you a great deal of amusement."

She'd not thank him for his smile, so he kept his face carefully expressionless.

"You think that's why I watch you?"

She turned her head and looked at him.

"The least you could do is deny it."

He shrugged. "Why deny it? I do watch you."

She nodded. "As if I'm a leg of lamb and you're a hungry wolf."

"The analogy is not far off the mark, Shona. I am hungry, but not for food."

"Revenge?"

He laughed. "Revenge? Perhaps."

Her face was flushed, tendrils of hair sticking to her cheeks. The dress she wore concealed her shape from inquisitive eyes, but he remembered her well enough.

A frown settled on her face, like a thundercloud on a sunny day. Now her eyes flashed at him, daring him in the way she always had.

Shona Imrie, proud and arrogant.

A bolt of lust hit him then, along with a certainty so strong it felt true. It wasn't anger he felt or betrayal. No, this feeling was need, pure and desperate.

He wanted her. He wanted her with seven years of wanting. He wanted her to sob beneath him, arch under him, admit she needed him more than anyone else. He had loved the girl, but the woman fascinated him.

Perhaps he simply needed female companionship. And her? Did she hunger for a man?

He'd tried to forget what she'd said, but despite his best intentions, his imagination had conjured up more than one scene of her and the Earl of Morton.

He reached out and slowly pulled her toward him. She pursed her lips together again, frowning at him. But he noted that she didn't jerk her arm away, and his grip wasn't that tight.

"I'd not thought to see you jealous, Shona Imrie."

"I'm not," she said, her face averted. "And it's no longer Imrie."

"You'll always be Shona Imrie to me, dear one."

She looked at him then, her eyes wide. "Don't call me that, Gordon. You've no right."

"Who else has a better right? You gave your innocence to me, and your heart, at one time."

He lowered his mouth to hers. She was, he realized in a flash of wonder and surprise, not pulling away.

The press of his lips against hers seemed to be a portal to a different time, when he was young and unschooled and she'd taught him with her soft gasps and moans of wonder.

He felt something open up inside him and cautioned

himself against it. He might lust after Shona Imrie, but he couldn't love her again. The pain of that first betrayal was still there, for all that it was seven years old.

His hands slipped behind her back, drew her forward until his arms could lock around her.

She made a sound in the back of her throat as she angled her head, and allowed him to deepen the kiss.

He wanted to touch her everywhere, strip her bare in the sunlight, cover her with kisses until she shivered and cried aloud. Even after all these years, he knew the texture of her skin. She'd always sighed when he'd kissed the underside of her breasts, or the curve of her waist. He'd run his fingers over her ankles to her toes, tickling her, giving her laughter in the middle of their loving.

She was his first lover, and he didn't think he'd ever forget anything about her.

When he released her, she didn't draw back, only laid her forehead against his jacket. The brush of her hair against one of his medals reminded him of the last time he'd seen her.

She'd come to see Fergus off to war and when her eyes had met his, there was a jolt of surprise in them. They'd not spoken, only nodded to each other as cordial as almost-strangers. Her husband had been with her, and he'd been shocked at the age of the man. In that moment, he'd known she'd chosen a title over a mere soldier.

A pity she hadn't waited a few years; he could have offered her a baronetcy. But he'd never be an earl.

He bent his head to brush a kiss on the top of her head, wondering why he didn't release her, push her away. He'd kissed her. He wouldn't have to wonder if she'd changed; she hadn't.

She still had the power to enthrall him.

Dangerous woman.

His cheek rested against her hair; he wished she would pull away. He wouldn't be the first. Courage in the face of every battle, even this one.

"Fergus told me about your father," she softly said. "I didn't know."

He should thank her for giving him a reason to drop his arms and step back.

"Most people end that sentence with an expression of sorrow. How dreadful that he's passed. How very sad that he died. You must be devastated."

She remained silent.

"But you aren't sorry he's dead, are you?"

A moment passed before she shook her head.

"What did he say to you that day? What did he say to make you run off to Inverness and marry your earl?"

The look of surprise on her face might have been amusing. He found, however, that he was devoid of humor at this particular moment.

She stared down at the floor.

"He said that you felt sorry for me," she said softly. "That if you offered for me, it would be out of pity. Or because Fergus was your best friend and you were aware of our plight."

"He played to your pride, Shona, and you let him win without a fight."

Before she could offer up a false defense, he held up his hand to halt her words.

"He bet that your pride was stronger than your love and he was right."

"That's not true."

He smiled. "It is, regrettably. I knew the moment he told me." At her look of surprise, he continued, "Did you think I didn't know?" he asked. "That he didn't use it as a weapon? Brag about your choice?"

She looked stunned at his words.

"He knew exactly what he was doing, Shona. He was brilliant at ferreting out an enemy's weakness."

"Was I the enemy?" she asked.

He nodded. "From the moment I fell in love with you." No doubt he'd smiled all the time. Or found a reason to laugh. He had probably been so filled with good cheer that anyone looking at him would know he was in love.

General MacDermond had wanted three things for his son, and none of them was love. Instead, he was to first acquit himself in battle. Gordon had done that, but more to save his men than to please his father. Second, to achieve a rank commensurate with his heritage. As Colonel of the Regiment, he was well on his way to making general. Third, to acquire an honor that would segregate him from others. He hadn't won the Victoria Cross, but he'd been made a baronet, an honor that had annoyed his father more than pleased him, since the general had no hope of obtaining it for himself.

Too bad the old bastard died before understanding that whatever accomplishments, whatever successes Gordon achieved from this moment on were his and not his father's.

"My father believed in the rightness of his cause. He believed he was at war and you were the enemy. If one tactic hadn't worked, he would have used another."

She stepped away from him, went to stand in the doorway.

"It would be easier if you weren't here," she said, her voice sounding tired.

"Must everything be easier for you?" He welcomed the sudden annoyance he felt.

"Must everything be so difficult?" Before he could answer, she turned to him. "Why didn't you tell me before?"

"Because he waited until you left for Inverness to tell me that you'd chosen your pride over me." He turned, looking through the window as if the view of the forest was captivating. "What was I supposed to do? Beg you to return?"

"You think it was pride that made me leave?"

"What else? I think it's the core of you. You're not simply a woman. You're Shona Imrie, the last female of the Clan Imrie. You have a position to maintain, an image to uphold."

He faced her. "It wasn't just your pride at work, Shona, but his. You wouldn't have liked the military. You would have chafed to return to Gairloch. So the two of you, filled with pride, warred with each other."

"And you were the one caught in the middle, is that it?"

He only smiled at that thought.

She held herself very still, her hands clasped in front of her. Her lips were still reddened from their kiss.

"You must hate me," she said.

"I hated you for a very long time," he heard himself saying. Words that bobbed up from the depths of his heart. A sentiment he wasn't even conscious of having, let alone expressing.

Surprise replaced the misery in her eyes. "Do you still?"

"It was Fergus who told me you were to be married," he said. "You lost no time encouraging the earl."

"I'd met Bruce before," she said.

"Evidently, he was quite the eager suitor."

Her face was oddly pale, as if the truth was a death-blow. He wanted, in that moment, to go to her and hold her, an idiotic impulse he didn't fulfill. He might lust after her, but he didn't trust her.

"You've no pride at all, is that it?"

"I loved you, but what I felt for you was purely love. It wasn't confused with status or title or pride." He hesitated a moment. Should he tell her the whole truth? "Loving you," he said, deciding that all of it must be aired, or none of it, "added to my life. When I decided that I needed to stop loving you, it made my life duller, but it didn't change me."

When she didn't respond, he smiled again. "Love isn't simple for you, Shona. It's twisted up in other emotions."

She turned, but before she could leave, he spoke to her back.

"You can live without love. But it's like color or flavor or music. It makes life something better, something worth experiencing."

She glanced back at him. "And that's what I was? Color or flavor or music?"

He thought of those years, his smile fading. "You were a rainbow," he said. "A feast. A symphony."

Then, she was gone, and he was done with confession, and freed of the truth, as well as the pain he'd held inside for years.

Chapter 18

Shona felt drained, as if she'd indulged in a fit of weeping. She had too many things to do to take time out to feel sorry for herself. Or perhaps she simply didn't want to think about what Gordon had said.

He'd known.

He'd known what his father had done and had seen it as a test, one she'd failed miserably.

Anger was a better emotion than despair.

She'd been his rainbow.

Had she failed him in some way? Was he right?

What did it matter, now?

Dear one—how long had it been since she'd heard those words, said in just that tone? Seven years.

Was he right? Had it been her pride? It hadn't felt like pride at the time. Hurt, that's what it had been. Pain and shame, that she couldn't be more than she was. Shona Imrie, once of the proud Imries, now destitute.

At the secret door, she grabbed the lamp, retrieved the box of matches tucked in the drawer in the base, and lit it again. She felt as if she'd aged forty years as she retraced her steps through the passages. In the library, she replaced the lamp on the table and stood staring at the wall, replaying the scene in the cottage.

When she'd asked him if he still hated her, Gordon hadn't answered.

She wanted to retreat to her bed, but that would be the act of a coward. For all her flaws and failings, she wasn't a coward. Rash, reckless, perhaps engaging in behavior that wasn't entirely ladylike—she would confess to all that. But she'd always faced the circumstances full-on and never backed down from a challenge.

Even if the challenge made her skin cold and her stomach lurch.

What she really wanted to do was go have a good cry, but she knew the minute she did, Helen would probably enter the room and want to know what was wrong. Or Helen would see her swollen eyes afterward, and be too curious to remain silent. For all of Helen's attributes, sometimes she cared too much.

She was supposed to lead Miriam around Gairloch this morning, but she hoped the Americans had forgotten. Instead, she went in search of Fergus. Thankfully, she found him easily, in the conservatory. He was sitting on one of the stone benches watching as Old Ned slept, fully clothed, on an adjacent bench, a half-empty bottle of whiskey cradled in his arms.

"Sometimes, I think he has the right idea," Fergus said, glancing up at her. "Maybe that's what I need to do. Remain sotted by day and night, buried in a bottle."

She sat on the bench and surreptitiously studied Fergus. His face was pale, and there was a white line around his lips. Navigating around Gairloch was difficult for him. He'd proven himself to be courageous to a fault, but sometimes, courage could be wearing.

She hoped he'd be brave enough for the truth.

They couldn't possibly have a party, a welcoming ball for Miriam and her father. Nor was there any need to do another inventory of the larder and pantry. No matter how often she counted it, the results were the same. The food was going to run out before the Americans left.

Now was the time to address their finances, but she found that she couldn't do it, not with the look on Fergus's face. He was three years older, but she felt absurdly maternal toward him right at the moment.

She placed her hand on his upper arm, patting it with a silly little gesture. Nevertheless, he glanced at her and smiled, obviously an effort but one she appreciated.

"We'll get through this," she said.

"Will we?"

She nodded.

"Do you think I'm proud, Fergus?" she asked.

Her brother laughed.

She frowned at him.

"What about arrogant?"

"You're an Imrie, Shona," he said kindly. "All Imries are proud and arrogant."

She didn't say anything for a moment. "That hardly makes us easy to deal with, does it?"

Dear God, what if Gordon was right? Could he be right? Had she allowed her pride to dictate their futures?

For now, however, what she felt for Gordon must be pushed to the background.

Old Ned still hadn't roused, and she watched him now, so utterly peaceful as he snored.

"What do you think he does all night?"

"Drinks," Fergus said. "Then he sleeps so he can get up and drink some more."

"I don't remember him drinking that much when we were younger."

"Maybe he didn't. Or maybe we just didn't notice."

Perhaps she should take up whiskey as well. Would she sleep better? Surely she wouldn't worry as much.

She sat back on the bench, looking around her. Once, her mother's garden had provided cut flowers for all the public rooms at Gairloch. Since her death, however, there hadn't been the staff to keep it fertile and weeded.

The conservatory, however, seemed to thrive on being abandoned. The plants and small trees that grew there did so in glorious profusion, stretching their emerald arms toward the clear glass walls and domed ceiling.

This was Gairloch's newest room, a present from her father to her mother. Knowing of his wife's liking for puttering in the garden, and her equal dislike for cold winter days, he'd commissioned the octagonal addition to be built just beyond the library.

The floor was made of the same stone as the rest of the castle, fitted with cunning drains at the corners and in the center of the room. In the middle was a pool, nearly four feet tall, adorned with a figure of a woman pouring water from a large amphora. Her father always joked that the sculptor had been so taken by her mother that he'd fashioned the statue in her likeness.

She hadn't had time to clean this room, and perhaps it was suffering a little from neglect. The pool should be drained and scrubbed, because there was an odor emanating from it. The fountain hadn't worked for years, and perhaps if it had, the water wouldn't be stagnant. Some of the larger plants had dropped leaves and they lay abandoned on the stone floor.

Would the Americans bring Gairloch back to its former glory?

"I always thought we led an enchanted life," she said. "That nothing could ever happen to us."

"It didn't, until we left Gairloch," Fergus said. "Maybe Gairloch's enchanted, and not our lives."

She turned to look at him. "Did you ever think we'd be here now? You, a decorated soldier, and me, a widow?"

"A countess," he corrected.

A pauper countess.

"Fergus, about the party—" she began.

"It's little enough to make up for you behaving like a child, Shona."

Both the words and his tone silenced her.

She finally stood, then leaned down and kissed his cheek, wishing that the truth wasn't suddenly a wall between them.

She left the conservatory, mounted the stairs, and caught sight of Elizabeth Jamison. Sometimes, Providence provided exactly what she needed at exactly the right time. In this case, the nurse.

She'd never before interfered in Fergus's life. But Fergus had never before gone to war or returned badly wounded. Nor had she ever seen him so dejected, so much so that she couldn't bear it. Something had been bothering him since he returned from India. Something that now had a name and a face.

"I need to speak with you," she said to Elizabeth.

She headed for the Winter Parlor where her mother used to sit and sew. This room, also, had not been cleaned or readied for visitors, but at the moment, it simply didn't matter. She glanced back once to see if Elizabeth was following. She was, but with a look on her face that indicated that the other woman didn't anticipate a conversation between the two of them.

She waited for Elizabeth to join her, then shut the door firmly behind the nurse.

"I need to know why my brother is so miserable when you're around," she said.

Elizabeth folded her arms on top of her pristine blue apron and simply stared at Shona as if she were one of the ghosts of Gairloch.

She exhaled a breath impatiently, walked to the settee by the window, and sat in a gesture that was less ladylike than impatient.

"Between you and Fergus, I've never seen such examples of obstinacy."

"What does Fergus say?" Elizabeth asked.

"Nothing," Shona said. "Because I haven't asked him."

"But you feel compelled to ask me?"

She motioned to the end of the settee, but Elizabeth remained standing.

"Ever since Fergus returned from India, he's been a different man. I thought, at first, it was his injury that caused him to be so moody. But it wasn't until we came to Gairloch that I realized it could be something else. You."

Elizabeth walked to the window, staring out at the view. "I don't know how to address a countess," she said softly.

"You call her Shona."

Elizabeth glanced over at her. "Mr. Loftus would not approve."

Shona made a face. "How you can abide the man, I haven't the slightest idea." But she came back to the point. "What is it between you two?" she asked, wondering if Elizabeth would confide in her.

Would she have spoken to anyone about Gordon? No, she wouldn't.

She stood, walking to the other side of the room. At the last moment, before she opened the door to leave, she turned back to face Elizabeth.

"Fergus is the only family I have left," Shona said. "I would do anything to spare him pain."

Elizabeth turned to face her. "He's walking quite well with his cane."

Shona folded her arms. "Not physical pain, Elizabeth, but that of the heart."

"Can you spare another person pain of the heart?"

The other woman's smile was barely an expression at all, but it held such sadness that she almost felt sorry for Elizabeth.

"I suppose you can't," she admitted.

"I don't wish to cause your brother any type of pain at all."

Shona returned to the settee and sat. "How did you meet him?"

Finally, Elizabeth said, "He came to visit his men. Every day, if he could. I warned him that it wasn't safe. We were losing men from diseases more than their wounds. But he still came. Only later did I begin to suspect that it wasn't just for his men."

She remained silent, letting Elizabeth speak.

"When I could, I met him in the garden." Elizabeth's smile was more genuine now. "Not really a garden, just a strip of grass with a few hearty flowers someone had coaxed to grow and a bench. Still, it was better than being in the hospital. For a little while, you had a feeling of hope, that death didn't win everywhere."

Shona sat up straighter, folding her hands in her lap. "How did you bear it?" she asked.

Elizabeth glanced at her.

"I wanted to do something to help."

Shona nodded. "When I cared for my husband in the last two years of his life, I felt the same. Yet some days were horrid."

"Most of my days in Sebastopol were like that," Elizabeth said. "We lost so many men that a day didn't go by without wagons carrying coffins up Cars Hill. But then, there were other times when a man we didn't think would live through the night rallied at dawn."

Elizabeth faced the window again. "You learn to take the smallest things and treasure them for the joys they are, and try to ignore the most awful things."

Shona nodded, feeling a curious connection to the other woman.

"I think one of the things that made it more difficult with my husband," she said, "was the fact that I knew there was no other result. It was a long, slow descent into death. All I could do was make the journey easier for him." She looked at Elizabeth, wondering if she should add that it was the first time she'd talked of Bruce's illness to anyone, even Helen. "I admire what you did."

Elizabeth only smiled, still staring out the window. "I felt good nursing. I felt clean."

Something about her demeanor kept Shona silent.

"Fergus is the Laird of Gairloch." Elizabeth stretched out her hands as if to encompass the entire castle. "And he's won the Victoria Cross."

Before Shona could speak, she added, "Did you know they decided to award the Victoria Cross to only one officer? Even though six officers had been selected to receive it, they all voted to give it to the one man who most epitomized gallantry and bravery. Fergus. A unanimous vote, I understand."

"How did you know that?" Shona asked, surprised.

Elizabeth shrugged, an embarrassed little smile curving her lips. "I made it a point to discover what I could after the Ninety-third left the Crimea. I wanted to make sure he was all right."

"At the moment, he's miserable."

Elizabeth didn't respond to that comment.

"I think my brother feels something deeply for you, Elizabeth. Even I can see that. Why else would he walk out of a room when you enter or refuse to look at you? And why do you ignore him so completely?"

She didn't know the way to convince Elizabeth, but she suspected it wasn't going to happen because of this conversation.

"Is it his leg? Is it because he was wounded?"

To her credit, Elizabeth looked shocked. "Of course not."

"Then, if you can't feel anything for Fergus, at least don't hurt him. He doesn't deserve that."

"Then you'll not interfere." Elizabeth's gaze was steady.

She only nodded, leaving the room and Elizabeth, wishing she'd never said anything, and feeling uncomfortably that she might have done more harm than good.

Chapter 19

~~~⌒⌒~~~

Magnus Imrie gave Brian MacDermond the land on which he built his house, as well as extending the hospitality of Gairloch for him and his clan—small though it was—until his house was finished. The land he wanted to buy, but Magnus wouldn't have it, saying it was his way of paying Brian back for saving his life in battle.

Brian saw her the second hour he was at Gairloch. He remembered the time well, marked it in his mind to remember. His own wife was standing next to him when Anne Imrie entered the Clan Hall. She stopped, blinked at him as if struck by the same overwhelming sense of knowing him, and then walked forward, a warm and welcoming smile gracing her lovely face.

He'd married Fenella when he was but a boy, but they'd worked well together. He had a fondness for her that was deeper than friendship, since she'd labored to bring their son into the world and supported Brian whatever his decisions.

At that moment, however, he knew that what he felt for his wife would never be enough for him. Not when the pain of loss struck him dumb even then.

As Elizabeth sat at the breakfast table the day after her talk with the countess—Shona—she wanted to counsel her patient that he wasn't eating according to his doctor's orders. But Mr. Loftus was annoyed, enough that she stored away her lecture for later.

Fergus wasn't at the table, displeasing Mr. Loftus, who wanted to ask him about the secret passages. When he grumbled about Fergus's absence, Miriam offered to go in search of him. The girl needed a chaperone. Or a governess. She didn't need to be alone with a handsome man in this cavernous castle. Mr. Loftus didn't look any more pleased than she felt when Miriam left the room.

Elizabeth almost wanted to warn Fergus that he was about to be assaulted by Miriam's charm. The girl had little decorum when it came to flirting. Miriam would flirt with a coachman if it occurred to her or would gain her something in the end.

Her mother would have called the girl a right little strumpet. But, then, her mother would have probably said the same about her, tending men's wounds and needs and not being married to any of them.

The work at Scutari and in the Crimea was a world away from this magnificent castle in the Highlands. Even working for Mr. Loftus was a pleasure compared to those days of laundry and scrubbing floors, long before they were allowed to even treat the wounded.

When Fergus had arrived at the Barracks Hospital, the very air felt different. He would stop and speak to each of his men, but his eyes would seek her out. He'd smile, just that, and her heart would flutter.

She pushed away thoughts about Fergus Imrie, wishing she'd known they were coming to his home before they'd arrived. Mr. Loftus, however, was very close-mouthed about his affairs. Or perhaps he simply didn't think it important to share details with her, since she was only his nurse.

A position that had seemed heaven-sent when she'd

applied for it in London. Her experience in the Crimea had seemed to impress the American and his bodyguard as well.

In truth, Helmut was more than a bodyguard. He cared for Mr. Loftus, pushing his wheelchair up steep inclines and carrying the man where his chair could not be accommodated. Why Mr. Loftus had not unpacked his enormous wheeled chair from the rear of the carriage was another question she was not to ask. Along with how long, exactly, they were to remain at Gairloch.

She wondered, sometimes, why Mr. Loftus had bothered to hire a nurse when Helmut performed most of the duties. And why bother to pay her, when he didn't listen to her cautions about his diet or the amount of spirits he consumed?

Without his chair, movement was difficult for him. Walking was a slow progress from room to room, and more than once, she'd been worried about him making it up and down the steep curved steps. Did Helmut carry him down the back stairs? That seemed almost too personal a question to ask.

"Tell me about your relationship with the laird," he said, startling her.

Two people in two days were suddenly very interested in her affairs. She could understand the countess's—Shona's—concern—but why was Mr. Loftus asking?

She laid her fork down on the edge of the plate. Cook had served her a fried egg, rashers, black pudding, and a potato scone this morning, as if she needed fattening. Her childhood, however, had taught her never to turn down a meal because the next one might be a long time coming.

"I've already spoken of it," she said, hoping he wouldn't press the matter.

"Is he a cad?"

She felt a surge of anger on Fergus's behalf. "Of course he isn't."

Mr. Loftus nodded. "I'll not have my Miriam associate with a cad."

"I was under the impression that Miriam was to be married," she said carefully.

He nodded again. "Until the day, there's always a better offer. A deal's not done until it's done."

Surprised, she stared at him. Was he thinking of pairing his daughter with Fergus?

Now, she really did want to warn him.

"We'll go to the Clan Hall," he said, pushing himself out of the chair.

Helmut nodded to her, his eyes dark and cold. The man disturbed her, but she couldn't say exactly why. Perhaps it was because he rarely spoke of his own volition. He didn't seem to have an opinion on anything. Whatever Mr. Loftus wanted, he did silently and with complete obedience.

Could a man's will be purchased along with his labor?

Why was she here? Hadn't she done the very same thing? But she'd been desperate for employment, and the American's salary was too good to turn down.

They left the dining room for the Clan Hall, Elizabeth silent behind the two men. She didn't ask why he was set for the larger room when he'd made himself at home in the library. Ever since he'd employed her in London, she'd discovered it was better not to ask Mr. Loftus any questions at all.

A few moments later, she watched as he directed Helmut to begin poking the section of wall that had opened when Shona had played ghost.

"It's got to be here someplace," Mr. Loftus said from his perch on one of the benches Helmut had moved in front of the fireplace. He pointed his finger at a likely-looking brick.

Elizabeth stood behind him, glancing toward the doorway occasionally, wishing that either Fergus or the countess would appear.

"Should we be doing this, sir?" she asked finally. "It's a family secret."

"I won't be put off by that chit," he said, annoyed. "If I buy her castle, then she'll tell me the secret? I'll not buy a pig in a poke."

She couldn't imagine Mr. Loftus ever being cheated by anyone, but surely the countess had a right to retain the knowledge of the secret passages until such time as Mr. Loftus purchased Gairloch.

"Perhaps the laird will tell you where the passages are," she said.

Miriam, however, hadn't returned with Fergus, a fact that Mr. Loftus didn't seem to notice. Where were they?

"Then go and find her," he said.

Evidently, like Helmut, she was to have a myriad of duties: nurse, peacemaker, and now chaperone.

An autumn day in the Highlands was the perfect place to be, last night's storm clearing the air. The ground was soggy, so Fergus had to watch his step, but even so, he couldn't imagine a more glorious day. The sky was a clear blue, the winds were blowing cold, stinging his eyes and chilling his skin. He should have worn a coat, but he didn't retreat back into Gairloch, enjoying the day too much for caution.

He stood in his mother's garden, long since gone to ruin. The weeds looked hardy, however, some of them almost as lovely as flowers.

One day, he'd take on the chore of readying the beds

again. When he was feeling more up to it. When his damn leg didn't ache all bloody day.

For now, he envisioned a future that could be, instead of a past he hadn't enjoyed.

Most men thought the army too regimented, but it had been exactly the opposite for him. His life had been too uncertain, never knowing where he'd be tomorrow. Would he be fighting in some damn hot place where he hadn't understood the culture, the language, or even the reason they were there? Or freezing his arse off in Russia?

No, he wanted certainty to his life, and Gairloch offered that to him. A line of permanence stretching back three hundred years.

He could see himself living here with the woman he loved, with their children laughing and playing throughout the castle. He'd teach them about their heritage. Sit them down in the library and oversee their study of the most famous books. Take the shields and spears down from the walls in the Clan Hall and allow each to hold them for a bit while he talked about the men to whom these weapons had belonged.

None of that would come to pass if Gairloch was sold.

Somehow, he had to convince Shona that more money wasn't the answer. Somehow, she'd have to come to grips with her memories of Gordon and realize that they could do very well at Gairloch with a bit of inventiveness.

"Have you seen Miriam?"

He didn't turn at Elizabeth's voice. Instead, he took a deep breath, wondering at the sudden rapid beat of his heart. His mind might realize that she'd rebuffed him, but his body had yet to understand.

"No," he said. "I haven't seen her."

She didn't say anything for a moment, but he could sense her growing closer.

"I think it would be better if you weren't alone with her," she said.

He turned, angling his foot correctly so no further pressure was put on his leg. He wasn't about to either wobble or fall in front of Elizabeth.

"Why, does she have designs on me?" he asked, forcing a smile to his face.

"I think she does," she said.

A curl had loosened from her coronet and he stared at it as if it were a magical tendril of hair. If he held it in his hand, would it wind around his fingers, ensnaring him as ably as Elizabeth had?

"I doubt Miriam Loftus would settle for a cripple," he said.

"I thought you a smarter man than that, Fergus Imrie," she said, frowning at him. "First of all, Miriam Loftus is a child. A cunning child, but no more than that. She toys with people because it amuses her to do so. Secondly, you're no more a cripple than I am." She surveyed him with a scorching look that took in his windblown hair and traveled down his body to his feet.

Even in the army he'd never been inspected so thoroughly. Or left to feel so lacking.

He had only one recourse—to retaliate. "Why did you never answer my letters?"

She twisted her hands together, looking down at them as if they held the answer to his question.

"Miss Nightingale told us not to form attachments. Men would come to think of us as angels, and imbue us with traits we didn't have. They'd fall in love with us out of gratitude."

"I wasn't your patient," he said. "And it wasn't out of gratitude. Perhaps it was due to lunacy, instead."

She glanced at him, her eyes widening.

"I was an idiot," he said.

She nodded.

"An absolute besotted fool. Who's exceedingly grateful that you've pointed it out to me."

She nodded again, her face carefully expressionless.

"Be careful of Miriam," she said. "And Mr. Loftus. I think he might prefer to marry into Gairloch rather than having to buy it."

He smiled, grateful to her for giving him a source of amusement.

"I could do worse than to marry her, don't you agree? Mr. Loftus could take himself back to America and leave me a very wealthy bride."

Without another word, she turned and left him.

By mid-morning, Gordon had arranged most of the crates and bags on one side of the cavernous floor of the Works.

He'd already received a shipment of potassium, but he'd paid double in freight what the material had cost. Once the dock was built, supplies could be sent directly from Inverness via the River Mor to the loch.

The Invergaire Works was ideally suited for a large production facility. He wished some of the staff were still employed, but the general had shut down the Works when he was in India, a way of demonstrating his power. Why not? He'd been safely in London while Gordon was in India.

Rani wasn't here yet, the tardiness surprising him. Today, they'd put the final touches on the explosive formula.

He walked to the other side of the workspace, hearing his boots echo throughout the space. In shape and structure, the Invergaire Works was not unlike Inverness Station, tall gabled roofs supported by metal beams and struts. The only difference was in the two smokestacks and the matching furnaces on the work floor.

He went to one of the furnaces on the far side of the building, opening the front metal door and allowing the heat to escape. Today, they'd begin to melt one of the ingredients in their blasting powder. Each step would have to be done using an infinitesimal amount of material due to the danger. Rani had already briefed him on the cautions.

The scurrying sounds indicated that they would need to rid the place of vermin. He'd also have to get around to cleaning some of the windows, but for now he wanted to rid the work floor of debris and accumulated signs of neglect. He grabbed the broom from its storage space and began to sweep, taking pleasure in this small task.

Each step was part of the journey, not only to making his own life, but to bringing a new industry to Invergaire Glen. Nothing was too small or too onerous a task. He wasn't, as his father had been, above certain chores. Need his boots shined? Have a subaltern do it. Need a glass of wine? Wave to his aide to attend him.

General MacDermond had been surrounded by men whose main function in life was to ensure that he was fed, shaved, outfitted, and made comfortable.

Not one of them had attended his funeral.

He heard another sound and glanced up, facing the one person he'd never thought to see.

Shona stood just inside the door, a shawl covering her shoulders and clasped by her gloveless hands.

"You should be wearing something more substantial," he said. "It's cold this morning."

She only nodded.

"Has something happened?"

She shook her head.

"What's wrong, Shona?" The silence wasn't like her.

He leaned the broom against the wall and began to walk toward her.

"Nothing," she said. She remained in place, her hands clasped around the ends of her shawl.

"Then why are you here?"

She looked around the Works, her eyes scanning from the floor to the ceiling.

"I've never been here before," she said. "All these years. Isn't that odd?"

"There was never a reason. Besides, it was dangerous."

She glanced over at him.

He told himself it wasn't fear he saw in her expression. Shona Imrie was rarely afraid. She turned in a slow circle as if the empty building was noteworthy.

"How did you get here?" he asked, wondering if she'd answer that question.

"I walked."

"You walked?" It was a good two miles to the Works from Gairloch.

She nodded.

"Why are you here, Shona?" he asked again.

"Mr. Loftus is waxing eloquent about his Scottish relatives in the library," she said. "With Helen as his audience. Miriam is complaining that she's cold and Elizabeth is eyeing everyone as if they're perched on the edge of illness. Fergus? He's taken himself off somewhere, again."

Not quite an answer, but he didn't challenge her.

She turned and walked away from him, keeping as much distance between them as she could. Even from here, he could smell her perfume, as if it trailed behind her like a scent marker. Very well, he'd be the hound to her fox.

But he wasn't going to beg for answers.

As she glanced over her shoulder at him, he modified that thought. Perhaps he would, after all.

In his hands was a broom, and his simple act of sweeping the floor had rooted her to the spot. She'd never seen Fergus do such a thing. Or her father. Or even Bruce. But Colonel Sir Gordon MacDermond was engaged, and happily so, if the look on his face was correct, in cleaning.

A lock of hair had fallen against his brow. He'd rolled up his sleeves to the elbow and there was dust on his black trousers and on the toes of his boots.

The sounds of her breathing seemed to echo in the cavernous space. She turned, the hem of her skirt swirling over the dust and looked around her, amazed at the emptiness and the sheer size of the Works.

But the strangeness of her environment was not what was keeping her silent now.

He was.

She forced herself to face him. "Do you still hate me?" she asked, a question that had been festering for days.

He looked surprised. "No," he said, beginning to smile. "I don't."

Did he feel anything for her?

His look was grave and steady, but she didn't back down.

"I need to ask you something," she said, daring herself.

He remained silent.

She'd come to appeal to Gordon for money. Now she couldn't. How could she? He stood there looking strange and familiar all at once. The boy buried in the man. A strong, well-built man who intimidated her just a little.

She shook her head and began to make her way back to the door.

He covered the distance between them with a few strides, grabbing her arm before she could leave.

"What is it, Shona?" he asked, his tone impatient. His grip, however, wasn't punishing. She could pull free if she wished.

He turned her to face him, placed his fingers beneath her chin, and gently urged her face up until she was looking at him. *Dear one.* He'd not been the only one to use that term. She'd always thought of him that way, until it was simply easier to hate him.

In the silence of the Works, she felt the past push in, over the barriers she'd erected, and into her mind and her heart. She felt swamped, overcome, and near tears.

Dear one. Do you like this? A kiss at the base of his throat. *Dear one, I love touching you.* Her fingers stroking his penis softly until he moaned. *Dear one, please, now.* Her body arching as he entered her, the teasing forgotten.

Seven years ago, he'd not yet gone away to war. Seven years ago, Fergus hadn't yet joined the army, since he'd lacked the funds to purchase a commission. Seven years ago, she was madly in love, and nothing was as important as this man.

She wished it were possible to turn back time, to give her a respite from this world, this life, and this existence. For a moment, she wanted to forget, to roll back the years, and pretend they hadn't happened. *Please*, and it was a solicitation to God or Providence, Fate, or any greater power, *let it be seven years ago.* Let her be Shona Imrie, not the widowed Countess of Morton. She wouldn't have experienced a marriage steeped in boredom and regret, and filled with hidden longings that kept her on her knees beside her bed in desperate prayer.

Or if that couldn't happen, then for a little while give her something to assuage her thirst, ease her hunger: a cup of water in the desert, a loaf of bread.

Or Gordon.

The minute she touched him, she'd be lost, incapable of thought. She wanted to study him, take in the perfection of his body, note the way the morning sun streamed in through the high windows and played across the planes of his face.

She wanted, dear God, to feel him.

She should run as far and as fast as she could. Instead, she stood where she was, drinking in the sight of him, feeling herself weaken, and tremble, and wildly excited about her own disgrace.

Chapter 20

Instead, she approached him. With slow, measured steps, she walked toward temptation, her body recognizing both want and need in the figure of Gordon MacDermond.

One step took her closer, until her shoes met the toes of his boots. A single slight sway, and her skirt flirted with the wool of his trousers.

Slowly, she placed her hand flat against his shirt. A simple white shirt created by a meticulous tailor, with almost invisible stitches and bone buttons. Had the tailor known that he would be covering a chest shielding a heart beating so steadily and with such honor? Had he known that one day, a woman would wish to tear the shirt off, uncaring for his hours of labor or the cost of the material?

Love me.

Words she'd often said, but never on this spot. Words that sounded too risky now. She gently placed her fingers on his cheek, traced the angle of his jaw, his cheekbone. She couldn't look into his eyes, keeping her gaze on her fingers. But the feel of him was the same. Warm skin, smooth from his morning shave. The almost dimple beside his mouth seemed to encourage her touch.

She stood on tiptoe to kiss him there.

At his sharp intake of breath, she smiled. He felt the

same, then, trapped inside restraint, desperate to break the shell that protected the people they'd become from the people they'd once been.

Her heart expanded, the joy she felt unexpected and shocking. She placed both hands against his chest, her fingers stretching up to his shoulders.

"No one ever kissed me the way you did," she softly said, pressing a kiss to his shirted chest. Beneath it, his heart beat as fiercely as hers.

Slowly, he lowered his head, waited until she lifted her head, then touched his lips briefly to hers, coaxing her mouth open. This was new and different and yet so familiar that her heart ached with remembrance. How many hours had they spent knowing each other's kisses? Testing what each other liked until their breaths were hot and their pulses raced.

Perhaps a woman never forgot her first lover. Or her first love.

Without saying a word, she unbuttoned one of his buttons, the one at the very top.

His hand slapped against hers.

She raised her gaze to his. In his look was a warning, and something else, a spark of hunger.

Wiggling her fingers out from under his hand, she continued on her task. An answer asked and given, yet no words passed between them.

He lowered his head, intent on doing the same to her. Sixteen buttons stood between him and her skin. A monstrous number of buttons, an almost impossible amount.

By the time she'd unbuttoned his shirt, however, he'd already finished with her bodice.

Twice, she glanced up at him. The first time, there was still that edge of caution in his expression. The second time, his cheeks had bronzed, his lips thinned.

Passion had always done that to him.

Her fingers were trembling as she loosened the last button and pressed her palms against the chest revealed by her explorations. Leaning forward, she kissed him on his bare chest, feeling both their hearts leap in excitement.

He made an inarticulate sound, grabbed her waist with both hands, and pulled her up to him.

Yes, kiss me. Please.

He was too slow. She framed his face with both her hands, held it still and placed her lips on his.

His mouth was hot, soft, and intensely talented. His breath was life. His tongue swept along her bottom lip, not in a gesture of coaxing as much as acquainting. A dance of the memory that was as seductive as his hands stroking her skin.

He pulled her with him, their feet dancing across the floor and into an alcove of sorts. She felt as if she couldn't breathe, her heart was pounding so quickly. And then breath didn't matter as much as the touch of him, the feel of his skin beneath her fingers. Her thumbs stroked his throat, pushed aside the shirt. She wanted, suddenly and desperately, to run her hands down his back, scratch at him with her nails, mark him so that he would always and forever remember her.

The tightness she felt inside loosened, became lax limbs, soft lips, and pooling warmth where she dampened from a single, lingering kiss.

He stripped her skirt and petticoat from her, tossing them anywhere; it didn't matter. She fumbled with the buttons of his trousers, annoyed when her fingers weren't as quick. His hand covered hers and he stepped back.

Don't question me now. Sanity might prevail. She might grow cautious once again when all she needed was this. Him.

Instead, he toed off his boots, unbuttoned his trousers, and stepped out of his clothing, all the while never moving his eyes from her.

Naked, he was even more beautiful than he'd been seven years ago. War had marked him, but it had also honed the shape of him. Muscular arms and thighs, a broad chest tapering down to a narrow waist. She ached to put her hands on his hips, splay them over his skin, reacquaint herself with the curve of each buttock.

But her eyes drifted to his penis, erect and unashamed.

As she watched, his hand brushed from the base to the tip, as if he pointed out the various attributes of such a marvelous weapon of pleasure. Please note the testicles, drawn up high beneath the nest of hair. See how the ridge along the engorged shaft pulses impatiently? Or how the mushroom-shaped tip, larger than she remembered, glistens in anticipation?

All for her.

The thrumming beat between her legs grew even stronger.

She slowly unlaced her corset, taking her time, teasing them both. He didn't move, content to stroke himself and watch her. His hands flattened against his thighs when she dropped her corset. After bending to grab the hem of the chemise, she pulled it over her head.

Bare now, her breasts throbbed, nipples hard.

Slowly, she removed her pantaloons, attired now in only her stockings and shoes.

He took one step toward her but she shook her head, the admonishment softened with a smile.

She removed her shoes, then bent to remove her stockings, one after the other. Unfastening one garter, she rolled down her stocking slowly. Then repeated the movement on the other leg. While he was still watching her, she approached him, a smile of anticipated delight curving her lips.

She was on her back, atop her clothes, before she could blink.

His arms bracketed her, hands spearing into her hair. He kissed her for long, endless moments, sending plumes of color behind her lids, making her breath race and her heart thud furiously.

His lips traced a path from one ear to the other. A kiss to her nose, to her closed eyelids, to her chin, and both cheeks. He'd never spoken Gaelic before, never murmured her name in such a fierce tone. Never said, "Dear one," as a punctuation for each kiss.

But he did now.

Tears hid behind her eyelids, dampening her lashes.

She wrapped her arms around him, hands flat on his back, feeling the power and the strength of his muscles. Widening her legs was an invitation. Today, she had no patience for more teasing, for slow, drugging kisses, or the sweep of his fingers over every inch of her body.

He raised up, positioning himself, his eyes never leaving hers.

Time seemed to still in that instant, as if this mating was somehow important. A moment to be heralded and remembered. Into her mind flooded all the memories of their loving when he'd worn that same expression, passion raging in his eyes.

Surrender had never been a necessary word between them. Instead, they'd come together equally matched, equally willing, equally passionate.

Nor was it changed now.

He surged into her, the force of their joining causing her to cry out, arch her head back, all the while gripping his shoulders with fingers transformed to talons.

All she could see or feel was him.

Dear one. Dear God.

Raising up, he kissed her, soothing her with a soft murmur, a promise in his eyes.

His fingers measured where he entered her, tested the welcoming slickness and danced along her folds.

Their gazes clung, each withdrawal coupled with a momentary feeling of loss, each thrust accompanied by a sigh of relief. Over and over, until it was too much, the sensations as pure and piercing as pain.

Her eyes fluttered shut when the peak came, when lightning flared behind her lids and pleasure held her heart still for one long, breathless moment.

His body convulsed on hers. A moment later, he kissed her temple and her cheek, his breath harsh in her ear. Her legs loosened around him, her feet lowering to brush his ankles. Her arms fell lax to the side, the backs of her hands brushing the dusty floor.

He kissed the dampness at the base of her throat, then the pulse there.

Silence ticked off the moments.

Words were perilous. They'd tossed so many words at each other of late, each one barbed and forked it was a wonder they didn't bleed to death from their conversations.

Her hand rose to rest against his back, the touch of him seeming to anchor her to this place, to the now of it. They were seven years older, but the connection was still there. So, too, the need that had knifed through her until it had been satisfied.

He'd taken her on the floor and she'd gone willingly.

Dear God, what had she done? Been unwise again.

"I've made another mistake, haven't I?" She stared up at the cobweb-draped rafters. "Coming here, first of all." Secondly, acting the strumpet.

He raised his head, but he didn't answer, his face set

in careful, noncommittal lines. Had he looked at his men in such a way? Had any of them been able to tell what he thought? She couldn't. Unless it was a whiff of contempt. That, she sensed only too well.

She gently pushed him away and he rolled over. Naked and spent, he was still beautiful. A work of masculine perfection, even his scars somehow decorating his body, not detracting from it.

She wanted to ask what the mark on his chest was from, or the one on his leg, but she didn't. He'd tell her or he wouldn't, but regardless of what he did, she would worry. For seven years she'd worried.

"Is there anywhere else you could be?" she asked softly. "Isn't there any duty that would take you to London? Or to Inverness? Or Edinburgh?"

"Shall I conveniently take myself off to war, the better to ease your conscience again?"

There it was again, seven years ago. Could they never get past that? Or not until she paid enough of a penance for it?

"I left Invergaire before you did."

"I remember," he said. "In fact, the recollection of those months is quite vivid."

"I can't do anything about seven years ago," she said. "I can't make things right. I can't undo my actions."

"No."

Such an ugly word, no. A sound, really, and little else.

"All I can do is concentrate on today."

She began to dress, donning her clothes more hurriedly than she'd removed them. She glanced down at her bodice to ensure it was buttoned correctly, arranged her cuffs, and pinned her hair back into place.

While she'd dressed, he had as well. His trousers were fastened but not the white shirt.

"Do I look presentable?" she asked.

He didn't answer, only nodded.

This man was a stranger, not the lover he'd been only a moment ago. So much the baronet that she asked, "What's it like being a baronet?"

"The same as being a colonel, or simply Gordon. I didn't change."

Yes, you did.

But she had, too, and perhaps that was the reason she suddenly wanted to weep, to flee from the Works and vow never to see him again.

The day had been an eventful one, the past marching back into Gordon's life and announcing in stentorian tones that it had never truly left.

Now he stood staring into the flames of the furnace as *if* they held the answer for his confusion. Despite the work he still needed to do, he couldn't stop thinking about Shona.

He'd been seduced. Not only had he gone willingly to his seduction, but he'd found himself stunned by the intensity of his response to her.

She wasn't the girl he'd known. He'd realized that when it was over and passion drained from him to be replaced by tenderness. She'd not teased him the way she had seven years ago. Instead, he'd seen sadness in her eyes, as if their loving had unleashed emotions she normally kept cloaked.

He'd been routed by her grief, left floundering on the bank like a salmon.

"The lady, she is gone?" Rani asked.

He turned to face his friend.

"The lady, she is gone," Gordon said. Refusing his offer to take her home, another example of the indomitable Imrie pride.

Had he hurt her?

"Many pardons for my tardiness," Rani said.

He began to button his shirt, glancing at Rani. "You weren't an audience to—"

Rani interrupted. "I saw the lady enter and did not do so myself. She is your lost love, is she not?"

Surprised, Gordon shook his head.

"I think, perhaps, she is. The woman who occupies your thoughts, to whom you wish to prove yourself." Rani smiled. "I, too, have such a woman. A blossom with deep brown eyes and lips that make me wish to kiss them."

He didn't know what to say to Rani's confession. An admission hardly seemed necessary since anyone could see how he acted around Shona. What kind of man takes a woman on a bare floor in the middle of a factory with no concern as to witnesses?

"I had an adventure last evening," Rani said. "It is why I am tardy. My room was in disarray. I believe someone thought to take my notes."

Surprised, he stared at Rani. "Did they?"

Rani bowed slightly. "I no longer take my notes with me," he said. "I keep them here," he added, tapping his temple with one finger.

"Someone wants to know what we've discovered," Gordon said.

"General Abbott, perhaps? He is with the army," Rani said. "They wish something, they take it."

As Rani should know only too well.

"Come and stay at Rathmhor," he said. "You'll be safer there."

"I am safe enough where I am," Rani said, shaking his head. "I am not known well, and I am left alone for the most part."

In other words, Rani preferred his privacy.

"Has no one in the village befriended you?" he asked.

The Scots were known for their hospitality, especially in Invergaire.

"I have talked at length with many men," Rani said. "Some are interested in who I am. Most are more interested in who I am not."

Rani was an expert at cloaking his words, but Gordon was getting better at deciphering what his friend didn't say.

"Prejudice is everywhere, Rani."

"This I know. I am not angry. I am different from your countrymen."

He put away the broom and headed for the office, Rani beside him.

"We're fortunate you were wise enough to guard your notes," he said.

"This is not the first time such a thing has happened," Rani said, not looking at him.

He stopped and faced the other man. "Why didn't you tell me?"

"I'm not entirely certain of it," he said. "Whoever was in my lodgings did not disturb much."

"Did they take anything?"

"This I do not know," Rani said in a subdued voice. "I do not write my notes from that night."

He couldn't think of a damn thing to say to reassure Rani, or himself.

We're interested in seeing what it can do. Abbott's words.

Just how far would the War Office go to obtain his blasting powder?

A surge of anger kept him silent. His superior officers had taught him restraint, especially in the presence of rampant stupidity. His own, in this case. First, he'd been effortlessly seduced, and secondly, he hadn't appreciated the threat General Abbott posed.

Which one was more dangerous: Shona or the War Office?

She hadn't worn her bonnet, and the wind was blowing briskly by the time she made it back to Gairloch. Her breasts ached, Gordon's seed was drying on her thighs, and shame spread over her skin like fire.

What had she done?

She hadn't even thrown up her skirts and asked to be taken. She'd taken off her skirts, instead. She'd been as naked as a babe in the Works, and allowed—no, solicited—her own abandonment on the floor.

The sight of Gairloch ahead was almost an admonition.

The sight of Fergus waiting on the road made her sigh.

"Have you been with Gordon?"

Did she even need to answer that? It should be written all over her face. Her lips still tingled with Gordon's kisses.

"I knew about the cottage," he said, startling her. "But I didn't say anything. I should have been a better older brother."

She kept walking, but slowed her pace so he could match it.

"What do you expect me to say, Fergus? That I was a foolish girl? I was." *And still am.*

"I thought you needed someone," he said. "Or maybe I just turned my back. But I won't allow it now, Shona. I'll have a talk with him."

She stopped, turning to face him. "You had a talk with him, before, didn't you?" Why had she never considered that? "You asked him to marry me, didn't you?"

"Why do you ask?"

She shook her head. "Don't avoid the question, Fergus. It's important. Did you?"

"If I had, what did it matter? He was going to do it himself. He loved you."

She turned and looked toward Gairloch. "It doesn't matter," she said, realizing it was the truth. "It doesn't matter at all."

She slowed her pace still more.

The fading sunlight flickered through the trees, tracking them. Sunset bathed the sky in orange, yellow, and blue as if reminding the world that night had nothing to recommend it in comparison.

"I'm not selling Gairloch, Shona," he suddenly announced.

She wasn't up to this conversation. She'd just bedded Gordon on the floor of the factory. Dear God, had she lost her mind?

"I want you to send the Americans away."

She stopped in the road and stared at him.

Fergus hadn't approved of her marriage; she knew that well enough. But in the last six months when she'd cared for him, their childhood bond had seemed repaired. Now, however, everything could come apart again, and all because of Fergus's love of Gairloch.

"You'll have to agree," she said, beginning to walk again. "I haven't any money."

"Surely, the bank will honor your credit," he said.

She glanced over at Fergus. How obtuse was her brother? Or was it her fault?

She stopped in the road again and faced him. "Gordon said that I treated you like a bairn," she said, wondering now if she had.

He looked startled at the comment.

"We should have had this conversation weeks ago. Months ago, perhaps." She blew out a breath. "I haven't any money in the bank, Fergus," she said. "I haven't had any money for nearly a year. There is no money anywhere."

"Don't be ridiculous," he said. "What about your portion from Bruce?"

"There isn't anything, Fergus. Bruce died penniless. I've been selling everything to buy food. I'm down to one bonnet, a lace-trimmed shift, and the clan brooch I can sell."

The look on his face was almost worth the mortification of admitting their dire straits.

"If you don't sell, we don't eat. It's as simple as that. I, for one, do not champion the idea of starving to death."

She strode ahead, desperate to be alone. She'd had about as much humiliation as she could tolerate for one day.

Chapter 21

Shona was tired, but sleep wouldn't come. Clanks and banging, and a distant hammering disturbed her sleep just as she was drifting off again. She tried to determine the source of the sounds. She'd been away from Gairloch for a number of years. Had these noises always been normal and she was just not accustomed to them?

She rolled over on her back, staring up at the ceiling. Perhaps she wasn't being kept awake by the noise as much as by her thoughts.

She'd made love with Gordon. In violation of sense, decorum, and decency, she'd bedded Gordon. No, not quite a bed. Not even a cot. A dusty floor. Why was she trying to pretend? She would have accepted a field of heather, prickly as they were.

She could still feel his touch on her skin, but then, she'd never been able to completely forget him. What did that make of her? A mental adulteress? Bruce had deserved better from her. In the end, when death had loomed, Bruce had held her hand, kissing her knuckles, and smiling at her with the last of his strength. "Thank you," he'd said, and those were the last words he spoke to her.

How could she have shamed herself so completely?

Because it was Gordon, and she'd always been a fool about him.

After another hour of tossing and turning, she finally realized she wasn't going to sleep. She sat up on the edge of the bed. Tonight, the moon lent a bluish glow to the shadows. She stood, pulled on her wrapper, and grabbed the oil lamp by its handle, hesitating outside her door.

Instead of heading toward Helen's room, she went in the other direction, taking the servants' stairs down to the first floor. The duties of companion did not extend to keeping her company when she couldn't sleep.

Perhaps a snack, something to drink. A little whiskey? Only if Old Ned had left a bottle about.

At the base of the stairs, the darkness was absolute. The lamp seemed almost abnormally bright, the yellow glow casting her shadow on the far wall. She moved it to her other hand so that the shadow fell behind her and was less of a presence.

Eight people slept above her—nine, if Old Ned was sleeping in the castle proper. Yet it felt as if Gairloch was deserted and almost otherworldly. Home to the specters of the past, the ghosts only a few acknowledged.

In this utter silence, it could easily have been three hundred years ago, when the Imrie Clan was at the height of their power. Or two hundred years ago, when their wealth was sufficient to support the entire clan. Or even a hundred years earlier, when their numbers had been decimated by the rising of Prince Charles, but their fortunes were still intact.

She heard a noise down the corridor, and stopped, holding her breath. Unlike the house in Inverness that groaned and moaned at night, each separate wooden strut singing in the darkness, Gairloch was made of stone. If she heard anything, it was either the ghosts or perhaps Old Ned, foraging for another bottle.

"Ned?"

She stood in the doorway of the Clan Hall. Shadows

fled before the oil lamp like frightened mice, but there was something wrong about the silence.

She heard the wail of a high note, sounding almost like the beginning of a piper's dirge. Stiffening her shoulders, she called out again.

"Ned?"

No one answered her, but something moved: a current of air, a drifting shadow.

The flame in the lamp flickered and she stopped, pressing her back against the wall. The feeling of something being wrong was even stronger now.

She wanted to pull her wrapper tighter around her body, scamper down the hallway, and race up the stairs to her bedroom. Instead, she stood there until she was certain nothing was moving in the darkness.

Her calm lasted until she heard another sound directly in front of her.

Someone was in the Family Parlor.

If Fergus's leg hadn't been bothering him, she would have summoned him. Or Helen. But Helen would have been too frightened, even with both of them investigating.

Perhaps it was only her imagination, coupled with a few fitful nights. Add Gairloch's atmosphere, and no doubt she'd conjured up something that wasn't there.

Be brave, Shona.

Talking to herself was hardly helpful. Did men do the same before going into battle? Had Gordon or Fergus? Had Gordon ever said to himself: *Don't scream. Don't make a fool of yourself, man.*

Somehow, she couldn't picture it.

She was Shona Imrie, the last daughter of the Imrie Clan. She had to do something. Racing to her bed would be the act of a coward.

Holding the lamp aloft in her left hand, she grabbed her

wrapper with her right and headed for the Family Parlor.

A shadow knocked the lamp from her hand, and as she was suddenly enveloped by it, her last thought was a curious one. Had she finally seen the ghost of Gairloch, or was she about to become one?

Someone was screaming. The sound speared through Shona's head, pinning her in place. She wished the woman would cease.

Was it raining?

She blinked open her eyes to find Helen kneeling over her, weeping.

"Oh, don't move, Shona," she said, pressing both hands against her shoulders.

She wanted to tell Helen that there was no need to hold her down; she couldn't move if she tried.

"Helmut's gone for Elizabeth," Helen said, another tear dropping onto her face. "Oh, dear Shona. Did you faint? Helmut said you fainted."

How ridiculous. She'd never fainted in her life. She would have told Helen so, but the effort to speak was suddenly too much. Instead, she had to make do with a slight wave of her hand.

Helen caught her fingers in a punishing grip as she rocked back and forth on her knees.

She was on the floor, evidently, since she could see the chandeliers of the Family Parlor above her. Turning her head slightly resulted in a lightning bolt of pain in the back of her head, as well as the sight of Fergus entering the room, followed by Elizabeth and Helmut. Another quarter turn in the opposite direction resulted in the vision of Mr. Loftus dressed in a garish plaid robe that had never been loomed in Scotland.

Only Miriam and Old Ned were missing from the tableau.

"What happened, Shona?" Fergus asked.

He lowered himself as far as he could without kneeling. His leg didn't bend well, and she knew if he got down on the floor next to her, he might very well need help to stand.

"I haven't the slightest idea," she said, which was the utter truth. "I couldn't sleep, so I came downstairs. I was going to get something to eat. I heard something in here and that's the last I remember."

Miriam entered the room then, standing in the doorway, and looking around her in bemused fascination. She rubbed at her eyes with one demure little fist, the gesture a child might make when first waking. But her hair was perfect, not netted or braided for bed. And the wrapper she wore was tied in an exact bow that spoke of deliberation and not haste.

Shona slowly looked around her, hoping to see something out of place. The only thing wrong in the Family Parlor was she, stretched out on the floor like a dead deer. She tried to sit up, but a wave a dizziness made her close her eyes and reassess the situation.

She opened her eyes when a cool hand was placed on her brow, to find Elizabeth looking at her intently. Her soft smile had vanished, the warm glance supplanted by a look of worry.

"What happened?" Elizabeth asked.

"She fainted," Helen said.

"I've never fainted a day in my life," she said.

Fergus had dragged a straight-back chair next to her, sat, and dropped his hand to hold hers. He glanced toward Elizabeth, but away when the nurse looked up. Elizabeth peeked in Fergus's direction, but he studiously avoided her gaze.

She'd never seen two people try so hard to ignore each other and fail so abysmally.

"Someone struck me," she said to Elizabeth, and turned her head gently.

Elizabeth carefully examined her, the nurse's indrawn breath a worry.

"Am I all right?"

"A cold compress, a little rest, and you shall be," Elizabeth said.

Gently, she pulled her hand free, testing a smile for Helen. It must have looked terrible, because Helen immediately began sobbing again.

"Really, I'm fine," she said, raising up on her arms. The distance from a supine position to a sitting one seemed too far to manage, especially since her head was aching abominably.

She looked toward Mr. Loftus, who was talking to Miriam too softly to be overheard. Evidently, he was giving her instructions to return to her room, because she abruptly turned and left the library.

So much for any concern Miriam felt. *Oh, did you fall, Countess? Are you feeling ill, Shona? Is there anything I can do?*

She shook her head, changed her mind about that decision, and bit back a moan with difficulty.

"Help me up, please," she said to Elizabeth, who was feeling the knot on the back of her head again.

The nurse grabbed an arm, supporting her back as she rose to a sitting position. Once she was upright, it took a few moments for her to acclimate herself to the sudden dizziness, and a few moments to realize that the oil lamp was sitting on a small table beside the door.

She hadn't put it there.

"I'm sorry you had an episode of dizziness, Countess," Mr. Loftus said. "It's a good thing I was around."

Slowly, her gaze traveled to Mr. Loftus.

Her stomach knotted.

"I didn't see you, Mr. Loftus."

"I came to get something to read, Countess and saw you there on the floor. Naturally, I fetched Helen."

The man could barely make it up the stairs on his own, and he expected her to believe he'd raced up them to summon her companion?

"It was indeed fortunate, Mr. Loftus," Fergus said, tapping her shoulder as if to recall her back to good manners.

"Are you absolutely certain someone struck you, Shona? Couldn't you have just fallen?"

She glanced at Fergus. What was the alternative? To pretend she'd fainted? Perhaps she should scream and wail like Miriam. Would that garner her any sympathy?

"Thank you," she said, looking over at Mr. Loftus. Her smile felt brittle, but evidently satisfied Mr. Loftus, because he nodded back at her.

She turned to Fergus. "I'm not certain what happened," she said, hoping that would be enough. She was not going to pretend to faint, even to appear proper and ladylike.

Helen stood, in earnest conversation with the American. Elizabeth and Fergus were still ignoring each other, and Helmut was at the door, staring down at her as if he'd discovered an incapacitated mouse on the floor. She wasn't entirely certain if he wanted to step on her or haul her up by her wrapper belt and dispose of her.

"Could you help me up?" she asked, and was assisted by Fergus, who grabbed one arm ineffectually, and Elizabeth, who was much stronger than anyone would suppose from her angelic appearance.

The two evidently brushed hands, because both of them jumped apart, causing her to bite her lip in impatience.

Once standing, she leaned against a chair, not feeling the least bit steady.

"I'm going to get Mr. Loftus a tray," Helen said. "Why don't you sit and rest here, Shona? I'll bring you some tea."

She slowly nodded, nearly falling into the nearest chair. As far as she was concerned, she wasn't going to move from the spot until she felt better.

"Do you always sleep fully clothed?" Fergus asked Elizabeth.

A sharp, indrawn breath was Elizabeth's only response.

Really, how much more of this was she to endure? Two obstinate people, each pretending the other didn't exist.

"You look as if you feel ill," Elizabeth said. "Shall we help you to bed?"

"No," she said. "A bit of tea and I'll be fine."

Or even some whiskey, if she could find a bottle Old Ned hadn't purloined, something to deaden this sudden, sharp pain in her head.

Helen disappeared into the labyrinth of the kitchen. Mr. Loftus took himself off to be waited upon, and even Helmut dissolved from his position by the door, leaving her alone with Fergus and Elizabeth.

"Someone struck me," she said.

Fergus turned and stared at her, but Elizabeth's reaction was far more interesting. She looked decidedly guilty.

"Earlier, Mr. Loftus was looking for the entrance to the secret passage," Elizabeth admitted. "I'm not certain if he found it. I was sent to find Miriam."

Fergus smiled. "A thoroughly charming young woman."

That comment was so odd that Shona frowned at him.

"You think she's an idiot," she said, ignoring Elizabeth's presence.

Fergus shrugged. "She's a wealthy idiot."

A horrible idea was taking root. "You aren't thinking of making a match with Miriam Loftus."

"Why is having a wealthy wife any different than a wealthy husband?"

They stared at each other.

"Did you resent my marrying Bruce?"

"To save me?" His lips twisted. "You could have married Gordon and saved yourself."

Surprise kept her speechless. Had he thought that all along? Bruce had been generous to her brother. Had Fergus resented that, too?

"Perhaps it's my turn to marry for money," Fergus said.

She stood, wobbling a little.

Something had to be done. Something now, before he gave any more credence to such an impossible notion.

"Fine," she said. "I'll go and flirt with Mr. Loftus."

Elizabeth's eyes widened.

"We'll have a test of it," Shona said. "Which Imrie can marry for money first."

Fergus frowned. "Don't be ridiculous."

Shona made her way from the room, an exit that might have been dramatic except for the fact that she needed Elizabeth's assistance. They left Fergus in the Family Parlor, no doubt planning his strategy for the hand of Miriam Loftus.

She really did feel horrible, and not all of it was because of the pain in her head.

Chapter 22

❧

S hona stood on the bluff overlooking Loch Mor. Busy white waves raced like children for the shoreline. A wintering wind tugged at her cloak, blew off her hood, and whipped her hair loose. Frantically, Shona grabbed at the mass of it, trying to stuff it back into some kind of order. Instead, it curled around her head, marking her as a plaything of the weather.

Twice now, she'd come to this exact spot and twice she'd turned away, the courage to walk down to Rathmhor slipping from her grasp like water.

Two days had passed since the accident in the Family Parlor. Accident—the word everyone called it. She knew it hadn't been an accident, and Elizabeth knew as well. The nurse had checked on her constantly the next day when Shona had taken advantage of the situation and simply remained in bed.

She would have still been there, with the sheets drawn over her head, if she hadn't been consulted on every single domestic crisis occurring at Gairloch. When Cook had appeared, nearly in tears, that had been the last straw. She'd had to get up, dress, and visit with Mr. Loftus, explaining that Cook didn't know how to cook eggs the way he liked them. This was Scotland, not New York, and surely he would like a nice bit of salmon for lunch?

As she left the Laird's Chamber, she realized that Fergus had more chance wooing Miriam than she had of tamping down her distaste for the very wealthy, over-indulged American.

Now, Mr. Loftus, Helmut, and Elizabeth were all in the library, Helen holding forth on the history of Scotland while Mr. Loftus pontificated about American history as counterpoint. Fergus was probably in the tower and Cook and Jennie were in the kitchen, which left her free to solve one of the problems confronting her.

She'd always had the ability to face the truth, even if it was unpleasant. Never before, however, had it tasted so bitter. She couldn't turn away today. No other option lay before her.

Her hand fisted, the jewelry in her palm biting into her skin. She only had one thing of value, and it was this, a brooch of diamonds and emeralds denoting the Imrie Clan crest, bequeathed to her on her mother's death.

Her stomach rolled at the idea of selling it, but now was not the time for sentimentality.

Wrapping her cloak more closely around her, she began walking toward Rathmhor when the ground rumbled with a dragon's roar. A plume of white smoke a thousand feet high shot up into the heavens, lighting the gray sky. Her feet trembled as the earth shook and, for an instant, she thought the world was ending.

Her ears rang with the explosion long after the sound ended. Wraithlike fingers of smoke swirled over her, the acrid smell becoming a taste. She coughed, waved a hand in front of her face and realized that Rathmhor was still obscured by a cloud of smoke.

Gordon was down there.

She began to run, her shoes easily finding the well worn path through the woods. Beneath the heavy boughs, the air smelled of winter. Past the cottage, to the other side of the trees, her heartbeats matching the rhythm of her running feet.

She halted on the road leading to the Works, on the other side of Rathmhor, her eyes wide, her face stiff with fear.

The smoke was being chased away by an impatient wind, but the smell lingered, a sharp odor that inflamed her nostrils, and coated the back of her throat.

Gordon was standing there, laughing.

Wrapping her cloak more closely around her, she slowed her pace to a walk, the fear transforming itself to calm, the calm changing to irritation, and irritation mounting to anger.

With Gordon was another man, one darker in countenance and shorter, whose laughter was as open and free. The two of them were attired in similar garb, white shirts and dark trousers, equally dirty.

They were staring at a deep pit in front of them, a hole so large it looked as if God had simply reached down and scooped out a handful of dirt.

She knew the minute they saw her because their laughter abruptly ceased.

He said something to the other man that she couldn't hear before turning toward her. Pasting a determined smile on her face, she walked toward him, stopping a few feet away.

"Did you do that?" she asked, gesturing to the hole in the ground. Her heart was still pounding, and she wondered if he could tell how afraid she'd been.

"Yes," he said, his voice sounding as carefree as a boy. "Or rather, Rani and I did." He put his hand on the other man's shoulder. "This is Rani Kumar, an expert at munitions. Rani, the Countess of Morton."

"Your Ladyship," Rani said, pressing his hands together prayerfully in front of him, and bowing from the waist.

She nodded, hoping to hide her confusion. She'd known that some of the East Indians had been friendly to Commonwealth troops, but to the extent that he would make his home in Scotland? What exactly were the two of them doing?

"I'm sorry if the explosion scared you," Gordon said.

"It startled us a bit, too," Rani added. "We weren't quite sure how large an explosion it would be."

She looked at both of them, not quite understanding. "But you set off the explosion even so?"

They both looked at each other, then at her before Gordon gave her a wicked, boyish, grin.

"We had to find out if we were right," he said.

"Did you not think you could be injured?"

His smile was slow, utterly charming, and equally maddening. "Were you worried about me?"

"Of course not," she lied, smiled in farewell to Rani, and turned on her heel, intent on leaving him.

She didn't hear his footsteps before he grabbed her elbow, and whirled her around to face him, forcibly reminding her of both his height and strength. She had to tilt her head back to look up to him and when she attempted to pull free of his grasp, he didn't release her.

"Were you worried about me?" he asked, his tone dropping, becoming low, almost seductive. If she were given to being seduced, she might have been charmed by his smile, but she wasn't.

However, she wanted, absurdly, to wipe his face free of dirt, especially a smudge on his upper cheek.

"No. I came to talk with you. Can you spare some time to speak with me?" she asked.

On her race to Rathmhor, she'd placed the clan

broach in her pocket. She felt for it now, reassured it was still there.

"Not at the moment, no," he said.

"It's important," she said. Honesty compelled her to add, "Perhaps not to anyone but me, but it is important."

The flicker in his eyes might have been surprise or something else. It was gone before she could tell.

He turned, leaving her to rejoin Rani. For a moment, she thought he'd simply dismissed her, but then they both glanced at her. An interruption, that's what she was, and if she wasn't devoid of ideas or time, she'd have turned and walked away.

How's that for pride, Gordon MacDermond?

Won't you be pleased to note how far I've fallen?

She wrapped her arms around herself, biting her lip to keep herself from saying something foolish. *Never mind, I'll find someone else. I wouldn't dream of disturbing your explosions.* Words that resounded in her mind, but never found a voice.

A person could suffer only so much shame until it became second nature. She was growing accustomed to humiliation. Besides, there was a certain freedom to being honest. Why should she try to portray herself as anyone other than who she was? The effort of doing so had been absolutely exhausting all these years.

He turned, finally, striding toward her, his face somber beneath the streaks of dirt. Rani was packing up the assorted items on the ground: rolls of paper, three small flasks, and a box whose contents were a mystery.

She suspected it would be better to leave it that way.

"Why are you exploding your land?" she asked when he reached her.

Gently, he turned her in the direction of Rathmhor rather than answer her. She gave a mental shrug, resigned to his silence. Evidently, she wasn't to ask him questions.

"It's a new invention, if you will," he said, almost to the door. "A new explosive. Too volatile in its current form, but when we have it perfected, it could be a revolutionary blasting powder."

"Why?"

He stopped, turned, and looked at her. "Why?"

She nodded.

"Why not?"

Hardly an answer, but he didn't apologize for it.

Opening the door, he stepped aside, allowing her to enter.

"I'll be with you in a few moments," he said, escorting her into the formal front parlor.

She nodded, turning to watch him. He hesitated at the door.

"I'm tired of war, Shona. If we can produce something other than black powder at the Works, I'd be pleased. I don't like feeling responsible for death. The new explosive can be used as a blasting powder. Not for killing."

She nodded again, stripped of speech by the passion in his voice.

Alone, she turned to survey the room.

All four walls were paneled in wood and polished to a gleam while the cove ceiling was oval in shape and painted brown. A cinnabar Chinese vase sat on a table beside an overstuffed chair upholstered in beige. A fireplace occupied the far wall, with two tall fireside chairs arranged on either side of it. A large portrait of Lieutenant General MacDermond hung over the mantel, dominating the room. Even in the likeness he looked stern and forbidding.

He knew exactly what he was doing, Shona. He was brilliant at ferreting out an enemy's weakness.

Had the general considered Gordon an enemy as well?

"Your Ladyship, how lovely you've come for a visit."

She turned to find herself facing a diminutive woman with a crown of white hair, her round face brightened by a welcoming smile.

"I'm Mrs. MacKenzie," the woman said, "the house-keeper. Sir Gordon asked that you be served refreshments. I've come to ask if you'd like scones or biscuits."

"That's not necessary, Mrs. MacKenzie," she said. "Truly."

She was here to beg, not be treated as a guest.

Mrs. MacKenzie, however, had the same look in her eyes as Helen when she was set on a point.

"It'll be no trouble, now, will it? Scones or biscuits?"

"Whatever is easier for you, Mrs. MacKenzie," she said, capitulating.

The housekeeper nodded, the smile once more in place.

When the housekeeper left, she walked to the window. From here, the tip of Loch Mor was visible, but not Gairloch, as if Rathmhor had turned its back on its nearest neighbor. The day was hinting at rain, and she wondered if the weather would interfere with Gordon's explosions.

Had he hated war so much?

She'd never talked to him about it. But then, she'd never told him how happy she was that he'd survived when so many others hadn't. Nor had she ever told him how much she'd prayed for him.

She glanced over at the portrait, making a face at it. The general would probably have been as happy with Gordon being martyred, as long as his sacrifice had been well publicized and posthumously awarded.

Three times she'd come to Rathmhor, each occasion remembered vividly. The first time, she'd come with her parents to celebrate the general's promotion. The second time, the Imrie family had arrived to mourn Gordon's mother's death. The third, she'd come alone in search of Fergus. Their aunt had arrived at Gairloch with news of their parents' death.

"You said you wanted to speak with me."

She turned to see him standing in the doorway.

"You've changed," she said, taking in his appearance. Another snowy white shirt, and pressed trousers. She missed his kilt. Was that something she should mention?

Not at the moment, perhaps.

"I didn't mean to disturb your explosion," she said.

"What is it, Shona?" he asked. "Fergus?"

She shook her head.

He entered the room but didn't sit. Instead, he stood with his back to one of the wood panels, his arms folded across his chest.

"Will you buy the clan brooch?"

"What?"

She pulled it out of her pocket. "The Imrie Clan brooch," she said. "The one from my mother. I need to sell it quickly, and I thought you might wish to buy it." She had to get the words out quickly before her courage left her. "I could sell it in Inverness, but the price might not be fair. Besides, I'd feel better if you had it, rather than sell it to a stranger."

"Why sell it at all?" He frowned at her. "Are you set on ridding yourself of everything that reminds you of your heritage, Shona?"

"Is that what you think?"

"What else is there? Fergus doesn't want to sell the castle, but you do. Does Fergus even know you're planning on selling the Imrie brooch?"

"It's mine," she said. "From my mother. I'm free to do with it what I will."

His mouth twisted. "You're still a Scot. Or are you trying to forget that, too?"

The truth was more difficult than she imagined.

She could leave now, walk out the door, and return to Gairloch. No one would know what she'd done. No one would ever know that she'd stood here, on the verge of tears, not angered as much as saddened.

Every word he said was true, but it was his version of the truth. What he saw, what he interpreted, what he believed. The reality of the situation was vastly different.

The knock on the open door was a welcome respite.

Mrs. MacKenzie stood there, directing a maid to place a heavily laden tray on the table between the two chairs.

"Mr. Kumar asked me to tell you that he'll meet you back at the Works, sir."

He nodded, his eyes never leaving Shona.

"That will be all, Mrs. MacKenzie. We don't wish to be disturbed."

The housekeeper's eyes widened, Gordon's face took on the appearance of stone, and Shona could feel the heat rise up her neck to her cheeks.

Chapter 23

"Why did you say that?" she asked after he'd closed the door behind the woman.

"Are you going to take the money and go live in London?"

"London isn't one of my favorite places."

"Then Inverness or Edinburgh?"

She stopped, folded her arms, and glared at him.

"I can't be intimidated, you know."

"Can't you?"

"No," she lied. "Certainly not by you." A second lie added to the first.

"Why are you selling Gairloch? Why the clan brooch?"

He'd accused her of having too much pride. She had none now. She straightened, dropped her arms, and faced him. Very well, if the price for survival was shame, then so be it.

"I haven't any money," she said.

Still, he didn't say a word, only continued to stare at her.

"If I can sell Gairloch, then at least I'll have enough money to get a little house for the three of us."

She felt her lips tremble, and bit them to steady them.

"Your husband left you nothing?" he asked, his tone curiously dispassionate.

"No. Nothing."

"You didn't make a wise choice seven years ago, did you? At least I still have money."

She turned and stared out the window again. She wanted to escape this room, him, and maybe even herself.

He came to stand behind her, so close that she could feel the warmth of him. She lowered her head, staring at her clasped hands.

"I'll buy your brooch, Shona," he said, placing his hands on her shoulders and drawing her back against his chest.

For a moment, she allowed herself that weakness, laying her head back against him, saying nothing when his hands stroked down her arms. When he embraced her, she closed her eyes, holding the moment aloft, special and rare.

She'd always remembered him, each moment shared with him, times of laughter and passion. At first, the memories had been weighted with joy. At the end, they'd carried only sorrow.

Rain, only hinted at earlier, wept against the panes. Long droplets lingered for a moment before slowly streaking the glass. The journey home would be a miserable one.

"I'll send you home in a carriage," he said, as if hearing her thoughts.

He'd always done that, anticipating her cares, understanding her unspoken concerns. Leaving him, leaving Gairloch would be so much easier if he'd behaved as he had in Inverness, haughty, annoyed, his anger all too easily discernible.

But in the factory, only days ago, each had forgotten anger. Only need had remained. And now? A certain bittersweet sadness that ached in her bones like the cold of the oncoming winter.

In a moment, she'd forget why she was here.

She took a cautionary step away before turning and facing him.

Before she could speak, to thank him, he asked, "How much do you owe?"

That was none of his concern, but she'd already descended into the ditch, she might as well tell him the whole truth. When she mentioned the amount, however, he didn't comment. Nor did he flinch, which she expected.

"I was running a household in Inverness for two years on air," she said. "Being the Countess of Morton gave me a certain cachet, but after a while even the butcher wanted payment."

"So, you couldn't have employed any of the footmen I saw," he said, startling a laugh from her.

"No," she said. "I couldn't. Now, Fergus has this idea of introducing the Americans to Invergaire. I don't know how I'm going to feed them for the next week, let alone find the money to entertain people."

His face changed, his eyes flattening to opaque discs she couldn't read. Suddenly, she knew he was going to say something that would hurt her.

"Did you ever love me?" he asked.

She turned to the window again, wishing the rain would come down harder and the thunder roar. She was in the mood for a brutish Highland storm.

Did you ever love me? How painful a question that was, merely because he shouldn't have asked it. He shouldn't have had to ask it. Didn't he know?

"The past is gone," she said dully, "and wishing it back won't make it happen. We're seven years older and wiser."

"Are we?"

She glanced at him to find him unbuttoning one cuff.

"What are you doing?"

"The purchase of your brooch has a condition."

Her eyes narrowed. "I'm not for sale."

One of his eyebrows arched up. "Really? Did your husband know that?"

Anger was a better emotion than tears.

She wanted to slap him. Or throw the odd little porcelain figurine on the table beside her at him. Or maybe even kick him in the shin, hard, with her stiff, heavy shoes. She wanted to do a great many things to Gordon MacDermond right at this moment, but loving him was not one of them.

He unbuttoned the other cuff with the same unhurried movement.

"I'm not going to bed you," she said.

He looked around the room. "I don't see a bed here, do you?"

She frowned. "You know what I mean."

"Indeed, I do."

He began to roll up one sleeve. She took a step sideways toward the door, narrowing her eyes at him.

"One last fuck as a gesture of goodwill."

"No."

"Oh, yes, Shona Imrie," he said, coming to her. His fingers danced along her jaw, raised her face. "Of your own accord, with passion in your eyes. Not reluctant. Not annoyed. Not grudgingly. I want a reminder of the girl I adored."

"I'm not your rainbow, Gordon MacDermond."

He smiled, the expression oddly sad. "Not at the moment," he agreed. "Maybe never again. But can we pretend, for a little while? I find I don't want to be seven years older and wiser."

The young man she'd known had been eager and enthusiastic about life. This man, hardened by war, both fascinated and frightened her.

He'd demand everything from her, including truth. No sophistry or pretense would be allowed. He'd love her until she shuddered in his arms, then love her again. He'd weaken her with passion until she was limp and sated.

A woman needed courage for that kind of liaison.

A woman would need to guard her heart so that she didn't tenderly stroke his back, or kiss his shoulder in the blissful aftermath of loving. A woman would have to protect her mind, so that his logic and his persuasiveness wouldn't overpower her will.

A woman of courage, strong heart, and sound mind might be equal to the task. She wasn't at all sure that described her.

But one thing stopped her from running from the room, or calling out to Mrs. MacKenzie and the maid. One thing only, the memory of seven years without him. His birthday passed, and she'd noted it, as well as other anniversaries kept secret between them, such as the first time they'd loved or when he'd returned from school and recognition sparked between them like fire.

She'd read Fergus's letters, hoping he would mention Gordon, terrified that he might and her voice would tremble when she read each letter aloud to her husband. She'd lain awake in her solitary bed, praying for her husband's health, her brother's safety, and the courage to forget Gordon MacDermond.

He walked to the door and held out his hand to her.

"I can't fight you," she said now. "I can't fight the world, the Americans, Helen, Fergus, and you. It's too much."

"I don't want you to fight me, Shona. I want you to come with me."

She'd arrived with her pride in tatters, yet this moment had nothing to do with pride, submission, or dominance.

Come and love me.

She'd never been confused about his feelings for her. He'd loved her, and with such single-minded grace that she'd often felt unworthy. How could he have asked her that question? *Did you ever love me?*

Was love enough?

She hadn't thought so at one time. She'd turned her back on it even though it was the only gift she could bring to him, the only offering she could make that was truly hers. The only thing she'd owned.

She'd not valued her love enough, and now?

Perhaps that wasn't a question she could answer. Or perhaps it simply didn't matter.

If she were wise, she'd leave now. But when had she ever been wise around him? Even as a girl, knowing that her virtue should be prized above all things, she had no hesitation in giving herself to Gordon. Not once, but many, many times in the years before she married. Unwise, feckless, rash—all words she'd labeled herself. Looking back, she hadn't understood how she could have been so foolish.

Now, watching his lips curve in a smile, she knew she could never have refused him.

She took a deep breath, released it slowly, trying in a vain attempt to calm herself. He didn't move, patient in a daunting way. Slowly, she began to walk toward him, her eyes never leaving his face. If she succumbed, it would be on her terms. Pride, rearing its head again, perhaps. But he wouldn't be the master. Instead, they would come together as equals, as they always had.

Placing her hand in his, she wondered at the heat of his palm. His fingers curled around hers, sharing his warmth. He pulled her from the room, gently but inexorably, intent on a destination he didn't divulge. This part of Rathmhor she'd never seen: a sturdy set of stairs, lacking both the difficulty and the protectiveness of Gairloch. He hesitated at the landing, glancing back at her, his face somber once more. He didn't speak, either to coax or to question.

The house, sturdy and square and resolute on the landscape, seemed to draw in around them creating a bubble silent and still. Mrs. MacKenzie and the rest of the staff weren't in sight. If they went about their daily duties, if they laughed and joked or even spoke, they heard none of it.

He turned once more, advancing up the steps, her hand clasped in his.

She didn't ask where they were going, didn't pierce the silence with questions. To perdition perhaps, that's where they were going. Never to heaven. Not with so many rules broken and dictates ignored. They would be the subject of a sermon from the pulpit at kirk. The minister would abjure them; the congregation would look askance at them if they were courageous enough to attend. They would be an object lesson to all lust-filled, improvident men and women.

But they might well be envied.

For now, her heart was pounding and her breath was tight. Lightning laced her blood and sent it tingling throughout her body. She grabbed her skirt with her right hand, her left firmly holding his, and followed him up the steps, intent on each tread as if it were a marker.

As she ascended the staircase, she descended into depravity.

She could almost envision being interrogated by a barrister of behavior:

On step three, Shona Imrie Donegal, did you not consider that while you had been fortunate in the past, you might become with child from this encounter?

No, Your Lordship. It did not enter my mind but a fleeting second.

On step six, Shona Imrie Donegal, could you not have pulled away?

With all ease, Your Lordship. I could have fled the house, run into the storm, and known myself safe.

Then why did you not?

Oh, Your Lordship, if I could explain that, I would not be here at all, standing before an imaginary justice, while a court of righteousness decreed my fate.

At the head of the stairs, he turned left, then left again. At the end of the hall, he opened the door to a room, so small that she turned and looked at him in surprise.

"The bedroom I had as a boy," he said.

Only a narrow bed, a ladder-back chair, and a bureau could fit in it. The curtains, deeply emerald, were cast-offs from another room, since the hems obviously had been refaced.

The rooms for Gairloch's staff were more luxurious than this monastic-like cell.

She disliked the pinch of her heart, the sudden wish to comfort him. He regarded her with a piercing stare, but the shadow of the boy was there, the son of Lieutenant General MacDermond, the father always to be addressed with military precision and bearing.

Yes sir, no sir, perhaps sir. Never Father. Never Da.

"I have a larger chamber now," he said. He came to stand in front of her, leaned down, the words bathing her cheek. "This is the only bedroom with a view of Gairloch. I want to take you here, where I imagined you so many times."

She could barely breathe.

"Give me the brooch," he said.

With trembling fingers, she reached into her pocket,

withdrew the brooch, barely noting when the clasp scratched her skin. She placed it on his palm, her head bent and looking at their two hands.

"Now give me your body."

Her head jerked up.

He reached for her collar, beginning her unveiling with practiced fingers. This was not the fevered coupling in the factory. This was slow and sure. An inch of skin, then more, a steady revelation that she wasn't quite the girl she'd been. Her body was riper, fuller, hungrier for love. She knew, now, what she'd missed.

Another few buttons, and she began to breathe harder, her skin heating, the feeling of helplessness growing. Not bending to his will but her own need. Her eyes closed slowly, savoring the sensations with trembling wonder.

She felt as if she'd imbibed too much whiskey, the strength of it mimicking what she felt at this moment. As if, even barely touching her, Gordon was rendering her sotted, drunk from him.

He smelled of clean linen, the lingering acrid scent from his explosion experiments, and soap. His fingertips were rough but gentle, and when they smoothed the skin they revealed, she shivered.

Her breasts tingled and tightened, the nipples drawn up and heated. Warmth pooled in secret crevasses; her legs trembled as if they could barely sustain her weight.

She opened her eyes to find him studying her. Too many years had passed for her to be able to decipher his look. Gently, she placed one hand on his cheek, feeling the silence press around her and into her.

He kissed the tip of her thumb, softly smiling in reassurance.

Didn't he know that she didn't fear the act with him? She never had. If anything, she was afraid of what she might give him beyond the pleasure they'd share with their bodies. Her heart, perhaps. Or her soul.

Would he capture it and hold it hostage? Or would he simply incinerate it, and return it along with her heart, an empty, shriveled shell?

Chapter 24

The storm made night of day, brought the wrath of God down on Invergaire Glen. Sheep scuttled to safety, hairy-faced Highland cattle steadfastly endured, and humans, depending on their experience with the weather, either looked eastward to the flash of blue and resigned themselves to a short, nasty spell or found shelter somewhere safe and dry.

At Rathmhor, Gordon was uncaring about the ferocity of the storm. As a flash of lightning illuminated the room, he realized the weather would have rendered his experiments dangerous had it occurred an hour earlier. Providence had gifted him with safety and now seduction as Shona stood in front of him with a solemn look.

His hands reached up slowly and parted her bodice, giving her a chance to step away. She only continued to look at him wide-eyed and silent. A sacrificial lamb awaiting its fate.

The idea of Shona playing the role of victim brought a smile to his face.

What a damn fool he was.

Did you ever love me? A question she'd never answered. One that held him immobile, studying her. The whites of her eyes were pink, as if she'd wept unknown to him. Her cheeks were flushed, and her lips full and slightly open. A mouth petulant for a kiss. He wanted to ask her again, demand an answer of her.

If she said no? Would he gently button her bodice, send her from Rathmhor in peace with only the memory of his chivalry? Or would he love her regardless?

If she said yes? Then he'd ask her if she could love him again. He'd humble himself, perhaps even beg.

He'd stood on a ridge at Balaklava, facing down several thousand Russian cavalry. At Lucknow and Begum Kothi, he'd fought the enemy hand to hand. As Colonel of the Regiment, he'd sent men into battle, positioning his troops to assault the enemy and protect the regiment's flanks.

A man seemingly without fear.

But he knew it now, and was kept silent by it.

Folding back the placket of her bodice, he bent forward, gently kissed the pulse at the base of her throat.

"Is this where you put your perfume?" he asked, the mental image of her doing so this morning somehow necessary to validate. He wanted snippets of scenes in his mind, to hold there regardless of what happened between them.

She nodded.

"Where else?"

A shake of her head indicated that he'd have to find all the spots himself.

Gently, he peeled the bodice from her shoulders, his thumbs trailing down her arms. How improper she looked, plump breasts hinting at freedom from their corset cage. Her skirt was next, and an array of fastenings that almost defied him. But he persisted, determined not to be stopped at this point. His fingers were clumsy, his heart thrummed in his chest, and his engorged cock was threatening to pop his trouser buttons.

What a damn eager fool he was.

He pushed the froth of petticoats, hoop, skirts down

to the floor, too impatient to bother with the proper care of her clothing. Wrapping his hands around her waist, he simply lifted her up and placed her to one side, kicking at the pile of garments until it was adequately subdued.

A kiss. He needed a kiss now.

He pulled her to him, lowered himself into the abyss that was kissing Shona, the darkness behind his eyelids sparkling with their own explosions.

"I'll name it Shona," he murmured against her lips.

She blinked up at him, her beautiful gray eyes misty. "What?"

"My blasting powder. I'll call it Shona powder."

A silly idea, one she greeted with a smile.

He leaned down, his forehead against hers. "You affect me the same way," he said softly. A confession he hadn't meant to make.

Before she could say anything, he kissed her again, his fingers working on her laces. He wanted her naked, pliant, eager, and on his bed.

First, however, he had to get the damn corset off.

He swore, which prompted her smile again, but he didn't care. There wasn't any hiding his eagerness, his near desperation. The corset finally done, he almost flung it across the room, but settled for tossing it to the mound of her clothes.

Now for the shift and beneath it, pantaloons with a touch of lace, pretty little garters, stockings, and shoes.

He couldn't wait.

Lifting her up, he deposited her on his boyhood bed, one not constructed for seduction. She rose up on her elbows, the look on her face a combination of surprise and amusement.

It was easier to get his clothes off.

He shouldn't have bothered to change after the experiments, should have just bodily transported her up here and have her watch as he bathed. Naked and wet, he could have turned to her, allowed her body to dry him.

The trousers were more difficult, due to the size of his erection. His cock was pointing at her as if it were a sentient being and knew its home.

The amusement had faded from her face, her attention focused on that part of him that stood at attention and trembled in her presence.

Naked, he stood and let her look her fill, until impatience had him unfastening her shoes, dragging her stockings off, and nearly ripping her pantaloons in his haste.

She never said a word, just raised her hips to allow him to pull off her clothing, sitting up when he addressed the issue of her shift.

Finally, finally, finally she was naked, the cool air pebbling her skin. He'd warm her.

His hands smoothed up her thighs, his thumbs playing in the nest of curls. She was damp for him, eager, spreading her thighs. A temptress who needed to be kissed again.

The bed was too small. He moved to place one knee on the floor, his hands on her thighs. His lips trailed a path up each leg to her hips.

She trembled.

He rose a little, kissing her from hip to waist, lingering at her navel, then trailing a chain of kisses to the underside of each beautiful, full breast.

Her indrawn breath evoked a smile from him. So, too, did the widening of her legs.

Come to me.

A siren's call, one he ignored for the moment.

He slid his fingers through her damp folds, pushing back his own eagerness to make her climax first. He wanted to see her, neck arched, eyes wide and wild, biting her lip to keep herself from screaming.

God, he wanted her to scream.

She lay trembling beneath his regard, unconcerned for her nakedness. But, then, any woman with her perfection of form shouldn't be worried about displaying it. She was a Greek statue come to life, alabaster given warmth.

He was filled with her, fingers damp, nostrils flaring with the scent of her arousal.

Bending his head, he tugged at one nipple with his lips, his mouth suckling her, the taste of her beating at the door of his restraint.

"There," he said, inhaling the scent of her skin between her breasts. "You put it there."

Loving her in the factory had been too quick. Here, it wasn't going to be different. Hell, it had always been that way. He saw her, he wanted her. He breathed in her perfume, he wanted her. She smiled at him, he wanted her.

Thoughts of her made him hard. Her laughter made him hard.

Her thighs widened and any thoughts of waiting were pushed aside by need.

He rose up, bracing his forearms on either side of her. Her lips were reddened, her cheeks pink, and he found it a surprising challenge to look into her eyes and not tell her how much he loved her still, perhaps always.

Instead, he surged into her.

"I'm sorry," he said, settling himself, sliding home with a feeling of bliss so sharp he closed his eyes.

He commanded himself to restraint, but it was easier ordered than done. He kissed her, pulling gently out, hearing her soft plaintive moan and feeling the same. He thrust deep, again and again. Shona gripped his arms, hips jutting up as she planted her feet on his narrow bed and rose to meet him.

A low, keening sound escaped her lips. Her eyes closed as she turned her head.

No mortal man could withstand the sight of Shona wild and helpless with passion.

He wanted to gather her up, keep her his, love her until the earth aged and tired. He wanted to pleasure her for a thousand years, feel her lips against his, her tongue, her breath.

Suddenly, he was close, too damn close to last. When he erupted into her, his climax was an explosion of its own.

He collapsed on her, made a mental note to shift his weight, but even that would have to wait until he was capable of moving. Her heart was racing. He bent his head, kissing her breast to soothe the thrumming beat. He laid his head beside hers. In a moment, he'd be able to breathe. His hand waved in the air as if to gain him time. Her hand weakly patted him on the back in wordless understanding.

He didn't stand a chance with her. How could he ever deny her anything? How could he ever not love her?

"What did you mean?" she asked a moment later, her voice trembling. "Why should I forgive you?"

He smiled into the pillow. "For being rash, too quick."

"Thank heavens you were," she said softly.

He supported himself on his arms, looking down at her. Her eyes were closed, her face flushed, but a smile sat happily on her full lips.

What a damn ecstatic fool he was.

"Did I please you?"

Her eyes opened, and he almost called back the question, foolish that it was. He kissed her, sealing the admission on her lips.

He moved to the side, his arm across her body. Her hand curled into a fist, rested at his waist.

Outside, the storm raged, nature a petulant child intent on gaining attention. He allowed his eyes to close, drew her next to him until they made do on the narrow bed. Her perfume wafted up from behind her ear, and he smiled.

He'd found another place.

When Shona woke, Gordon was gone.

She turned her head to the right to see that the storm had passed, the window revealing a clear and cloudless afternoon. She hadn't heard him get up, dress, and leave. At least she'd slept, something she'd not been able to do well for days now.

Sitting up, she surveyed the room. He'd put her garments in some order, folding them neatly and placing them on the chair beside the bed. How odd that she felt more embarrassed about him touching her garments than about bedding him.

Sometimes, she amused herself.

At the foot of the bed was a leather pouch. Frowning, she reached over, opened it, and stared at the contents. Inside the pouch was enough money to keep her—and the residents of Gairloch—until the castle was sold.

Only a fool would weep at this moment.

But she'd never been wise around Gordon.

Shafts of sunlight pierced the remaining gray clouds. The storm had left the air smelling of spring, a curiosity since winter was approaching with vigor. The road to the Works was strewn with fallen leaves and small branches that hadn't been able to withstand the winds, and in the distance, the windows of Gairloch glittered like tear-filled eyes.

Gordon guided his horse around the worst of the debris, his attention only partially focused on his destination. Why had he confided in Shona? He'd vowed not to trust her, yet he'd told her his plans as well as his thoughts.

She'd always had a way of piercing his guard.

Perhaps it had something to do with her confession about finances. Her expression had been wary, as if afraid he'd ridicule her. Instead, he'd wanted to take her in his arms and promise her that he'd protect her and keep her safe. He wanted to make the world a safer place for her. He wanted to stand between her and what caused her discomfort or worry, and if that didn't make him a besotted idiot, he didn't know what did.

He wasn't going to think about Shona asleep in his bed, a soft flush coloring her face even in sleep. He wasn't going to think about how damn hard it had been to leave her.

He suspected, however, looking toward the Works, that history would repeat itself. They'd never have a future together. Shona would continue to hold on to her pride. It was part of who she was, after all. When her parents had died, she'd mourned them, but carried on. Evidently, she'd done the same when her husband died. Stalwart, brave, and arrogant—words he would forever use to describe her.

But such rigidity made it impossible for her to bend, and he wasn't going to accept less than what he deserved. In this case, a woman who loved him wholly and completely, who would put him above all others.

He'd spent years trying to win his father's love, only to realize that his father was incapable of that emotion. He wasn't going to make the same mistake with Shona.

He'd treated Rani badly, abruptly abandoning his partner for Shona, and he'd have to apologize for that.

But the morning hadn't been a total waste. They'd learned that the second formulation was more stable. The third, using kieselguhr, assisted in the nitration process.

The Works was proving to be ideal for the production of his new blasting powder. The supply of acid for the nitration process was obtained from a company near Edinburgh, and the kieselguhr was found in deposits along Loch Mor.

In addition, Rani was a brilliant chemist.

The carriage at the front of the main building of the Works was a curiosity. The fact that three men left it as he dismounted was only interesting, not alarming.

He remembered one of his sergeant's favorite expressions: *Don't stand out, sir; it draws fire.* Just what kind of fire were those three about to deliver?

Attired in a similar fashion—long frock coats, tall silk hats, and suits of black, respectable serge—they immediately reminded him of London bankers. The similarity didn't end with their clothing. Each had an expression of somberness, as if they'd come to announce a death. Perhaps he'd been wrong to liken them to bankers. Undertakers would do as well.

"Sir Gordon?" the tallest of the three said. His hair was a pewter gray, marking him as the eldest of the three.

"Yes?"

Gordon halted where he was, cautious because he disliked surprises. The three of them were most definitely unplanned. He fingered the Imrie Clan brooch in his pocket as if it were a talisman, something to keep him safe.

"Might we have a moment of your time?"

"Might I inquire as to why?"

The spokesman smiled. "A matter of some urgency, sir. We've come to offer you a business proposition."

Curious now, he strode to the door, opened it, and motioned the three inside. They followed him across the cavernous space in single file, mutely, a solemn procession of middle-aged men.

He'd cleared out the accounting manager's office for his own use and stood behind an ancient wormwood-riddled desk facing them.

"What matter of some urgency?" he asked.

Less than a quarter hour later, they left the office in the same manner, leaving him stunned and silent.

Chapter 25

*L*ove of country had been bred in Brian MacDermond, fueled by talks of breaking free of the yoke of England. He'd fought for Scotland and would do so again, but fighting was one thing, living in an uneasy peace another.

Life had narrowed for him. There was no more talk of freedom, only whispers of how to endure the English rules. They'd taken the pipes from him, forbidden him their use. But his canny clan had hidden more than one instrument, and from time to time, he took himself up to the bluff overlooking Loch Mor and eased his heart with the sound.

Some hinted that he might well be reported to the English, sent away to be imprisoned in an English gaol, or hanged to make a lesson of him.

But when the anguish was too great to bear, and the emptiness of his soul too great, Brian MacDermond defied the cowards, took up his pipes, and played to the gorse, the deer, and the eagle.

He met her there, where she'd come to hear him play in defiance of all that was safe and proper. The laird's wife, Anne, with her soft and sad smile. On the bluff overlooking Loch Mor, they revealed each to the other, and Brian found that there was something else other than the pipes that could give him peace: Anne Imrie.

Anne, with her black hair and brown eyes, and her shy smile as if uncertain in the way of it. A good Inverness lass, she was, a distant cousin of a distant cousin of the laird.

They talked of their children, then they talked of freedom, of rumors of more laws to choke down the throats of good Scotsmen everywhere. They never talked of his wife or her husband, a man he'd come to call friend.

Nor did they ever speak of what they felt, one for the other, or the fact that when night came, each had begun to long. Not for what they had, but for what could never be.

The preparations for the entertainment welcoming Mr. Loftus and Miriam to Gairloch were also accompanied by Mr. Loftus's indisposition.

For three days now, the American had been laid up in the Laird's Chamber, so vilely ill that even Elizabeth looked a little pale after caring for him. Helmut had taken himself off, finding duties requiring his presence outside the sickroom, even taking his meals in the stable.

As annoying as Mr. Loftus was, he didn't deserve to be quite that ill. Twice, Shona had called for the doctor from Invergaire Village, and twice he'd come, examined Mr. Loftus, and pronounced him healthy except for an incipient case of gout and a love of too many rich foods. He'd put the man on an abstemious diet, refused him whiskey, announcing dire consequences if the American didn't obey his strictures.

Two hours later, Helen had been seen sneaking up the stairs with a dram full of whiskey, and tray of slices of mutton adorned with one of Cook's white sauces.

The second time the doctor had come, he'd looked at Shona as if she were guilty of poisoning her guest.

Out of fondness for Helen, she hadn't said a word, but she had given the other woman a stern look. A warning for Helen not to accommodate Mr. Loftus's gluttonous desires regardless of her tender heart.

She suspected, however, that someone had, behind her back, provided him whiskey or the food the doctor expressly prohibited.

Miriam hadn't been the least upset about her father's illness. She waved it away with a comment to the effect that: "Papa probably just ate something bad for him." Otherwise, she was content to involve herself in each part of the preparations for the entertainment to welcome her to Invergaire Glen.

"We don't have many musicians," Shona said, two days ago. "We've drums, pipes, flutes, and a fiddle. Those will have to suffice."

Did the silly woman know they wouldn't be playing waltzes for her, but a series of country dances? The party might ostensibly be to welcome Miriam, but it would also be for the villagers and the rest of the invited guests.

As well as announcing the departure of the last of the Imries from Invergaire Glen. Now, that was a thought guaranteed to depress her.

Resolutely, she grabbed the book in which she'd been making notes, and retreated to the Violet Sitting Room, a parlor on the second floor so named because of the expensive French wallpaper depicting bouquets of the flower.

As she closed the door, another explosion sounded at Rathmhor. For days, Gordon had been experimenting with different strengths of blasting powder. When people had first rushed out to see the cause of the horrendous sound—all but poor Mr. Loftus and Elizabeth—she'd wanted to tell them not to bother. It was just Gordon.

She hadn't seen him since he'd left a bag of money at her feet.

Shouldn't he, at least, have called on Fergus? Or had he decided to ignore their friendship?

"I shall have to travel to Edinburgh for a dress suitable to wear," Miriam said, flinging the door of the sitting room open.

"The party will be held in three days," Shona said, startled. "You haven't the time."

"I haven't anything to wear."

She bit her lip, thought about her words before speaking, then attempted to moderate her tone.

"Miriam, you're a princess to the people of Invergaire Glen. I've seen you wear dresses to dinner that would awe them. It isn't necessary to purchase anything new."

Miriam's mouth twisted into a moue of dissatisfaction. "Perhaps you're right," she said with a toss of her head. "Besides, I doubt I could find a dressmaker to my requirements in Edinburgh."

She kept a smile on her face because she was an Imrie, and no one was going to best her, least of all Miriam Loftus.

"What are you wearing?" the other woman asked.

The question took her aback. "I haven't given any thought to it," she said. Really, what could she wear? The one good dress she had was black. She was exceedingly tired of black.

Miriam eyed her with a narrow-eyed gaze.

"You're not going to wear another black dress, are you?"

She sat up straight and pinned a smile to her lips. "I'm just out of mourning," she said.

"Black doesn't favor you at all."

She didn't know what to say to that.

"I have something that might fit you," she said. "It's

much too large for me. I never had the alterations done because the dress didn't suit me."

"That isn't necessary," she said, the smile now anchored in place by sheer determination.

"Then I'll go and have Elizabeth fetch it for you," Miriam said, as if she hadn't spoken.

Elizabeth wasn't her maid, but that comment was never uttered. Why speak, when Miriam never listened?

Miriam simply turned and left the room without another word, leaving Shona to stare after her in dismay.

Was she going to be trapped, by manners, into wearing some hideous castoff from the American girl? Her last public outing before she left Invergaire Glen would be as a frump.

The Imrie pride had been supplanted by the Imrie humiliation.

She frowned at the doorway for a few moments before bending her head to her task again. She'd already planned the refreshments, and they would cost her a sizable portion of the money she had. That, and feeding Mr. Loftus and his party for the next several weeks. She'd arranged to have several women from the village come and scrub the Clan Hall and the adjoining Family Parlor to a shine, since the guests would be mainly in those rooms.

The piper she'd hired had refused to be paid, saying that it was an honor to perform at Gairloch. She'd almost kissed Rory in response. Of course, she hadn't, since such a thing would have embarrassed the older man, but she hadn't been able to keep tears from welling in her eyes.

Helen tapped on the door frame, then crept into the room on timid feet. They'd barely talked since yesterday, when the doctor had called upon Mr. Loftus again.

She glanced up at Helen, put her journal down on the table, and studied her companion. Something was wrong, and it was evident from the puffiness beneath the other woman's eyes that Helen had been weeping.

"What is it?" she asked.

She'd allowed herself the profligacy of a small fire, and the room was warm, the sunlight welcoming.

Helen sat on the opposite chair, staring fixedly at her clothed knees.

"Helen?"

"Have you ever found yourself miserable because of something you've done?" Helen asked.

"Many times," she said. "What are you feeling so guilty for?"

"Being unwise," Helen said promptly.

She blew out a breath. "Don't tell me you took Mr. Loftus some whiskey again, Helen. Or some scones? He isn't to have any of that."

Helen shook her head, the other woman's demeanor so filled with misery that she really was concerned now.

She leaned forward, placing her hand on her friend's arm. "Helen, tell me, please."

"I think history has a way of repeating itself, don't you?"

What a curious question.

"In what way?"

"You tell yourself you're not going to do what you've done before, but when the circumstances are similar, you do the very same thing that you once did. What happened to all the lessons you learned? What happened to the misery you felt?"

She sat back, staring at Helen. How had the other woman known? She'd returned to Gairloch soon enough, both after the incident at the Works and at Gordon's home. She'd never confided in the other woman, but now it looked as if she was being censured for her behavior.

As well she should be.

Helen was only a few years older, but in some ways, she had more maturity. Perhaps it came from nursing her father for so many years. Or from being rendered destitute by his death. In that, they had something in common.

"I've been lonely," she said. "Which is no explanation for losing my mind around the man. I see Gordon and the world falls away."

Helen was looking at her strangely.

"I can't change the past, Helen. You're right, though. I can do something about my behavior now."

"What would you change?" Helen asked. "If you could?"

She picked up her journal, opened it, but didn't see any of the writing, or the careful columns of numbers. Instead, the page was a blur.

"Seven years ago, Gordon's father came to me. He told me that Gordon was going to offer for me, that he was going to do so because he and Fergus were friends, because he knew the extent of our dilemma."

She put her finger in the book to mark her place and held it close.

"We didn't have any money, you see." She sighed. "Same situation as we find ourselves in now, I'm afraid. The general said that not only would it be a marriage made in the name of pity, but it would keep Gordon from his destiny."

"You evidently believed him, because you married my cousin."

She nodded, looking away. This room had been decorated by her mother, who loved all things French. Had she truly loved the wallpaper pattern? Or simply because she'd had to order it from Paris? All those bouquets were rather overwhelming, not to mention that they seemed to change color in places, from light purple to blue.

"Was it out of spite?" Helen asked. "Is that why you married Bruce? To prove to Gordon that someone wanted you?"

Startled, she could only stare at Helen. The thought had never once occurred to her, although Fergus had questioned the speed of her marriage. She'd told herself it was because they had no money. But they hadn't had any since their parents' death. She'd reasoned that there was no need to delay, that Bruce was an eager bridegroom.

Had it been more than that?

Silence stretched between them, and she knew Helen wanted a response. How did she tell her the truth? Perhaps simply by uttering the words.

"I came to love Bruce," she said. "I was prepared to live my life with him. I wanted to make him happy."

Helen didn't say a word to ease her confession or halt it.

"But what I felt for Gordon was always different. I'm not sure I can explain it."

Words couldn't hold what she felt for Gordon. Ever since she was a girl, he'd occupied a special place in her heart—a niche created just for him. When he went away to school, she'd been inconsolable. When he returned, the world looked like a different, friendlier, place. Her heart seemed to beat faster in his presence, and even her breathing seemed to try to keep time with his.

They'd spent hours discussing things, arguing or agreeing. With Gordon, no topic was out of bounds. No question was too absurd to ask.

Perhaps there had been a little spite to her decision to marry Bruce. *I'll show you, Gordon MacDermond. Someone wants me, and not out of pity. An earl, a man with a title and a fortune. So there!*

How did she admit that?

How did she explain the pain she'd felt? Even if she had discounted the general's words, a part of her would have always wondered if he was right. She hadn't wanted Gordon's charity. Nor could she stand between him and his future, or take more from him than she could give back.

Helen frowned. "What did he say when you told him you were going to marry someone else?"

Oh, dear, Helen really did know the most pointed questions to ask, didn't she?

She stood, placing the journal on the table in front of her. Suddenly, she wanted out of the room, away from Helen's pointed questions.

"Did you at least tell him how you felt?"

Shona turned and faced her companion.

"What could he have said?"

Helen sat back, wide-eyed. "Did you never speak to him? Never explain your actions?"

She shook her head.

For seven years, she'd kept her own counsel, determined to make the best of her marriage and forget Gordon completely. He'd appeared in her dreams, instead, and in her thoughts when she didn't guard them well enough.

"You would have been happy," Helen said, not waiting for her to find the courage to answer. "Happier than you were with my cousin."

She waved her hand toward Helen, set to respond that she'd loved Bruce, but the other woman didn't give her the chance.

"Instead, you chose to believe the general," Helen said, "because it was easier."

Shona stared at the other woman for a moment, allowing the shock of that remark to penetrate.

"No," she said. "I believed him because he was right."

Helen didn't comment and perhaps it was just as well. The lies Shona had told herself for years were beginning to crumble around her.

"Does it matter?" she asked. "I can't change the past."

"You might not be able to change the past, Shona, but are you going to repeat it?"

"I don't know what you mean."

Helen shook her head. "You know. He's there, just over there," she said, pointing in the direction of Rathmhor. "Have you ever told him how you felt about him? How you feel now?"

Shona looked away, wishing she'd left the room.

"By your silence, I take it that means no," Helen said. "Don't let this chance slip by. Because there'll come a day when you want to undo the past, just like before, only you won't be able to. Don't let your pride stand in the way."

"It isn't pride," she said, wishing it were. "If it were something I'd done, I could fix it. It's him." She looked over at Helen, the mist of tears making the other woman appear blurry. "He doesn't want me."

"And how do you know that?"

"I'm here. He's there. If he wanted me, he'd come to Gairloch."

"Do you want him? Do you love him? Perhaps it's time for you to say it."

She turned away from Helen, walked to the doorway, and pretended an interest in the carving on the door.

Love wasn't a word they'd ever exchanged. They simply knew, in a way that transcended words and made a mockery of oaths.

"What if it's too late?" she asked softly.

"After death, it's too late," Helen said. "Until then, you have a chance to make wrong things right."

Did she? Lust still bound them, and perhaps need. Was it too late for love?

"What have you done?" she asked Helen, wanting to change the subject desperately. "You said you were miserable because of something you've done."

Helen smiled. "It doesn't matter now," she said, shaking her head. "I might have been unwise, but I've never been as foolish as you."

The indictment stung but, then, truth often did.

Chapter 26

"**D**ear St. Bridget," Shona said, staring at her reflection.

Helen and Fergus had managed to move her mother's pier glass into her room when Mr. Loftus was on one of his foraging expeditions. Now, in the light of the oil lamp, she was dumfounded by her own reflection.

"I can't go anywhere looking like this," she said.

When she'd first seen it, the dress hadn't looked at all frumpy. Although it was a strange red color—the shade of old red wine—the garment had looked to be proper enough. She hadn't counted on her own attributes filling it out so well.

Her shoulders were bare, and it was quite obvious that she was endowed with, well, large breasts, since more than half of them could be seen.

"I think it's quite shocking," Helen said from behind her.

"I know," she said. "Too shocking."

"Not at all," Helen said, surprising her.

She glanced over her shoulder at her companion.

"Shona," Helen said, "this is the last occasion you'll be entertaining at Gairloch if Mr. Loftus purchases the castle. If Fergus won't agree to sell, you still can't afford to have another gathering here."

That was true. Of all of them, Helen knew the full extent of her finances, or lack of them.

"This is your farewell appearance as an Imrie of Gairloch. Why shouldn't you leave them with a sight to remember?"

"Shocking?"

"No," Helen said, regarding her solemnly. "Magnificent. The dress really does suit you. Do you think Miriam knew?"

"If I said no, then that would mean she thought it would be a disaster. I choose to pretend that she was gracious and accept her generosity."

Helen smiled in approval.

The dress really was beautiful. In addition to being snug at the waist and a bit deep in the bodice, it was adorned with sparkly bits on the straps that fit over her arms, and draped to her elbows. She hadn't the slightest idea of fashions in America, but she knew Invergaire Glen had never seen a dress like this.

"You've been a proper widow all these years, Shona. Perhaps it's time for you to be a little shocking."

Had Helen forgotten her confession a few days earlier? Did Helen want her to show up in Gairloch's Clan Hall half undressed?

From the glint in her eyes, yes.

"You might as well catch a certain Scotsman's attention," Helen said.

"Better me than Miriam." She turned toward Helen. "Isn't she supposed to be engaged? Why isn't she pining for her intended?"

Helen looked amused, which was equal parts vexing and embarrassing.

"I don't think she cares for her intended. It's a match Mr. Loftus arranged. This trip is a bit of a consolation for her, I think. As is Gairloch. He means it as a wedding present."

That idea was simply annoying.

"That isn't to say," Helen added, "that she couldn't convince him that another suitor was more suitable."

"Someone with a title," she said dully. "First Baronet of Invergaire."

"Or Laird of Gairloch," Helen said.

Twice in the space of a few minutes, she'd been struck dumb. Was there no end to Helen's confounding comments?

"Fergus? Could she be interested in him?" Perhaps Fergus hadn't been jesting that night in the Clan Hall. She couldn't imagine ever being related to Miriam Loftus.

Finally, she found her voice. "I really do look different, don't I?"

"No, you look like Shona, only dressed up for a party." Helen smiled and touched her arm. "Let me help you with your hair," she said, leading her to the vanity.

All conversation about Miriam Loftus blessedly ceased.

Gordon knew his own failings all too well, one of them being feeling a sense of anticipation as he walked toward Gairloch.

Shona had sent him an invitation to the party. If he had any kind of sense, he'd decline. But she's also written a note on the back: *Thank you, Gordon, for your generosity.* She'd invited Rani to the party as well, a gesture that pleased him, even though Rani had declined. Not a surprise, since his friend wasn't comfortable in social situations.

Shona had always been a master of the verbal thrust and parry, capable of delivering the perfect quip at the perfect moment. In that one sentence of thanks, however, she'd revealed a vulnerability, and in her invitation a generosity of spirit.

Perhaps he was a fool to come to Gairloch again, especially for an occasion such as this. Was he supposed to celebrate the arrival of the Americans to a place that had proudly belonged to an ancient clan? Were the Imries simply to go off meekly, counting their coins? The idea of either Shona or Fergus doing so was a little difficult to accept.

No, Shona would go shouting and yelling defiance. She'd have that look in her eyes that said her pride was up.

I haven't any money.

Her eyes had been clear when she'd said those words, her face set in an expression of stoic endurance. What had she suffered in the last seven years?

Perhaps the Imrie pride wasn't as stiff and unrelenting as he'd thought.

He could always offer marriage to Shona Imrie Donegal, a thought that had him stopping in his tracks. Would she accept his suit? No, he wasn't going to put himself in that position again. He'd learned, the last time, that it stung to be rejected. No, more than that. She'd wounded him, damn it, and he'd taken years to heal.

He had enough to do rather than appear at Gairloch like some idiotic suitor. He wasn't. She'd made it all too clear that she didn't want him except in bed or to act as her banker.

Shona Imrie wasn't going to call the tune. No one was, a comment he'd made this very afternoon when the three men—bankers, as he'd originally thought—appeared at the Works again.

"We represent a consortium of interested buyers, Sir

Gordon," the spokesman said, "who are very interested in your discovery."

They didn't want the Works. They wanted the blasting powder he and Rani had developed. They evidently wanted it badly enough to offer a fortune for it, the amount they'd offered today staggering him, once more, into speechlessness.

He'd be wealthier than he ever dreamed. So would Rani.

"But if we take our invention to the market ourselves," Rani had argued, "we will be as rich."

What concerned him most wasn't the fact that the men they represented wanted to purchase their discovery, but the single-minded intensity with which they pursued the point.

"Is the army involved?" he'd asked. The surprise on their faces was indication of their answer even before their spokesman denied the War Office's involvement.

"Do you want the blasting powder enough to steal it?" Rani asked.

This time, all three men looked insulted. Rani only shrugged.

Even though Gordon had given them no encouragement—the opposite, in fact—they'd visited the Works three times. Once, when he met with them initially. The second time, when they had badgered Rani, and the third, this afternoon, when they'd arrived unexpectedly, insisting on meeting with both of them.

After their departure, Rani said, "The English see something, my friend, and they do not walk away. They want it. They take it."

He wondered if Rani was talking about his own country and the Empire's blunderings there. In that, they had some common ground. He might be a former officer of the Crown, and a baronet for his troubles, but in his heart, he was all Scot.

The line of carriages and wagons circling around to the Lower Courtyard attested to the success of this gathering. Torches lined the road for nearly a mile, ready to be lit when the Highland night finally darkened.

Even in the darkness, Gairloch would lord it over the countryside.

Shona Imrie did the same.

But she'd changed, hadn't she? Become more reticent, less vocal, her thoughts hidden by a calm and placid expression.

If he only had a bit of magic in his hand, he'd wish for the years to roll back. He'd be simply Gordon, striding across the glen between the houses, visible for all to see. He'd call on her with his pride stuffed in his pocket, and his heart in his eyes, and beg her to be his bride.

Come with me, he would have said, the accent of their homeland in his voice. And if she'd refused, instead of accepting her rebuff as an answer, he would have spirited her away like his border reiver ancestor.

They'd have made their home in their own place, a spot not far from here that they could build themselves. *This is the house we made*, they might have said to a passerby, or a relative come calling.

Instead, they served the past, both of them, a true son and daughter of Scotland.

A quarter hour later, Shona's hair was done, done up with so many pins that Helen had to go and fetch more from her bedroom. Helen had also, surprisingly, insisted on dusting her face with powder, and applying a salve to her lips.

"Just so it reminds you to smile," Helen admonished. "And no, don't go chewing it off."

"I know how to behave in public," she said, feeling like a child.

Finally, she was ready, and she walked to the other side of the room to look at herself again. The woman in the mirror had color on her cheeks. Was there something in the powder Helen had used? Her hair was pinned above her ears, falling in curls to her shoulders.

She wanted to cry.

"You've made me beautiful," she said, the sound of tears in her voice.

"You've always been beautiful," Helen said. "You've just been too miserable to notice it."

"You've made me noticeable, too," she said.

Helen nodded. "Not one person will fail to recall the exact moment you arrive, Shona Imrie Donegal. You look the proper Countess of Morton."

"I do, don't I?"

If she'd had any of the jewelry Bruce had given her, she would have worn it tonight. But those items had served a better purpose than simple decoration by supporting them in the last two years.

Would Gordon think her beautiful? Was she foolish even to wonder?

She turned to Helen. "Now, shall I help you?"

Helen shook her head. "I'm not one for parties," she said.

She sat on the bed, throwing the shawl and fan to the side. "Then, I'm not going, either."

"You don't need me to give you moral courage, Shona."

"No, but I need you to enjoy yourself. Ever since we've come to Gairloch, you've been at everyone's beck and call. I think you need to dance a little, weep at the pipers, and maybe even drink a wee dram of whiskey."

"Really, I'd be much happier reading a book in my room."

"Then so shall I."

Helen frowned. "Really, Shona."

She only smiled. "How long will it take you to get ready?"

"You won't go without me?"

She shook her head.

At the door, Helen looked back. "You really are very obstinate, you know."

Her smile grew wider. "Yes, I know."

When Helen was gone, she stood, brushing the wrinkles from her lovely borrowed dress. Rather than go and look at herself again, she walked toward the windows, staring out at the Highland night, the light gradually fading. In a few hours, the sky would blacken, but for now, she could see the approach to Gairloch and the procession of vehicles carrying the guests to the castle.

When darkness fell, the flames in the lanterns would toss shadows against the leaves of the overhanging trees. The stars would shine so brightly that it would seem heaven had been brought closer for this event.

Tonight, the pipes would play, welcoming the world to Gairloch. Tonight, the skirling sound would speak to another time, but one just as fraught with confusion and despair. Peace covered the Highlands like a warm blanket, but the world away from here was not so serene, and Scotland's sons had gone to war again.

Many of their guests tonight had done the same, some of them returning, like Fergus, with scars visible to all. Some of them were perhaps like Gordon, outwardly perfect, but affected just the same.

How could she bear it if anything happened to him?

What if one of his stupid explosions went wrong? Would anyone even let her know?

She pressed her fingertips against the cool glass, closing her eyes as she did so. On this night of celebration, when it seemed the past was hand in hand with the present, she whispered a prayer of protection for both men she loved.

And there she was, like a gift from God, a test for his patience and his pride.

The light was behind her, and she was a red-hued shadow, but he'd know Shona Imrie anywhere. Even in his coffin with her a weeping visitor. The last shreds of his soul would reach out to her, and thank her for the comfort of her tears.

Tonight, he had to either leave her or love her for the sake of his mind and his heart. He couldn't wonder what might have been or what could be.

He had to know.

Chapter 27

As the hostess, an Imrie of Gairloch, she should have been the first to greet each visitor at the door. She would have been, too, if Helen had not insisted on two things: that Fergus serve in that role, and that she should take care with her own appearance.

Very well, both had been accomplished, and she was on her way down the stairs, carefully lifting up her skirts and hoping her bodice stayed up as well. Her face warmed when she realized that the crowd of people were beginning to look up. Not only that, but they weren't talking, as if a wave of silence was moving slowly through Gairloch.

She halted, halfway down the steps, clenching the wooden banister so tightly she wondered if she'd crush it.

"Smile," Helen said from behind her.

She'd been in social positions before. Bruce hadn't entertained much, but when he had, she'd certainly comported herself well. He'd often complimented her afterward. When they'd attended various functions in Edinburgh and even London, she hadn't been a wayward chit, but a gracious guest.

But here, and now, she suddenly forgot everything she'd ever learned from her mother and in the intervening years. Every person she'd ever known in her childhood looked up at her, a mass of people spilling out of the Clan Hall, silent and . . . what? What were they thinking? What did they want of her?

The minister she'd known since she was a child looked a little surprised. So, too, his birdlike wife. Sarah Imrie McNair, a cousin, who was holding a cup and staring up at her wide-eyed. Her brother, Magnus, was actually leering at Shona.

Had they all forgotten what she looked like?

Helen whispered something else to her, some instruction, and she nodded, descending another step, glancing down at herself to ensure her bodice was in place.

Gordon stood talking with Fergus, a glass of whiskey in his hand. He'd dressed for the occasion in his formal uniform with kilt and black jacket. His black hair had been brushed until it shone. He laughed at something Fergus said, and the sound traveled up her spine.

He was the most beautiful creature in the world.

At that moment, he glanced in her direction, his smile fading. A room separated them, dozens and dozens of suddenly silent people. Because he was looking up at her, she managed the last few steps. Keeping her eyes on him, and only him, she ignored the silence. She reached the bottom of the steps, uncertain what to do. Gordon rescued her by pushing through the throng and offering his arm.

"You're beautiful," he said softly.

"I thought the same of you," she said, to his obvious surprise.

Her hand felt cold on his arm, or was that only because he was so warm? His gaze heated her from the inside out.

"I'm so glad the dress was able to fit you," Miriam said, her voice carrying across the room.

The spell was broken, the noise level increasing. She

might have been a fairy princess, but her reign had lasted only minutes.

The American girl was suddenly there, only feet away.

"It's a lovely dress," Shona said, forcing a polite smile to her flaming face.

"It looks lovely on you," Miriam said. "How fortunate that it didn't fit me."

Must everyone know she wore a borrowed dress? Or was that the reason behind Miriam's sudden, and unexpected, generosity?

At the moment, she would have been just as happy if the stone floor opened up and swallowed her. Better yet, perhaps she could escape through one of the secret passages and just disappear.

She removed her hand from Gordon's arm.

"Shona."

She glanced up at Gordon. "Thank you for coming to my rescue," she said. *Please don't let him say something kind at the moment.* She really couldn't bear if he was kind.

Moving away, she met with the musicians, giving them instructions on when to begin playing, and then gave the signal to the piper.

At first, the sound was muted, so that only a few of the guests glanced around, confused. Then, as he came down the corridor leading to the Clan Hall, all the guests pressed into the doorway to see him.

The procession was a simple one—the piper playing the Imrie Clan tune, a haunting melody heard at momentous events. As Laird of Gairloch, Fergus was next, his advance a little slow because of his limp. Next, she followed, secondary to her brother, only because he was laird.

In other times, the rest of the family would follow, but she and Fergus were the only Imries left. Their guests parted to allow them to enter the Clan Hall unob-structed, a sign of fealty and respect.

When the procession was over, she moved through the crowd, greeting people she hadn't seen for years, accepting their compliments about the castle, the night, and her own appearance with more equanimity than she'd thought possible only minutes earlier. She smiled until her face ached, allowed herself to be hugged, her cheek patted, her arm stroked, and recalled the past with every other person.

Yes, her parents would be happy to see her and Fergus looking so well. Yes, Gairloch looked lovely at night. Yes, it will be sad to leave the castle. Yes, the food is wonderful, is it not?

Colonel Sir Gordon, First Baronet of Invergaire? Yes, it was a great honor he'd been given, secondary to Fergus's own award of the new Victoria Cross. They should have had a celebration simply for that. Yes, what a pity Fergus had been wounded, but he looked so much better now. Yes, it was impossible to know if he would always limp.

As to the Americans, Mr. Loftus seemed amenable, and that daughter of his was quite a lovely girl. Will they be living here? Yes, it will be strange not to have any Imries living at Gairloch. Who is that giant following him around, and that beautiful blond girl who never smiles?

She supervised the refilling of all the platters of food on the table, gave instructions to fetch another barrel of whiskey, and took a small sip of her own glass when she had a moment. Gairloch whiskey went straight to her stomach, warming the cold places she'd pretended weren't there for the last hour.

Every time she turned around, Gordon was within

sight. Every time she spoke to one of the older villagers, and he brought up her childhood, she felt him close. Twice, she turned to find him watching her, a curious, almost speculative look on his face.

Granted, she was wearing a dress that was more revealing than any she'd ever worn, but surely that wasn't why he was looking at her in that fashion. Besides, Gordon knew quite well what she looked like without any clothes at all. For that matter, he knew what made her moan and what pleasured her.

Not thoughts she should be having in the midst of two hundred people.

The next time she saw him, she frowned. He smiled in response, which only flustered her.

Finally, she found Fergus sitting in a quiet corner and joined him.

"You should be among our guests," he said.

"At the moment, I need a respite from our guests."

The Family Parlor had been transformed for dancing, and the musicians made up for any lack of talent with their enthusiasm. Several times, instead of dancing, the guests had begun to sing along with the tune.

She should have been warm, but the broad double doors had been left open to the autumn night, and an occasional gust cooled the air.

Mr. Loftus was holding court in the Clan Hall, his gouty foot propped up, his usually taciturn face transformed by a smile. Several villagers clustered around him, no doubt inquiring as to the changes he'd make if the sale of Gairloch happened. Money, in this case, could soothe any worries the inhabitants of Invergaire Glen might have.

If Gordon danced, she hadn't seen it. Nor was she all that interested in whom he might pick to be his partner.

Not one little bit.

Fergus was staring out at the crowd, his face somber. He wasn't having a good time and wasn't at all shy about showing it.

Once, she might have been able to tease him from his mood. But his aura of privacy was so intact that she knew he wouldn't speak of what was bothering him.

That didn't mean, however, that she was going to refrain from badgering him.

"Haven't you and Elizabeth talked to each other yet?"

He frowned at her. She was growing tired of being on the receiving end of her brother's glower.

"You have to agree to sell Gairloch," she said, abruptly. "If you had enough money, Elizabeth would agree to your suit."

"Are you suited to give advice, Shona? I would have thought your own life rather a mess."

That was too true not to feel a twinge of hurt.

"I'm not your mother or your nurse, but you need someone to care for you, since it's only too evident you need someone's help."

She threw up her hands at his expression.

"I'm not talking about your leg, brother. But your heart."

He frowned at her again.

She stood, shaking her head at him.

"Are you two fighting again?"

She turned to find Gordon standing there, a glass of whiskey in each hand. Wordlessly, he handed one to Fergus.

"No, we're not fighting," she said. "We have differing opinions, that's all."

Gordon only smiled, nodded to an acquaintance, then excused himself absentmindedly, as if he was bored with her presence.

She watched him for a few moments, then turned to find Fergus smiling at her.

"You still love him," he said, the words soft enough that they didn't carry.

"Don't be ridiculous."

His smile held an edge of pity.

"You still love him."

Really, he had to stop saying such things.

"If I'd been commanded to marry Gordon, I would have and no doubt been very happy until the end of my life. I knew all his attributes, those qualities a wife must learn in time."

"When have you ever done what anyone commanded?" Fergus asked with a smile.

She ignored the comment, intent on her confession. "But in the last seven years, I've trained myself only to see his flaws."

"Has he that many?"

"He's proud, stubborn, and impossible," she murmured.

"Qualities that could be spoken of you," he said, turning his head to watch her.

She wasn't going to answer that.

"I'm thinking he's had to be that way, to become his own man," Fergus said.

Surprised, she turned to look at him.

"Gordon's entire life has been spent trying to either escape his father or make him proud." He leaned back against the wall. "In the end, he didn't care about the old man's opinion." He looked up at the ceiling. "I'd venture to say that there are few people's opinions he does care about." He slowly turned his head and regarded her. "Is yours one of them?"

Without an answer, she left him, intent on their guests. With any luck, none of them would mention Gordon.

* * *

"They don't like each other very much, do they?"
Miriam Loftus said.

The woman was drenched in scent. If nothing else,
the overly flowery perfume should have warned him of
her approach, but he'd been lost in his own thoughts.

"Who?"

"Sir Gordon and Shona."

The comment was so absurd that, for a moment,
Fergus didn't know what to say. But when his amusement vanished, he realized that Miriam was seeing exactly what the two of them wanted others to see.

"They've been friends for years," he said cautiously,
unwilling to divulge his sister's past to anyone.

"He's quite magnificent," she said. "In his kilt, I mean."

Annoyed, he glanced at her. He was dressed in the
same uniform.

Elizabeth had looked at him, earlier, then pointedly
away. Did she remember the Crimea?

When one of his men died, she'd announced it to him.
More than once, she'd held his hand in wordless comfort. It hadn't seemed fair that, after having survived his
wounds, a man perished from disease. Elizabeth had understood the danger, even cautioning him that it wasn't
wise for him to visit so often.

"Doing so might put you in harm's way," she'd said
one day.

"Would you care?"

Her lovely face had changed, the calm look changing
to one of distress. He'd left not long afterward, embarrassed at revealing his uncertainty. That was before he'd
garnered his courage and confessed his love to her.

Nothing was more insecure than a man in love. Or
perhaps a man in love on the eve of battle.

Miriam said something and he pushed away the mists

of memory, turning his attention to her once again. Another point not necessarily in her favor, that Miss Loftus always seemed to know when she wasn't the sole object of someone's thoughts.

How could he ever have thought to court her? The idea of doing so was loathsome, even to save Gairloch.

She moved away, finally, skirting the dancers, smiling as she was complimented. She would be a poor chatelaine and the castle deserved better.

He wished the fool well who was to marry her. She'd run him a merry race, that was for sure. Or perhaps marriage would settle her, but he sincerely doubted it. Marriage didn't convey substance, and that was lacking in Miriam Loftus's character. Life was not all about what could be purchased or acquired, a fact the young woman had yet to learn.

Gordon arrived with another glass of whiskey.

"Are you prescient?" he asked, reaching for it.

"Just being a friend."

A comment fraught with memory. He wasn't disposed to think of the past with any kindness right at the moment.

Gordon sat in the same chair Shona had occupied only a few minutes earlier.

"It's time for me to be a protective older brother," he said.

"Is it?" Gordon said, not sounding the least interested.

"It's a miracle I didn't become an uncle seven years ago," he said. "But I'm not altogether certain that same luck will hold."

Gordon's expression changed. Now he had his interest. Damn time, too.

"You knew?"

"The whole countryside knew, or did you think your trysts in the cottage were secret?"

He could tell, from the other man's look, that Gordon had thought exactly that.

"Don't you know that the Imries have been fodder for gossip for years? We're entertainment for the village, if nothing else."

"Why didn't you mention it before?"

"What, and admit you've been seducing my sister? I would have had to beat you to a pulp. A little difficult after you became my commanding officer."

Gordon stared down into his glass. "I deserved it."

Fergus sighed.

"You deserved some measure of blame," he said, a moment later. "But so does Shona." He looked toward the Family Parlor where she'd disappeared. "What Shona wants, Shona normally gets, and it seemed she wanted you."

He almost smiled at Gordon's look of surprise, but he was feeling a little vulnerable at the moment himself, so he spared himself the amusement.

Elizabeth was standing behind her patient, and every time he glanced in her direction, she glanced away, leaving him no doubt of two things: she was watching him just as he was watching her, and she didn't want him to know it any more than he wanted her to know he was acting like a lovesick swain.

Dear God, they were all pathetic.

"Leave her alone," he said to Gordon, a little harsher than he intended. "She hasn't had it easy these last few years. I don't want you to take advantage of her again."

"I have no intention of doing so."

How damn stiff and righteous Gordon sounded. He and Shona, however, were combustible in combination. Anyone—other than Miriam Loftus—could see that.

"Isn't there anyone in England enamored of you? Some bride you could bring back to Rathmhor?"

"I've met a few women."

He sat back, his gaze intent. "Someone in particular?"

"One or two. The daughter of the regimental surgeon seems to fancy me. A Miss Thompson." Gordon glanced in his direction. "And you? Did you ever tell Elizabeth how you felt?"

With one hand, he gestured toward his bent leg. Reason enough not to speak.

"Plan on remaining a cripple always, Fergus?"

Surprised, he glanced over at the man who'd always been his friend, then his commander, and now an irritant.

"You won the damn Victoria Cross, man. For courage under fire. I'd never thought you'd be a coward now."

He stood, albeit with some difficulty. "Perhaps it's best if you leave now."

His anger grew at Gordon's easy smile. One part of him knew that he was using Gordon as a scapegoat, that his frustration and rage were only partly due to the other man. He was damn tired of being betrayed by his body, by being inept and easily tired. His leg hurt; his heart hurt, and he was more than a little worried about the future.

Right now, however, he couldn't solve all those problems, but he could solve one—Gordon.

"I mean it. Leave."

"Such hospitality," Gordon said, standing.

Another point of irritation, that Gordon topped him by two inches.

"Get out of Gairloch. Leave my sister alone and get out of Gairloch."

"Or what, Fergus? You'll fight me? You've become too much a coward for that."

His fist connected with Gordon's chin with a resounding crack. He hoped to God he'd broken the other man's jaw.

But Gordon didn't look overly disturbed by the blow. Other than rubbing his jaw, the other man didn't move. The least Gordon could have done was fall to the ground.

He gripped his cane hard with one hand, and turned, his aim to get as far away from Gordon MacDermond as humanly possible. Unfortunately, Mr. Loftus took the opportunity to shout out an instruction to Helmut. He glanced in their direction, and found himself face to face with Elizabeth.

He really had had enough tonight.

She was just going to have to see him limp, damn it.

He turned back to Gordon. "Go back to England. Go marry your Miss Thompson. Leave Shona with some reputation."

On his way out of the Hall, he saw Shona standing there, her face carefully expressionless, her eyes flat.

She'd heard it all, then.

"You've won," he said. "I'll sell the castle. Americans can live here for all I care. I don't care anymore."

In the silence, he gathered up the remnants of his dignity and made his way from the Clan Hall. This time, there was no piper to lead the way.

Chapter 28

They'd certainly given all the inhabitants of Invergaire Glen enough to talk about, hadn't they? The final appearance of the Imries would be fodder for gossip for years to come.

She tilted her head up, pressed a smile on her face, and faced Gordon. She should say something witty right now. Something cutting, perhaps, to let him know just how much she didn't care that he'd been talking about a Miss Thompson.

Poor Shona Imrie, gave her virtue and innocence to Gordon McDermott. Then, just when you'd think she would have learned better, she fell in love with him again.

He was coming closer, and her smile, anchored with such determination, was wobbling.

She turned and walked in the other direction.

"Are all Scotsmen so foolish?" Elizabeth asked, finding Fergus in the west tower. Did he think himself invisible? Everyone knew this was his favorite place at Gairloch. "Even when there's no reason for them to be?" she added, drawing near.

Fergus didn't turn when she spoke, answer, or acknowledge her in any way.

"I'm not going away, you know. Even though it's apparent you very much wish I would."

"I adored you from the beginning," he said, staring out at the night-darkened landscape. "I've plighted my damn troth to you on numerous occasions. I've bared my heart more than once. And now," he said, turning to face her, "you come to my aid? Why? Because you like to see me laid low?"

"Is that what you are?" She regarded him somberly. "I think you're in a bit of a temper. Are you feeling very sorry for yourself as well?"

"Go away, Elizabeth," he said, turning back to the window.

"No," she said. "I don't think I will." She took a few steps toward him. "Your sister thinks I've avoided you because of your leg," she said. "I know that's not true of me, but I'm beginning to wonder if it's true for you."

She approached him, placed her hand on his shoulder, feeling the rebuff in his movement away from her touch.

"Do you think I care about your leg?" she asked.

He didn't answer.

She sighed.

"My family isn't as proud as yours, Fergus."

He didn't say anything, only shook his head. Repudiation in a gesture.

Very well, it must be the whole truth, then.

"I never received your letters," she said. "But if I had, it wouldn't have mattered."

He turned and faced her. "So you've said. Is that what you came to tell me? I understand, Elizabeth. You want nothing to do with me."

"Oh, Fergus, it isn't that."

"Then what the hell is it?"

An indication of his anger, that he swore in front of her.

She straightened her shoulders. "I can't read. I never learned."

For the longest moment, he only studied her. She looked away, then back at him, determined to be done with this once and for all.

"My father was a thief. My mother was a prostitute. My brothers are skilled at many things, none of them legal."

"I didn't want to marry your family, Elizabeth."

She didn't know what was more disturbing about that statement—the fact that he'd wanted to marry her, or that it sounded as if he'd changed his mind.

"I come from London. Kensington, a battleground in its own way. My mother had seven children, three of whom died before they reached the age of three. The rest of us were sent to work almost as soon as we could walk by ourselves. Some occupations were not those to boast about."

Elizabeth turned her hands, staring at her palms. "I've gotten used to washing," she said softly. "But before Miss Nightingale, I might have gone weeks without a bath. It's what I knew. I'd never seen the broader world or even imagined it. I was simply trying to survive, and I somehow thought it was the same for everyone."

He didn't speak, so she continued.

"I became ill one day and was taken to Middlesex Hospital." She stared down at the wood floor. "I didn't know it was cholera until later, or that Miss Nightingale herself had been my nurse. When I heard she was going to treat the wounded, I begged to go with her. I was willing to learn anything I could."

She wondered if he knew this confession was difficult for her. It seemed he did, because he reached for her. She put both hands in the air, palms toward him. She really couldn't finish her story if he touched her.

"I had no other place to go, Fergus, but that's not why I wanted to be a nurse. I found that by helping others, I could forget where I came from." She took a step toward one of the windows.

"Miss Nightingale taught me everything," Elizabeth said. "I learned to speak like her, to dress like her, to be better than I was. I learned nursing to heal myself, then realized I could be a help to others."

"You're as far from your past as we are from London, Elizabeth."

She looked at him.

"Do you think I give a damn about your family, Elizabeth? I've got a family that goes back three hundred years, and a pittance to my name." His arms stretched outward to encompass the whole of Gairloch. "I'm laird of this great and grand place, and I haven't the funds to repair the roof or buy sheep."

"Well, good," she said.

"Good?" His eyebrows rose. "Good?"

"You're a very imposing man, Fergus, being the Laird of Gairloch. And winning the Victoria Cross. If you have no money, then it means we're alike in one way."

"You have more than me."

"How can you say that? I've nothing but what Mr. Loftus pays me. No family, no honors, certainly no history to call mine."

"You have something of infinite worth to me," he said. "My heart."

How easily he could steal her breath.

"But I have nothing to offer a wife," he said.

"Oh, how can you say that?" she said, going to him and placing her hand on his chest. Her other hand went to his cheek where it rested, her thumb brushing the corner of his mouth. "You're such a handsome man."

"One who loves you, Elizabeth."

She looked up at him.

"I've never stopped."

Oh, neither had she. Tears misted her eyes.

"With your wounds, Major Imrie, you really do require some ongoing attention."

Surprisingly, startlingly, wonderfully, he smiled.

"Are you offering to be my nurse, Miss Jamison?"

"I believe it's a position commensurate with my experience, Major Imrie."

"I've only a paltry sum available to pay you."

She looked around the tower. "But a magnificent place in which to live, sir. Surely, that should count as something." Reaching out, she touched one aged brick. "You aren't going to sell it, though, are you? Gairloch is part of you. You're part of it. I would hate to see anyone but you living here."

"I don't see any other option," he admitted.

"There must be one, Fergus."

"We'll figure it out, Elizabeth," he said.

Her eyes filled with tears because her heart was so full.

"Together, though, all right?" He reached for her. "I don't want to ever lose you again."

She smiled through her tears.

In the next moment, he kissed her for the first time. Somehow, it seemed right to wait until this moment, this place with the stars shining down on Gairloch's tower, and even the air holding its breath around them.

A storm was coming. Shona could feel it in the moisture in the air, in the soft night breeze that carried with it a hint of rain. A storm would mirror her mood, allow her to weep in the onslaught of it. She could stand in the courtyard and raise her face to the sky and no one would be able to tell she wept. But would her tears be from frustration, anger, or grief?

She fled—a thoroughly improper act, since she was hostess—to the library, a room that had always been a sanctuary for her. She could smell the musty volumes, the oiled leather of the covers and feel herself settle and calm.

As a child, she'd played a game of closing her eyes and walking down each narrow aisle, being able to tell exactly which section she was in by the shape of the books and how they were shelved. The travel books were larger and thicker, and had a great many maps that folded out, making them among the most cumbersome of volumes. But the books on alchemy, almost certainly forbidden when they were first written, were the most fascinating. Certain books had been written in Latin, and contained drawings she didn't understand. Others had cloth covers that hadn't worn well in the last two hundred years. Some were leather, kept from cracking by careful oiling.

The light from the hall streamed into the room, leaving shadows in the corners. She moved to the table beside the secret panel, lighting the lamp there before sitting on the nearby chair. Years ago, she'd arranged to have this chair moved into the library, so that she might sit and read in peace.

Now, the room was a haven, a place to remember, as well as a refuge.

"Are you hiding again, Shona Imrie?"

She stood, facing Gordon.

"Donegal," she said, tilting her head up. "My husband was Bruce Donegal, the eighth Earl of Morton."

"As if I could forget," he said.

"You never seem to remember."

He was looking at her as if he'd never seen her before, or was he storing up the sight of her for his trip to England? For his marriage?

She hated him at that moment, with every bit of pride she had left.

"Should I be warmed by the fact that you're here, and not thinking of some London miss?"

"Are you jealous, Shona?" he asked, his smile almost smug.

"Jealous? Why should I be, Gordon? You're here, instead of there, aren't you?"

He approached her, devilment in his eyes. "Indeed I am," he said.

He took a few more steps toward her, stalking her, as if she were a Highland deer, and he a hungry predator. Well, she wasn't going to allow him to back her into a corner.

She stood her ground, folding her arms and staring at him. When she noticed the direction of his glance, and the fact that her pose only accentuated her bosom, she dropped her arms and frowned at him.

"What do you want?"

"I could say you," he answered, a curious smile curving his lips. "But that's not how this game is played, is it, Shona?"

"What game is that, Gordon?"

"Our thrust and parry. Our constant give and take. If we could be united, I don't doubt we could accomplish all manner of things."

He reached out and stroked a finger along her arm. She took a step back, out of range of his touch.

"But we're united only in lust, aren't we?"

Did he think to seduce her here, in the library, while two hundred people partied on the other side of the door?

He strode forward, gently pushed her up against a bookshelf, blocking her escape.

Glancing down between them, at the sight of her

breasts pressed against his chest, he softly said, "I like your dress. I would prefer it, however, if you wore it only for me. The sight of all those other men ogling you has put me in a bad mood."

"So, your mood is all their fault," she said.

"And yours."

"Mine?" she asked, surprised. "I've barely spoken to you all night." Instead, she'd been very careful to avoid him.

"I know," he said. "Perhaps that's what put me in such a bad mood." His finger traced her bottom lip. "Your lips need kissing," he said.

One of Gordon's kisses was a snare.

"I don't want you to touch me," she said. "I want you to leave me alone."

"Does the great Shona Imrie Donegal, Countess of Morton, always get what she wants?" he asked, his tone low and almost fierce.

She didn't respond. What could she say? That she'd not gotten what she'd truly wanted for seven years?

He startled her by cupping his hands around her breasts outside her dress. Her traitorous body immediately reacted to his touch. Her nipples hardened as her pulse beat increased and her breath grew tight.

And all he did was stand there and hold her.

"I could take you here," he said. "Against one of the bookcases. Or the wall. A kilt makes it easier, you know."

He could and she wouldn't fight him. Fight him? She'd probably urge him on. But what she'd learned in the Clan Hall kept her from reaching for him.

"Go away. Or did you just come here to ogle me yourself?"

He smiled. "I've a mind to kiss you," he said in a

thick brogue. "But I think right now that would be a dangerous thing."

She only stared at him, reminding herself that he'd spoken of a woman in London. She would not be a substitute, a surrogate for another. Did he love her? The question kept her silent.

He surprised her by grabbing the material of her sleeve, that scrap of fabric slipping down her arm, and pinning the Imrie Clan brooch there. Once fixed, he patted it as if to keep it in place.

"If you want a better position," he said, "you should have worn a more substantial dress."

Her gaze flew to his face.

"I never meant to keep it," he said, stepping back.

"I won't take your charity, Gordon MacDermond," she said.

His face changed. His eyes, those beautiful blue eyes of his, flattened.

"No, you won't, will you? You won't take anything from me. Except lust. Well, Shona, I've decided that I'm a bit more particular in my bed partners."

What did that mean?

She went to remove the brooch, but before she could, he turned and walked away, leaving the library, as proud and as stubborn as any Imrie.

Now, she truly did want a good cry, but there was hardly time for it, was there? Perhaps she could indulge in a little histrionics after the party was done, and the guests all sent home with visions of something other than either Fergus or herself indulging in a fit of temper.

A sound nudged her from her self-pity. At first, she thought it was someone coming into the library. Pressing her cool hands against her heated cheeks, she hoped for calm and some form of composure.

*Dear Lord, please don't let me make a fool of myself
again.*

The noise, however, was coming from inside the passage. As if someone was struggling to get out.

She pressed the release and watched as the secret door
swung open.

A second later, everything went black.

Chapter 29

In all her life, Helen Paterson had never had such a delightful time. She danced a series of country dances, despite the fact she didn't know the steps to any of them. Her companions thought it great fun whenever she stepped right when she should have stepped left or vice versa. Once, she turned around and realized she shouldn't have turned at that moment, and joined in the general hilarity.

She'd also sipped whiskey. Well, perhaps it was more than just a sip. The world became a warm and amber-tinged place, where people smiled at her, and wished her well. She felt so grateful to each and every one of them that she wanted to kiss and hug them all.

Evidently, she wasn't to hug everyone she saw, because that only made people laugh more. She wasn't the least offended. Who could be angry at laughter?

The longer the party kept on, however, the more she was conscious of a vague and troubling notion. Finally, when the dawn sky was visible through the open front door, she figured out what it was.

Shona wasn't at the party.

Fergus had reappeared in the Clan Hall with Elizabeth on his arm. They'd danced together, to the surprise of both Mr. Loftus and his daughter. Twice, in full view of the entire gathering, he'd kissed her on the cheek.

That had garnered the approval of everyone, except for the Americans.

Would Shona have been pleased?

A question Helen intended to ask the moment she was located. Where on earth could Shona be?

Around dawn, the guests began leaving. The poor cook and the maid had served everyone a hearty breakfast. Even dear Mr. Loftus had partaken. She'd spied him sipping some whiskey and only shook her head at him when he glanced in her direction. He really did need to be taken in hand.

She had the most curious feeling of dizziness when she stood, and wondered if it was the aftereffect of the amount of whiskey she'd sipped. If so, she really didn't want to sample any ever again. And this growing headache, was that a remnant, too?

How did people consume the stuff on a daily basis?

A few minutes later, she stood at the door behind Fergus and Elizabeth, waving to the departing guests.

"Have you seen Shona?" she asked, when there was a lull in the farewells.

Fergus shook his head before glancing toward Elizabeth, who left to tend to her patient.

"Mr. Loftus will need to hire another nurse," he said.

Did he think that such an announcement would surprise her? It had been obvious from the moment Elizabeth had come to Gairloch that they were smitten with each other.

"Do you think Shona went to bed early?"

How very strange, if so. But it had been all too evident that Shona was uncomfortable since the moment Miriam announced she was wearing a borrowed dress.

He glanced up the stairs where Elizabeth was following behind Helmut and her employer.

"Fergus," she said, frustrated at his inattention. "Shona. Why would she have left the party?"

He finally concentrated on her. "Gordon left early. Perhaps she left with him."

A thoroughly shocking thing to do, of course. Even as surprising was the fact that Fergus had suggested it.

She left him to finish the farewells, following the others up the stairs. They would all sleep the day away. Miriam had probably already retired. But she discovered that Shona had not.

She wasn't in her room, in Helen's room, or in the public rooms of Gairloch.

As the morning sun set the dew to sparkling, Helen told herself that she was being foolish. Shona was a grown woman, more than capable of taking care of herself. It was quite evident that she'd gone off with Gordon. If that were the case, she'd only be embarrassed by Helen continuing to look for her.

With great reluctance, she went off to her own bed, hoping that the feeling she was getting was only the punishment she received for imbibing whiskey and nothing else.

A harsh voice spoke to her, the sound of it rising and falling like a sighing breath. "I've got you now. You won't bother anyone."

The echo of it seemed to linger for hours, followed by the sound of receding footsteps.

Shona closed her eyes, but the pain didn't go away. Slowly, she raised her hand to her head, and felt something warm and sticky on the side of her head. Blood?

She was lying on the floor of the passage. She blinked, but that didn't make it any easier to see. She was in total darkness, so complete that it felt smothering. Rustling sounds somewhere ahead of her made her try to sit up. She wasn't going to be nibbled on by a rat.

Deciding what to do, however, was a little different from actually accomplishing the feat. The pain grew as she raised her head higher, supporting herself on one forearm. Nausea, swift and unexpected, made her take a few deep breaths before continuing.

Suddenly, it was simply easier to rest. To close her eyes and pretend this was only a dream.

Chapter 30

The song of the piper hung in the clear air. A signal,
then, to be away.

Anne was leaving with little, feeling as she did that
most of it belonged to her husband. Her sons, dear God,
she was leaving her sons, but they were of an age now
to barely note her living, and probably barely note her
absence.

For the first time in her life, she was going to do
something forbidden and dreadful, for the most wonderful of reasons. She and Brian were going away, to
live together where the world would think them man
and wife. He was going to say farewell to his new home,
and she was going to say good-bye to all she'd held dear.
Until, of course, she'd fallen in love with him.

The world would not understand, and God would
not forgive, but she knew how Eve had felt in the
Garden. Even though God had forbidden her, she'd felt
compelled to eat of the fruit anyway.

She'd lain with Brian and felt no shame. Dear Heav-
enly Father, she'd only felt unclean when her husband
had come to her bed days later.

A sign, then, that she should not regret what she did.

They would have each other to love and comfort
even if the rest of the world shunned them. What was

the world, anyway, but people with narrowed eyes and long noses?

She was taking only her silver brush, a gift from her mother at her wedding; a miniature of her parents; and a lock of hair from each of her sons. She would never forget them, although after today, they would probably never mention her name again.

Slowly, carefully, and with great stealth, she made her way to the corridor linking the Clan Hall to the kitchen area, then ducked into the newly built map room. Magnus was very fond of maps, and had shelves built to hold all of them. When she'd mentioned that the room would make a fine library, he'd ignored her as he did most of her pronouncements.

Would he even notice she was gone?

The secret door was easily opened. Each week one member of the clan was given the responsibility for seeing to it that the passage was kept clear and the doors functional. After all, it was an escape route for them if they were ever trapped in Gairloch, just as it was an escape route for her, now.

Shona made it to her knees, resting a moment as dizziness almost forced her to the ground again. Finally, she got to her feet, leaning weakly against the door. Reaching out, she grabbed the pull for the door release.

Nothing happened.

She closed eyes, waiting until the dizziness passed, and tried again. The door didn't open.

She'd simply misjudged, that was all. All she had to do was to remain calm, trace her fingers up the stone wall, pull down on the handle as she had so many times. The door would open slowly and she would slip into the library.

When she pulled on the release, nothing happened.

She was not going to panic. She was, after all, an Imrie. But even more than that, she knew the passages well. How many times had she traveled through them? A hundred? Two hundred? If there was something wrong with the door release into the library, there were at least ten other doors.

All she had to do was remember how to navigate the passages.

She sat, knees drawn up, with her back to the door. The effect of pure darkness was disorienting. Even if she blinked, she couldn't see anything.

A sound startled her, sounding so much like a sigh that she called out. "Who's there?"

No one answered.

She wrapped her arms around her knees, wishing she'd worn anything but the crimson dress. Her arms were cold, and her back felt like ice where it rested against the door.

The next closest door was in the Clan Hall. She got to her feet, turned left, and slowly began walking, counting her paces. Her right hand stretched out to the stone of the far wall, and she fervently hoped she didn't encounter any insects going about their lives in perfect darkness.

Ahead was a small rectangular bar of yellow-white light. She began to smile as she made her way to it.

Standing on tiptoe, she looked out into the Clan Hall. The dancing had spilled out from the Family Parlor, and now people were engaged in one of those country dances she'd learned as a child.

She was certain to scare the lot of them when she emerged from the passage. Then, too, she would reveal the presence of the secret passages. But she wasn't about to wait here until the room was cleared of guests.

Reaching up, she pulled on the bottom of the torch

holder. The door didn't open. She pulled on the latch again, and only heard a noise like metal grinding on metal. Had something been wedged between the opening mechanism and the door? In the darkness, she traced each part of the latch as far into the door she could. The hasp ended in a sharp edge, as if it had been sawed through.

Had that happened with the door to the library?

The faint panic she'd been able to subdue earlier was growing now.

She banged on the door with both fists. This section was brick on the other side. That, coupled with the noise of the party and the music, meant that no one heard her.

"I'm in the passage!"

Not one person turned to look toward the fireplace. "I'm here!"

Another minute of banging on the door brought the realization that she wouldn't be heard in the Clan Hall. But she could make her way back to the larder. There was a small door below the bottom shelf. Granted, she would have to crawl on her hands and knees, but she didn't care. Right now, she very much wanted to be out of the passages however it was accomplished.

She turned back the way she'd come, following the passage as it sloped downward. The closer she came to the kitchen, the more she could smell the food they'd served tonight. Smells of salmon, claret-cooked beef, shortbread, cottage pie, and Gairloch cake, a confection filled with fruit and nuts, flavored the air.

Her stomach rumbled, reminding her that she hadn't eaten.

The moment she entered the larder, she'd prepare a plate for herself.

She felt the wooden framework of the door and slowly slid to her knees, all the while conscious of her pounding head. Blood had dried on her cheek, and it itched. She hadn't used this door since she was a child, but the mechanism was the same.

Reaching for the latch, she pulled at it with all her strength. When it didn't budge, she braced her shoulder against the door and pushed.

Nothing happened.

Too late, she recalled that they'd moved the barrels of flour and salted fish against the door. Sheer force would not open it.

What was she going to do if she couldn't open one of the doors? What if she couldn't get out?

Shona Imrie, calm down. She had at least eight more doors to try. Surely they couldn't all be broken.

But was that the right word? It felt as if they'd been damaged on purpose, as if someone really didn't want her to escape.

Had Miriam done this? Had the American woman not forgiven her after all, and this was some horrid joke at her expense? Was Miriam going to release her after a few hours when she was suitably chastened?

Miriam could release her right at the moment and she'd be grateful. She was cold, hungry, and didn't like being in the secret passages when they were so dark.

But she was not going to cry. She was an Imrie.

Oh bother that. When had being an Imrie ever given her an advantage? When had being herself ever given her an advantage?

Shona Imrie, proud and arrogant. Look at Shona now, on her knees, fighting back tears. She pressed her hand against the clan brooch. Her heart and her head hurt. Her heart because of what she'd said and done. Her head because of someone else.

The dark, dank silence stretched until Shona could hear only the booming of her heart, its rhythm oddly worrying. Was it beating too loudly, too fiercely? Was it going to stop in fright?

For pity's sake, Shona, you're an Imrie. Be a little more courageous. But she couldn't see anything, and courage was infinitely easier in the sunlight.

Something filmy and sticky touched her face and she impatiently brushed it away. She didn't mind spiders, actually, as long as she could see them. Right now, she couldn't see anything.

Wasn't there a torch at each door? What did it matter when she had no matches?

She made her way down the passage, realizing that she was so disoriented that she wasn't certain exactly where she was. Sitting down on the dirt floor, she drew up her knees.

Two choices faced her—to wait until morning when she was bound to be discovered, or find her way to the door to the loch. The journey was so familiar that she should be able to do it even in the darkness.

The idea of waiting wasn't appealing at all, especially since she was growing colder by the moment.

"Where are you going, Anne?"

A shudder traveled through her.

Slowly, she turned and faced her husband. Magnus stood holding a torch, the passage door closed behind him.

"With a pack and your best dress on, and your hair fixed as it was the day we wed. Where are you going, Anne?"

"What are you doing here, Magnus?" she asked.

He advanced on her, his thin, cruel smile warning enough.

"Where are you going, Anne?"

"Why do you care?"

"You're leaving with him, aren't you?"

Once, he'd been a handsome man, but cruelty had marred his features, making them sharper. "Brian, the piper. The one man who owed me nothing but friendship."

"He's your friend, Magnus."

"What kind of friend steals my wife?"

She was not his to steal. She wasn't his possession, like his horse or his sword, but saying such things to Magnus would only result in a blow. Her husband cared little for her, except as a vessel for his seed, or a mare to bear his children. Once her duty was done, he'd discarded her.

"You'll not leave me, Anne."

He grabbed her arm, but not tightly. Such kindness was not like him.

"Where are you meeting him?"

When she didn't speak, he shook her. "Tell me."

"I'll stay with you, Magnus. Just leave him alone."

"How sad you sound, Anne. Do you love him so much?"

She knew better than to answer that.

"Where, Anne?" *His grip was tighter, and his smile had disappeared.*

She shook her head, then closed her eyes when he twisted her arm behind her.

"Tell me."

She would hold out as long as she could. Hopefully, Brian would wait for her only so long. When she didn't come, would he return to Rathmhor? Or would he leave, as he'd planned?

Please, God, she thought, *make him leave before she told Magnus that he was waiting for her at the end of the passage, where the door opened to Loch Mor.*

By the time Magnus carried her, broken and bleeding, through the passages and into the cave, Anne no longer felt any pain. All she could think about was that she'd betrayed the one man she'd ever loved.

If there was a God, let Brian escape before Magnus and his followers found him.

Pride propelled Magnus forward, not love.

She and Brian had sinned, though, and because of that, she didn't struggle when Magnus wrapped the chains around her wrists. When he spat in her face and told her, in words that reeked of blood and vengeance, what he was going to do to her lover, she only stared up at him weakly and wished him tormented to death.

When they brought Brian to her, only a spark of life left in his body, she curved herself over him, wept, and welcomed heaven.

Helen couldn't sleep.

A few minutes later, she crept into Shona's room, her heart lurching at the sight of the empty bed. She returned to her chamber, dressing slowly, wondering if she dared do what she felt most compelled to do.

She might cause a scandal if Shona was with Gordon. But what if she wasn't?

She finished dressing, plaiting her hair and attaching it sensibly in a coronet. Smoothing her hands over her bodice, she stared out at the view. Fog skirted the ground, obscuring the dawn as well as the path to Rathmhor.

She'd be wise to simply remain at Gairloch until the morning was well advanced.

But something was wrong, a feeling that had been creeping up on her as the hours progressed. After settling the bonnet on her head and tying the ribbons with firmness, she nodded to herself just once.

For good or ill, she was going in search of Shona.

* * *

The cold woke Shona.

She was sitting with her back to the wall. Blinking didn't make the darkness any less absolute. She'd had time to acquaint herself with the blackness, but familiarity made it even less tolerable.

How many hours had passed since she'd been trapped in the passages? Enough time to deduce that six of the doors she'd found had been tampered with so they didn't work.

Enough time for the party to dissolve? If she could find her way back to the Clan Hall, perhaps someone could hear her now.

If she could find her way back.

She'd finally collapsed hours ago, when, despite how long she walked, she couldn't find the door to the loch. Nor could she find her way back to the pantry door.

Had she ever been in this part of the passages?

She rose to her knees, brushing her hair away from her face. Slowly, she stood, wishing she wasn't so confused. If she turned left, the ground sloped upward, but not necessarily to the Clan Hall; she'd discovered that a few hours ago. If she turned right, the ground sloped downward, but she'd learned that this passage didn't lead to the loch. No doors opened in this section of passages. Nothing was familiar.

She had never been here before, and it was all too evident that she was, like it or not, on her own. Alone.

She was Shona Imrie and she was terrified.

Chapter 31

"**I** do beg your pardon," Helen Paterson said, her plain face contorted with worry.

She glanced toward the housekeeper, and Gordon nodded to Mrs. MacKenzie that he would handle their unexpected—and early—guest.

"Some tea, perhaps?" Mrs. MacKenzie asked, and he shook his head. This was not, he surmised, a call to discuss pleasantries.

"What is it, Helen?" he asked, when his housekeeper left the room.

"I didn't know quite how to ask," she said. "If she was here, asking might have caused a scandal. And if she wasn't, just implying that she might be here might be shocking as well."

"Are you talking about Shona?" he asked patiently.

She nodded, her bonnet bobbing up and down fervently.

"She isn't here. Did you expect her to be?"

The bouncing bonnet was joined by flaming cheeks.

"She isn't at Gairloch, you see, and I thought she might be with you."

He grabbed her arm, and the bonnet abruptly stopped. "What do you mean, she isn't at Gairloch? Where is she?"

"That's it, Sir Gordon, I don't know. I haven't seen

her since she left the Clan Hall. I believe you followed her, did you not?"

He nodded. But their encounter had lasted only a few moments. Where had Shona gone, then?

"If she isn't here, Miss Paterson," he said, returning to the reason for her call, "where could she be?"

She blinked at him. "I don't know, Sir Gordon. But I'm very worried."

That simple statement from the eminently practical Helen Paterson concerned him more than anything else she'd said.

Shona turned left at the crossroads, the disorientation making her hesitate. This couldn't be correct. The floor of the passage was sloping uphill now, but she didn't see the light from the Clan Hall.

Stopping, she placed both hands flat on the walls on either side, forcing herself to calm. She closed her eyes, took several deep breaths, and pushed back the panic. She wanted to race down to the loch, open the door, and breathe deeply of the chilled night air. She didn't want to ever smell the sour tinge of old earth again. Or the dusty air of the passages.

Opening her eyes, she faced the blackness, retracing her steps mentally. Right now, all her earlier travels through the passages counted for nothing. She was truly lost.

Something skittered across her left hand. Jerking her hand back, she gripped her skirts, pulling them upward so as not to drag on the floor, and turned, going back the way she came.

Where was the crossroads?

How did she lose it?

Oh, dear God, was she doomed to walk Gairloch's passages like the ghosts were said to do? Right at the moment, she wouldn't mind a ghost of two if, for no other reason than to keep her company.

As if hearing her thought, a plaintive sound hung in the air. The last, lingering notes of the pipes, or a ghost's sigh.

She flattened her back against the wall, knowing that she was holding onto her courage by a thin hair, a filament as fine as the spider's web that clung to her cheek. She brushed it off, repeating the words that hadn't brought her any strength so far. *I'm an Imrie. I'm Shona Imrie.*

Perhaps she was simply a foolish woman, one who'd been guilty of too much arrogance in the past. Gairloch, after all, had not been an accomplishment of hers, but that of an ancestor. Being the Countess of Morton was only a title acquired through an effortless marriage. What had she earned by virtue of her own effort?

She'd survived these past two years, handling circumstances that would have tried anyone. She'd cared for Fergus and Helen and kept a roof over all their heads, never mind that it looked as if she would be tossed into gaol for not paying her debts. Still, every morning she'd attempted to look on the bright side, and find a way out of her predicament.

There, an accomplishment of her own, but one about which she could hardly brag.

Her entire life was going to perdition, and she was tired of pretending that it wasn't. Her marriage to Bruce had been a disaster, a polite, mannerly, boring disaster, because she'd been desperately in love with Gordon the whole while.

She'd been wrong. Love was necessary. It wasn't separate and apart from other emotions. Instead, it wound itself through a person's heart and mind and soul. She'd felt jealousy because of love, done stupid things because of love, risked everything because of love.

Once, she'd said that she, Shona Imrie, would be no man's charity. She, Shona Imrie, would not go begging to any man. So she'd said seven years ago. So she'd said a few weeks ago. So she'd said a day ago. And now?

Gordon, save me.

When Gordon and Helen arrived at Gairloch, Mr. Loftus was holding court at breakfast over a pile of rashers, scones, and what looked to be colcannon. The subdued clink of silverware on china, their murmured voices seemed normal, commonplace, and wrong to Gordon.

Helen made a sound of disapproval after a glance at the American's plate.

"Rashers are not good for you, Mr. Loftus," she said, making a clicking sound with her tongue. "Really, Elizabeth, have you no concern for your patient?"

"I'm afraid Elizabeth has resigned her position, Miss Paterson," Fergus said, standing. "She has agreed to marry me."

Gordon felt as if he were split into two people. One was standing there in the doorway to the dining room. The other was clapping Fergus on the shoulder and congratulating him on the news he just announced.

The bruise on his jaw still hurt, so he doubted Fergus would welcome his good wishes. His old friend surprised him by standing, saying something quietly to Elizabeth at his side, and rounding the table. He tensed, more than willing to fight him if that's what the other man wanted, but later. Right now there was another, more urgent matter.

"Have you seen Shona?"

That stopped Fergus in his tracks. He frowned, and said, "When?"

"This morning. Or last night," he said with a look at Helen. "Anytime."

"She seems to be missing," Helen said. "Her bed has not been slept in."

Fergus didn't say anything for a minute, then turned back to the dining table. "Has anyone seen Shona since last night?"

Miriam was picking at a piece of toast. "No, but I do hope something hasn't happened to her. After all, that was a very expensive dress I loaned her." She smiled up at them guilelessly, "She did realize it was just a loan, didn't she?"

Fergus didn't answer, moving on to Mr. Loftus whose attention hadn't veered from his meal. Helmut wasn't present again. Neither was Old Ned, but that was to be expected given his nocturnal habits.

"Sir," Fergus said, "have you seen my sister?"

The American only shook his head.

Fergus turned and looked at him. He could almost hear the question Fergus didn't voice in front of the ladies. *Did you take Shona home?* If she'd agreed to come home with him, he would've taken advantage of her willingness. Hell, he would've kept her there, and to perdition with the gossips and the whole of society.

He only shook his head.

"Then we should do a thorough search of Gairloch," Helen said. "I've only looked in the public rooms, Fergus."

"I'll take the second floor," Elizabeth announced, standing.

Fergus nodded, moving to her side. Evidently, he had plans to accompany her.

Miriam didn't bestir herself to offer to search. Neither did anyone ask her. Gordon didn't have the patience for her apathy.

"It wouldn't hurt to look through the public rooms again," Helen said. "I might have missed her."

He doubted that was the case, but smiled at her in reassurance. "Then do so, by all means. Perhaps Cook and Jennie can see to the third floor while I go search the outbuildings."

"Where could she have gotten to?" Helen said.

He patted her on the arm, a touch to substitute for words he didn't have.

Perhaps Shona had gone to Inverness to sell the clan brooch, an idea that had occurred to him on their walk back to Gairloch. He wouldn't put it past her. Sometimes, Shona's pride was almost a living thing, an entity of its own.

After reaching the stable, however, he realized that she couldn't have traveled to Inverness. She didn't have a carriage and the American's coach was still in the stable.

An affable Ned was smiling and singing as he was mucking out one of the stalls. He studied the man for several moments. Ned wasn't entirely sober. Instead, he teetered on the edge of drunkenness.

"Have you seen Shona, Ned?"

The older man whirled, pitchfork raised in front of his chest like a weapon.

"It's like to scare a body to death when you come up on a man like that," Ned said. "I thought you a ghost, I did."

"A ghost?"

"The Gairloch ghosts, sir. The piper and his lady, wandering the passages trying to find each other."

He only nodded, hoping he wouldn't have to endure a drunken soliloquy. Ned's addiction to the bottle had to be addressed before he drank himself into an early grave.

"Where's Helmut?"

"The German?"

Ned walked to the door of the stable and pointed west. "Out riding one of the horses. He don't like Gairloch, mostly. Dark days do him in, and he hates the rain, he do."

"The other horses are here?" he asked. "None of them are missing?"

Ned shook his head.

"Do you think the Americans will mind if I borrow one of their horses?"

"Better to be exercised than standing in their stalls getting fat," Ned said, and went back to singing his song.

He headed in the direction Ned had pointed, hoping to God Helmut held the answer to Shona's disappearance.

The wall abruptly changed from a straight line to the beginning of a curve. Shona pulled back her hand, surprised. Her father had told her that there were places in the passages where previous generations of Imries had hidden their weapons. Or, as after the Forty-five, they used the caverns to hide their kilts and pipes and any silver that might be confiscated for their participation in the rebellion. She'd never found any such caches, but the experience of the last few hours had taught her that she didn't know the secret passages as well as she'd always thought.

Another instance of her pride holding sway.

What good was pride when nothing else was left? Why should she pretend anymore? Pride hadn't warmed her heart, or held her, or made life any easier. Let the world see exactly who and what she was.

She stumbled on something, the metallic clank unexpected and jarring in the silence. Bending down, she patted the ground until she found it, following the chain to the end.

Falling to her knees, she bit back a scream, knowing that no one could hear her anyway. No one but her companions in this secret cave.

By mid-afternoon, they'd finished searching Gairloch from the ground floor to the towers. Shona wasn't to be found.

"Would she have taken the boat out on the loch?" Elizabeth asked Helen.

The three of them were standing in the Clan Hall, having separated from Mr. Loftus and his daughter. Neither of them seemed overly concerned about Shona's fate. At the beginning, Miriam had treated her disappearance like a game. Now, it was evidently palling, since she'd retreated to her room for some occupation or another.

"It's a damn deep lake," Fergus said, frowning at both of them. "And cold. If something happened to her . . ."

None of them completed that thought.

"No," Gordon said, entering the room. "She wouldn't do that. Besides, all the boats are accounted for."

"Then, we should start looking over the glen," Fergus said. "She might have fallen and injured herself."

Gordon nodded. "The drivers already are, with Helmut commanding them."

"Helmut?"

"Evidently, the man has a dislike of Gairloch," Gordon said, glancing toward Fergus. "He told me the ghosts are too brazen here, not like in his homeland. He's been awakened for the last two weeks by their banging and tapping, but this morning was the last straw. The *bean tuiream* woke him up."

"The weeping woman?" Helen asked.

Fergus nodded. "Shona used to say that the *bean tuiream* was a sign that something momentous was about to happen to the Imries."

"Momentous? Or terrible?" Helen asked.

"The *bean tuiream*?" Gordon asked, turning. He stared at the brick wall, then walked toward the fireplace. "Has anyone looked in the passages?"

"No," Fergus said, joining him. "But Shona knows these passages better than anyone."

"Maybe something's happened to her," Gordon said pushing back his sudden fear.

Fergus reached up and pulled at the brick that released the door.

"It's not opening."

"She could be trapped," Gordon said, tracing his fingers along the almost invisible line marking the hidden door.

Fergus didn't comment, only pulled on the brick again.

The door wasn't opening.

Fergus stepped back and looked at Gordon. "I'll go to the stable and get some tools."

Gordon nodded.

The moment Fergus left the room, Gordon walked to the fireplace, grabbed the poker, and in glorious disregard for the antiquity and value of the mantelpiece, raised the poker and began to break the bricks.

Shona was in there; he knew it. He knew it because of the sick feeling in his gut, the cold feeling down his spine, and the fact that the damn door wasn't opening as it always had.

Chips of masonry went flying so fiercely that Elizabeth and Helen stepped back.

"What can I do?" Helen asked over the noise of his assault.

Get out of my way. Let me get to her. Dear God.

He only shook his head in response, unwilling to stop even to be polite. Grabbing the other end of the poker, he slammed it into the wall overhand, like a spear. A small opening appeared next to the seam marking the door.

"Shona!"

The larger the gouge appeared, the louder he shouted. The sound of her name became a rhythm, a drumbeat he shouted every few seconds.

"You'll let the ghost out!"

He glanced over his shoulder to see Old Ned barreling toward him, a hammer clutched in his fist. He rolled along the wall just in time to avoid the blow.

Ned was as tall as he was, but not as fit, so he was easily subdued. Not before, however, landing a blow on his already bruised chin.

"What the hell have you done, Ned?" Fergus said, helping to hold the man.

"I trapped the ghost. You can't let the ghost out!"

It took the two of them to lead him to a chair. Gordon handed the hammer to Fergus who stood over Ned with the hammer in one hand and his cane in another.

Gordon turned back to the fireplace.

What if Shona had been in the passage all this time?

And an even worse thought—had Shona been the *bean tuiream*?

•

Chapter 32

They found her an hour later, in a small cavern off one of the passages.

The torchlight illuminated a scene out of a nightmare. One skeleton was chained to the wall. The other lay with head propped next to the first. By their clothing, he could tell one had been female and the other male.

Shona sat next to them, too close to becoming just like those lost souls.

A line of dried blood stretched from temple to cheek, and the rest of her face was spotted with dirt. Her lips were bitten raw, and the deep, shadowed crescents brushed by her lashes were the same color as her eyes.

He dropped to his knees beside her, pulling her gently into his arms. Slowly, and with great care, he removed her hand from atop the two still clasped together. The bones clicked as if to protest the loss of their living connection.

She moaned, and he brushed her tangled hair back from her face as he held her, cheek against his chest. He heard the others come in behind him, then just as quickly step back. In a moment, they would have time with her. Right now, she was his, just as she'd always been his.

"I love you, Colonel Sir Gordon MacDermond, first

Baronet of Invergaire," she said, her hoarse voice painful to hear. "If you've a woman in London, you'll just have to forget her."

He lowered his head until his cheek rested against her forehead, feeling his heart expand.

"I've no one in London, dear one."

She pressed her hands against his chest. "I think I've loved you always, from the moment I first saw you, all those years ago."

"And I you, Shona Imrie Donegal. You were Fergus's annoying little sister for so long, until one day . . ."

"I worked on you," she said softly. "I decided I was going to have you forever and ever."

"So you did," he said, wanting her to stop talking, to let him simply hold her.

"But I've been thinking," she said, insistent on speaking. "You were partly right."

"On which occasion?" he asked, smiling.

"You were right about my pride. But I'm thinking you have a bit of your own." She raised up and looked up at him. "You could have come after me before I married Bruce. You could have put your own pride aside, Colonel Sir Gordon."

His lips quirked. "So I could have," he agreed.

"That's the past," she said. "I'm thoroughly tired of the past. I must be focused on the future, Gordon."

"Another point of agreement."

"I have no money," she said. "But I'm very much afraid I have to marry for money, again."

"Will you?" he asked, feeling the most absurd wish to laugh.

"I need a rich husband," she said, nodding.

He bent down and kissed her forehead, wondering if she would accept a proposal here and now.

"I bring nothing to you, Gordon. Nothing but love.

Fergus should live at Gairloch, and he can't bear to part with any of his shields or claymores."

Amusement was a strange feeling to have in conjunction with this other emotion, one that threatened to swamp him, and open up his chest so that he might give her his heart.

"I've no need for weapons," he said. "I've had my fill of them of late."

She sighed, then surprised him by sitting up and motioning Fergus inside the little cave, followed by Elizabeth.

Turning to him again, she placed her hands on either side of his face, staring into his eyes as she spoke the words slowly and somberly.

"I will consent to be your wife, Gordon MacDermond. Will you consent to be my husband?"

He smiled. "I will consent to be your husband, Shona Imrie Donegal, and cherish you for the rest of your life. Will you consent to be my wife?"

"And love you forever? With my whole heart, Gordon."

He heard Fergus say something, but he wasn't paying much attention, because right at that moment, he was looking at Shona.

He loved her—every proud, haughty look, every small mysterious smile, every toss of her head, and every single glance of her fog-colored eyes. The enormity of the love he felt for her nearly choked him.

Softly, gently, and tenderly, he kissed her.

Chapter 33

Shona sat in the chair by the fire.

Gordon stood by the fireplace, close enough to be needed, and smiled down at her.

"I've done as you asked," he said, "and summoned the lot of them here."

She only nodded, queenly in demeanor, but he was close enough to see that her lips trembled.

You should have rested more.

An admonition he wouldn't make. Nor would she have retreated to her bedroom. She was set on something, something she wouldn't tell him.

Mr. Loftus was the first to arrive, leaning heavily on a cane, his recent indulgences in wine and rich foods revealed by his gouty limp. Instead of being accompanied by Elizabeth, he was escorted into the room by his daughter, Miriam's lovely face wearing the sheen of boredom. She helped him sit on the end of the sofa, then took a seat on the opposite sofa.

"You don't look the worse for your experience, Countess," he said.

She only nodded in response.

But Gordon knew Shona Imrie Donegal as well as he knew himself. Her lovely gray eyes were shadowed, and she was still too pale. In a few hours, he would take her from here, and heal her in the only way he knew, with attention, conversation, but mostly love.

Miriam remained silent, an oddity from her. But perhaps the frown he'd given her warned her that he wasn't in the mood for any of her idiocy.

Helen was next, bustling into the room with hands clasped in front of her. He gave her a smile, indebted to her for her persistence in finding Shona. Surprisingly, she took a seat on the sofa beside Mr. Loftus, sending a winsome smile in his direction. He studied her, wondering if his suspicion was correct.

Cook and Jennie entered the Family Parlor just in front of Fergus, with Elizabeth on his arm. Fergus just stared back at him.

He'd have to make amends there.

Cook and Jennie moved to stand behind the sofa on which Miriam sat, but Shona shook her head. "Take a seat on the sofa," she said, and after a moment, they did, albeit reluctantly.

Old Ned had been sent to Rathmhor, under the care of Mrs. MacKenzie. Since the woman abjured any type of alcohol, even Scottish whiskey, she would watch over Ned until he could turn his back on spirits. Shona had made the decision after a conversation with the caretaker.

"Ned," Shona said, "have you been making sure the doors don't work in the passages?"

"It was the only way to keep the ghosts out."

"And you've been doing this at night?"

He nodded. "It's when you have to catch them. They wander through the hallways, always whispering, always trying to scare me."

Endless days of drinking Gairloch's whiskey had evidently addled Old Ned's wits.

"Did you strike me in the Clan Hall, Ned?" she asked.

He looked shamefaced, his eyes never quite meeting hers.

"That were a mistake, Miss Shona. I thought you were one of the ghosts come after me when I was sealing up the door."

"Did you lock me in the passage, Ned?"

He shook his head vehemently. "I wouldn't do that, Miss Shona." His face changed, his eyes dancing with merriment or self-congratulation, Gordon wasn't sure which. "I did trap me a ghost last night, though. The *bean tuiream*. Dressed all in red, she was. I got her good and fast, I did."

"Where is the madman?" Mr. Loftus said now. "When I buy Gairloch, I'll not have him in the place."

Gordon was an expert at reading Shona's expressions. He wondered if the others realized how enraged she was at this particular moment. He smiled, caught Fergus's eye, and almost laughed.

"I'm not selling Gairloch to you," she said very quietly and very firmly. "We're not selling," she added, glancing at Fergus.

"Does that mean, Father, that we can finally return home?" Miriam asked. "I'm very sorry, but I truly cannot abide Scotland. It's very cold and very empty, isn't it?"

"I apologize if you're disappointed," she said, ignoring Miriam and addressing her remark to Mr. Loftus.

"Oh, I doubt he's all that disappointed, Shona," Gordon said. "You didn't come to buy Gairloch, did you?" he asked, staring at the older man. "You were prepared to do so, if necessary. But that's not the real reason you're here."

Loftus didn't say a word, merely flicked his hand at Helmut, who was instantly at his side.

"No need for protection, Mr. Loftus. Just tell the truth."

"What are you talking about, Gordon?" Fergus asked.

"Somehow, he learned about the blasting powder. Was it you behind the burglary of my partner's lodgings?"

The American didn't say a word. Neither did his daughter, who viewed her father wide-eyed.

"He came to discover our formula," he said. "And if he couldn't steal it, to buy it." He studied the American. "All I want to know is how you knew? Did you have a spy in the village? Someone who conveyed the information to you?"

Shona turned to him. "The inspector. That's how he knew. He sent a man to look at Gairloch before we arrived. He probably stayed in the village."

Gordon folded his arms, and leaned back against the mantel, a deceptively casual pose that was as false as Shona's composure.

"Is that what happened, Mr. Loftus? You decided that my blasting powder would add to your considerable wealth?"

"You should sell it to me," Loftus said. "I could make you a fortune."

In Loftus, he saw his father, two men similar in their need for power. He wasn't going to take orders from anyone anymore. Not because of patriotism or paternal fealty or even greed. He was going to decide his own future.

"I think we can do quite well on our own," Gordon responded. He turned to Fergus. "And so could you, if you'd like to throw in your lot with us. I still need a manager for the Works."

"I need a position," Fergus said. "Now that I'm to be married."

Shona sent a surprised look to her brother, then smiled.

"But I won't be a model employee," Fergus added.

"You weren't a model soldier," he responded.

"The queen didn't agree." Elizabeth frowned at him, moving closer to Fergus.

Gordon couldn't help but smile. His friend deserved someone who would be as fiercely loyal as Elizabeth seemed to be.

"Oh, he's brave," he told Elizabeth. "But he's apt to argue with a command as obey it."

"Just the sort of employee you need," Fergus said, smiling. "You have a tendency to be an ass from time to time."

They grinned at each other, and just as quickly as that, they were friends again.

He was not, however, finished with Loftus. "You're the one behind the men trying to buy me out, I take it?"

The older man didn't answer, but there wasn't any need for words. The acknowledgment was there in the American's eyes.

"We'll be gone in the morning," Mr. Loftus said, standing.

Shona only nodded in response. He left the library, Helmut following in his wake.

Before Miriam followed, she turned to face Shona.

"You're a very strange countess," she said. "I can't imagine that any of my friends will really believe you existed. You swear and you're quite rude. Besides," she added, "you're not at all discreet. Or do you think that no one knows you two are lovers?"

Helen's eyes widened.

Shona, however, only smiled.

"You'll have to tell your friends that I'm a Scottish countess," she said calmly. "That makes all the difference."

"Is it like wearing a kilt?"

"Entirely," she said.

Gordon held his laughter until Miriam left the room. He came and stood in front of Shona, stretching out both hands. She placed hers in his, her eyes clear and focused on him.

"It's time to go home," he said softly.

She nodded.

"You're going to Rathmhor, then?" Fergus asked.

"With my wife, yes," he said.

Fergus shook his head. "Leave it to both of you to do it that way. I can't say I'm surprised."

"What have they done?" Helen asked, her gaze flicking between them.

"He married her. She married him. In the passage," Fergus said. "A declaration of intent witnessed by other people is as binding a marriage as any other in Scotland. But the Reverend John McIntyre will not be pleased," he added. "He'll declare it a penny marriage."

"That's because he'll want to preach dour pronouncements over us, first," Gordon said. "Or perhaps he simply wants a celebration."

"We have a lifetime to celebrate," Shona said, her gaze never moving from him.

Fergus eyed Elizabeth speculatively.

"No," Elizabeth said firmly, taking two steps back and holding up her hands. "A minister, please. I'm English. Not a Scot."

"You'll be a Scot soon enough. After all, you'll be the Laird of Gairloch's wife," Fergus said.

Shona glanced at Elizabeth. "You'll be an Imrie. Definitely not English." She looked at Fergus. "And you'll not be telling her about the feet washing."

"What? Feet washing?" Elizabeth said, but no one was answering.

"And you're a MacDermond," Gordon said, looking down at her. "Finally."

What happened between Fergus and Elizabeth would have to wait. What the rest of the Invergaire thought would simply have to wait. His blasting powder would have to wait.

He wanted to be alone with his wife.

His wife.

Shona stood on tiptoe and kissed him.

The whole damn world could wait.

Epilogue

❧

Sometimes, she was completely and totally con-
founded, as now.

Shona stared at the letter, then waved it at Gordon as
she entered his library.

"You'll never believe it," she said, standing beside
his desk.

He didn't give her a chance to talk further, merely
grabbed her skirt and pulled her over to sit on his lap,
not an easy feat considering she wore three petticoats
and her skirts were fulsome enough to cover his papers.

He kissed her soundly just as she was about to explain.

"It's from Helen," she said, somewhat breathlessly a
few minutes later.

"An explanation why she's left us alone for nearly a
week? Not that I mind," he said, and proceeded to kiss
her again.

They did this so often that it was a wonder he was
able to get any work done on his blasting powder. When
she said that to him, he merely laughed and kissed her
again.

Why did she always feel as if she'd imbibed Gairloch's
whiskey after kissing him? Whiskey that Mrs. MacKenzie refused to serve now that Old Ned was on her staff.

So many changes had occurred in just a week. Old
Ned was walking around dressed in clean clothes, his

eyes looking a little red, his beard shaved clean. Mrs. MacKenzie watched him as if he were a thief in their midst. Poor man, he took his life in his hands if he ever so much as thought of taking another drop of drink.

They had, amid a solemn ceremony, buried the man and woman from the passages in Invergaire. A small pack had been found in the cavern, as well as a set of pipes, leading to speculation that the two had been the laird's missing wife and Brian MacDermond. Would they ever know for sure? Perhaps if the ghosts of Gairloch were never heard from again.

The interment had been a very uncomfortable gathering, as it turned out, since Reverend McIntyre frowned at her and Gordon the whole time. He'd not liked the idea of an irregular marriage and was determined to have them wed, again, this time before the entire congregation.

She had no objection. She'd marry Gordon a hundred times over.

"No," she said now, pushing away from him. "You really need to read this."

She held out the letter for Gordon to read, retreating to the chair beside his desk. Not that his lap wasn't a perfect place, but some of the proprieties should be observed.

For a time.

He quickly scanned the letter, his answering smile indicating that this was no surprise to him.

"You suspected as much?" she asked. "Did you know Helen was going to marry Mr. Loftus?"

"Didn't you see how much she doted on him? She might become a wealthy widow in a few years."

Shocked, she stared at him. "You make her sound quite conniving."

"Not at all. But she did manage to snare the wealthiest man in the group." He handed her back the letter. "You could have married him, you know."

"And be exceptionally wealthy," she added, nodding. "There is that."

If she could have tolerated the man.

She placed the letter on top of the desk and crawled back onto his lap. "But I wouldn't have been happy," she said, wrapping her arms around his neck.

"Are you?"

His look was direct, his beautiful blue eyes holding only love for her. She laid her head against his shoulder, thinking that the world was a lovely place as long as Gordon was in it.

He'd once said that love wasn't simple for her, that it was twisted up in other emotions. This last week had been a lesson learned, and a foretelling of the future. Love for Gordon was pure, uncomplicated, direct, and endlessly satisfying. A rainbow, a feast, and a symphony.

"With my whole heart," she said. After that, it was difficult to think because he was kissing her again.

"Ah, but you'll soon be a great deal wealthier than Mr. Loftus," he said, when she pulled back, intent on luring him upstairs.

"Will I?"

How very curious not to care all that much. A roof over her head, some security was all she'd wanted. Instead, she got Gordon. She already was a wealthy woman.

She placed her cheek against his, wishing she didn't have the most curious wish to weep at the moment. Joy was the reason for these tears, not sorrow.

"Aren't you curious?"

Pulling back, she looked at him. "You evidently want me to be," she said, smiling.

"I've sold the blasting powder to the War Office."

Surprised, she stared at him. "Have you?" she said cautiously.

"And to the consortium. And to Mr. Loftus."

She began to smile. "Can you do that?"

"I can. It's the only way to ensure that it's used correctly, I think. It will temper the War Office's use as well." He glanced down at the letter on his desk. "They were bound to discover the formula sooner or later."

"Have you a plan for all this wealth?"

He smiled. "The Works need to be fitted to make the new blasting powder. Plus, I've had an idea to transport it to Inverness using Loch Mor."

She raised one eyebrow. "You have been thinking," she said.

"There will be a great many more people in Invergaire Glen in a few months."

"And some won't be here," she said, thinking of Helen.

"We can go to America, if you wish, make sure she's settled in. And meet other Americans. Something tells me they're not all like Mr. Loftus and his daughter."

"I'd like that," she said, taking a moment to kiss him again.

"There's another absence I need to tell you about," he said a few moments later. "Rani's going back to India."

"After he's become wealthy?"

"He wants to help his country," he said, "and who could blame him? Also, I think a woman is at the heart of it."

She smiled. "Aren't we always, dear one?" She bent and placed another kiss on his lips to mark her place there, on his body, in his heart, forever.

Author's Note

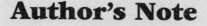

The first passenger elevator was installed in a New York City department store in 1857.

Alfred Nobel set up Works in Ardeer, Ayrshire, in 1871 to manufacture nitroglycerine. Sir Andrew Noble is considered the father of the science of ballistics. A physicist and gunnery expert, he devised a method to increase the firing accuracy of guns. I've taken both Nobel's and Noble's achievements and combined them for Gordon MacDermond.

Kieselguhr is another name for diatomaceous earth.

According to *Scottish Customs* by Margaret Bennett (1992, Polygon), *bean tuiream*, or mourning woman, refers mainly to a professional weeper, hired to mourn at a funeral. The word *tuiream* means to mourn for the dead, while *bean* means woman or wife. I've borrowed the term *bean tuiream* for one of the ghosts, the weeping woman.

Gairloch is also a town in the Highlands with a history dating back to the Iron Age.

After 1845, poor relief in Scotland was administered at the parish level. Several parishes in the east of Scotland operated smaller poorhouses such as almshouses, parish cottages, or parochial houses.

Kensington is now a very fashionable part of London but it once housed slums.

In Scotland, an irregular marriage didn't require the auspices of any official, religious or civil, but was as binding, as long as it was held before witnesses.

The Ninety-third (Sutherland Highlanders) Regiment of Foot was a Line Infantry Regiment of the British Army. It was united with the Ninety-first (Argyllshire Highlanders) Regiment of Foot in 1881 to form the Argyll and Sutherland Highlanders.

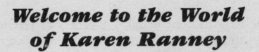

Welcome to the World of Karen Ranney

Turn the page to explore
other wonderful romances
Karen Ranney has in store for you.

A Highland Duchess

The beautiful but haughty Duchess of Herridge is known to all the *ton* as the "Ice Queen." But to Ian McNair, the exquisite Emma is nothing like the rumors. Sensual and passionate, she moves him as no other woman has before. If only she were his wife and not his captive . . .

Little does Emma know that the dark and mysterious stranger who bursts into her bedroom to kidnap her is the powerful Earl of Buchane, and the only man who has been able to see past her proper façade. As the Ice Queen's defenses melt under the powerful passion she finds with her handsome captor, she begins to believe that love may be possible. Yet fate has decreed that the dream can never be—for pursuing it means sacrificing everything they hold dear: their honor, their futures . . . and perhaps their lives.

Sold to a Laird

Lady Sarah Baines was devoted to her mother and her family home, Chavensworth. Douglas Eston was devoted to making a fortune and inventing. The two of them are married when Lady Sarah's father proposes the match and threatens to send Lady Sarah's ill mother to Scotland if she protests.

Douglas finds himself the victim of love at first sight, while Sarah thinks her husband is much too, well, earthy for her tastes. Marriage is simply something she had to do to ensure her mother's well-being, and even when her mother dies in the next week, it's not a sacrifice she regrets.

She cannot, however, simply write her mother's relatives and inform them of her death. She convinces Douglas—an ex pat Scot—to return to Scotland with her, to a place called Kilmarin. At Kilmarin, she is given the Tulloch Sgàthán, the Tulloch mirror. Legend stated that a woman who looked into the mirror saw her true fate.

Douglas and Sarah begin to appreciate the other, and through passion, Douglas is able to express his true feelings for his wife. But once they return to England and Douglas disappears and is presumed dead, Sarah has to face her own feelings for the man she's come to respect and admire.

A Scotsman in Love

Margaret Dalrousie was once willing to sacrifice all for her calling. The talented artist would let no man interfere with her gift. But now, living in a small Scottish cottage on the estate of Glengarrow, she has not painted a portrait in ages. For not even the calming haven in the remote woods can erase the memories that darken Margaret's days and nights. And now, with the return of the Earl of Linnet to his ancestral home, her hopes of peace have disappeared.

From the first moment he encountered Margaret on his land, the Earl of Linnet was nothing but annoyed. The grieving nobleman has his own secrets that have lured him to the solitude of the Highlands, and his own reasons for wanting to be alone. Yet he is intrigued by his hauntingly beautiful neighbor. Could she be the spark that will draw him out of bittersweet sorrow—the woman who could transform him from a Scotsman in sadness to a Scotsman in love?

The Devil Wears Tartan

Some say he is dangerous. Others say he is mad. None of them knows the truth about Marshall Ross, the Devil of Ambrose. He shuns proper society, sworn to let no one discover his terrible secret. Including the beautiful woman he has chosen to be his wife.

Only desperation could bring Davina McLaren to the legendary Edinburgh castle to become the bride of a man she has never met. Plagued by scandal, left with no choices, she has made her bargain with the devil. And now she must share his bed.

From the moment they meet, Davina and Marshall are rocked by an unexpected desire that leaves them only yearning for more. But the pleasures of the marriage bed cannot protect them from the sins of the past. With an enemy of Marshall's drawing ever closer and everything they now cherish most at stake, he and Davina must fight to protect the passion they cannot deny.

The Scottish Companion

Haunted by the mysterious deaths of his two brothers, Grant Roberson, tenth Earl of Straithern, fears for his life. Determined to produce an heir before it's too late, Grant has promised to wed a woman he has never met. But instead of being enticed by his bride-to-be, Grant can't fight his attraction to the understated beauty and wit of her paid companion.

Gillian Cameron long ago learned the danger of falling in love. Now, as the companion to a spoiled bluestocking, she has learned to keep a firm hold on her emotions. But, from the moment she meets him, she is powerless to resist the alluring and handsome earl.

Fighting their attraction, Gillian and Grant must band together to stop an unknown enemy from striking. Will the threat of danger be enough to make them realize their true feelings?

Autumn in Scotland

Betrothed to an earl she had never met, Charlotte Haversham arrived at Balfurin, hoping to find love at the legendary Scottish castle. Instead she found decaying towers and no husband among the ruins. So Charlotte worked a miracle, transforming the rotting fortress into a prestigious girls' school. And now, five years later, her life is filled with purpose—until . . .

A man storms Charlotte's castle—and he is *not* the reprehensible Earl of Marne, the one who stole her dowry and dignity, but rather the absent lord's handsome, worldly cousin Dixon MacKinnon. Mesmerized by the fiery Charlotte, Dixon is reluctant to correct her mistake. And though she's determined not to play the fool again, Charlotte finds herself strangely thrilled by the scoundrel's amorous attentions. But a dangerous intrigue has drawn Dixon to Balfurin. And if his ruse is prematurely revealed, a passionate, blossoming love affair could crumble into ruin.

An Unlikely Governess

Impoverished and untitled, with no marital prospects or so much as a single suitor, Beatrice Sinclair is forced to accept employment as governess to a frightened, lonely child from a noble family—ignoring rumors of dark intrigues to do so. Surely, no future could be as dark as the past she wishes to leave behind. And she admits fascination with the young duke's adult cousin, Devlen Gordan, a seductive rogue who excites her from the first charged moment they meet. But she dares not trust him—even after he spirits them to isolation and safety when the life of her young charge is threatened.

Devlen is charming, mysterious, powerful—and Beatrice cannot refuse him. He is opening new worlds for her, filling her life with passion . . . and peril. But what are Devlen's secrets? Is he her lover or her enemy? Will following her heart be foolishness or a path to lasting happiness?

Till Next We Meet

When Adam Moncrief, Colonel of the Highland Scots
Fusiliers, agrees to write a letter to Catherine Dunnan,
one of his officers' wives, a forbidden correspondence
develops and he soon becomes fascinated with her even
though Catherine thinks the letters come from her husband, Harry Dunnan. Although Adam stops writing
after Harry is killed, a year after his last letter he still
can't forget her. Then when he unexpectedly inherits the
title of the Duke of Lymond, Adam decides the timing
is perfect to pay a visit to the now single and available
Catherine. What he finds, however, is not the charming,
spunky woman he knew from her letters, but a woman
stricken by grief, drugged by laudanum and in fear for
her life. In order to protect her, Adam marries Catherine, hoping that despite her seemingly fragile state, he
will once again discover the woman he fell in love with.

The Highland Lords: Book One
One Man's Love

He was her enemy, a British colonel in war torn Scotland. But as a youth, Alec Landers, earl of Sherbourne had spent his summers known as Ian, running free on the Scottish Highlands—and falling in love with the tempting Leitis MacRae. With her fiery spirit and vibrant beauty, she is still the woman who holds his heart, but revealing his heritage now would condemn them both. Yet as the mysterious Raven, an outlaw who defies the English and protects the people, Alec could be Leitis's noble hero again—even as he risks a traitor's death.

Leistis MacRae thought the English could do nothing more to her clan, but that was before Colonel Alec Landers came to reside where the MacRae's once ruled. Now, to save the only family she has left, Leitis agrees to be a prisoner in her uncle's place, willing to face even an English colonel to save his life. But Alec, with his soldier's strength and strange compassion, is an unwelcome surprise. Soon Leitis cannot help the traitorous feelings she has when he's near . . . nor the strange sensation that she's known him once before. And as danger and passion lead them to love, will their bond survive Alec's unmasking? Or will Leitis decide to scorn her beloved enemy?

The Highland Lords: Book Two
When the Laird Returns

Though a descendant of pround Scottish lairds, Alisdair MacRae had never seen his ancestral Highland estate—nor imagined that he'd have to marry to reclaim it! But the unscrupulous neighboring laird Magnus Drummond has assumed control of the property—and he will relinquish it only for a King's ransom . . . and a groom for his daughter Iseabal! Alisdair never thought to give up the unfettered life he loves—not even for a bride with the face of an angel and the sensuous grace that would inflame the desire of any male.

Is Iseabal to be a bride without benefit of a courtship? Though she yearns for a love match, the determined lass will gladly bind herself to Alisdair if he offers her an escape from her father's cruelty. This proud, surprisingly tender stranger awakens a new fire inside her, releasing a spirit as brave and adventurous as his own. Alisdair feels the heat also, but can Iseabal win his trust as well as his passion—ensuring that both their dreams come true . . . now that the laird has returned?

The Highland Lords: Book Three
The Irresistible MacRae

To avoid a scandal that would devastate her family, Riona McKinsey has agreed to marry the wrong man—though the one she yearns for is James MacRae. Had she not been maneuvered into a compromising position by a man of Edinburgh—who covets her family's wealth more than Riona's love—the dutiful Highland miss could have followed her heart into MacRae's strong and loving arms. But alas, it is not to be.

A man of the wild, tempest-tossed ocean, James MacRae never dreamed he'd find his greatest temptation on land. Yet from the instant the dashing adventurer first gazed deeply into Riona's haunting gray eyes, he knew there was no lass in all of Scotland he'd ever want more. The matchless lady is betrothed to another—and unwilling to break off her engagement or share the reason why she will marry her intended. But how can MacRae ignore the passion that burns like fire inside, drawing him relentlessly toward a love that could ruin them both?

The Highland Lords: Book Four
To Love a Scottish Lord

Hamish MacRae, a changed man, returned to his beloved Scotland intending to turn his back on the world. The proud, brooding lord wants nothing more than to be left alone, but an unwanted visitor to his lonely castle has defied his wishes. While it is true that this healer, Mary Gilly, is a beauty beyond compare, it will take more than her miraculous potions to soothe his wounded spirit. But Mary's tender heart is slowly melting Hamish's frozen one . . . awakening a burning need to keep her with him—forever.

Never before has Mary felt such an attraction to a man! The mysterious Hamish MacRae is strong and commanding, with a face and form so handsome it makes Mary tremble with wanting him. Already shadowy forces are coming closer, heartless whispers and cruel rumors abound, and it will take a love more pure and powerful than any other to divine the truth—and promise a future neither had dreamed possible.

The Highland Lords: Book Five
So In Love

Jeanne du Marchand adored her dashing young Scotsman, Douglas MacRae, and every moment in his arms was pure rapture. But when her father, the Comte du Marchand, learned she was carrying Douglas's child, Jeanne was torn from the proud youth without a word of farewell—and separated not long after from her newborn baby daughter. Jeanne feared her life was over, for all she truly cared about was lost to her. Can the power of love prevail?

Once Douglas believed his lady's loving words—until her betrayal turned his ardor to contempt. He cannot forget even now, ten years later, when destiny brings her to his native Scotland, broken in spirit but as beautiful as before. His pride will not let him play the fool again, although memories of a past—secret, innocent, and fragile—tempt him. Can passion lead to love and forgiveness?

After the Kiss

Margaret Esterly is desperate—and desperation can lead to shocking behavior! Beautiful and gently-bred, she was the essence of prim, proper English womanhood—until fate widowed her and thrust her into poverty overnight. Now she finds herself at a dazzling masked ball, determined to sell a volume of scandalous memoirs to the gala's noble host. But amid the heated fantasy of the evening, Margaret boldly, impetuously shares a moment of passion with a darkly handsome gentleman . . . and then flees into the night.

Who was this exquisite creature who swept into Michael Hawthorne's arms, and then vanished? The startled yet pleasingly stimulated Earl of Montraine is not about to forget the intoxicating woman of mystery so easily—especially since Michael's heart soon tells him that he has at last found his perfect bride. But once he locates her again, will he be able to convince the reticent lady that their moment of ecstasy was no mere accident . . . and that just one kiss can lead to paradise?

My True Love

Anne Sinclair has been haunted by visions of a handsome black-haired warrior all her life. His face invades her dreams and fills her nights with passionate longing. So the beautiful laird's daughter leaves her remote Scottish castle, telling no one, to search for the man called Stephen—a man she does not know but who fights in war-torn England, a place she has never seen. Stephen Harrington, Earl of Langlinais, never expected to rescue this unexplained beauty from the hands of his enemy. And yet, when their eyes first meet, he feels from the depths of his soul that he should know her . . . that he needs to touch her, and keep her by his side forever. For unknown to both of them, they are in the center of a centuries-old love . . . a love that is about to surpass their wildest dreams.

My Beloved

They call her the Langlinais Bride—though she's seen her husband only one time . . . on their wedding day, twelve years ago.

For years naïve, convent-bred Juliana dreaded being summoned to the side of the man she wed as a child so long ago. Now her husband, Sebastian, Earl of Langlinais, has become ensnared in his villainous brother's wicked plots—and has no choice but to turn to his virgin bride for help.

Juliana now finds herself face-to-face with a man so virile and so powerful that she's fascinated by him—just as he asks her to go against everything she holds true. Sebastian never counted on being enchanted by the beauty of this innocent angel he intended to keep as wife in name only—and he dares not reveal to her the secret reason why their love can never be . . .

Upon a Wicked Time

Tessa Astley is everything a duke should want in a wife. A breathtaking beauty with a reputation that is positively above reproach, she desires nothing more than the love of her husband, the man she's long pined for.

Only Jered Mandville doesn't want a soul mate, just a proper duchess hidden away on his country estate to beget heirs. He certainly doesn't see a place for his bride in his decadent life in London.

Tessa won't let her fairytale slip through her fingers. She'd do anything to win Jered's heart. So Tessa starts a campaign to win her husband's heart by invading his home, his reckless adventures, and his bed—all to prove to her cynical duke that even a happy ending can be delightfully wicked . . .

My Wicked Fantasy

Mary Kate Bennett was married too early, widowed too young, and left to fend for herself without a penny. Her path was never meant to cross with Archer St. John's, except for a terrible carriage accident with the wickedly handsome Earl of Sanderhurst. Mary Kate awakens in a mysterious lord's bed to a life more luxurious than she could have ever imagined, facing a man she's never met before, but instinctively knows . . .

The whispers about Archer follow him wherever he goes. Had the reclusive nobleman murdered his unhappy countess? When Mary Kate enters his life so unexpectedly, the bold earl is convinced that she has all the answers he has been searching for. So why can't he think of anything else besides her decadently red hair, her luminescent skin, and the feelings this vibrant, spirited beauty evokes within his masculine soul?

Their love can be a fantasy, or it can be strong enough to entwine their destinies forever.

READING LOG

My Wicked Fantasy

Mary Kate Bennett was married too early, widowed too young, and left to fend for herself without a penny. Her path was never meant to cross with Archer St. John's, except for a terrible carriage accident with the wickedly handsome Earl of Sanderhurst. Mary Kate awakens in a mysterious lord's bed to a life more luxurious than she could have ever imagined, facing a man she's never met before, but instinctively knows . . .

The whispers about Archer follow him wherever he goes. Had the reclusive nobleman murdered his unhappy countess? When Mary Kate enters his life so unexpectedly, the bold earl is convinced that she has all the answers he has been searching for. So why can't he think of anything else besides her decadently red hair, her luminescent skin, and the feelings this vibrant, spirited beauty evokes within his masculine soul?

Their love can be a fantasy, or it can be strong enough to entwine their destinies forever.

READING LOG	